The Condor's Head

An American Romance

BY THE SAME AUTHOR

Tales of History and Imagination
Umbrella
Jem (and Sam)

A Chronicle of Modern Twilight
The Man Who Rode Ampersand
The Selkirk Strip
Of Love and Asthma
The Liquidator
Fairness
Heads You Win

Very Like a Whale

The Clique

Non-fiction
The Theatre of Politics
The Subversive Family
The British Constitution Now
Communism (Ed.)
Mind the Gap

The Condor's Head

An American Romance

Ferdinand Mount

Chatto & Windus
LONDON

Published by Chatto & Windus 2007

2 4 6 8 10 9 7 5 3

First published in Great Britain in 2007 by
Chatto & Windus
Random House, 20 Vauxhall Bridge Road,
London SW1V 2SA

www.randomhouse.co.uk

Addresses for companies within The Random House Group Limited can be found at:
www.randomhouse.co.uk/offices.htm

The Random House Group Limited Reg. No. 954009

A CIP catalogue record for this book is available from the British Library

ISBN 9780701181208

The Random House Group Limited makes every effort to ensure that the papers used in its books are made from trees that have been legally sourced from well-managed and credibly certified forests. Our paper procurement policy can be found at:
www.randomhouse.co.uk/paper.htm

Typeset by Palimpsest Book Production Limited, Grangemouth, Stirlingshire
Printed and bound in Great Britain by
Mackays of Chatham plc

Contents

'Happiness is a new idea in Europe.'

Louis-Antoine de Saint-Just, *The Spirit of the Revolution*, 1791

'We hold these truths to be sacred and undeniable; that all men are created equal and independent, that from that equal creation they derive rights inherent and inalienable, among which are the preservation of life, and liberty, and the pursuit of happiness.'

Thomas Jefferson,
original draft for the Declaration of Independence

For Julia

who climbed the fence

Uncle Bob's Cabin

'Waambek-k . . .' a pause, some minute variation in the breeze coming in from the back porch, and 'wambbik . . .' then the breeze so faint I could not feel it myself but, even so, 'aamkk'. It was a slatted half-door that didn't reach the ground or the ceiling, once sea-green but most of the paint had peeled off and its tremulous flapping against the flimsy doorpost sounded like a protest. The catch had fallen off too and there was no way of wedging it because of it not reaching the floor. She stretched out her arm to hold it shut. I could see her long fingers curled round the edge. But that took her too far away from the shower-head, so she gave up and left the door to its own devices. 'Waamkh' – why was the noise fractionally different each time? Now it swung open again, six or eight inches this time, and I could see the lank tow of her wet hair slopping across her pale lemony shoulder. Then she must have bent forward to let the water run over her shoulder or to pick up the soap from the tin dish on the wall and I had a glimpse of her bottom, just the top of it and the beginnings of the curve and the shadow of the dimple, and 'waamck . . .'

I turned back to the *National Geographic*, which was the only reading matter in the place because according to Wizz it was the only magazine his uncle considered worth a dime. The article I was reading was about the many medicines to be extracted from plants in the Amazon jungle, which the natives have known about for centuries but which Western medicine has only just discovered. There was a picture of a stringy Indian, naked except for a rather exaggerated cache-sexe, standing by a bleeding tree. Sharing the same page was a doctor in a white coat with a grim smile on his face, and 'waaaa . . .' And I saw three-quarters of her as the door swung open wide; her head was turned away but her body wasn't and I saw the surprising swell of her thigh and beyond her thigh the tips of the sandy fuzz. '. . . Ammmgkk.' And I tried to concentrate on the text, in which Dr Donald Ohrstrom, presumably the man in the white coat, was explaining that the medical profession was not to be blamed for its reluctance to explore the potential of forest medicine because it was like shooting at a needle in a haystack.

I couldn't take the strain any more, so I got up and walked out on to the front porch. The paint was peeling here too. Uncle Bob had handed the place over to Wizz four or five years back, but Wizz had been finishing his master's and had not had the time to do it up. Besides, he liked the peeling look – interior decorators spent hours with a blowtorch to achieve the same effect, he claimed. Anyway Wizz was an outdoor type, though you would never think it to look at him, he was so slight and the lick of fair hair across his bulging brow gave him an air of fragility, the sort of boy who invited bullying. In fact, Franco said, when the two of them had fetched up together at this strange boarding school out in the wilds of Idaho – he on a scholarship, Wizz's old man paying Wizz's fees – it was always Wizz who came in first on the big trek at the end of term, Wizz who had the fastest time for swinging across the creek on the rope strung between two thirty-foot pines. To see him stripped down swinging the axe on a stack of timber would have made Charles Atlas eat his heart out because there he was, this nine-stone weakling with no muscles to speak of, knocking the hell out of these enormous pine logs. He was no slouch either on the academic side, which was heavily geared to Homer and Plato and he had already inhaled them back East. Whereas at South Philly High the classics were closed books, except to Betsy Paglia who sat two desks away from Franco and was a prodigy even then.

Francesco O'Mara, as he was christened (at Saint Joseph's of course), came from pretty much the toughest part of the City of Brotherly Love. His father worked in the meat market, his mother was a nurse, he being Irish obviously and she Italian. Franco dodged between his two ancestries depending on which crowd he was running with at the time. If with the wops, he was Franco Mara, full of twinkle and swagger.

If with the Irish, which was the more likely because the street they lived on was Irish, he was Frank O'Mara, a stonier personality with the makings of a hard man about him. It was a mistake, Franco explained, to see his fellow Hibernians as full of blarney and bonhomie. The Philly Irish took a decidedly chilly view of the world, which had helped him to survive out at Fournier College.

That peculiar institution had been founded by Edward P. Fournier in 1925 with a view to reconstituting the moral fibre of the American race. Edward P. had made a packet in the stock market and decided that the only answer was to build his own college and raise a new cadre of leaders far from the enervating influences of the East Coast and the Ivy League. And each year since then a clutch of young men, no women, had been carefully selected, without regard to income or background (though until recently all white; there had been trouble about that), and shipped off to Idaho to learn how to become leaders of men.

It was an austere place, Franco said, like a monastery without God. The first generations of Fournier men back in the Twenties had built the bunkhouses with their bare hands, living in tents until they had carved the first cabins out of the stands of pine on the lower slopes of Cat Mountain. Just before the war the class of '36 or maybe '37 had learnt a little dynamiting and quarried some stone from the now bare hillside. They built a plain four-square lodge for EPF, but the old man refused to stay in it when he visited (they used the lodge as a sickbay now), preferring to bunk down with the Adjutants, as he had dubbed the permanent staff, a skeleton crew because the students mostly taught each other. They also drew up the rules themselves and looked after the discipline though there was not much call for it.

'You see, the selection procedures were pretty damn accurate, so most of the guys were leaders already, chilly, inner-directed personalities who were always thinking one move ahead, you know, like how is this going to play with the Old Man, how will it look in my final report, oh, and will this be for the good of the school.'

'I wasn't like that at all,' Wizz said. 'I was an innocent youth who knew nothing of the world.'

'Oh Wizz, come on. I've never seen any seventeen-year-old with so much natural self-confidence.'

'You must have been so sweet,' Polly said.

'I'm rather sweet now, don't you think?'

You could see what Franco meant, though. For all his willowy figure and the poignant lick of fair hair, William Short Stilwell did have an air of command about him, a hint of the seigneurial.

When we had been buying the groceries down in Leconfield, the girl at the check-out treated him with an instinctive respect although he had not been in any way condescending. But there was something else about him too, a slightly detached, almost mournful quality, as though he used to be part of the scene he was in but had somehow lost his place, perhaps for a reason he himself was unaware of. Even when he was at his most entertaining, telling his long, artful stories, this glimmer of sadness was never quite gone, so that a racy, even raucous anecdote appeared to carry some tragic ulterior meaning.

We all loved Wizz, Franco because he had lightened those stern days at Fournier, I because he was the first American I got to know properly and his laconic humour and unashamed enthusiasms came fresh to me, and Polly because, well, she could talk to him like you could talk to a girl but without any of the bitchy competitive stuff that always crept into being friends with another girl.

She had met him when she had come over for a year's postgraduate study on trade cycles, and then he had gone to England for a year at the LSE and stayed with her parents in Camden Town. When Polly's younger sisters Mel and Terps were home from school, they were all on top of each other in the tall stucco house and Wizz said he felt he was turning into their long-lost brother, which none of them minded a bit, although they told him that brothers had never been on the agenda, because their father, John Castle, had conceived the absurd project of fathering nine daughters who would all be called after the classical muses. He got as far as three before his American wife Anne called a halt. Still, Polyhymnia, Melpomene and Terpsichore were there as witnesses to this hopeless enterprise, like three arches of an enormous unbuilt nave. Mr Castle, known as Turret to his daughters, had one of those brains that was good for learning Latin and Greek and solving crossword puzzles but was otherwise spark-free. He toiled away in an old-fashioned merchant bank, which had been taken over by a less old-fashioned merchant bank and then submerged in a huge

American bank where his services were of uncertain value. He was clinging on by his fingernails, dreading his annual appraisal. His consolation – and it was a glorious consolation – was his daughters, free spirits whose long solemn faces belied their unbridled characters. Polly in particular liked to exaggerate her solemn look while talking dirty, a trait immediately spotted by Wizz: 'Polly, why do you always look like a particularly glum twelfth-century saint when you're talking about fucking?'

'Oh, do I? I just thought I was looking thoughtful.'

We had come to Uncle Bob's Cabin, as Wizz called it, the night before. When we were unpacking, there was a violent storm. All night the trees outside were cracking and wailing, and the mosquito panels never stopped rattling (nor did the shower door). The next morning there was driving rain that lasted through the afternoon. We ventured outside for a walk through the pines, our sneakers skidding on the wet pine needles and splashing through puddles flecked with sawdust from the fresh-cut timber, but the rain drove us back in again. So we sat indoors reclining on the shabby old bunk seats by the windows, re-fuelling on junk food and cans of beer from the coolstore. After wearying of the *National Geographic*, I turned back to *The Adventures of Augie March* (I had just discovered the big sloppy American novelists), but now and then I found the texture a bit chewy and I would glance across to the other three: Franco was reading his way through the novels of Fanny Burney for his thesis on The Rise and Fall of Sentiment in Mid-Georgian England, sitting crosslegged holding the little blue book with its gold-embossed cover between his hairy paws, looking like a chimp especially pleased with itself because it thinks it is reading; Polly drying her hair while slowly absorbing the *Vogue* and *Marie-Claire* she had brought with her. She was a trained economist now (her special paper on Kondratieff's Long Wave Theory had been the pick of the year), but when she was off duty she liked to veg out in a feminine style. Wizz, by contrast, could not sit still; in fact, could not sit at all and was constantly on the move fixing things, rigging up the new gas canister we had brought from Leconfield, securing the mosquito frames, nailing down a loose floorboard, dusting off the wicker chairs on the porch, shunting the garbage out into the yard (if you could call it a yard, it was really just a clearing in the scrub where Uncle Bob had once tried to grow vegetables – a few mildewed artichoke stalks were still poking through the long grass). His homely industry gave the scene an unexpected uplift, which he did not fail to notice: 'In the American frontier home,' he descanted in a sing-song schoolmarm voice with his wet anorak still over his head, 'everyone had his or her allotted task. While Mom saw to the domestic chores, the boys stuck at their studies in the hope that one day they might get to go to college in far-off Omaha, Nebraska, while little Polly was growing up fast and learning how to be a woman.'

'Can it, Wizz,' Polly said without looking up from painting her toenails.

The rain was still sluicing down outside and a pleasant feeling of security stole over me, a feeling of being on the inside for once in my life. I felt so close to them all, although Franco I had just met for the first time and I only knew Wizz through Polly. My life had been so closed-up, solitary. Nobody's fault but mine. If anybody needed to be taken out of himself it was me and this, I thought with something close to joy, was what was happening to me here.

Perhaps I felt so relaxed because I was tired. I had only landed the day before and it had been a weary five-hour bus ride to the depot at Leconfield where Wizz had met me in the pick-up. So my defences were down and I said in an unguarded way, not my style at all, something about what a great welcome they had given me and how at home I felt.

'Enjoy it while it lasts,' said Franco, stretched out on the bunk seat with his wet sneakers propped against the stove.

'How do you mean?'

'We're great at saying hi to new people. In fact, saying hi is what we do best. We can become best buddies over a single beer. But it doesn't go any deeper. You will see when you have been among us a while longer that Americans have no gift for intimacy. There is no intimacy in American literature. Just when you think you are getting really close, somehow we aren't there any more.'

'Well, where are we then?' Wizz enquired, rather sharply.

'Getting ready to say hi to the next guy.'

Even stretched out on the bunk Franco still had that prehensile look, as though he might tumble over at any minute and curl his hairy fingers round the next branch.

'So Americans never really fall in love, not in books anyway?'

'Oh, sure, we fall in love, with a whale or a river or with some millionaire across the bay who we don't know at all; in fact, that's the point because if we did know him properly we'd realise what a total prick he was. Mostly we fall in love with ourselves and that's fine because that's a lifelong romance. But what we don't do is fall in love with another person, I mean love in the sense of singling her out – OK, him too – from the rest of the human race and living for her and with her so intensely that the rest of life is flat and trivial, and if it breaks up your life is shattered. There's nothing like that in American literature.'

'What about *Love Story*? Or *Gone with the Wind*?'

'I said literature.'

'But books don't necessarily have anything much to do with life. Even if your theory was true, it could be something to do with the way we write, not the way we live,' said Wizz, sounding distinctly nettled. 'After all, we're obsessed about relationships, half the self-help books you see in the stores are about how to improve the quality of our relationships.'

'The stores are also full of books telling you how to improve your cooking. That doesn't mean that we love to cook – in fact, it means the opposite, we prefer to go out and take away. We'd like to learn the language of intimacy, but we can't even pronounce the menu.'

'So where did we go wrong?'

'Did I say anything about going wrong? Going ahead would be nearer the mark. We've merely jumped the romantic stage, moving in one tidy leap from Puritanism to pure egotism without stopping at the love station. In any case the romantic project was always doomed to be self-cancelling. If you put the holiness of the heart's affections in the number one spot, then the holiness of the heart's disaffections has to be number two and pretty soon divorce gets to be as big a deal as marriage. You rightly observe, my dear Wizz, that these relationship therapy books are on the self-help shelf. If there's a bookshop with a *self-sacrifice* section, I haven't found it yet.'

'Is that why you're reading all those crappy eighteenth-century novelettes?'

'Yeah, because I want to pinpoint the moment at which decomposing

Christianity transmutes into this new secular religion. Just precisely when did people switch over from the idea of giving yourself totally to Jesus to the idea of giving yourself totally to another human being? C. S. Lewis had it down to the troubadours. But courtly love looks to me more like a literary convention than a life-changing thing. It's only when Christianity segues into its final Protestant phase that the idea of love breaks free and takes over. Without the Christian ideology of self-giving the whole shebang is inconceivable. Outside Christendom, there's nothing like it, nothing at all. In any other culture a person who gives up everything for love is regarded as a moral idiot, on a par with a junkie or an alcoholic.'

'And what do you think?' Polly sounded nettled too.

'What do I think about what?'

'Is a person who gives up everything for love like an alcoholic?'

'Oh I don't have opinions. I'm your friendly neighbourhood analyst, I just ask questions and listen to the answers and murmur as I take my fees, there is no cure for this disease.'

'Come off it, Franco. If this passion thing was just a phase we've skipped or we're growing out of, is that good or bad or don't you care? Have we lost something precious or are we well rid of it?'

'You really wanna know?'

'Yes.'

'Well . . .' Franco was face down on the bunk now, stretching out his paw for his beer can and squeezing it flat when he found it was empty. 'Well,' he said, 'it's hard for us to judge at this distance in time. It must have been a bad moment when people realised that their love was no more immortal than they were. But they still had the consolations of the flesh, screwing and kids and so forth, so it wasn't so bad as when they discovered there was no God. For that there was no consolation.'

'How can you be so sure people don't feel as passionately any more?' Wizz sounded personally aggrieved.

'Oh, people, I don't know about people. I'm only a literary scholar, for Christsake, not a goddam sociologist. For all I know, people may still be killing themselves or each other for love. All I can say is that nobody much is writing about it, nobody worth reading anyway. Joyce couldn't even mention the word, he was so freaked out by it.'

He yawned and sat up, stretching his arms above his head in his relaxed simian style. As I got up to fetch a couple more cans from the coolstore, I became aware how tight the atmosphere was. Both Wizz and Polly were looking away from Franco in strained postures, as though they had to force themselves not to look at him. How sharp their questions had been, how seriously they had taken him, considering there we were, half-pissed with our wet clothes steaming on the rickety drying rack, with the gamy aroma of Wizz's stew simmering in our nostrils. They were like believers in the old faith, undeclared ones perhaps, who were finding it hard to keep mum when they heard it abused as obsolete.

As Franco stretched out a hand to take the beer, I caught the look that Wizz gave him. Then, as I was turning back to the creaky wicker chair I was sitting on, I saw Polly looking at him too. There was no mistaking those two looks, partly because the looks were so alike. The gaze was intense and yet at the same time distraught, like the look of someone witnessing a terrible accident or, no, being part of the accident and so shocked that the eye cannot focus, glassy and wild at the same time. That is a confused description but then it is a confusing thing to catch, the look of someone ravening for love.

I had not realised till that moment that either of them was in love with Franco. They never stopped teasing him and making monkey jokes, and I had taken all of that at face value. Presumably each of them knew about the other, or perhaps they didn't. Perhaps they were each as blind as I had been, having eyes only for that sprawling figure on the bunk seat whose hirsute fingers were now happily clasped round the next can of Budweiser.

Wizz's stew came and went. I cannot remember much about it, dark and chewy I think. I was so unsettled by the violent currents of feeling that had now broken into our idle talk (assuming that it had been idle and Franco had not been deliberately teasing either or both of them). We could not find a topic that suited us and so jogged about restlessly from one to the next: memories of people they had in common from their various colleges, why Johnson had decided not to run again, how long it would be before there was a black president, whether you could actually teach literature or even if you could whether you should. Then Wizz told us something about the people who lived in this part of the state who were not really German but Dutch or some other nationality that I have now forgotten.

But what I do have a sharp memory of is Wizz getting up to poke the stove and sneaking another look at Franco as he passed, this time not so wild, more the look of a collector who cannot stop looking at the piece he has just acquired, scarcely able to believe his luck. And Polly stretched out opposite with her long arms drooping over the edge of the bunk and a soupy smile on her solemn face as she looked at Franco too. And I wondered whether I was not a little bit in love with her, or perhaps I did not want to be left out of this roundelay.

It was a relief when we agreed to turn in.

'Being wet is so tiring.'

'So is being smashed.'

'Being wet *and* smashed is the worst.'

I was already in my only dry T-shirt and my boxer shorts, so all I had to do was grab an old blanket from the box under the bunk seat and throw it over me, grunting goodnight to Franco who was doing the same in the opposite bunk. Wizz turned down the wick on the oil lamp and wished us goodnight, then shepherded Polly along to the two tiny bedrooms either side of the passage out to the yard. They were both in white T-shirts and he had his torn old beige shorts on and she was just in her white knickers because her jeans were still damp. They looked like a couple of castaways.

We lay quiet in the glimmer of the lamp, listening to them brushing their teeth in the shower room. I expected Franco to start off on some midnight homily but he did not utter. In fact, he lay so still I thought he must have gone to sleep the moment his head touched the pillow.

Perhaps I had dozed off myself but it seemed like only half an hour later (I did not check my watch) when I saw Franco get up from his bunk and walk slowly across the room. I imagined that he was going out the front to piss in the wet bracken – no, imagined is not the right word, that is what I hoped.

But he went the other way, down the passage. Halfway along he stopped, or at least the creak of his footsteps stopped, and there was a tingling silence. Was he pausing before taking the plunge? Or could he not remember which was Wizz's door and which was Polly's? There had been some business about Wizz giving up the slightly better of the two hutches to her, but Franco might not have known which was supposed to be the better one (I had put my head round both doors and could not see much difference). Or – and this was a more unsettling thought still – perhaps he did know which of them was sleeping where, but could not make up his mind which door to try. How was I to presume which way his fancy went?

I have never forgotten that silence although it happened so long ago. Each second of it seemed dragged out, separate from the moment before and the moment after. I could just hear the flickery throb of the stove. The silence was so heavy I felt I could touch it.

Then a door opened, a flimsy creaky noise, and closed again with a little thwap and I heard the voice of an English girl. Not that I could hear her actual words, she was keeping her voice down, just the slightly higher pitch of the vowels. Then murmurings, so low that it was soon hard to tell which of them was talking. Then silence again, nothing but the throb of the stove. And a few minutes later, rhythmic, tentative at first then gathering pace, those other noises.

I woke late, at least it seemed late. Stale beer, headache, stale fumes from Franco's French cigarettes, Franco's bunk still empty, grey light straggling under the stubby flounces of the curtains. In the little galley – too cramped to call it a kitchen – I heard a kettle steaming and there was Wizz fully dressed, grimly placing bacon strips on a filthy griddle.

He brushed aside my sleepy good morning. 'Today', he said, 'you and I are going down to the city. You said you were longing to see it.'

'Did I?'

'If you didn't you should have. It's the greatest city in America.'

'Won't the others –'

'We must leave the lovebirds to it.'

We ate our blackened bacon and scalded coffee without either of us saying a word. Wizz looked pinched, as if he had lost weight overnight. I imagined this was how he would look when he was sixty, though there was not a line on his face.

'Could you give me a hand with the gas? Let's try not to wake them.'

We lugged the spent cylinder into the back of the pick-up. We must have looked like a couple of murderers humping the body.

'I've left a note,' he said, jumping into the driver's seat, leaving me no time to fetch my anorak. He drove down the twists and turns of the mountain road with the intent ferocity of a rally driver. His pace did not slacken as we came out of the woods, and we drove through scattered villages and orchards heavy with fruit until we came to the general store in Leconfield where we dumped the empty cylinder and picked up a couple of pieces of junk mail directed to Uncle Bob (who had died three years earlier).

I hoped his mood might lighten after we hit the freeway and he did begin to talk a little, in a clipped sort of way.

'I have to visit our lawyers, Chisholm and Daly, known in the family as Chisel and Dally.'

'How impressive.'

'We're trying to break up Uncle Bob's trust. My cousin Marve's getting married and he wants out.'

The explanation seemed to depress him, whether because of the impending bother or because he did not care for Cousin Marve was hard to tell.

After a couple of hours' steady driving, mostly through a light drizzle, we reached the outer suburbs of the city. The first lights were red and Wizz turned to me with an anguished twist to his mild features. 'Look,' he said, 'I don't mind about them fucking, they can fuck themselves stupid for all I care, but he shouldn't play around with other people's feelings just because he doesn't have any himself.'

'Oh, are you—'

'Because it's all crap what he was saying last night. Love *is* the most important thing in life.'

'Even in America?' I said, trying to lighten the tone.

'Sure it is. Hell, we take everything else seriously, why wouldn't we take this seriously? We're the last romantics in fact, always were, always will be.'

'So nothing's changed?'

'You don't believe me? Listen, I'll show you something.'

He drove on down the long avenue, putting his foot on the accelerator as though he had just received an urgent summons. Soon the suburban lawns and the wide sidewalks gave way to streets with older four- or five-storey houses with iron fire escapes zigzagging down their fronts. Then in another ten minutes we were driving though a city park with broad lawns and fine old trees and public buildings in red brick with classical façades and Doric pillars. The rain was bucketing down now.

'There,' he said, pulling up at the next intersection and pointing dramatically to one of these classical buildings on a quiet side street. 'You go in there and ask the librarian to tell you the story of William Short.'

'Who's presumably some sort of ancestor?'

'I always said you were smart. Ask him to show you the letters, oh and the bust too. He's a friend of mine and he loves to do the spiel. And then you come back and tell me that Americans are incapable of romance.'

He was still boiling with rage, and to cool him down I didn't ask any questions but said, all right, I'd give it a whirl. So I got out of the pick-up and padded across the sopping grass towards the imposing portico. I wondered whether it had only just occurred to him to put me through this experience, whatever it was, or whether he had it in mind even before we left Uncle Bob's cabin. Either way, it would kill an hour and keep me out of the rain. I did not imagine that the story would occupy my mind, off and on, for the next thirty years.

A flustered lady in spectacles opened the door to me. She had a startled air as though this was a door she had never opened before.

'Oh,' she said, 'you're wet. You'd better come in.'

Wizz helped me, of course. In fact, he kept nagging at me to carry on. He liked to call himself my commissioning editor, and he doubled as my research assistant. On his time off from Stilwell Short, the family boutique brokers he had gracefully subsided into, he would go to the Historical Museum or the Phil Soc and copy out stuff for me in his tidy hand with the epsilons for 'e's. Sometimes on afternoons in the spring he coxed a four on the Schuykill river and I liked to think of that slight figure sitting there in the library in his cox's cap and muffler, though he told me he changed out of his city clothes down at the boathouse. But he never offered any comment on the material he sent me or asked to see any of the work in progress and the only time I asked him what he thought about some episode or other he declined, saying, 'You're the romancer, I'm just the editor.' I think he wanted an impartial witness, but witness to what exactly? Was I supposed to prove Franco wrong about the history of love? Or did he want an outsider to tell a story that would make his fellow Americans, possibly the rest of us too, feel differently about something, about themselves perhaps? That would certainly be an ambitious enterprise, to put it mildly, but beneath his modest exterior Wizz concealed his fair share of ambition.

I

The Landing

'Simmon, Simmon, where is that boy, never there when you want him, I know he does it apurpose,' Madame Suard called in her quick high English, which still had a French buzz to it, though she had been keeping her boarding house in Philadelphia for ten years and more. To call it a boarding house is to do her establishment some injustice. What Madame Suard kept was a *French* boarding house, serving the best wines from Bordeaux and offering her guests cooking of a refinement found only in two or three houses on Society Hill, Dr Physick's for example and Mayor Powel's. It was a fine old mansion of the type they were already calling colonial, on the best part of Walnut Street, the low seventies, with blue panelled shutters, gabled roof, shed dormers and a perron so polished it might have been marble. Perhaps it was; Madame Suard insisted on the finest materials in all departments, napkins of Breton lace, chests and tallboys of New England cherrywood in all the twenty-dollar bedrooms and the table silver of such a quality that those of her guests who fancied themselves in such matters were constantly arguing whether the epergne was by Storr or de Lamerie, which gave her the chance to tell them it was in fact fine Boston work and she had bought it round the corner at Mr Twite's on Locust Street and for half the price they had hazarded, for she was enough of a Frenchwoman still to boast of *belles économies*, even at her exalted level.

'Simmon, *enfin*,' she said, as the long skinny youth finally surfaced from the kitchen quarters where he claimed he had been polishing that very piece of silver, pointing by way of proof to the green apron he wore like an English butler. The double 'm' in his name is not, as you might think, a misprint. He insisted on it and bridled when anyone tried to write him down as Simon, explaining that it was short for Persimmon, which he had been christened, though the pastor did not care for it, because as a baby his father claimed his bulbous orange head was indistinguishable from the fruit of that tree. Mrs Suard had been fetched by this story when she first heard it and for several weeks called him Monsieur Persimmon, until Simmon asked her not to because the other boys were laughing at him.

'Simmon, there's a crate from France for Mr Short just come in on the tide.'

'Must be a powerful wet crate if it floated all that way.'

'Don't be sassy, Simmon.'

He liked the way she pronounced sassy, as if it were the most delightful thing in the world to be. In fact, he liked Mrs Suard a whole lot. She spoke to the boys the same way she spoke to her boarders, as though they were all a little backward and needed to be geed up if any sense was to be got out of them.

'It was shipped over on an American boat, the *Marquis'* – she pronounced it in the French way, mark-ee, and that was neat too, he thought, though why an American boat should be called after a French aristocrat he could not imagine.

'It is named for the great Marquis de Lafayette,' she said, not for the first time reading his thoughts. 'He is a hero for the Americans too, because he fought for both our nations.'

'Uh – uh.' Simmon hauled in this information with some negligence.

'So here's five dollars for the carriage and you'd best take the wagon. The boy from the Landing says the crate is not so big but it is very heavy.'

'Yes, ma'am,' said Simmon with a little more *empressement*. He fancied he cut a fine figure standing up in the little cart flicking his whip across the mule's hindquarters, but only when out of sight of 70 Walnut Street, for Mrs Suard did not care to see the mule tickled up.

Simmon sniffed the spring air as he went through the yard down to the little stable at the back. He pretended to flick the whip at the red tulips and gillyflowers in the beds along the brick path but never touched a petal because Mrs Suard might be watching from the window of her small study where she did her accounts and wrote out the menus in that curly hand of hers, which Mr Short always said made him feel he was back in the Palais-Royal.

Harnessing up old Beetle took less than five minutes the way Simmon reckoned it. He claimed he could be at the Landing within half an hour of receiving an errand and no sweating. Straight down Walnut Street, past Independence Hall, or the State House as older Philly people still called it, and you had a clear run. Mrs Suard always sent Simmon because he could write a fair hand, and the other yard boy, George, could barely scratch his mark and someone had to sign off the bill.

Simmon had always been the brightest of the brood. That, after all, was why he was a free man holding down a position of trust in the big city, while his brothers and sisters were still back in Georgia. How had he gotten all the way up here? That was something of a mystery and even Mrs Suard, who was dandy at asking questions, had not got to the bottom of it. The most that Simmon had vouchsafed was that there was a minister in the next parish, the one who had been willing to christen him by this heathen name and who was notorious for his advanced views (Simmon had put it differently but nigger-loving was not a word that Mrs Suard cared to use to Mr Short, even in *oratio obliqua*) and would sometimes take on a bright houseboy and teach him the rudiments, which the older planters didn't hold with at all because once they could read and write, where would we all be and we should hearken to Parson Malthus over in England who said that literacy among the lower orders was the gateway to perdition. Anyway, that would explain how Simmon could read and write but not how he had managed to travel all those miles crossing five state lines without being caught, not to mention the Savannah, the James, the Potomac and goodness knows how many other rivers. There was a suggestion that the minister's services might not have been confined to the instilling of literacy, but Simmon clammed up on the subject. Perhaps he was not quite sure of the details himself or perhaps he preferred to forget.

'Simmon, Simmon, wait, boy.' He was turning out of the side lane into Walnut Street when a middle-aged man burst out of Mrs Suard's front door, gasping for breath.

'Why, g'morning, Mr Short, how are you today?'

'I must come with you.'

'Lordy, Mr Short, I don't need no help. They know me down at the Landing. My name's good for most anything there.'

'I don't doubt it,' said the middle-aged gentleman hopping up on the wagon with some nimbleness and settling himself beside Simmon. 'But I wish to make sure of the package and convey my thanks to Captain Hillard in person.'

'Ain't right for you to be sitting up in this old cart. I'd have had George sweep it out if I'd known you was coming with me. Or we could have harnessed up the carriage.'

'Oh, I've travelled in worse tumbrils than this, Persimmon, my boy.'

The middle-aged gent was sandy-haired and slight of build, though beginning to run to fat a fraction (it would have been an insult to Mrs Suard's cooking not to). He was wearing a high-collared velveteen coat that matched pretty close his mop of hair. There was an uncomfortable alert sort of look in his eye, as though he had an idea of what you were up to and didn't much like the sound of it, and when his face relaxed his mouth had a sad turndown, though he was always cheerfulness itself to Simmon. He had come out in some haste and he was still tying his snowy stock as he sat down on the old plank seat.

'Walk on, Beetle. Tell him to walk on, we can't wait all day. I have business with the Chesapeake Canal people at noon. I shall probably be late, well, no matter,' he said all in much the same breath, digging out his gold watch from the fob pocket of his blue waistcoat and glaring at it as at some acquaintance who was in the habit of giving him trouble.

'Must be a mighty important package to keep the Chesapeake Canal waiting.'

'It is, Simmon, you're right.'

Persimmon Williams cocked his head in Mr Short's direction in the expectation of further particulars. But Mr Short just smiled and said nothing.

After a pause: 'Worth a few dollars I dare say, massa.'

'Worth a lot to me. And don't call me massa if you please. We're not in Georgia now.'

'Yes, *suh*,' Simmon replied smartly.

'And easy with that whip, boy. This isn't a chariot race.'

'Yes, suh.'

The dogwood was not quite out yet. Even so the pink and white blossom was clustered so thick on the branches that you could scarcely make out the library and the Philosophical Hall behind – all in that dignified red brick that made Philadelphia the finest city any place in Simmon's humble opinion, and he had heard Mr Short express the same opinion too.

'That dogwood smells mighty fine,' Simmon remarked a few blocks further on.

'Not dogwood, Simmon, azalea – *canadense* if I'm not mistaken. Mr Jefferson had those plants sent up from Monticello when they weren't above eighteen inches tall.'

They were passing the site of the Pennsylvania Savings Bank, which was building at the corner of 3rd Street in a cloud of white dust. The workmen were sawing great chunks of stone for the pillars, in the Greek style of course, everything had to be Greek in the new Athens. Most of the masons had tied cloth kerchiefs round their heads to keep the dust off their hair. They gave a raucous cheer as the cart went by and one of them shouted something Simmon could not quite catch. Well, it was an oddity to see a middle-aged gentleman in a velveteen coat sitting in a common grocery cart with a Negro boy who looked as if he had been pulled through a briar patch backwards. But Mr Short did not pay much heed to what other folks thought, that was what Simmon liked about him.

Beetle trotted over the little rise and all at once they could see the Delaware river spread out before them and the low hills of New Jersey beyond, and on the shining expanse of water a great mass of ships that jostled around the quays like flies around a rotten squash.

'*Mark-ee*'s berthed on the south quay, Mrs Suard say, captain name of Hillhead'.

'Hillard,' Mr Short corrected, 'and the ticket's marked S.H.I.'

'Yes, suh.'

But Captain Hillard was not on board for them to pay their respects to. In fact, the entire company seemed to have abandoned ship in favour of the quayside taverns. Only a couple of coloured hands were to be seen gloomily swabbing the decks. These two remnants agreed with some reluctance to conduct them down the companionway, which smelled horrible of cheese and leather and vinegar and another nastier odour, and it was a relief when they found S.H.I. almost immediately.

It was a big square crate, some four and a half feet high, wrapped in travel-stained burlap and secured with greasy cords to the central pillar to stop it sliding. And heavy too.

God, how heavy it was. It took all four of them to push it across the hold to a position below the open hatch from which they could winch it up on deck.

'Reckon it weighs a ton at least,' one of the hands said, wheezing and purple in the face from the effort.

Even with the winch the crate came up painfully slowly and they had the devil of a job to lift it over the ship's side and let it down into the waiting cart, which gave an alarming creak as it took the full weight.

'Don't you dare drive back the way you came, Simmon, or you'll shake this old cart to pieces.'

'Sure thing, suh, I'll take her back as slow as if we were taking a poor body to the graveyard.'

He was as good as his word and they proceeded back up Walnut Street at a pace that would have made a funeral procession look frisky. Even so the cart continued to give out ghastly creaks and to judder from side to side, and they had to stop to tie the ropes tighter to the pegs to prevent it from sliding about. Beetle could barely manage the last upward incline, gentle though it was, and to lessen the weight Mr Short got out and walked alongside the cart until they reached the Savings Bank again. His walking alongside enhanced the funereal impression, and a couple of the ghostly masons bowed their heads and folded their hands on the handles of their bandsaws in mock reverence, chuckling mightily the while.

At the top of the rise Mr Short remounted, but they maintained this sedate pace until they reached the corner of the lane by No. 70, where Beetle, delighted to be close to home after this gruelling excursion, pricked his mangy old ears and on the slight downward slope picked up speed to something approaching a trot, and the crate strained horribly at the ropes and Mr Short threatened to be obliterated by it, the cords rubbing fiercely against his blue vest and the corner of the burlap inflicting severe damage on his left toe.

'We had better unpack it out here in the yard,' Mr Short said after he had regained his composure. 'I understand there are several items inside and if we break them up into separate loads we can carry them up without killing ourselves.'

Simmon summoned little George to give assistance or rather to give orders to. And with the aid of little George's pocket knife they soon had the cords cut and the burlap stitches unpicked, and the shroud fell away to reveal the sturdy firwood bars of the crate and the straw densely packed inside.

'Is it an animal?' George enquired.

'Is you an idiot?' Simmon riposted. 'How would an animal breathe inside that canvas and anyways you ever heard of an animal that didn't have no smell?'

George took this reproof in silence and began hammering at the bars with a vehemence that provoked Mr Short to tell him to go gently.

It was not long all the same before George had freed up one side of the crate and they began pulling out the straw in handfuls. Mr Short had taken off his coat and laid it on the bench at the end of the yard by the door to the stable. There was a light glistening of sweat on his forehead as he smoothed away the wisps of straw and pulled out a parcel wrapped in rough cloth.

'Books,' snorted George as Mr Short unwrapped half a dozen finely bound volumes.

'Just cos you can't read, there's no cause to be so high-toned,' said Simmon.

Mr Short took out a little grey cloth notebook and began to check the volumes against a list he appeared to have handy for the occasion. 'Three volumes by Monsieur de Chateaubriand, four volumes of Humboldt's essays, ah, and these must be the letters of poor blind Madame du Deffand. What a woman, she was before my time, of course, but they say an hour in her company surpassed any other pleasure in Paris.'

He was caught on the edge of a reverie, squatting by the gillyflowers, holding the books up to the sunlight, seeming almost unconscious of his helpers. George, making up for his earlier disdain, carefully took the books from Mr Short and began dusting them with his sleeve before laying them down on the cloth they had been wrapped in, although they did not really need much attention, being in remarkably good condition after their long sea voyage.

Simmon had meanwhile been pulling out the rest of the straw and the remaining contents of the crate were exposed to view.

'Lordy,' exclaimed George, 'he's an ugly great crittur, aint he?'

The three of them peered at the marble bust, gleaming white amid the cracked and dusty straw. It was a little larger than life and its beaky face gazed back at them from the broken bars of the crate with something of the disdain of a wild animal kept in a menagerie for public amusement. The gaze was ironic, sidelong, uncannily lifelike, but above all it was scornful. One of the onlookers might have just made a remark that the bust thought utterly contemptible. The bust had a wig on it streaked with highly incised and subtly planed locks that looked as if they had been dressed and powdered five minutes earlier. A series of drill holes defined the shadowy recesses of the wig's roll over the ears and down the neck. As they gently levered him out of the broken crate, they could see a long queue tied with a broad and heavy bow such as in Philadelphia only a lady would wear. This luxuriant mane flowed down the back all the way to where the carving stopped. In front, the negligent lapels of his coat opened to reveal a crumpled waistcoat and a froth of fine cravat. But it was the expression that stayed with you. How cold it was, more frigid than the marble it was carved in, with that half-smile on the lips that was more contemptuous than any scowl.

'Who is he?' George asked, awestruck.

'Got his name here on his arm, any fool can see that,' Simmon said with some scorn. 'Mr Hoodun Fakit, that's his moniker.'

'No, no, Simmon, that's the signature of the man who carved it, Monsieur Houdon.'

'Why's it say he faked it then?'

'*Fecit* is Latin for made it,' Mr Short said, stepping to one side to admire the bust from a different angle, so taken up with the contemplation of it that he seemed unaware his fine black boots were trampling the flowerbed.

'Come on, boys,' he said when he had done, 'let's take it inside and put it in the parlour.'

Simmon, who was quick to notice such things, noticed that Mr Short's voice had gone thick somehow as if he had a frog down his throat. And it was as much out of kindness as curiosity that he persisted in asking so who was the marble gentleman if he weren't Mr Fakit.

'Oh,' said Mr Short, still sounding thick in the throat though a little recovered, 'it's the Condor.'

'The Condor?' Why did none of these people have plain ordinary names like Persimmon Williams?

'D'Alembert called him that, le Condor. It's a species of vulture. You find them in California, and the Andes too. Look, see how hunched he is, how his neck goes back into his shoulders, and look at his great beak.'

But Mr Hoodun Fakit had done his faking so admirably that the two boys could see nothing but a marble gentleman with a sniffy sort of smile on his face.

'So it's a nickname then, not his real one?' Simmon persisted.

'Of course. Permit me to introduce you to the Marquis de Condorcet, the finest mathematician of his age and the most daring philosopher, perpetual secretary to the Academy of Sciences, a loyal friend to Mr Jefferson and to your humble servant.' Mr Short made a humorous little bow. He had recovered his voice now but Simmon saw that there were tears on his weathered cheek.

'So he sent you this statue all the way from France as a keepsake?'

'No, he's long dead, Simmon, more than twenty years back. He killed himself, took poison.'

'What did he do that for?'

'Well, they had arrested him and he was in jail and he knew he would be sent to the guillotine.'

'There weren't much point to it then, poisoning himself if he were going to have his head chopped off anyway.'

'I suppose he didn't want to give them the satisfaction, preferred to do it by his own hand.'

'My,' said Simmon. George said nothing but stood there squinting at the bust, then rubbed his eyes because the bust was so dazzling white in the sunlight that it hurt him to look at it too long.

'I'm very glad to have it,' Mr Short said ruminatively, 'but I had forgotten how large it was. I really don't believe it will fit into my modest quarters here. I had best give it to Philosophical Hall, that would surely be the most fitting place for it in any case. He was such a friend to our country, he was one of "*les Américains*" as they called them, but oh dear.' He began to look sorrowful again, but this time he shook himself and said quite tartly, 'Now then, look sharp. I want to have it sitting in the parlour by the time Mrs Suard comes back from Locust Street. I mean to give her a little surprise.'

Gingerly they hefted the great marble along the brick path and up the back steps, and through the pleasant gloom of the hallway. The shutters were still drawn to in the French fashion to keep the rooms cool, as Madame Suard insisted, and the parlour was especially murky. Mr Short smoothed a square of burlap on the round table so as not to spoil the veneer and very carefully the boys lowered the bust on to it. The three of them stood back for one last look.

In the murk the bland noble aspect of the bust had disappeared. Instead, the head looked hunched, menacing, poised to strike. The flappy lapels of the coat suggested furled wings, which might be going to unfurl the next minute.

'Yeah, I reckon that's a vulture all right,' said Simmon.

'Thank you, boys, thank you,' said Mr Short, already turning back into the hallway as he fumbled for a coin to give them. 'I must make haste or I shall be late for the canal business.'

The boys went their separate ways, Persimmon down below to finish up the silver and George off into the garden to begin a little desultory hoeing of the flowerbeds. Most of the other gentlemen boarders being at their bureaux, 70 Walnut Street returned to its usual slumbrous calm.

It must have been nearly an hour later that Mrs Suard came back from her business at the drapers – replacing all the table napkins and a quantity of the bedlinen too, a matter involving considerable expense and therefore prolonged negotiation with Mr Macmanus, the tight-fisted manager of the store. She was tired and a little out of breath as she came through the parlour on the way to the study, unpinning her hat as she went, as she was in the habit of doing.

At first Simmon thought the cry came from the street. Was it the tail end of some hawker's yell, the earlier part of it obscured by the rumble of the cart? Yet it seemed to come from directly above his head, just where he had heard Mrs Suard's heavy footsteps only a few seconds before he heard the cry. Anyway, he was sure it was a woman's scream.

He found her in the parlour, lying half on the floor but with her head lolling against the upright settle, which she had pushed sideways in her fall. Her hat lay crushed beneath her black skirt. She was just about conscious now and she was mumbling words he couldn't get the hang of, but it was clear enough she had fainted, clean away was his guess. Well, women did faint, he knew that, and she was an old lady and it was a warm day especially when you hadn't gotten used to the heat, it being the first days of spring, but he blamed the marble gentleman because there was something about the marble gentleman that was damnably spookish. It was the marble gentleman who had made the tears run down Mr Short's cheeks, and now he had given Mrs Suard a seizure. It was Simmon's view that the quicker he harnessed up Beetle again and took the marble gentleman down to Philosophical Hall, the sooner this house would be a place fit for decent folks to live in again.

II

French Lessons

From his bedroom he could just see a corner of the courtyard. His little attic salon gave on to grey slate roofs that had a flat shimmer after the rain (it had rained every day for a week), but the bedroom faced south and caught the sun when there was any to catch. Yet it was not just for the sun that he liked to lie on his iron bedstead and look out of the window with his copy of Cornichon's *Grammaire de la langue française* idle on his lap. What amused him were the glimpses he caught of Lilite as she came and went through the big green door into the street. How sweet and regular her habits were. Mass at eight o'clock on Sunday mornings and on saints' days of which there seemed to be a remarkable number. Such a lot of saints, he teased her, we don't have half so many in America, it must be because we are so ungodly. Oh, but you will soon discover them, she riposted, America is the land for discoverers, *n'est-ce pas*? Then she would explain who they all were – St Hubert the patron saint of hunters, St Jude the patron of lost causes. Oh, I'll take him, William said, that's what my French is, a hopeless lost cause. Oh, but Monsieur Short, she giggled, you are making such progress. William, please call me William, he said, there must be no ceremony between us, we Virginians cannot abide ceremony. Well then, she said, you may call me Lilite. I have three Christian names, Anne-Hippolite-Louise. I love the middle one best because it is the most *singulier* but it is too long to be employed *en famille*, so Maman always calls me Lilite or Lite when she is *pressé*.

Then there was the music lesson at ten. She went to the ancient Monsieur Renard, whose father had taught the exiled royal family of

England and had seen the Old Pretender proclaimed King James the Third at the palace gates. Monsieur Renard was too grand to touch their own inferior harpsichord, insisting that Lilite should come to the apartment he rented in the *basse-cour* of the chateau.

Then in the afternoon she would take a walk with her friend Cloclo along the two promenades which were the glory of St Germain, the *grande* and the *petite*, both with such breathtaking views of the city, then back to the rue de Lorraine through the Jardin Anglais, hurrying a little, her cheeks pink, as she slammed the door behind her so as not to be late for dinner, her mother being impatient to begin, food being one of the few pleasures remaining to her in her frail state of health.

At first Lilite would not let him walk with them at all, let alone replace Cloclo when Cloclo was detained elsewhere. Maman would not approve. But Monsieur Short had a way with mamans, always had had even when he was seventeen or eighteen. There was something about his slender figure and the way his soft sandy hair flopped over his brow and his round questioning eyes that made mothers take pity on him. Or perhaps it was those tremulous downturning lips that did the trick. Handsome he was not and had never thought he was, but he was conscious of a certain melting power where the sex was concerned. Above all, he knew how to make them laugh. He could make men laugh too but in a rowdier style. Back in Virginia he had been a stalwart of the first Phi Beta Kappa and a founder member of the Flat Hat Society where they knew how to enjoy themselves as well as debate the eternal verities in the highest tone you could wish for.

Anyway, it did not take more than a couple of weeks before William had his licence to walk out with Lilite and Cloclo. Then Cloclo came down with *la grippe*, but Madame Royer granted an extension of the licence. She thought he was looking pale as a consequence of all his studying and in her book health trumped propriety.

So out they went together just the two of them in the damp February air, which really could not be expected to do much for anyone's pallor. And he strolled beside her on the high terrace under the bare twigs of the pleached limes. Usually they would stop to take an ice on the terrace or a plate of *croquignoles*, the fancy biscuits the café arranged delightfully in the shape of a fan, or even the *pâté de guimauve*, a sort of marshmallow he abominated but which Lilite loved best of all.

William noted down the cost of all these items in livres and sous in his little grey cloth account book, just as Mr Jefferson had advised him to do.

'There, monsieur, I mean William, you see Notre Dame, the two towers, and the dome that is the Invalides where the old soldiers go.'

'I like the way you say it, Wee-yam, as though I were a small sweet potato.'

He touched her arm as he tried to explain the joke, which was not easy because *pomme de terre douce* was not the equivalent of sweet potato. But how huge the city was. Boston and Philadelphia were small towns by comparison. And how it was growing. Even at this distance you could see the dust and the smoke and the scaffolding of the great new hotels and offices that were spreading out along the boulevards. The Comte d'Artois had on his own account registered building plans covering three or four acres north of the Champs-Elysées, a couple of blocks down from the *villino* that Mr Jefferson had fixed on for his ministry.

'It is called the Hôtel de Langeac,' William's master had written, 'though I fear the poor Marquise de L. had but little joy of its possession, for scarcely was the construction complete when she was forced into exile for reasons I may tell you when we next meet. But it is a fine modern building that I wager will remind you somewhat of my dear Monticello. The design is by Monsieur Chalgrin, one of the coming men who regard the architecture of their elders such as Gabriel as but an insipid parody of the true tradition of Vitruvius.'

How characteristic it was of his master to rhapsodise thus over architectural matters and to delay to the end of the letter the more germane intelligence: that William, having mastered the French language, was soon to begin on his duties as Mr Jefferson's secretary, for Mr Jefferson had finally received his appointment to succeed Mr Franklin as minister to France. The previous secretary, the saturnine Mr Humphreys, was off to London and it was time for Wm (as we may call him now and then, for that was how he signed his name) to start earning the thousand dollars a year that Mr Jefferson was paying him out of his own pocket until the Congress could be persuaded to stump up.

There was but a week left to try his luck with Lilite. So far all he had managed was to plant a kiss on her slender fingers as he was helping her on with her mantle.

'There, am I not learning a few French courtesies, Lilite?'

'But you must not linger so long, it is not polite.'

'Not linger so long when I *baiser* you, how could I not?'

'And you must not say *baiser*, that is not polite either.'

He chose his moment to tell her that he was leaving. It was in the late afternoon and the little upper landing was almost dark; in fact, Lilite had just brought up a fresh candle to place on the old commode that stood there.

He could see her catch her breath as he told her and her bosom heaved with what he immodestly assumed to be deep emotion. He took the candle from her and put it down and embraced her with such vim that she gave a dear little gasp. He kissed her on the lips and for an instant she made as if to break away, then she kissed him back.

Twice more he managed to kiss her, once on the landing again and another time behind the café on the terrace (when her lips tasted of marshmallow) and both times she responded, there was no doubt of it.

But then the very next morning after the marshmallow kiss as they were sitting over breakfast Madame Royer said, 'Monsieur Short, I have some joyous news to impart.'

'I am very glad to hear it, madame, please do not keep me in suspense.'

'My daughter Hippolite is engaged to be married.'

He could scarcely get out the words of congratulation, let alone enquire who the lucky man was to be, but Madame Royer needed no egging.

'He is a most serious young man, Monsieur Henri Denis, he is a *juré-prieur* by profession.'

'A *juré-prieur*? Forgive me, madame, I fear my French is not yet . . .'

'He sells objects, like so, biff.' She mimed the action of a hammer falling.

'You mean he is an auctioneer.'

'Quite so, monsieur, in France it is a most respectable profession,' she said defensively.

But Wm was no longer listening. He had eyes only for the

treacherous, secretive Lilite who was sitting opposite him blushing as well she might. How had she managed to carry on her courtship under his eyes? Or perhaps there had been no courtship worth the name and she had merely been knocked down to the highest bidder, as the serious Monsicur Denis would doubtless put it. Why, even so, had there been no word at Madame Royer's table of the impending contract? Back in Virginia there would have been joshing for weeks before the announcement, not to mention endless financial discussions. But here in France, not a word, not a gesture and apparently nothing to prevent a marshmallow kiss. He would never understand the French and he certainly could not understand the cheerful smile that Lilite was now giving him.

'We very much hope that you will honour us with your presence at the wedding ceremony, monsieur, I need not say how welcome you will be.'

'I should be honoured, madame,' Wm replied, offering a frigid bow from his sedentary position.

But Wm's months at St Germain were not entirely passed in a state of despondent chastity. By way of exercise, he had taken to riding an old hack from the livery stables through the rolling chestnut woods of Marly. The retired captain of cavalry who kept the stables was most helpful, giving him the address of a house just outside the gates of the park where other forms of exercise might be obtained.

'I suggest you try Wednesday,' Captain Pommeau said, 'towards the end of the week they are very busy and as for Sunday, oh *mon Dieu*.'

It was a little white house on a steep cobbled street where the wet leaves gathered and his horse slipped on the leaves although they were only going at a walk because he was looking for a green lantern in the shape of a dolphin as instructed by the Captain. Wm jumped off and tied the reins to the hitching rail and tugged at the iron bell rod. There was a mournful jangle, more like the tolling for a funeral than the promise of pleasure.

A long interval. Wm felt his heart thumping against his heavy coat. It had been quite a time, after all. The thought of the first time came back to him, every second of it, from the moment when he had been fooling around with his Skipwith cousins out at Green Bluffs and one of them – it must have been George, he was always the forward one – squeezed him down there in his crotch and said, why, Cousin Will is quite grown up, I think he's ready, and he had said, ready for what? And George had said, why, Ma Scranton of course, and the two of them had laughed when they saw he had no idea what they meant.

They took him to Richmond that same afternoon, a hot dusty August afternoon when the Queen Anne's lace was so tall you could scarce see over the low hedges of the pastures. They went towards the river, the end where the gloomy brick warehouses stood. It was a part of town he had never been to, irregular rows of shabby clapboard houses with patches of mangy grass between them and glimpses of the sluggish dirty water beyond. He remembered how he had stood disconsolate in the front parlour, while George explained their requirements to Ma Scranton, who looked a severe sort of person, more like a governess than someone in her line of business, although Johnny Skipwith claimed that he had had her when he was a couple of years younger than Wm and she was a real goer. Anyway, he remembered her looking at him ruminatively, like a tailor sizing up a client, and saying, 'Yes, I think Dolly would do.' She had a little varnished wooden board beside her chair with bell pulls fixed to it, about half a dozen of them. And what he also remembered was the way she selected the cord she wanted and pulled it without needing to look at it or interrupt her conversation which was about the terrible state of the roads and how the mayor had a growth in his stomach and wasn't expected to last the week.

Dolly was small and friendly-looking, with ginger curls. When she put out her hand to him, he shook it like a clumsy country boy, and she laughed but not unkindly because what she intended without much in the way of ado was to take his hand and lead him off upstairs. So she took his hand again while they were still laughing and off they went up the polished wooden stairs, she turning brightly to ask had he driven far. They weren't in the little bedroom above a minute before she had unhooked her green taffeta dress and had nothing on but her shift and was putting a fresh towel on the bed. He began fumbling with his buttons and hopping on one leg to kick off his shoes, but she said, 'Don't worry, there ain't no rush. Besides, I kind of like slowcoaches.' And after he finally managed to shuck off his underclothes, she slowly drew the shift over her head and there she was.

That was the moment he remembered with the sharpest pang of

pleasure – no, it was too intense to be called pleasure exactly – her standing there with her small madder-tipped breasts staring back at him, and the carroty fuzz down below. And the way she leant forward to cup him as George had done, only infinitely more gently – well, she hardly had to lean, she was so tiny – and murmured, 'I think you'll do, George's cousin, what did you say your name was, I think you'll do nicely.'

As for what followed, that went like a breeze or a blur, he scarcely had time to register his surprises, how slippery the whole business was and how rough, he had not imagined it would be so rough but he was glad, proud even, that he somehow knew this was the way it had to be and judging by her exclamations of pleasure he had just about hit it on the head (he smiled now to think how innocently he had judged her cries). And when it was over she patted him on his damp back and said, 'You see, I knew you would do, I can always tell.' And the room was full of the scent of rotten lime blossom.

Then came the awkward moment which he cursed himself for not having consulted George about. He thanked her and then he mumbled, so as not to be thought to be sneaking off, should he pay her up here and the only time in all the time he knew her (because he came back half a dozen times for a refresher) her good humour snapped and she said, 'Didn't they teach you nothing? I don't talk to my gentlemen about money. Ma handles the business side.'

That was all years ago now, long before he went up to William and Mary and started moral philosophy, which was a very modern course including economics, political science and something newfangled called sociology, and that was when he took up with Louisa Gedding who was a very modern kind of girl and had the run of her house most of the time because her widowed father travelled in leather goods – saddles, bridles, portmanteaus and the like – and was on the road upstate half the year. He fancied himself to be hopelessly in love with Louisa and bemoaned the difference in their social stations (though it beat her why he had to refer to it in the first place) and he wished they could run away to Kentucky and live as man and wife on the frontier, which she said was stuff and nonsense. She didn't believe him either when he said that without her Richmond was the gloomiest place in the world and if she would not go with him he would go out West anyway and die a rich frontier bachelor with a broken heart.

Something of those first feelings of apprehension and desire came to him again as he stood for what seemed an unbearable eternity on the damp step of the house with the green dolphin, with the autumn leaves blowing about him in the dusk and his tethered horse snorting steamy breaths under the chilly light of the moon, which was near the full.

By now both he and the horse were stamping their feet to keep out the damp. He pulled the bell again and this time the door half opened almost immediately, and a flustered little maid peered out. 'Sorry to keep you waiting, m'sieu. I was upstairs helping the ladies.'

He started up the lower step expecting her to open the door fully to him, but she did not budge. 'I'm afraid we're closed tonight. They're all going out. It's a special order.'

'Couldn't I just come in and arrange, you know, another time.'

'Well . . .'

'Who's that, Boubou?'

'A gentleman, madame, I think he's foreign.'

Which Wm did not care for, having been so often complimented on his accent.

'A foreign gentleman? Well, don't leave him freezing on the doorstep.'

Boubou opened the door, muttering that she had been told to admit no one, so how was she to know.

As he came into the hall, a woman in a swirling silver evening gown came down the stairs to greet him with both hands outshetched. If she was indeed the madam of the house, she was a far cry from Ma Scranton. For a start, she was no more than thirty-five and she had golden curls to toss about her heart-shaped face. Her nose might be a little thin and suspicious-looking and her eyes were somehow disconcerting too, but she seemed full of sport and Wm thought, as Dolly had once thought of him, that she would do.

'You could not have come on a worse night, monsieur. I am so sorry' (she said this last in English). 'One of our best patrons has commanded the entire establishment to follow him on some mad excursion of his devising. The girls are beside themselves with excitement. They don't get out enough, you know. I am always telling them but they would die rather than put one foot in front of the other. He is such a fine gentleman, I fear I cannot give his name, I am under strict instructions – I am to call him Monsieur R. Oh, he is a man of such a generous and amiable character that I would not disobey him for all the world.'

As she was rattling on, Wm could hear the chattering and giggling from upstairs and she was still talking when they started to come down, five or six of them, laughing as they descended in a rustle of skirts and a cloud of perfume. He was gawping at them, so lost and so enchanted that he scarcely heard madame enquire after his own name so that he might be better received in future, if he could find it in his heart to forgive her and come another time.

'You may call me Mr S,' Wm said with a confiding grin.

Just then the doorbell rang again and this time Boubou was quick as a whippet and had the door open, and a tallish gentleman in a blue riding coat decanted into the hall in no time. The blue gentleman stared about him as lost in admiration as Wm had been.

'My dear Madame Sylvie, I fancy I must have landed upon the isle of Cythera. I have never seen such beauties and you are the queen of them all.' He bent to kiss her hand before shaking off his heavy coat and handing it to Wm. 'Would you be so good as to put it in the first carriage, the one in front of the door. Though the air is damp, your house is so warm and welcoming, madame.'

'This is, er, Mr S. He is a valued client.'

'Oh my dear sir, a thousand apologies. I had understood that the house was to be closed tonight.'

'Indeed, monsieur, I gave the strictest instructions, but Mr S called quite unexpectedly.'

'Ha, did he now? Well, he could not have come to a better place.'

Monsieur R came up to Wm very close and examined him as intently as if he were inspecting a miniature with a view to purchase. He did not seem much put out by Wm's intrusion on his private party and the more he surveyed him, the better he appeared to like what he saw. 'You are a fine fellow, sir. The ladies must hang around your neck.'

'Well, I don't know about that.'

'You are English, no, American?'

'American.'

'I like that. A republican. I too am a republican, though I scarcely dare confess it in this house, eh, Madame Sylvie. Our hostess is a devout monarchist. She has been known to wait on Her Most Christian Majesty, at the hospital, am I not right ?'

'You must not tease me, monsieur.'

'Oh, but I must, teasing is my *métier.*'

As they bantered on, Wm in turn looked closer at Monsieur R. He was a pretty fine fellow himself, in his late forties perhaps and run to flesh only a little, with a quick bright look and full lips that seemed to bubble as he talked. But when he paused for thought, as he did now, something harder, cruel even, came into his features and his face seemed to sag a little, like the face of an old comedian coming off the bright stage into the dark wings.

'You are a disappointed man, sir, don't deny it. You come here expecting all the elixirs of pleasure and you find the house closed at my orders. I cannot be the agent of your disappointment. You must come with us, Mr S. We shall explore the alphabet together and a good deal else besides.'

'B-but—'

'No buts, m'sieu. I insist. Pleasure must be shared, don't you think, or it is but sad sport.'

'You are too kind, I—'

'The kindness will be all yours if you fall in with my desire. Come, ladies, *en voiture*, we are off to the island of love.'

He clapped his hands and shooed the girls towards the door, bussing and patting them as they passed, accepting Wm's mumbled thanks with a dismissive wave.

They tumbled into the two coaches waiting outside. With a guilty start Wm remembered his faithful horse, but before he had managed to mention it he saw the little maid unhitching the animal and leading it off through the archway to the side of the house. 'There is no better stabling in Marly than ours, monsieur. Your horse will pass as pleasant a night as I trust we shall.'

Wm found himself seated next to Madame Sylvie with Monsieur R and the darkest of the girls opposite. He could feel the warm bulge of Sylvie's flesh against his own and the dark girl negligently rubbed her silky calf between his legs as the carriage began to rumble down the street towards the gates into the forest.

He abandoned himself to the moment and did not worry about the likely expense of this excursion or even its destination, still less about what Mr Jefferson would think.

They were deep in the forest now and the leaves deadened the sound of the wheels, and they could hear the other girls laughing in the carriage behind as they passed under the great trees. Wm began trying to work out which direction they were headed in – it was certainly not the road he had come on – but there were so many avenues criss-crossing one another that he soon gave up the attempt and let his body jog in time with the vibrations. He greedily drank down the white wine that Monsieur R uncorked from a gilt tantalus under his seat. It tasted of gooseberries and he enquired the name of the vineyard, which he resolved to pass on to Mr Jefferson who was halfway to acquiring one of the finest cellars in Paris. He wondered what TJ would say if he should add to the details of its provenance – a small property in the Sauvignon country belonging to a cousin of Monsieur R's – that it tasted even better if you were drinking it rolling along at night in a coach seated beside a brothel keeper with one of her girls rubbing against your legs and a mysterious voluptuary opposite. Even Madame Sylvie had condescended to stroke his thigh now, while the dark girl was leaning across Monsieur R, but he could not see exactly what she was doing, for her extravagant black tresses blotted out the view and the carriage was in darkness anyhow because the trees blotted out the moonlight.

The carriage took a sharp turn uphill, jolting over a stony track and shaking the passengers upright and out of their compromising positions. Then it stopped and with an even sharper jolt turned out of the road. Immediately in front of them there was a rocky wall, composed of gigantic boulders. For an instant it seemed as if the coachman had taken leave of his senses and meant to dash them against the wall. But in another instant the carriage had somehow passed through an aperture in the wall – a close thing, the ladies cried out and he could hear the wheels scraping against the rock – and they were out the other side. Instead of the high trees they now found themselves in a grotto, at least it seemed like a grotto from the tumble of great stones covered with moss and ferns that surrounded them. But the weird thing was the flickering light that played over the place. He twisted his head to see where the light was coming from, and on top of the rocks he saw an extraordinary apparition.

It was the figure of a satyr, horned and goat-legged, leaping along the crest bearing a burning torch. Then, following Madame Sylvie's pointing finger, he looked across to the other window and there was another of these eerie creatures with its torch casting erratic light over the dripping cave.

'Oh, how dreadful,' the dark girl exclaimed.

Monsieur R said nothing but tapped the glass behind him and the coachman drove on through a narrow defile and out into the woods again. Almost immediately the trees began to thin out and the moonlight straggled through the branches. What was that odd shape just coming into view? At first he thought it might turn out to be merely the gable end of a woodman's cottage, but then there was no doubt of it, there in the middle of Marly forest there reared up a stone pyramid, like the funereal monuments of ancient Egypt. What pharaoh had chosen to be entombed here so far from home? Wm could not be sure of the size of the pyramid, the moonlight was deceitful, and he looked back to enquire particulars of Monsieur R but that gentleman was lying back in his seat with his eyes closed and his bubbly lips agape while the dark girl busied herself in his lap.

Wm turned back to the window, but the pyramid had passed out of view and they were emerging into a rolling park, which dipped down to a lake or stream in the distance with the moon shimmering on its drowsy waters. This seemingly tranquil scene began to restore Wm's nerves somewhat and he was about to turn back to Madame Sylvie to remark on the pyramid and the strange creatures in the grotto when an even stranger apparition rose up in front of his eyes.

It was a broken column of white stone shining with eerie brightness under the light of the moon. At first glance it might resemble one of those fragments of antiquity that littered the classical pavements of old Europe, but in no time Wm realised that this was like no broken column he had seen in the engravings of Signor Piranesi or the capriccios of Hubert Robert. For a start, it was fully fifty feet high and twenty feet broad, larger in height and circumference than any column he had ever met with. The building of which it appeared to be the sole remain must have been unimaginably vast, the Parthenon would be no bigger than a cowshed beside it. The walls of the column were fluted in the Greek style, but no Greek pillar had ever had windows let into it, and such bizarre windows, ovals and lozenges, nothing classical about them at all, and there were great cracks and fissures striating the gleaming surface as though an earthquake had struck it. And was there not something horrid about its proportions? The straight lines did not seem to be quite straight and the curves did not seem to be regularly curved. At first he fancied that the whole column was leaning one way, then he thought it was leaning the other, or perhaps backwards. What earthquake could have wrought such damage and who could have built such a looming monstrosity in the first place? It was without a doubt the oddest structure he had ever seen, if indeed he had really seen it and the thing was not a phantasm of the night. He stared back at it until it was lost to view, for the carriage was now descending the gentle slope into the park, or what he thought must be a park, though it was hard to be sure of anything in this landscape of nightmares.

In the distance he espied the vestiges of yet another ruined building, presumably destroyed by the same earthquake that had shattered the enormous white broken column. He had an impression of Gothic tracery, a pointed arch perhaps, but by now he was too jangled up to make anything of an exact survey.

The carriage was slowing now and he could hear the coachman shouting, 'Whoa there, my beauties, enough now.'

Monsieur R sat up and shook himself. 'Here we are, *my* beauties, welcome, a thousand welcomes.'

They stepped down into a blaze of light from two flaming torches and Wm wondered whether the satyrs had been running behind them all the way from the grotto, but as his eyes blinked in the dazzle he discerned that the torchbearers here were not satyrs but two Chinamen in long brocade coats and pointed scarlet hats. And behind them there was a Chinese palace with its own lights blazing, so exquisite and ornate and improbable that the only possible explanation was that he really had fallen asleep after all the gooseberry wine and was now in the middle of a hallucination.

'Come in, come in, it is damp out here,' said Monsieur R, chivvying his guests down the steps of the coach. In fact, it was only the dank night air that convinced Wm that he was still in the Ile-de-France and not in some perverted fairyland.

They wandered wondering under the tasselled eaves of this dreamland palace and through its cascading hangings and brocaded pelmets into a large salon painted with an infinity of birds and flowers and Chinamen tittupping over little wooden bridges and up snowcapped mountains and through little gardens that had no flowers but only queer-shaped rocks in them.

On the long table at the end of the salon there was a huge supper laid out: lobsters and crayfish and oysters on silver dishes, and turkey and swan and guinea fowl and wild boar glazed with the most enticing sauces, and beyond them castles of spun sugar and trianons of ice cream.

'Always feed them first, be sure to give 'em oysters too. There's no aphrodisiac like a bellyful of oysters,' Monsieur R whispered into his ear. Wm suddenly wondered whether taking up his invitation – well, being swept along by it – was really such a good idea. At any rate the girls needed no encouragement to attack the feast and they were soon crunching and munching everything in sight. Even so, Wm was conscious of an irritable impatience afflicting his host. Monsieur R's thumbs were twitching and his geniality was fraying.

'Come along, ladies, come along,' Wm could hear him muttering, though it could not have been more than half an hour since they had stepped out of the coach. Monsieur R himself scarcely ate at all and took only a couple of sips from the glass that was handed to him by one of the tiny Chinese servants.

Wm ate and drank little more. He was in too confused a state, bewildered by what he had seen so far and apprehensive of what might be to come.

A brusque gesture from Monsieur R. Then from somewhere there came a tinkling of bells. The girls, whether forewarned or not, seemed to recognise this as a signal and they put down their plates and glasses with an untidy clatter and turned towards Monsieur R with expectant looks, one or two still wiping the last skeins of sugar from their lips.

'Now, my dears, it is time to take ship for the island of love. If you would kindly wait here a moment while your captain prepares himself.'

Monsieur R walked off with little excited steps towards a latticed bamboo staircase and disappeared up it.

Silence fell among his guests. Then the girls resumed their chatter and a couple of them sneaked back to the supper table to finish their wine or scrabble up a few last delicacies. But they had not long to wait. From above their heads there came the sound of a tinny gong. The tiny servants – they were a good six inches shorter than Wm who was after all no giant – scurried to form a line leading to the stairs and with little birdlike gestures they beckoned the guests to ascend.

Wm followed the rest of them up the bamboo stairs. They came into a smaller room, a library to judge by the bookshelves that lined the walls. But there was no sort of desk, only three or four low divans arranged in a circle. Monsieur R stood in front of the marble fireplace. He had discarded the clothes he had travelled in and was now dressed in a Chinese brocade robe that came down to his knees. His legs and arms were bare. Without any preliminaries he said in a hoarse urgent voice, 'Now, ladies, to horse!'

He took the dark girl over to the nearest divan and motioned her to kneel on it. Then, as she was settling herself in this position, he clicked his fingers at the next girl, a blonde with a round surprised face: 'You, over there, the same.' Then he flung up the skirts of the dark girl and gazed at her bottom, which was bare. 'You, the same please.' The surprised-looking girl who had by now clambered on the next divan and had to twist her neck to follow Monsieur R's instructions, slowly hoisted her skirts. 'Those drawers. Madame Sylvie, did I not give instructions about the drawers?'

'It was cold, monsieur,' said the fair girl, at the same time taking down her drawers, which now hung limp and white at her ankles.

'Now Monsieur S, let us start together and see who reaches the winning post first.'

Their host undid the brocade loops on his coat, which revealed that he was naked underneath and aroused. He advanced on the dark girl and began thrusting in a deliberate passionless rhythm. He might have been at a gymnastic exercise. There was nothing for it. After all, what else had Wm rung the bell at the house with the green dolphin for in the first place? He unbuttoned the flap of his breeches and was relieved that he was upstanding to a respectable extent. He advanced on the girl with the surprised face, wondering whether he ought at least to enquire her name before engaging, but she saved him the trouble: 'I am Amélie, m'sieu,' she said. 'I was in the other coach' – as though to reassure him that she was not some impostor who had strayed in without an invitation.

'You are very pretty, Amélie,' he said, staring at her sallow buttocks for a moment before he started. Without meaning to, he found himself pumping pretty well in time with Monsieur R, as though they were two pistons in the same engine. This methodical in-and-out motion engendered a certain mental detachment from the matter in hand. The same seemed to apply to Monsieur R.

'You are a university man, Monsieur S?'

'Yes, sir.'

'Harvard, I assume.'

'No, William and Mary. It is in Virginia.'

'I know it of course. And what did you study there?'

'Moral philosophy, political science, political economy too, it is a very popular subject now.'

'An excellent choice. I too am an economist, you know – not so fast, please, my dear – Turgot spoke warmly of my analysis of the net product. Ah, ah, not so fast, I tell you. I was one of the physiocrats, we are out of the fashion now but . . . that's enough.'

Monsieur R abruptly interrupted his analysis of the ups and downs of the physiocrats and disengaged, holding his glistening member with care as though it might break if he let go of it, and turned towards another of the divans where a third girl had already taken up her station, lying on her back this time. Wm continued at what he was doing, unsure what was expected of him, until he was interrupted by a muffled bellow from his host: 'For God's sake, sir. We have to give all the ladies a turn.'

Obediently Wm followed his host's example, moving on to the next divan. Madame Sylvie, he noticed, did not seem to be included in the tour but merely followed in their wake, caressing those girls who were not for the moment engaged, like a cook who must keep all the dishes on the hob regularly stirred or they will spoil. He himself was going at it as hard as he knew how, but he was not so distracted in his frenzy as to be oblivious of a prospect which he found decidedly unsavoury, viz., that in the next round he must start pounding in Monsieur R's leavings. And he was devoutly relieved – well, devoutly was perhaps not the *mot juste* – when there was an anguished yelp from the next divan and Monsieur R expired on top of the fifth girl whom he had only just broached. His brocade coat settled over him like a counterpane. Wm could just see the face of the fifth girl trying to extricate herself from being smothered flat. He himself carried on but making every effort to finish off as quickly as possible, not fancying the idea of Monsieur R exercising what no doubt was the host's privilege of standing voyeur. Which was precisely what happened.

'My God, sir, I admire your stamina,' gasped Monsieur R. 'They instruct you well at Harvard.'

'William and Mary.'

'Quite so. Half a dozen times a night, that was the way it used to be, but now, pouf.'

'You are magnificent, sir.'

'You really think so? Well, I cannot deny that I have had some distinguished compliments in my time. You have heard no doubt of Madame de –' And he whispered a name which Wm failed to catch and thought it impolite to ask to have repeated.

They were sitting side by side now on one of the divans. The sweat was pouring off Monsieur R and his face was as red as a turkey's wattle. Wm had taken off his shirt and breeches and his body was sticking to the itchy brocade of Monsieur R's robe. The girls were sitting all tumbled together on one of the other divans, while Madame Sylvie reclined alone sipping meditatively from a tall Murano glass, which one of the tiny servants must have brought her while they were at it.

So, Wm thought, this is an orgy and all things considered there was a lot to be said for it, though there might have been more to be said for it without Monsieur R. Even so, after a few glasses of brandy, which is what the tiny servants were pouring them now, he could not be sure how much of it had really happened and how much of it he would remember in the morning.

Monsieur R and Madame Sylvie were whispering together now, she with her head cocked on one side and smiling in a way that Wm found less taking than when she had first greeted him. Monsieur R was shaking his head, with an air of faint dejection. Then he shook himself and advanced towards the tumble of girls and bowed first to them and then to Wm. How formal the French were, Wm thought, they even bowed to you when they had just put their pricks up every orifice you possessed.

'Our revels now are ended,' Monsieur R said in English and he clapped his hands. The girls might not be well versed in Shakespeare but they were as quick as anyone to know when a party was over and they got up, straightened their dresses and ran their fingers through their tousled hair as though they had just risen from the most undisturbed sleep.

The party trooped back downstairs and the two men followed after them, Wm still buttoning up as he went. Yes, he thought, it was like waking from a dream, everything felt cold and clammy. The candles had guttered low in the salon and the little Chinese servants were chattering among themselves as they piled up the last of the silver plates.

The moon had gone down by the time the carriages started back up the park. In any case he was too drowsy to look out for the strange edifices. Too drowsy and too depleted. Perhaps that was why fucking had this sad side, because there was nothing much left of you after it was over, or that was how it seemed anyhow. There was a word to describe the feeling, but in his fuddled state he could not bring it to mind. He had thanked Monsieur R as effusively as he knew how and asked if he might contribute to the expenses of the evening, and Monsieur R had said that of course there could be no question of it, but his refusal was also frosted with melancholy, as though he had suddenly become conscious of how sad it was to pay for one's pleasures.

'Oh, by all means give the girls a little something, but do not feel obliged to be extravagant. They are only village girls, you know, and I would not want them to be spoiled.'

And Wm could see how eager Monsieur R suddenly was to be rid of them all. Spent, that was the word. Funny that the same word should do for both sorts of draining. And as he fell asleep with his head lolling against Amélie's bosom, he felt cold and sticky and at last – how his Skipwith cousins would have mocked if he had confessed it – ashamed.

But the shame took only a day or two to fade – he could, after all, remember so little of the evening with clarity – and he was back at the sign of the Green Dolphin the following week to see Amélie, who was the one he had taken a shine to, and she, he flattered himself, to him. Thereafter he made a regular appointment with her (he liked to be regular even in his irregularities) for Wednesdays at four o'clock and they came to call him Monsieur Mercredi. Ever afterwards the sound of horses' hooves slipping on wet cobbles would revive the ecstasies of those Wednesdays and his rides home up the avenue of ancient chestnut trees, sore but happy, to the nourishing soup and lamb gigot at the rue de Lorraine. The Wednesdays broadened his French vocabulary. But the expenses he incurred at the Green Dolphin were not recorded in his little grey account book. Even bookkeeping had its limits.

Before he went to Paris there was another rite of initiation, of a rather different sort. Mr Jefferson had to be presented to the King and naturally he must be supported by the gentlemen of the legation. TJ did not care much for ceremony, to say the least of it. The old customs of the Virginia back country were good enough for him. But when in Paris . . .

So on the seventeenth of May just as the city was enjoying a visit from the sun, that almighty physician as Mr Jefferson put it in a letter to Mr Monroe, a little procession of open carriages set out from the Americans' temporary headquarters (the Hôtel de Langeac was nowhere near ready yet) and trotted up the Champs-Elysées to take the road to Versailles.

The presentation of a minister plenipotentiary was a peculiar affair, grand of course, yet at the same time intimate, since the new legate handed over his letters of credence, not like lesser envoys in the dazzling splendour of the Galérie des Glaces, nor in the scarcely less dazzling pomp of the Throne Room, but in the relatively domestic surroundings of the King's Bedroom.

Barely had they clattered up the Queen's marble staircase lined by a hundred Swiss guards in full fig than their little procession was standing in the famous Oeil-de-Boeuf with only a couple of Swiss barring the way to the bedroom, which belonged to the old palace and looked out on to the pink courtyard, the part of the palace Wm loved the best. Here Louis XIV had died, here he and his successors had conducted their levees and their couchees. Even when the King was not there, anyone passing through had to make a bow to the bed, for this was the very heart of the matter, the locus of royal potency.

As they waited, the door in front of the Americans opened to admit some flunkey or other, and it was just possible to catch a glimpse of them all grouped under the great brocade hangings: the court officials, the pages, the dukes and princes and, in the middle, sitting bolt upright like a plump hen on her nest, the King.

The *introducteur* (as they had learnt to call the pop-eyed little master of ceremonies), who was standing at Mr Jefferson's left with the Captain of the Bodyguard, whispered something in Mr Jefferson's ear and the new Ambassador moved a few steps forward with that strange shambling gait of his. TJ was a thin man, skinny even, but somehow his clothes always seemed too small for him. He was accounted stiff in company (he had nothing of Mr Franklin's easy charm), yet there was something loose, off-centre, canted to one side about him whether he was standing or sitting. He had a curious vacant look too, as though his mind were elsewhere, but unlike most dreamers he was the very reverse of taciturn. Indeed, he spoke almost without ceasing and he would talk to anyone.

When Wm as a boy had first met Mr Jefferson, he had been taken aback by the deluge of talk. Another man would have said on being introduced, ah, so this is my dear wife's young cousin and asked Wm how he did and whether he was getting on at school. But Mr Jefferson instantly hared off on a discourse about the difficulties of protecting vines in a Virginia winter, about the recent incidence of smallpox among his slaves, about whether he, Wm, should practise law when he came of age or immerse himself in agriculture or both or neither. It was unsettling, overwhelming, but irresistible.

And three years ago when poor Mrs Jefferson had died and her relict had taken to riding all day in a distracted haze, seeking out the wildest woods and loneliest pastures, Wm had thought it a great honour that, after Jefferson returned soaked and exhausted to Monticello, he would often send word across the river that he would be glad if his cousin would join him for dinner as he had need of his advice. Since Wm was then the greenest, most newly qualified lawyer there ever was, it was not likely that he would have much learned counsel to offer, although he was later able to dispose of some minor items of Mrs Jefferson's estate, notably her rights in the Shelton and Wayles properties, for which service Mr Jefferson paid him the generous fee of thirty-five pounds sterling. But what the distraught widower wanted was company and Wm now being an orphan (his father having died soon after Martha Jefferson) they became attached to one another and there was no impropriety in Mr Jefferson declaring that he looked on Wm as his adoptive son.

Wm returned this affection from his heart, and his concern for his new father's well-being had redoubled three months earlier after they met again in Paris and the terrible news came from Virginia that TJ's two-year-old daughter Lucy had fallen martyr to the complicated evils of teething, worms and the whooping cough. It had been after Lucy's birth that her mother's health had so rapidly declined. And their successive deaths had brought what Jefferson called 'my unchequered happiness' to an irreparable end. Sunk in melancholy, he had withdrawn into his studies, buying books in shoals as distracted scholars tend to do, his tall shambling figure to be seen in the afternoon among the booksellers in the arcades of the Palais-Royal or mooning along the quays talking at random to startled promenaders. He had brought his elder daughter Patsy, not yet twelve, with him to Paris (the younger Polly, still only five years old, had been thought too young to come over just yet), but as a dutiful parent he had lost little time in enrolling her in the most fashionable convent school, the Abbaye Royale de Panthémont, and her visits to the embassy were all too rare to comfort the buttoned-up widower. Besides, Patsy was sad and lonely herself.

Thus Wm was anxious that his master might sink into one of his trances and forget where he was and what he had to do. Indeed, he saw him turning to engage the Captain of the Bodyguard on some no doubt irrelevant and probably inopportune topic, the superiority of Mansart to Le Vau as an architect perhaps or the problems of obtaining manure for his new parterres at the Hôtel de Langeac. If not firmly shepherded, he might wander off in the wrong direction to examine the tapestries in an adjoining chamber.

At this very moment, however, the doors were flung open and the fussy little *introducteur* propelled Mr Jefferson into the *chambre du roi*. The moment he caught sight of Mr Jefferson, the King put on an expression of mild but gracious surprise, as though he had expected someone entirely different and rather less agreeable to come through the door, then he removed his great feathery hat and rose to his feet. Mr Jefferson, still seeming somewhat absent from the proceedings, advanced into the chamber, bowed, advanced again, bowed again, advanced another three paces exactly as prescribed by the *introducteur* and bowed yet again – all most perfectly executed. The King sat down and put his hat back on. So did Mr Jefferson. Everyone put their hats back on. Mr Jefferson began his oration. He and Wm had concocted this flowery discourse between them, with a little help from the Comte de Cheverny who was the stage manager of these proceedings and, though Wm had to say so himself, it sounded like the genuine article. TJ's French was mediocre at best, not a patch on the standard Wm had now achieved with the aid of Lilite and his tutor at St Germain, but something about his loose rustic twang gave his words a certain dignity.

But what was so gloriously risible was that every time Mr Jefferson mentioned the name of Their Most Christian Majesties (either one of them) he had to take his hat off, and so did the rest of them, and as there weren't above two sentences at a trot that failed to refer to Their Graciousnesses, the hats were going up and down like grasshoppers. Then the whole thing happened again, only with the King doing the talking. Then the gentlemen of the legation were presented, which was Wm and Mr Humphreys, who was not only a disagreeable fellow but was at that moment packing his traps for England, so Wm could see no reason why he should have hitched a ride on this wagon.

Then the Americans had to make their bows all over again but going backwards this time. When they had rehearsed these manoeuvres back in the temporary legation, Mr Jefferson had shuffled and all but tripped, and that old wooden floor was nowhere near as shiny as the marble of Versailles. But somehow TJ did it now as perfectly as a dancing master. He always came up to the scratch when Wm least expected him to.

And when they were all done and Mr Jefferson and his gentlemen were back in the Oeil-de-Boeuf, they scarce had time to catch their breath before the Comte de Cheverny came through the door, banged his tall gilt staff and summoned them through to dine in the Salle du Conseil.

Now this particular Salle lay on the far side of the King's bedchamber, so they had to troop through there again, though this time there was no King to bow to, but of course as they passed the royal bed all the courtiers made a low bow. Wm kept his eyes fixed on TJ to see which way he would jump, because when the details of the custom had been vouchsafed to him by Monsieur de Cheverny he had exclaimed that this must be the most ridiculous custom in the history of humanity. But could he alone remain upright en passant, a solitary heron amid the bobbing ducks?

Not for the first time the great man found an ingenious solution. As he came up to the huge contraption with its swirling falls of deep red velvet and its nodding plumes at each corner, Mr Jefferson paused and turned, lowering his head a little to one side as though to inspect some object of interest in the vicinity of the bed, perhaps the fine needlework on the royal pillow. You could not have said that it was a bow in the full sense, but you could not have said that it was not a bow at all. Wm and Mr Humphreys imitated this ingenious manoeuvre as best they could, thereby giving to bystanders the impression that this was some peculiar American form of salute.

As he passed through the chamber, Wm was conscious of a disagreeable odour. He had heard tell that the plumbing at the Château de Versailles had not had the benefit of modern improvements, certainly not of the kind that were being installed at the Hôtel de Langeac to Mr Jefferson's precise specifications – it would not be the first water closet in Paris but it was still enough of a novelty to be the object of excited enquiry from everyone who had been shown around. At Versailles, by contrast, it was hardly an exaggeration to say that nothing had been altered in that respect since the death of Louis XIV. Hard-pressed courtiers, expected to stand on ceremony for hours at a stretch, would relieve themselves where they could (the stairwell was a favourite spot). But in the King's own chamber William had not expected such courtly effluvia, unless of course what was reaching his nostrils was the King's own.

He was relieved to pass through into the Salle du Conseil where the fragrances were altogether more enticing. There must have been covers for fifty at the long table and the servants were already handing round oysters and lemons and what the gilt-edged menu card said was a *croustade à la béchamel.*

'The sauce is named for Monsieur le Marquis de Béchamel, he was maître d'hôtel to le Roi Soleil,' the plump lady on Wm's right hand informed him. She went on to declare that although Monsieur de Talleyrand claimed that the French had three hundred and sixty sauces the classic tradition only countenanced four: the béchamel, the velouté, the allemande and the espagnole, although the last named she personally thought a vulgar intrusion worthy only to grace a peasant's table.

'Ah,' she said as the waiters approached in a magnificent line bearing huge gilt tureens wreathed in steam, '*le potage.*' She spoke with a reverence that was both sonorous and hushed, as though she were explaining to some latecomer in church that the Host was just about to be elevated. Having supped Madame Royer's good bourgeois cooking for nigh on six months, Wm was by now accustomed to the homage paid in France to the pleasures of the table and was amused to find that the passion reached to the highest levels of society, for he had established by squinting at the little silver cherub whose chubby hands clasped his neighbour's *place à table* that he was seated next to Madame la Princesse de – but he could not quite read her name in the curly court script.

'It is a *potage à la condé*, one makes it with partridge and haricot beans. The legend is that *le grand* Condé's chef, Vatel, first prepared it for him when he was fighting against the Spanish in the Ardennes where the partridges are so plentiful, but my grandmother said this was a fairy tale, she had tasted the soup at the Prince's own table years before the Ardennes campaign.'

As each dish was set before her, the plump Duchess had some fresh anecdote to offer or some criticism – too much salt here, more rosemary needed there – so that as the banquet wore on, Wm's head began to swim, not least because of the glasses of Margaux and Yquem chasing each other down his gullet. And it was something of a relief when the signal came for them to rise to their feet while the King passed among them.

His Majesty passed down the long line of distinguished faces, many now flushed by the sumptuous dinner and by the proximity of royal personages. Close up, he himself seemed even less distinguished than when Wm had first caught sight of him through the open door but even more endearing. He had the air of a portly grocer who likes to stand outside his store and pass the time of day with his customers. You would never have picked him out in a crowd.

'And you are?'

'Er ah, William Short, sire, Mr Jefferson's secretary.'

'Shott, Shott,' the King tried out the word as though sipping a strange liqueur.

'Yes, sire, it means *court* in English.'

'Well, it is a very *court* name.'

Everyone within earshot erupted in hysterical, uncontrollable mirth. It appeared to be the greatest jest ever cracked in the history of France.

'Yes, sire, it is.'

'And you are a very *court* man.'

The first jest had clearly been no more than a pipe opener, a mere hors d'oeuvre. This was the cruncher, the joke of jokes. To speak of gales of laughter would be a criminal understatement. This was a hurricane of hilarity. Madame la Duchesse looked as if she would faint for excess of amusement. The pop-eyed little *introducteur* was heading for an apoplexy. Everywhere eyes were weeping tears down powdered cheeks, raddled faces contorted with guffaws. If there was anyone in the entire company who was sticking to Voltaire's precept that an honest man never laughs, Wm could not spot him.

William himself was too steady a fellow to be much concerned about his stature but if his interlocutor had been anyone other than the King of France he would have retorted that there couldn't be much in it between the two of them where height was concerned, not more than an inch at most.

'Your Majesty is most perceptive,' he said, bowing as low as he knew how, feeling (a) that he was showing himself to be a true courtier and (b) that it was not a trade he greatly cared for.

'My dear, here is Monsieur Shott. His name means *court* in English and he is a very *court* man, is he not?'

Renewed hysteria in the ranks, abated perhaps a tad by anxiety not to drown out whatever masterpiece of wit the Queen might have to contribute to this feast.

At first Wm could not see her. She was a few yards behind the King and obscured by his bulk and by the *introducteur* who was whispering the names of the guests to the King whenever he wearied of asking for them himself in his own brusque inimitable style. She had not been at the presentation, and this was to be Wm's first glimpse of the celebrated Marie Antoinette. He had to admit he was disappointed (in fact, he wrote to his old friend Preeson Bowdoin who was consul down in Nantes, that at the Phi Beta Kappa ball her dance card would have been darn near blank). She had grown a little dumpy like her husband and her long-nosed sallow face bore an expression that was not exactly radiant. Perhaps it was her pouting lower lip and long jaw that gave her a disagreeable air and a somewhat puzzled one too, as though she did not know quite what to make of the scene in front of her though she must have attended a thousand such occasions.

'What?' said the Queen.

'Monsieur Shott. His name means *court* in English and he is a *court* man.'

'Ah,' she said, not changing her expression to any noticeable degree. 'Good day, monsieur, I hope you are well.'

The King, however, warmed by the success of his wisecracks, was in fine form and soon branched off into what Wm knew to be his favourite topic: statistics, for Louis was a man of his time (that was part of the reason he was so popular) and he shared the popular mania for figures.

'You came here by Le Havre, did you?' he enquired of Wm, leaning forward intently (their statures certainly were much of a muchness).

'I did, sire.'

'That is only fifty leagues distant. If you had come by Calais you would have traversed a distance of some seventy-three leagues though you would have endured a shorter sea journey, barely ten leagues.'

'Is that so, sire?'

'I speak in French leagues of course, your English leagues are longer, by precisely twenty-two per centum.'

'I did not know that, sire.'

'You ought to know it, monsieur. I make a note of these things, do you see? Make a note of it, that's the secret.'

'So Mr Jefferson always tells me, sire.'

'Well then, he's a sensible fellow,' said the King, though he sounded a little nettled that someone else had got in first with this invaluable advice. But then cheering up, he tapped Wm on the chest and said, 'Do you know what I would most dearly love to possess, monsieur?'

'I have not the least idea, sire.'

'What I would love to possess more than anything else' – and here he came so close that Wm could scarcely breathe for the clouds of powder and the overpowering fragrance of His Majesty's eau de Savoie – 'what none of my scientists can devise for me is a machine for counting how far I have ridden. Naturally I keep a careful daily record of the hunt, the woods we have been through, the game we have killed, the weather – that I record minutely – but the total distance traversed, that is the missing factor.'

'It is a gap, sire.'

'But surely, sir, a simple extrapolation of the principle of the pedometer—' Mr Jefferson pressed forward brimming over with enthusiasm.

'The pedometer?' The King stood back, staring at Mr Jefferson in hope and wonder.

'Yes, sir, a simple step-counter, or way-wiser as we call it back home. I have mine here, I never travel without it' – and he brought out from his vest pocket a small round silver device resembling a watch. 'Some of these appliances have a string attached to the leg which jogs the indicator at each pace, but this more advanced model responds to the rocking motion of perambulation. It would surely be a simple matter to adjust it to the stride of a horse whether trotting or galloping. I find the thing indispensable in my walks about your fine city and have heaped up a compendium of useful information. It is for example a distance of eight hundred and twenty double steps from the place Louis XV to the corner of the rue de Berri where we hope very soon to open our legation.'

'Eight hundred and twenty steps, really?' The King looked at him in amazement as at a man who has raised a regiment of skeletons from the dead.

'Double steps,' corrected Mr Jefferson.

'But those would be your steps, the steps of a tall man. If Monsieur Shott was wearing the appliance, they would be shorter steps, would they not?'

And holding the pedometer in front of him, the King gave a

demonstration of tiny mincing steps, which had the entire court rendered incapable with mirth yet again.

'Yes, sir,' said Mr Jefferson with a wintry smile, 'there would need to be some adjustment made.'

And he began to suggest modifications: how, for example, the little lever on the rim of the pedometer might be connected to a ratchet that would govern the rocking mechanism. Mr Jefferson liked to go into such matters in some detail and was as a rule unwilling to come out again until he had scraped the bottom of them. But before he was finished, the King had handed the pedometer to a tall, thin, melancholy-looking attendant lord in a silvery-grey coat that flapped about his knees. This left His Majesty's hands free to dig out a fob watch and flip open its lid. He executed this manoeuvre with an unmistakable impatience that ruffled the surrounding courtiers as though a chilly breeze had got up.

At that moment, apparently summoned by an unseen signal, a burly fellow in a red hunting coat materialised at the King's elbow. As he bent forward, Wm saw the curly golden horn slung round his neck on a scarlet tasselled cord.

'The horses are in the garden court, sire. I saddled Bécasse as you said, anyway Boniface is still lame. We should get a couple of hours' hunting before the light goes. We'll draw the lower woods at St Eustache.'

'What about Marly? You promised we would try the Abreuvoir.'

'There's no time, sire, it's too far.'

'No time, no time?' The King's lower lip stuck out like a cross child's.

'No, sire, you'd have to turn round and come back the moment you got there.'

'Damn these ceremonies, damn them I say.'

He glared round at the nearest courtiers as though they had personally designed the whole intolerable rigmarole.

'Well, well, good day to you, good day.' He nodded briskly at Mr Jefferson and the other Americans, and turned away muttering, 'St Eustache, St Eustache, that's no place for a serious hunt.'

And in a moment the royal party was gone, gone in fact while some of the older guests were still straightening up from their low reverences. The atmosphere relaxed. Several of the gentlemen set about having their glasses refilled and the ladies began to fan themselves with a vigour that might have seemed indecorous before the King.

'This is yours, I believe, monsieur.' The nobleman in the flappy silver coat handed the pedometer back to Mr Jefferson.

'You do not go hunting with the King, sir?'

'Not today. I am Master of the Wardrobe, not Master of the Hunt. Besides, these little *banlieue* hunts are scarcely worth getting in the saddle for. I never like chasing an exhausted stag through some cottager's vegetable patch. But the King would carry on hunting if he were galloping down the Champs-Elysées.'

'You have not met my new secretary, Mr Short.'

'No, I have not had that pleasure.'

'This is the Duke de La Rochefoucauld, William.'

'This, I believe, is the American style.' The Duke advanced and shook Wm's hand in a vigorous bony greeting.

Although Wm had already seen something of what Paris was pleased to call the best society, this was his first fully fledged duke and it was something of, no, not a disappointment exactly but a surprise. The Duke's voice had an awkward cracked tone to it, but he was as friendly as you could wish, there was nothing magnificent about him. He might have been a superior type of schoolmaster or, well, he might have been Mr Jefferson's brother, they were so alike in the way they conversed.

Wm knew one fact and one fact only about this particular duke and this was clearly the moment to deploy it. They had not finished shaking hands before Wm brightly ventured, 'You are to be congratulated, I believe, sir, on having translated the constitutions of all the American states into French. It must have been a Herculean labour.'

'It must indeed, Mr Short. But I fear that it was not I who undertook it. That is the work of my cousin Louis-Alexandre. He is the political one in our family. My interests are more agricultural, as Mr Jefferson knows to his cost, for I have quizzed him on winter fodder until he must have been desperate to see the back of me.'

'You must find that the life at court interferes with your rural pursuits,' said Wm, cursing himself for trying to be so smart.

'It does, but the King is an excellent fellow at bottom and I would not leave him for the world. In any case I dare not because my mother bought the post for me and she would never forgive me.'

He smiled at the unthinkability of defying his mother and Wm smiled too.

'If you would care to meet my cousin, Mr Short, we may run into him on the Tapis Vert. He told me he would take a turn down there. Like me he finds the air in here too stifling.'

He led Jefferson out through the long windows at the end of the room. Wm followed with Mr Humphreys whom he cared for even less when Humphreys explained what an elementary blunder it was to confuse this fellow who was the Duc de La Rochefoucauld-Liancourt with his cousin who was just plain Duc de La Rochefoucauld and all the grander for it.

'These are the people you will need to cultivate, Short. They call them "les Américains" at the moment, you know, but when this country gets itself a proper constitution these are the men who will be running the whole outfit. I should give anything to be here to see it, but then between you and me I would not be a whit surprised if they don't send me back here as minister when TJ goes home.'

They came out on the great terrace and began strolling down towards the shimmering stretches of water below, shading their eyes against the afternoon sun. The scent of the gillyflowers and some other tall pink-and-white flowers that Wm did not recognise was so intense that it seemed to drown out Mr Humphreys's self-interested burble. Even so, occasionally Wm heard the voices of Mr Jefferson and the Duke in their earnest incessant talk. Now and then he managed to pick out the odd word because Mr Jefferson's French was still so rough and the Duke dropped in the odd English word to help him out – 'manure', 'nitrogen' and 'Norfolk plough', for example, though he pronounced it 'plowg'.

As they emerged on to the huge green lawn that undulated down to the basins and canals beyond, the Duke hailed another tall gentleman who was just coming out from the beech hedges to the left. It was not surprising that they were cousins. They had the same serious awkward way with them, but the plain Duke as Wm thought of him had a soft stammer in his voice and a milder look in his eye. He was older too, a couple of years past fifty at least, and his unpowdered hair was iron grey. You could not have called him good-looking, for he had a big broken nose too large for the rest of his face and an old scar running down his cheek.

'Mr Short is a great admirer of your translations,' the other Duke said.

'Oh, you have read them. I am so p-pleased.'

Wm did not deny this imputation, although the closest he had got to the work in question was to see it bound in green morocco on the marble table in Mr Jefferson's hall. Instead he again murmured something to the effect that it must have been a very great labour to compose.

'Yes it was, I m-must confess. It is not simply that my English falls a long way short of your excellent French, monsieur. It is also that I am so uncertain of the nuances of so many English phrases. Take for example that excellent phrase in your Declaration of Independence: "the pursuit of h-happiness". How precisely should that be translated? Is it a pursuit like the pursuit of b-billiards or a pursuit like the pursuit of a stag? If I render it as *poursuite,* that is like *la chasse.* For the other meaning I must use some word like *occupation* or perhaps even *j-j-jouissance.* Tell me, which is it to be? Is it our right to enjoy happiness or only to chase after it?' Once the Duke had got launched, he spoke in an eager breathy rush, fearing perhaps that if he slowed down the stammer would get the better of him.

'Well, sir, we have no less a person than the author here with us, let him pronounce,' said Wm, rather boldly, he thought, because Mr Jefferson did not always care to be publicly challenged as the author of that celebrated manifesto.

'Yes, yes, Mr Jefferson, you are the horse's mouth as they say. Tell us, which did you intend?'

They had reached the end of the rolling lawn now and they all stopped, looking enquiringly at Mr Jefferson. He took out a handkerchief and mopped his brow. It was a warm afternoon, but he was not much inclined to perspire. To his surprise Wm had to conclude that the innocent question had disconcerted his employer.

'That is a most pertinent enquiry, sir, and I am not entirely confident that I have the answer to it. I would not like it to be thought that I chose the words purely for their euphonious impression, although

I do hold that they have a certain ring to them. But now that you confront me with a choice of senses, I confess that I am not entirely enamoured of either of them.'

'Not either of them? How can this be, monsieur?'

'Well, if we choose the sense of enjoyment, which may well be the sense in which we Americans most commonly use the word pursuit, that would indicate a certain complacency, would it not? We would be demanding our liberty in order that we might recline in unfettered indolence upon whatever bed of roses might lie to hand. That is not how our strenuous forefathers would have envisaged their task in life. It would certainly bear little relation to the burdens and privations that they endured in the early years of their migration to the American colonies.'

'Then we are to pursue h-happiness in the other sense?'

'You hound me, sir, and you do not find me wholly at ease here either. There is a restlessness, I might almost say a dissipated quality, about a man who chases after happiness to the exclusion of all else – virtue, honour, ambition. He resembles that butterfly flying about this statue here, of Apollo if I am not mistaken, he rests nowhere and will not stay to feed upon any particular flower. Our religion teaches us that we must not strive too earnestly after happiness or we shall never attain it. Indeed, it becomes nigh impossible that we should, for no sooner have we reached a perch that from a distance appeared the most desirable abode that we could conceive of than we must imagine a newer, yet more blissful resting place. Thus neither the enjoyment of happiness when we have it nor yet the chasing after it when we have it not entirely contents me. The purpose of my few imperfect words was but to specify that a sound political constitution will enlarge and not deny nor inhibit the possibilities of both. Therefore I am of the opinion that my words allowed of a useful ambiguity that came to me, so to speak, out of the ether and was not constructed by any conscious operation of my brain.'

There was a silence when Mr Jefferson had done. The two Dukes looked gratified to have had the meaning of that noble declaration untangled for them by its author, and Wm too was gratified even if he was not greatly the wiser, though he would not have dreamed of confessing his perplexity to Mr Humphreys who, however, was less reticent.

'What on earth does TJ mean by all that stuff?' he muttered, but Wm merely gave a superior smile as of an adept to whom the whole argument was mother's milk.

'Well, perhaps we need not worry the question to death,' Liancourt said. 'Surely we ourselves show the answer. We are enjoying these gardens and this fine weather, yet at the same time our legs are carrying us towards other delights – the lake, the Trianons, perhaps even Her Majesty's rustic retreat. Happiness comes to us in perambulation, you might say.'

'You have saved my bacon, sir,' said Jefferson. 'I hope you will allow me to filch this charming metaphor if I am ever vexed by the question again.'

Wm happened at that moment to be looking at the other Duke, the plain one as he had come to think of him, and was taken aback to see that after all he did not seem best pleased by Jefferson's exposition. His Grace's mild long face was contorted by what looked like a spasm of impatience, perhaps even anger.

Then Wm became aware that in fact the Duke's attention had wandered. He was no longer looking at his companions but at something that had caught his eye in the middle distance. Wm followed the direction of his gaze but at first could see only the great shimmer of the canal stretching away to the horizon. Then he caught sight of a canoe being paddled across the shorter arm of the canal in the direction of the Grand Trianon. Nothing unusual about that. Canoes were all the go in Paris now. The smart thing was to have one built in Canada, by Indian craftsmen, or have one sent over as the gift of a distant Canadian cousin. In reality most of them were run up at Desailly's boatyard just upstream of the Ile St-Louis. But still it was unusual to see a canoe being paddled – and rather erratically too – at Versailles on an afternoon of diplomatic audiences.

'I told her not to,' the Duke muttered. 'It would embarrass my c-cousin Liancourt and in any case I would have preferred her to walk with me, but she said she would s-suffocate on a day like this, she had to be on the water.'

For the first time Wm realised that the two people in the canoe were young women, and as they came closer to the bank of the canal, one of them took off her big straw hat and waved it at them.

'My wife,' said the Duke with a despairing gesture.

The canoe followed a zigzag course to the bank where two servants were waiting to moor it and help the ladies up the stone steps. The elder of the two was fair and perhaps not as young as Wm had first thought, though still with a charming expression. The younger, presumably her maid or companion, was dark and slight and bright-eyed, and you could see how sportive she was from the way she tossed the paddle to the servant. Yet she was also the one who had waved her straw hat at them. Perhaps the Duke had been deceived in the strong light – the sun was burning now – or perhaps he had not really meant to suggest that the one waving the hat was his wife.

But no, it seemed that Wm was the one who was deceived, for it was the dark young woman to whom they were presented as the Duchess.

She held out her hand to him. 'Oh, but we are so wet,' she said and there were drops of water still running off the hairs of her slender forearm and her little hand was damp, like the hand of a child who has just come in from playing. 'We are such bad rowers, monsieur. Madame d'Astorg was sure we would drown.'

'Nonsense,' the fair lady said, 'I had every confidence in you, Rosalie.'

'You must be an expert oarsman, monsieur?'

'No, madame, I fear not. In my country we leave the canoes to the Indians, they are so much better at it.'

'Ah, then you must despise us. I am sure you think that rowing is not a suitable occupation for ladies.'

'I think nothing of the sort, madame.'

'Oh, you have to call me Rosalie, everyone does. My true name is Alexandrine Charlotte, but Rosalie is so much prettier, don't you think?'

Rosalie sounded a little winsome to Wm's ear, but he said nothing and bowed an amiable assent.

'We are trying to match the informal m-manners of you Americans, you see,' the Duke said, but he did not ask Wm to call him Louis-Alexandre. And it was clear that his ill humour was not entirely melted, for he could not resist telling his wife that she should not have asked the servants to bring the canoe all this way since they and the cart on which it had been loaded were needed urgently at the farm. She took the rebuke negligently, like a child who is already thinking of something else and is in any case certain of her parents' affection.

But the Duke persisted: 'They must have started before d-dawn to get here and they will not be home until long after nightfall. It is too b-bad, my dear, and it is even harder on the horses.'

'But Pierre wanted so much to see Versailles – did you not? – and Jeannot too.' The men turned from loading up the canoe on the wagon and gave blushing grins of agreement.

'Well, it must not happen again. In any case at home we have our own dear Seine to paddle in. Monsieur Short, you must come and teach my wife how to row in running water instead of a stagnant pond.'

Wm said that nothing would give him greater pleasure. He rather liked the Duke's style of dismissing these magnificent waterways. All the same, how could she be his wife? He must be twice her age at least. Of course he knew of elderly men back in Virginia who had taken much younger wives, usually to breed children or to join up adjoining estates. Old Mr Popkiss had married Sarah Topping when he was sixty and she was barely twenty-one, but Sarah was born matronly. But when Rosalie took her husband's arm and beseeched him not to stay angry with her, she seemed more like a wheedling daughter than a full-blown duchess.

'You will come, won't you? Tell Mr Jefferson he cannot come without you, to La Roche-Guyon I mean. You will love it and you will teach us all to row.'

'But you must believe me. I have never rowed so much as a skiff back home.'

'You Americans are so modest.' She did not seem to listen much to what a fellow said to her, but that was no great matter. He had met girls like that before. When they were on the wing, it was as much as you could do to keep up with them.

'It will be quite a large party. We are celebrating your war of independence, you see, so Monsieur de Lafayette will be there. And then we very much hope Monsieur de Condorcet will be of the party too, but he is so elusive. You know Monsieur de Condorcet, everyone knows him, though he says he is so unsociable.'

'I fear I have not yet had that pleasure.'

'Oh, but you must have. I am sure you have seen him, he looks so.' She hunched her shoulders and tried to make the most of her modest height by walking on tiptoe with a strange stilted gait, at the same time drawing her skirts round her like folded wings.

'My wife is less fitted to m-mimic Monsieur de Condorcet than anyone I know,' said the Duke, laughing. 'He is nearly two yards tall and looks like a vulture. That is why we call him le Condor, after the great vulture of Peru.'

'Travellers have seen them in the far west of our own country too, I believe.'

Wm professed a great longing to meet this enchanting vulture and it was a sincere profession, for it would be Rosalie who would bring about the meeting and nothing could be more pleasant than to watch this dark sprite dancing around these tall solemn men, like the little girls he had seen dancing round the marble statues in these shrubberies.

The sun had gone off the great glassy stretch of water and big bruised clouds were gathering over the woods.

'You will soon learn, Monsieur Short, that the s-sun never shows his face too long in the Ile-de-France,' the Duke said, looking up at the broody skies.

Behind them they could hear the slam of the cart's back board and the rattle of the iron pegs and chains slipping into their holes. In a couple of minutes Jeannot was geeing up the sleepy nags to make their way back to La Roche-Guyon.

Wm felt a sudden gloom descend on their little group. He had a sad face, the Duke, when it was in repose. Mr Jefferson too had that look when he had just finished expounding his latest enthusiasm, as though returning to a natural melancholy which only his restless curiosity could keep at bay and which his recent bereavements had deepened.

They roused themselves to make sprightly goodbyes, brightened by plans and promises to meet again in no time, at La Roche-Guyon, at the Opéra, at the new embassy (Rosalie could scarcely wait to view the famous water closet that Mr Jefferson was installing). This was only an intermezzo, no, an overture to an endless fête.

They turned back towards the great palace, all six of them walking a little quicker on the return journey up the great green carpet. The long façade had lost its golden glow now the sun was off it, and it suddenly looked grim and heavy.

III

Chalkface

He came to know the road so well that years later when he was far away, in Spain or Holland or back in Philadelphia, he could unwind it in his head like one of those child's panoramas that turn on a spindle. And he could single out from all those later occasions the very first time he travelled it. It had been in the early days of summer when the white candles were still on the chestnut trees and the lime leaves had not yet lost their shimmer. He could recall, so sharply, the quiet rumble of the carriage wheels through the forest of St Germain, the huge canopy of the ancient trees, then the sudden bright light as they came out to the edge of the river and the louder rumble of the wheels on the wooden bridge they crossed to cut off the bend. He leant forward and pressed against the dusty window to see the curve of the Seine and the chalky cliffs following it round to Mantes-la-Jolie. He could just see the twin towers of the cathedral the other side of the river, like a plainer Notre Dame set down in the countryside.

The sun was fully out now over the bosky meadows, but it would not have mattered if he had been looking out on dreary ploughland under heavy rain, for his heart was so brimming with hope that it seemed capable of flooding the universe. Even the jolting of the carriage and the smell of the minister's newly waxed leather seats felt as though they were part of some vast conspiracy to make him happy.

Mr Jefferson was talking about air balloons. 'It is my distinct impression that the form of a pear is best suited to catch the upward currents. The more globose shape of Monsieur Robert's balloon appeared to dwell in the air more securely, I agree, but that may have been the effect of the hydrogen. I gather that Monsieur Montgolfier still prefers hot air.'

'Indeed, sir, does he so?' Wm hazarded dreamily.

'It may be that some gas as yet unknown will bear aloft the Montgolfiers of the future, when they shall be our charioteers not merely from one side of Paris to the other but from Paris to Philadelphia.'

'Monsieur Blanchard managed to find his way across the Channel, did he not?'

'Yes, but he was merely carried by the prevailing wind. I had the honour of conversing with Monsieur Blanchard when he visited Philadelphia and he explained to me that . . .' But the particulars of Monsieur Blanchard's explanation were lost in the rattle of the traffic as they came into a village, which was packed solid with carts and carriages. At first Wm thought that it must be market day. But he spied a procession coming out of the parish church and he heard a bell ringing from the tower. A village wedding perhaps, but then he saw the sturdy youths in plum-coloured doublets and breeches carrying a sort of wooden howdah decked with flowers on which a female statue in a scarlet-and-gold robe juddered precariously.

'This, I fancy, must be the festival of Sainte Geneviève de la Rivière,' said Mr Jefferson, taking out his notebook. 'She is said to have been martyred on this spot and her remains thrown into the river for refusing to surrender her virginity to the invading pagans, Goths or Huns I forget which, although the *Encyclopédie* tells us that no such person ever existed and that, as is so often the case, the Christian myth merely enshrouds some earlier custom, no doubt one involving human sacrifice.'

Wm thought he preferred the story of Ste Geneviève, whose simulacrum was now being carried across their path. All the men in the crowd had removed their hats as she passed and although Wm was out of sight behind the dusty windows of the carriage, he took off his hat too. Mr Jefferson paid no attention and continued to discourse upon the tradition of river sacrifice, which he said had probably been brought to France by the Gauls. But again his words were drowned as the crowd began to sing a dirge. The four sturdy youths were now taking the howdah on to a rickety flight of steps leading down into the river. They waded into the water at a deliberate pace until it was up to their waists. Then they released the saint and she began to float in an erratic motion downstream, the howdah now transformed into an ark. Within a minute or two she was lost to sight behind the willows that leant out over the water.

The flowers that had been strewn about her came away from her conveyance and drifted across the river in long straggling wreaths, some snagging on logs or overhanging branches and waving lazily on the current long after Ste Geneviève herself had gone to her watery grave.

'She'll sink inside five minutes,' the coachman said. He had hopped off his seat and was leaning against the wheel enjoying the scene and smoking some foul tobacco in his pipe, the fume of which was curling through the open window.

Wm knew that he would remember the sight for ever: the juddering ark, the stiff little saint in her scarlet-and-gold robe, the flowers waving in the water and the coachman's tobacco. Even Mr Jefferson stopped taking notes and put his head out of the window alongside Wm.

It was not much above an hour after Ste Geneviève that the road took a sharp turn up the hill into the side of the chalky cliff, then twisted back towards the river through a larger, more prosperous-looking village, and the coachman leant back and shouted to them that this was La Roche-Guyon. In a minute they could have seen that for themselves because as they came round the bend in the village street there, unmistakably, was the great chateau, its creamy turrets and colonnades standing proud of the bare chalk. It was virtually in the middle of the village, there was no park to separate it from the humbler dwellings, and in another minute or two there they were in the castle yard with the white chalk directly above them and the plain Duke with his big nose and sad scarred face trotting out to meet them. And there she was in her straw hat, carrying under her arm a rough wooden basket full of spring flowers as if she were going to strew them before her guests.

'There, you see, we are t-t-troglodytes here,' the Duke said, gesturing at the great cliff of white chalk above them, almost too dazzling to gaze at in the midday sun, and indeed on an upper ledge further along there were openings cut into the chalk with dusty wooden doors let into them.

'You are most gracious to welcome us so,' TJ said.

'You mean, to c-come out? Ah yes, when I was in Norfolk Mr Coke came to his gate to meet us and I thought that we must learn to do the same service in France.'

All the same, there was a constraint about his greeting, as though he were acting under orders. And it was with some continued awkwardness that he led them under the arch and up a winding stair. He might have been a newly employed footman who did not yet know his way about the place.

He brought them into a great chamber, a gloomy room hung with vast tapestries that had a shabby look to them, or perhaps it was the bright light outside that made it seem so tenebrous. Wm's eyes took some minutes to adjust so that at first the figures congregated at the far end looked like mourners in inky black. They seemed preternaturally tall too, or it might have been the little Duchess skipping ahead of her husband like a frolicsome puppy who enhanced their stature.

There were introductions. The other Duke, Liancourt, they knew already. Then there were a couple of learned abbés who had not the advantage of the English tongue but speedily complimented Wm on the excellence of his French, prompting Mr Jefferson to remark that Mr Short was the true ambassador because he was the only one who understood what people were saying to him. Which sentiment Mr Short himself heartily (but silently) endorsed, since he it was who had to issue the visas, write the letters of introduction for distinguished visitors, compose the greater part of the official dispatches, persuade the bankers of the Low Countries to stretch out the repayment of the enormous American loans (the most important business of the lot), and into the bargain proof-read the text of TJ's *Notes on Virginia*, while His Excellency himself strolled about Paris (never neglecting to enter his pedometric readings into his journal), bought rare books and made botanical and architectural excursions.

Wm was so pressed for time that he ventured no commentary upon the content of TJ's Virginia notes as opposed to their punctuation and spelling (never his master's forte). He passed over in silence Jefferson's remarkable assertion that in reason Negroes were much inferior to whites and in imagination dull and tasteless. According to TJ, no black had ever uttered a thought above the level of plain narration, although he was prepared to admit that 'in music, they are more generally gifted than whites with accurate ears for tune and time and they have been found capable of imagining a small catch' (William wondered if Mr Jefferson had ever listened to the melodies that wafted up the hill from the vineyard huts at Monticello). And this inferiority could not, so the great liberal statesman and trumpeter of equality averred, be ascribed to the manifold injustices attendant upon slavery. It was not the condition of the Negroes but nature that had produced the distinction. These airy sentiments took Wm's breath away, but he knew there was no point in contesting them, even if he had had the leisure for it. On matters of principle TJ was hard to budge.

Now they were being presented to the elderly lady seated in the high-winged *fauteuil* at the far end of the room. She had a bright look in her eye and a crinkling smile, which promised more than mere courtesy.

'This is my dear m-maman,' said the plain Duke. The Duchesse de La Rochefoucauld d'Enville put out her hand to Mr Jefferson, who shook it warmly in the American style and then in turn introduced his secretary Mr William Short.

Again she held out her hand, but Wm – possessed by what whim he could not calculate either then or afterwards – bent low and kissed it with an address he had not thought himself capable of.

There was a ripple of what? Astonishment perhaps, then light-hearted applause.

'You see, madame, how fortunate I am to possess a secretary who is so frenchified already, although I was arrived here before him.'

Wm thought he detected a hint of aigritude in Mr Jefferson's tone, though his words were amiable enough. He could not be sure whether his master deplored his lapse from the frank and manly manners to be expected of Americans or whether he did not much care that Wm should be the centre of attention, perhaps a little of both.

'You are most welcome, sir. My granddaughter has told me that you are an adept in the art of canoeing.'

'Your granddaughter, I fear—' he babbled.

'Ah, I see I have confused you,' the Duchess said. 'My granddaughter is also my daughter-in-law. It was for all of us a great happiness when my daughter's child consented to marry my son. He had been on his own so long after his first wife died. I could not have imagined any greater good fortune than that she should come here to console my lonely widowhood.'

'My dear maman, you know less of s-solitude than any woman in France,' the plain Duke said, waving a long bony hand at the assembled company, which must have been fifteen or twenty strong.

'You are all very kind to come so far to amuse a poor old woman,' Madame d'Enville said, clearly not meaning a word of it. 'Rosalie,' she called out, beckoning her granddaughter/daughter-in-law, 'you must not allow me to bore Monsieur Short. Let him first kiss some other more delightful hands.'

Rosalie took him over to the group standing by the long window, through which he caught a glimpse of the orchards leading down to the river, which meandered in parallel with the sandy road. The members of this group all had their backs to this entrancing view and were listening intently to a tall, beaky-nosed, sandy-haired young gentleman who seemed to like the sound of his own voice. At least that was how a stranger might have described him, but Wm was not a stranger, for he had first met Monsieur de Lafayette back in Virginia when they were both nineteen years old.

How had he viewed the great hero then? With admiration certainly, for his dash, his pluck, his readiness to give his life for the cause of liberty. Lafayette was, after all, very nearly the richest young man in France. Brought up as an orphan by adoring women deep in the country, he was so surrounded by servility that when he crossed the boundary of his own huge estates he was amazed that the peasants no longer raised their caps to him. He could have frittered away his life in all the amusements that Paris had to offer. Instead he chose to cross the seas in search of revolutionary glory, at the risk of a squalid death in an American ditch. All this Wm could only admire and, to be frank, envy.

But then there was Lafayette's vanity. This was, alas, much worse than the ordinary vanity of a young man who glances in the looking-glass to make sure that his hair is brushed and his cravat knotted. It was an all-consuming self-passion. Ill-natured people said that Lafayette counted any day wasted that he had not sat on a white horse and waved graciously to a large crowd. If you caught him unawares, he could dispense practical sense. With his back to the wall he knew how to fight his way out better than any man. Nobody could deny his dauntless resourcefulness. But in the last analysis there was for him one person and one person only in the world who really mattered and that was Marie Joseph Paul Yves Roch Gilbert Motier de Lafayette.

He was friendly, though; that could never be denied either. He greeted old acquaintances with the same effervescence as he embraced fresh causes to fight for and new notions to spout about. And he greeted Wm now as though they were long-lost brothers who had been separated by shipwreck for twenty years, rather than, as was in fact the case, having last met briefly two weeks earlier at a Thursday at Madame d'Houdetot's.

'Did I tell you, my dear Short, of my most recent travels among the Indians of your country? It was a remarkable affair,' he said, turning back to the gentlemen and a lean pock-marked lady whom he was already addressing and so not giving Wm time to say that yes, he had in fact given him a full account of those travels on his passage through Virginia the preceding year. 'I had the honour to accompany the Commissioners of the Congress on their journey to Fort Schuyler to make peace. These gentlemen were good enough to remember that I had had some earlier intercourse with the leaders of those Indian nations and they perhaps saw in me the spirit of that France which had always been the Indians' friend and protector. The Indians had even bestowed upon me the title of the Great Kaweyla and the Commissioners were of the opinion that my words might reinforce the effect of the brandy and the bracelets that we had brought with us as peace offerings. It was bitterly cold in that country, colder even than I remember in my first winter in America, that terrible winter of Valley Forge and Brandywine. I had brought my new mackintosh and had my valet cover it with gum to keep out the cold. Unfortunately the gum had melted on the voyage and the *Courrier de Paris* in which he had packed the garment was stuck to it for all to read. I was, my friends, a walking newspaper.'

There was a titter at the thought of the gallant Marquis striding through Indian country covered in old newspaper like a tramp trying to keep himself warm.

'My teeth were chattering when I was invited to say a few words to the assembled tribes. Listen, I said, to the advice of the Great Kaweyla. Let my voice rush among the nations like that of the health-giving wind which in summer announces the rains.'

But the advice of the Great Kaweyla was interrupted by a clapping of hands from the other side of the room where Madame d'Enville was seated in her great chair. It was her son who beckoned them over and motioned the footmen to bring up more chairs.

'We are promised a rare treat,' he said in his quiet, serious, stammering voice. 'My mother has prevailed on Monsieur de Condorcet to say a few words upon his new p-project, which I understand he is to present to the Académie des Sciences next Thursday.'

'I had to implore him, I am quite weak with the effort of it.' Madame d'Enville looked anything but weak. Her eyes, paler than her granddaughter's but no less bright, seemed to gaze into your head, enquiring what have you to contribute, what do you think about that then? The faded pink bonnet and the froth of lace at her neck were suitable to the dignity of an old lady – she must be over seventy since her son would not see fifty again. Yet her gaiety was so abundant that her old lady's costume seemed almost like a disguise.

Wm could not afterwards work out whether Monsieur de Condorcet had been walking on the loggia and been whistled up by the Duke, or whether he had merely been lurking behind Madame d'Enville's chair, perhaps reading a book until he was called for.

At all events Condorcet made an entrance, there was no other word for it. Not an entrance such as Lafayette might have made, flamboyant, waving to the crowd as soon as he appeared. On the contrary, Condorcet came into view with an air of timidity and reluctance, almost as though some invisible mechanical device was propelling him towards the assembled company. His mannerisms were much as Rosalie had shown in her little mimicry by the side of the canal at Versailles: the hunched craning attitude, the arms flapping at his side, the stilted walk. Yet when Rosalie imitated him, she could not help making the whole effect vivacious. Her vulture seemed about to flap its wings and take off.

The real Condor, though, appeared a more listless creature, drained of the physical vitality that Rosalie radiated, partly because he was deathly pale. He must have been forty at most, but it was inconceivable that he should ever have been young.

There was a pause, which Monsieur de Condorcet seemed in no hurry to bring to an end.

Eventually the Duke felt obliged to make good the promise he had given. 'You were, I think, going to tell us something about the application to politics of the science of p-probability.'

'I should much prefer to talk about oysters,' Condorcet said. His voice was reedy and might have had a sardonic edge had it not been so feeble and hesitant.

'Oysters,' the pock-marked lady almost shrieked, carried away by the sage's wit.

'I had some excellent oysters in Brittany, in the neighbourhood of Quimper. They were small but the flavour was more refined than that of the larger specimens to be found further along the coast, at Brest for example.'

'I trust there was an "r" in the month, monsieur.'

'That, madame, is a common fallacy based upon the coincidence that the summer months in our calendar happen to lack that letter. In reality one may eat oysters at almost any season provided that the temperature of the sea does not surpass a certain degree.'

'But probability, sir—'

'The lobsters of that region too—' Monsieur de Condorcet persisted.

He was interrupted by a sharp rapping noise, the noise of Madame d'Enville's folded tortoiseshell fan on the wooden arm of her chair. 'My dear friend,' she said, 'if you persist in discussing crustaceans – a subject on which I fancy I know very nearly as much as you do – I shall myself begin to discourse upon probability and that would be a fate worse than a bad oyster.'

Condorcet looked at her with an expression that might have passed for affection and then without apology or hesitation he embarked on the subject he had been ordered to embark on. This lack of any caesura or change of tone gave to his discourse a curious uniform flow, as though probability were but another species of shellfish.

'It has for a long time occupied my attention, as it did that of my friend d'Alembert, that the truths of the moral and political sciences must be capable of the same detached scrutiny, the same methods of proof, as the truths of nature.'

He paused, either to catch his breath or to signal that this was the end of his preamble. The pause allowed a middle-aged gentleman in a green coat to remark in a negligent way, as though talking to the ceiling, 'I say, that was a funny business, the way old d'Alembert popped off.'

'There was nothing humorous about it, sir. Monsieur d'Alembert was an ornament to the human mind. He was also my oldest and dearest friend. And in his death he was as noble as in life.'

'No, I mean the way they kept out the curé for fear the old boy might cave in at the last moment.'

'You are mistaken, sir. Monsieur d'Alembert had no wish to see a priest, not the slightest. The curé of St Germain was politely received on the first occasion he called, but the fifth or sixth time he knocked at the door the servants had to be instructed to send him away.'

'But who instructed them, that's what I'd like to know.'

'I was party to the decision, sir, if that is your insinuation. Just as I was happy to accompany his body to the cemetery where at the insistence of your precious priests it was tossed in the common ditch without tombstone or memorial.'

'Not my priests,' the gentleman in the green coat muttered, but Monsieur de Condorcet had moved on, or rather moved back to his original topic.

'It is no disservice to my old friend if I venture to observe that in one crucial respect he was mistaken. He sought for truths in society that might be proved with the certainty that we expect from a proof in mathematics. But in the human sciences – that is, those sciences whose goal is to teach us how we should act – man must be content, as he must be in the conduct of daily life, with probabilities.'

'Probabilities.' The pock-marked lady sighed as though it were the most sensual word in the dictionary.

'The correct method in this sphere is not to seek out truths that may be rigorously proved, for no such truths exist or none but the trivial, but rather to choose between probable propositions and above all to estimate their relative degrees of probability.'

'Ah yes,' murmured the pock-marked lady in Wm's ear, as though she too had wished for nothing more than to estimate probabilities in just this fashion.

'You all know how in agriculture we experiment with seeds to see which will give the heaviest crop on a chalky soil such as we have here at La Roche. And we learn from trial and error at what density the seeds are to be sown and which on average is likely to be the best week of the year in which to sow them, so in politics we must use the tools of science to improve the results.'

'That is all very well, monsieur, but seeds don't have votes. In elections we're at the mercy of the popular will. One chap promises the moon and all the local halfwits vote for him, nothing scientific about it at all.' The gentleman in the green coat looked about him with an ill-suppressed air of triumph.

'Then at the very least we ought to ascertain the popular will in a more scientific manner, if only to confirm how imbecilic it is.'

'Well, there's no mystery about that. The fellow who gets the most votes is the winner.'

'Can you be sure of that, monsieur? Let us take a simple practical example. Suppose there to be sixty voters and three candidates: Monsieur A, Monsieur B and we must not forget Madame C, for in any serious inquiry it would be unscientific to omit one half of the human race. And let us further suppose that twenty-three of the voters give their voices to A, nineteen to B and only eighteen to Madame C. Under our present laws A would be elected the legal representative of his fellow citizens and poor Madame C would retire to her knitting. But suppose that we have asked our voters not merely to vote for one candidate but to range all three in order of preference. It might emerge from this deeper inquisition that A's twenty-three voters preferred Madame C to Monsieur B and that B's nineteen voters preferred her to Monsieur A. Thus we would find that it is Madame C who has forty-two votes and who enjoys the real majority of the voters and who ought therefore to be elected.'

There was quite a hubbub, compounded of bafflement and outrage. How could the candidate who had finished third be accounted the true winner?

Condorcet looked around him with a thin smile. Yes, Wm thought, now he does look like a bird of prey and one that has just spotted a juicy field mouse.

'It is a p-paradox, sir, a wonderful p-paradox.' The Duke was lit up by the thought of it, struggling with the noun but recklessly returning to it in his enthusiasm. 'I am sure that posterity will come to call it Condorcet's Paradox.'

'No I say, though,' remonstrated the man in the green coat. 'Old A won't stand for it, bet you he won't. He won fair and square and now this lady is put up in his place. He probably doesn't agree with women in politics anyway. I'm not sure I do, there's separate spheres, I always say. There's going to be one hell of a row, it'll come to blows I shouldn't wonder.'

'Science has always had her trials, monsieur. Remember Galileo. In the end the truth will prevail over men's minds.'

Condorcet looked about him for any further challenge, but for the moment nobody seemed eager to take him on.

'I say, Condorcet, can you tell me what the scientific probability is of my bay beating Chartres's roan?' The gentleman in the green coat had bobbed up again, undeterred by previous rebuffs. Rosalie told Wm later that he was Monsieur de Vernon, a local landowner who had heard about Madame d'Enville's celebrated intellectual parties and had begged to be included. The Duke had given in to this request from a childhood friend and was now wishing he hadn't.

But Monsieur de Condorcet was delighted by the request. 'At this moment, sir, I confess that I cannot, I have not the evidence. But suppose your horse were to gallop a mile and you were to time him on your fob watch and Monsieur de Chartres or his groom were to do the same with his horse. Then I would be able to estimate the probability of your horse winning the race and indeed to calculate the margin by which he might be expected to win. In due course the State might draw up a register of such timings so that all the horses in France might be graduated according to their speed and endurance. This would naturally assist the breeders in choosing the best stallions and mares to improve their stock.'

'But would it not take all the sport out of it, if you knew in advance which horse was going to win?'

'My dear sir, the English who are far in advance of us in so many matters have already devised a solution to your anxieties. Those horses that are deemed superior must carry thin lead plates of such and such a weight in their saddle-cloths, to even up their chances. These weights are known in English as "handicaps". Thus uncertainty of outcome is restored by strictly scientific methods.'

'He is a walking encyclopaedia, is he not?' breathed the pock-marked lady in ecstasy. Certainly the breadth of knowledge displayed by Condorcet was dazzling – oysters, elections, horse races. There seemed no end to it.

Wm felt a sharp nudge in his back and on turning round discovered that Lafayette was elbowing him aside in order to reach the front of their little group and had already begun speaking as he did so.

'You know, monsieur, that there is no greater friend to probability than myself. In military questions I have sought in my poor way to apply the scientific method at every possible opportunity. Yet I beseech you also to recognise, monsieur, that there are phenomena in nature which science is as yet powerless to account for. We may only record the effects of such influences.'

'Influences, what influences?' Condorcet interrupted in a harsh voice that seemed reinforced by strong emotion.

'I speak of those influences which, if rightly understood and encouraged, may prove the greatest boon to human happiness that our enlightened century has yet seen.'

'What influences, sir? Be plain with us.'

'I think you know what I am talking about, sir.'

'You refer, I have no doubt, to the despicable antics of that Austrian charlatan.'

'I refer, my dear Condorcet, to the new science of animal magnetism and its healing properties, which may revolutionise medical science if its progress is not obstructed.'

'Monsieur Mesmer is not worthy to be called a man of science.' Condorcet's voice was shrill now, he was almost gabbling in his passion.

'His medical qualifications are not, I think, inferior to your own.'

'One may be a doctor and still be a charlatan.'

'He is a close friend of Monsieur Mozart.'

'He could be Rameau's nephew and still be a charlatan.'

'Have you not heard how he cured the paralytic fever of the Chevalier du Haussay? Or how the Comtesse de Malmaison was entirely crippled from the waist down until she visited Dr Mesmer's establishment?'

'The most superficial acquaintance with medicine shows many cases where apparently incurable conditions undergo spontaneous remission without any clear explanation. We must realise, my dear Lafayette, that medical science is in its infancy. That is why it is so vulnerable to quacks like your confounded Dr Mesmer.'

'M-Mesmer – I had hoped never to hear that name in my house. And I forbid it to be uttered again. The man is a scoundrel and a m-menace.' The Duke had been attending to some business at the other end of the salon and he broke into the middle of the group with a startling force that seemed foreign to him. Recovering his calm a little, he again begged Lafayette in the name of their friendship never to mention that name in his presence. Lafayette bowed in assent but with an ill grace and the bystanders began to move away as though to break up the atmosphere, which could scarcely have been more charged if it had been inspissated with Dr Mesmer's magnetic fluid.

Wm felt a light touch on his arm and turned to see Rosalie who to his surprise seemed to be on the verge of giggling. 'My husband feels so strongly about mesmerism, you know. He takes science almost as if it were a new religion – perhaps it is.'

'And you do not?'

'Oh, I am only an ignoramus, but I do confess I would like to see Dr Mesmer's bath if only to see how the trick is done. Will you take me there one day, or would Mr Jefferson disapprove too?'

'Mr Jefferson would certainly disapprove no less than your husband, but I rather think it may be my duty to investigate this phenomenon, on behalf of the American people, you know.'

'And I on behalf of the French.'

There was a commotion behind them and Wm turned to see a dark young man, no more than a boy, with bright eyes like Rosalie's.

'I say, Ro-Ro, wasn't the Condor splendid, the way he tore poor old Vernon to shreds?'

'This is my little brother Charles who thinks Monsieur de Condorcet is the new Messiah. Charles, this is Mr Short who as you can see is an American but speaks French rather better than you do. You had better make friends with him immediately or I shall be very cross.'

'She has a foul temper, monsieur. My life wasn't worth living until

I grew bigger than she was. As you can see, she is very much older than I am.'

'What have you done with your two handsome cousins?'

'I cannot imagine that they could be any more handsome than you two,' said Wm, feeling that he ought to take a hand in this badinage.

'I didn't know that Americans could be such disgusting flatterers,' said Charles, 'anyway, the point is, it's a joke. François and Alex are our Liancourt cousins and we think them a bit plodding.'

'They haven't got a chin between them and they spend all their time massacring small feathered creatures.'

At this moment two more young men came in from the loggia, making a good deal of noise. One had a game bag slung over his shoulder and the other had a fowling piece under each arm, the barrels and the silver chasing on the stock glinting in the last of the afternoon sun.

'Is the lecture over yet?' one of them called out.

'Just as well you missed it. You wouldn't have understood a word.'

Wm noticed a surprising pugnacity about Rosalie's brother. His delicate marmoset's face, his long eyelashes and his cherub's mouth were at odds with the spirit he showed his two heavy cousins, each a good four inches taller than he was.

'I don't know why Charles swallows all this nonsense, he used to be such a sensible little boy.' The fairer of the two, who had the long face of his father Liancourt but a blobbier look to him, sighed. 'I'm François and this is Alex. Our father tried to make us read the *Encyclopaedia* but luckily we're too thick.'

'Much too thick. All they think of is joining the army so they can start shooting people instead of sparrows.'

'I think the less you see of these two the better, Monsieur Short. I shall give you a tour of the house instead. Let me tell my grandmother, she always likes to know where I am.'

She went over to the old lady at her light skipping pace that made everyone else in the room seem so slow and bulky. Wm thought how strange they would all seem to most people back home: Rosalie the granddaughter and daughter-in-law, yet at times not seeming like either, more like a daughter who cannot bear to be too long away from her mother; the Duke less like a son than an unfailingly considerate husband; the young brother-in-law who was at the same time a nephew and who seemed like a decent fellow and apparently found nothing odd in the situation, and lord knew what double kin those two cousins were; and the old lady not old at all but dressed up in bonnet and lace to give that impression. As for the relationship between the Duke and Duchess, well, that he could not fathom at all, could not begin to see the true substance of it. He supposed it must be what they called a marriage of convenience and to his sturdy American spirit that was a repulsive conception. In any case, was it not forbidden in the table of affinity at the back of the prayer book, probably somewhere in *Leviticus* too? Yet he could not deny that there was affection between the two of them and not just a torpid middle-aged kind of affection either. The whole arrangement seemed entirely harmonious, all three of them showed every sign of contentment. All that was lacking was a child. The Duke must surely long for the heir that, so far as Wm knew, his first wife had not borne him before her untimely death. And Rosalie herself must wish to fulfil her natural destiny. But he could detect no hint of strain or anxiety between them.

'We are released,' Rosalie said. 'I would not have you think that my grandmother is my jailor, it is just that she cannot bear to miss any entertainment.'

'Then could she not come with us? I am sure she would have much to tell me about the history of the house.'

'There are steps, oh such steps. She cannot bear to exhibit her infirmity even among friends. Come.'

She led him at her charming scurrying pace through the long anteroom into the old part of the house which recalled its sterner military origins: the guardrooms, the lookout window, the three-foot-thick wall of the first fortress on the site, which the Duke's librarian claimed was Gallo-Roman but the Duke had pooh-poohed the idea. And then back again through the Duchess's little drawing room and the state bedroom with its great scarlet swags and the tossing scarlet plumes at each corner of the enormous four-poster, which the last king had slept in during his visit, the visit that had gone so badly, Madame d'Enville said, because Louis le Bien-Aimé had just discarded his last mistress, the famous Madame de Pompadour, and had not a good word to say to anyone.

'Now,' she said, 'are you ready for a climb?'

They had come down a narrow passage past the doorway into a strange little chapel cut in the rock. They peeped in and nodded at the elderly servant morosely sweeping the dust. At the end of the dank gallery that led from the chapel Wm could see stairs, white chalky stairs twining upwards.

'You must count the stairs,' she said. 'No two people ever reach the same figure. According to legend it is because the devil comes in the night and adds to their number or takes some away to bemuse us. In fact it is because one is so out of breath and cannot count properly.'

He thought she was exaggerating and skipped up the stairs after her, following the twirl of her skirt up round bend after bend. Soon he had to admit he was running out of breath in the damp, chalky air and the elbows of his new sky-blue coat were white with chalk dust as he brushed giddily against the walls. At every third or fourth bend there was a window cut into the chalk and he stopped to catch his breath on the pretext of wanting to look out through the rusty bars over the steepling woods and the curling river and the fields beyond.

'You are not as fit as you think, monsieur, I can feel your heart thumping. Oh, I have left a mark.'

He looked down and saw the white outline of her small palm on the lapel of his coat, like a medal, he thought, or a buttonhole. 'It does not matter in the least. I am already as white as a pierrot.'

He stood up and cut a clown's caper in the narrow space and knocked his head on the low ceiling, and she laughed but he did not care. The light imprint of her hand on his heart was still burning in his mind.

'We cannot repose here or we will never reach the top.'

She seemed inexhaustible. The staircase must have turned on itself a dozen more times and she was still babbling without a pause for breath, about how the Norman knight had murdered Guy de La Roche while he was at Mass in the keep and sent his body on a raft down the Seine to warn the knights of the region not to stray beyond their boundaries and how – but she was two bends ahead of him and he could not hear what she was saying. It was as much as he could do to stagger up the last few steps and come out blinking into the fresh air, dripping with sweat and his mouth and eyes full of chalk dust.

'Well?'

'Well what?'

'How many steps were there?'

'Oh, I forgot to count. It was as much as I could do to breathe, madame.'

'Rosalie, I told you to call me Rosalie, everyone does.'

'I could be the exception and you would remember me all the better.'

'Only for your pomposity. You may shorten it to R if Rosalie offends you as a name.'

'Very well then, but I must be William to you.'

'Weelleearm. Is that right?'

It sounded charming to him and he said so, though he suspected she might be mocking him and could in fact pronounce his name perfectly well. He wished he were more adept at this repartee. The badinage that had sounded well enough when he was walking with Lilite at St Germain seemed so lame in this company. Which made him feel disloyal to Lilite who was not, it had to be admitted, quite as witty as she was sweet.

Still recovering his breath, he looked around him. They were standing on top of the cliff. Far below they could see the river snaking through the haze, and the orchards and the green fields stretching to the horizon. Around the ruins of the old fortress the woodmen had recently cleared the hazel and chestnut brushwood. The sawdust was still thick upon the last of the bluebells and the boughs were almost white where they had been slashed and coppiced.

'There it is. Is it not fine, my grandmother's arch?'

He followed her pointing arm and took in the classical portico that had been stuck on to the ancient masonry where the sides met at an acute angle. It was no doubt an admirable portico, the pediment was nicely proportioned and the twin pillars that supported it might have come straight out of Vitruvius's copybook. Yet Wm had to confess, if only to himself, that it looked out of place on these remains of a more barbarous time. All he said to her was, 'It is splendid, I wonder what Mr Jefferson might think of it.'

'Do not hide behind your master's skirts. You do not care for it, I can see. I knew you would not. Nobody young likes it a bit. We do not wish our civilisation to put a smiling face on such grim relics of the past.'

'Well—'

'There, you are thinking I have brought you all the way up to show you my grandmother's *bêtise.*'

'You must not put words into my mouth. I do truly think it is a handsome piece of work. Surely we should not shrink from trying to improve upon the work of our ancestors.'

'You are a diplomat, monsieur, but I know exactly what you are thinking. I can read you like a book.'

'A very dull one, I fear.'

'On the contrary, Will, I cannot wait to turn the page.'

She said 'Will' with barely a trace of accent, so she had been teasing him before, just as she was teasing him now by shortening his name to suit her fancy. He was nettled to feel himself such a slow partner in this game, for back in Virginia he had been accounted quick enough and the Flat Hat Society had elected him Beau of the Year, though that was a double-edged honour, not without a hint of chaff in it.

'You cannot fool me, monsieur. You Americans like to play the simple peasant from the backwoods, but in truth you are like oriental pashas. Your estates are ten times the size of ours and you have regiments of slaves to obey your lightest whim.'

'Not me, madame. I am the proud possessor of a couple of patches of the Tidewater country, which produce more frogs than tobacco, and I haven't a single slave to my name.'

'Not one? Poor Will. No, I don't believe you, I never heard of a Virginia gentleman without slaves.'

'We sold them all when my father died.'

'Ah, then you are a slave trader – oh, I am sorry, Will, I did not mean to offend you.' He had gone red with anger, and she apologised in the same moment that she teased him.

'No, it is a fair comment. The truth is that we did not know what to do for the best, my brother and I. We had our two sisters to think of. But cash was so scant after the war, the sale raised a very poor sum. We might just as well have freed them, but then our neighbours would never have forgiven us. We tried to place them as well as we could. I still feel remorse whenever I run into one of them on someone else's farm. They are pleased to see me, I think, at least they say so. But you will think that a sentimental delusion, I dare say.'

'No, you must not think me so hard. Anyway, how can any of us in France reproach your institutions when we still have the *corvée*? Those poor wretches who are forced to build our roads are no better than slaves.'

'I know we Americans may seem clumsy to you—'

'No, no,' she interrupted, 'never. You are more than a match for us. It is only that you prefer to roughen your surface while we waste our time polishing our veneer of civilisation.'

'Rosalie, you are too cruel. I have spent the past year polishing myself so hard I scarce recognise my face in the mirror any more, it is so shiny, and you refuse to notice.'

'On the contrary, I think your shiny face is adorable. You will keep your side of the bargain, won't you, and take me to Dr Mesmer's the moment we get back to Paris?'

'But what is he to cure you of?'

'Don't worry, by then I shall have thought of something. When you have been a little longer in our country you will realise that no Frenchwoman is ever without her pet maladies.'

IV

The Iron Wand

'Shall I call for you then? At four o'clock? It will take us half an hour at least to cross Paris and they say it is wise to be early or one may not be admitted to the first session.'

'No,' she said after a pause (she was not given to pausing, so he noticed her hesitation and remembered it), 'I think it would be better if I were to collect you at the Hôtel de Langeac.'

It was his turn to hesitate. 'I am not sure that would be wise. Mr Jefferson is generally at home at that hour and he might be . . .'

'Might be what, Will?'

The way she spoke his name – or perhaps her using it at all – unmanned him and he lost hold of what he meant to say. 'Well, I do not think . . . that is, he disapproves of animal magnetism, you know. He would not care to see me wasting time on such an excursion. We are very busy with the Dutch bankers just now and our people back home are anxious to see matters concluded.'

'My husband disapproves too, as you know. That is why I do not wish you to come to us. Monsieur de La Rochefoucauld has taken to you so much and he would be sure to quiz you.'

Though they used each other's first names readily enough now, her husband was still Monsieur de La Rochefoucauld to both of them and would, he thought, remain so until they became a good deal more intimate, perhaps not even then. How puzzling the French were. There was the awkward question of the second person singular. Lilite and he had begun to *tutoyer* in no time, but there seemed no question of that with Rosalie. Was that because she was a duchess or simply because she was married?

'Well then,' she said, 'let us meet halfway. Why not the back of the Palais-Royal. I am told it is a great place for assignations.'

Her dark eyes were brimming with mischief. She was wearing a gauzy dress of sprigged muslin, pale lilac and high-waisted in the new style, which made women look innocent and childish.

'I shall be lurking under the arcade. You will recognise me by my mask and black cloak.'

Even though he did not resort to disguise, he had hoped to sneak out of the Hôtel de Langeac without attracting attention. But Mr Jefferson was always on the qui vive. His curious vacant gaze never ceased questing for some fresh object and the distinctive sound of his shambling gait penetrated every room in the embassy (which was only a modest building on an acute-angled corner site, like a wedge of cheese). Wm was in the circular hall putting on his light September coat when he heard his master's footsteps coming from the salon.

'Where are you off to this fine afternoon, William?'

'The Palais-Royal, sir.'

'There is no better place for an excursion. We would benefit from such an institution in Virginia. Our womenfolk would appreciate the convenience of a covered mall where they might make their purchases and meet their acquaintances.'

'They would indeed.'

'In the northern states where the winters are harsher, such a thing would be even more valuable.'

'So it would, sir.'

'Well, I must not keep you. Ah, by the by, since you are taking the carriage – I see Vendôme harnessing up in the yard – might you be so kind as to drop in on Labiche? He has a copy of Monsieur d'Argenville's treatise on the laying out of gardens that he has put aside for me.'

'I should be glad to pick it up for you.'

'You are a good fellow, William.'

And despite his irritation at being thus waylaid, Wm found himself melted once again by the smile that hurried across Mr Jefferson's sad face as though it had no business there.

*

'Why are you carrying that huge book? Do you expect mesmerism to be so tedious?'

Wm told her about his errand for his master. Rosalie said that she too had told her husband that she was going to the Palais-Royal and he had told her to be sure to take the coachman with her if Madame d'Astorg was not available, for the place was full of dangerous characters. They laughed in sympathy at the half-truths they had told and were grateful that the embarrassing topic of animal magnetism should cloak the greater embarrassment that they did not care to name. Wm had already been in receipt of Mr Jefferson's strong views on the empty bustle of Paris, the flirtations and dissipations of its inhabitants, and the indifference to the conjugal fidelity that was so dear to the chaster hearts of their fellow Americans. TJ had even got wind of Wm's flirtation with Lilite and adjured him to come home like a good boy. Only a day or two earlier he had said, 'William, as your adoptive father, though I could not value your services here more highly, I think it my duty to remind you of yours, which is not to leave it too long before you return to Virginia to seek a bride.' Wm had blushed and mumbled something about needing to establish himself in the world first. But he knew that Mr Jefferson continued vigilant on his behalf, which is why he had asked Vendôme to drop him off at the Louvre end of the Palais-Royal, where there was no danger of the coachman (a beady fellow) spying the Duchess and he could walk through the stately avenue of limes, pick up TJ's book from Labiche and meet her at the other end.

Her carriage rattled to a halt outside an imposing mansion in the rue Coq Heron. Tall bronze torches were flaring either side of the porte-cochère and a footman in livery rushed forward to lower the steps, giving three piercing whistles as he did so.

'Do you greet all your guests so?' Wm enquired.

'Three vistles is for nobility,' the man said in a rough German accent.

'But I thought Dr Mesmer treated rich and poor alike,' Rosalie said gaily. 'This is said to be the only place in Paris where persons of every class mingle freely, soldiers, farmers, nobles, prostitutes, abbés—'

'Even Americans.'

'Oh, I think not. Americans are much too healthy to require Dr Mesmer's services.'

They were inside the hall now and a valet scurried forward to take their coats. The hall was cavernous and dark. Heavy drapes deadened the noises of the street. From the next room there came the sound of delicate music, like a harp but somehow more liquid and resonant.

'That is Monsieur,' the valet said, 'you may watch him play if you wish,' and he led them through the door on the left into a smaller chamber.

The room was almost as dimly lit as the hall. Wm could only just make out a heavy-looking man in a silk robe standing at a box-like instrument, in shape much like a harpsichord but larger and with an open top, over which his pudgy hands passed to and fro with surprising dexterity. As Wm's eyes grew accustomed to the umbrous half-light (there were but two candles in the room), he could see that the man's hands were passing over rows of glass tumblers and it was from these that this strange liquid sound flowed. Wm thought he recognised the melody and as he turned to Rosalie she whispered, 'It is an air of Monsieur Mozart's. Dr Mesmer was his patron, you know, back in Vienna, although he himself had little money to speak of. Now he could afford to commission a dozen operas. They say he makes five hundred louis a month from these seances.'

'And that is Dr Mesmer? He looks like a pork butcher.'

'But doesn't he play divinely?'

The divine pork butcher abruptly stopped playing and drew a purple cloth over the glasses. Then he bowed to the half-dozen people who had gathered in the little music room and motioned to them to pass by him through the door into the chamber beyond, which the valet was already holding open for them.

As they walked past Dr Mesmer's burly form, he bowed again and Wm found himself trembling, he could not think why. Was some vibration from the musical glasses still present in the room, or was there a draught coming from somewhere? Perhaps he was just shivering a little. It was a cool night and there was no fire lit in the music room.

They came into a much larger salon, also dimly lit. Somewhere in here too there was music playing, apparently from some kind of small organ, though he could not see the instrument. The room was dominated by two enormous wooden tubs, both some fifteen feet in diameter and perhaps two feet deep. Each tub was covered with a slatted wooden lid. Through holes cut in these lids there protruded iron rods to waist height. The rods were bent at the top so that they could be easily grasped by the persons sitting round the tub, ten or twelve of them being already seated, leaving only a couple of places free for Wm and Rosalie.

As Wm sat down, an elderly lady with a prominent goitre thrust out her hand impatiently, gesturing with her head that he should grasp it. 'Quick, quick or the fluid will be lost.'

Her other hand was fiercely gripping the iron rod in front of her as though she would lose her balance if she let go. He reached out to take the iron rod in front of him. The metal was cold to the touch and he began to tremble again.

'Is this your first visit, monsieur?' the elderly lady murmured to him in hushed tones. Now that she had turned her face to him he could see how the goitrous swelling entirely filled the far side of her neck.

'It is.'

'Monday is always a good night.'

'Why so, madame?'

'Monsieur Mesmer magnetises the bottles on Monday morning, so the electric fluid is fresh. I had that from his chief assistant Monsieur d'Eslon.'

'The bottles, madame?'

'There, in the tub under the lid. They are arranged like the spokes of a wheel, so they pass the magnetism from one bottle to the next through the water, which is itself magnetised so that the effect is redoubled. Monsieur d'Eslon was good enough to have the lid removed and show me because I am such a good patient.'

'And madame, pardon me for asking, but you are deriving great benefit from the treatment?'

'Dr Mesmer is a genius,' she said simply. 'But now we must pay attention. Ah, I see it is time to change hands.'

Wm too saw the signal from a dignified gentleman dressed in a purple silk robe at the far end of their tub. For an irreverent moment Wm fancied that they were all seated at a gaming table and that the dignified gentleman was the croupier. Many of the patients looked as if they would have been quite at home in such a setting. But he pulled himself together and hastened to follow the actions of the lady with the goitre who had slipped her right hand out of his left and grasped the rod with it, reaching out to her neighbour on the far side with her left hand, which had previously been grasping the rod. Wm imitated her and gripped Rosalie's hand, which felt warm and human.

'Are you cured yet?' she whispered.

'I still haven't decided what I'm suffering from.'

Rosalie stifled a giggle as the other patients round the tubs fell silent.

Dr Mesmer had entered the room. There was just enough light to see that he was wearing a purple silk coat of the same design as the dignified gentleman's. He was bearing before him a long iron wand, beautifully wrought. He might have been a verger in a cathedral. He approached the circle of patients round the tub (Wm had counted that there were sixteen of them) and bowed his head to each patient as he passed. It was a solemn sort of nod he gave but somehow intimate too, the sort of nod that a verger might give the altar he passed in front of twenty times a day. He made a circuit of each tub, then paused for an instant, his head sunk on his massive chest, seemingly lost in complex thought. Was he gathering his therapeutic forces or making some diagnostic calculation? The hushed breath of so many gathered in the two circles created an atmosphere of suspense and expectation that Wm began to find unsettling. And the room was so cold. Once again he became conscious of a draught of air that carried a curious musty smell like rotten apples.

With an abrupt movement Mesmer raised his head, as though he had at last come to a conclusion. Then, lowering the wand slightly and pointing it out in front of him, he approached the nearest patient, a rough-looking elderly man with a red carbuncular face. The man stood up and rolled down the grubby canary stocking on his right leg, and clasping his knee in both hands raised his trembling withered shank.

Dr Mesmer bent forward, seemingly to inspect the miserable limb, then with great deliberation applied the wand about halfway up the old man's calf. The touch appeared light but firm and lasted perhaps five seconds.

The man's whole body shuddered visibly and he let go of the leg, which immediately trembled with considerable violence so that he had to sit down with a thump to avoid falling over. Mesmer paused in front of the patient for a further five seconds as though to make sure that the treatment had been effective, before passing on to the next patient, a youngish woman who made an awkward curtsy to him. But Wm kept his eyes fixed on the man with the red face who was still stricken with convulsions the whole length of his body. Far from quietening as Mesmer passed on, he seemed to be increasingly affected. His head began to roll from side to side and he was shaken by a barking sort of cough that sounded close to laughter.

'He is one of our most sensitive patients,' the lady with the goitre whispered. 'With some of us the magnetism may take half an hour or more to make its effects felt, but with him, pouf, he goes straight off. In five minutes he'll be in the *salle des crises.* Look, here comes Monsieur d'Eslon already.'

The dignified gentleman held out his hand to the old man who consented to be led away through a small side door previously concealed by draperies.

'He'll be as right as rain in there,' the lady with the goitre said. 'The walls are padded with the softest silk, it is impossible to harm oneself.'

'Have you yourself, madame . . .'

'Certainly not, monsieur. My affliction does not produce such gross symptoms. Monsieur d'Eslon conducts new patients there to reassure them.' But she spoke with a hint of wistfulness as though one's treatment might not be complete without a spell in the *salle des crises.*

As Mesmer approached – he was only three patients away now – Wm became uncomfortably aware that he would have to exhibit some kind of malady if he was not to be unmasked as a fraudulent intruder. What would happen if he indicated some supposedly defective limb or region of the body and Dr Mesmer were able to tell at a glance that there was nothing wrong with it?

He was deflected from these alarmed thoughts by the sight of the lady with the goitre half rising from her seat and leaning forward to press her neck against the bent end of the nearest iron rod. She was still holding his hand and so pulled him towards her as she rose, and he had a glimpse of the dark shiny rod pressing into the discoloured flesh of her swelling. Being pulled so close to her he could feel her trembling the whole length of her body.

Then she turned round to face Mesmer. She was still holding Wm's hand and he could sense her bracing herself as she bowed to the doctor, who then raised his wand to the side of her neck where the other rod had been only a few seconds earlier. He held it there, this time for what Wm thought an unconscionable period, then gently took it away. She sank down in her chair, no longer trembling but apparently exhausted of all energy, quite unlike the man with the carbuncles in her reaction.

While this was going on, Wm had stopped fretting about what his own malady should be and to his relief an answer came to him. He suddenly remembered that a few months earlier when he had still been at St Germain and paying regular visits to the house with the dolphin over the door his horse had slipped on the wet leaves in the street and had thrown him. It was not a bad fall (the horse was only walking at the time) but he had come off at an awkward angle and twisted his back. The next morning he had found it difficult to stand up straight and he had to go about at a half-crouch for a week or so.

So when Mesmer stood before him and gave his by now familiar little nod, Wm nodded in reply and then turned round to face the tub again and, inclining forward, twisted his arm round and tapped his back in what he thought might be a plausible region.

There was a short pause during which he maintained this twisted posture. Then to his surprise he felt the tap of Mesmer's wand not anywhere on his back but on the top of his shoulder rather as though he were being dubbed a knight. He had read in a newspaper that with some medical complaints the seat of the disease or infection might lie in a different place from that in which the pain was experienced. Perhaps the muscle causing the supposed inflammation lower down was located up in the scapular region.

Wm waited. Surely the rod would be applied again, perhaps for a longer period, as with the other patients. But nothing happened. Then it dawned upon him that the tapping on the shoulder might be not so much part of the treatment as purely designed to attract his attention.

He turned round and faced the doctor again. Mesmer's eyes burnt like hot coals out of his broad pudgy face. He was a large man, a head taller than Wm, and he seemed to bear down on the young American as though he would drive him into the ground by the sheer intensity of his gaze. But his voice, when he came to speak, was soft with only faint traces of a Viennese accent and it had no hint of oppressive force in it. 'You are very welcome, monsieur. We are always glad to see observers at our sessions. Only thus can science hope to advance.'

He tapped him on the shoulder again with his wand, a light casual tap, a friendly dismissal. Then he moved on to the next patient who was Rosalie.

Although she had teased him about the illnesses that he might counterfeit, he had not quizzed her as to what she herself would say. She was so quick-witted she would think of something at a minute's notice. At any rate he was sure that she would extract full value from the encounter.

Instead of merely bowing to the doctor like the others, she went up close to him and murmured a few words to him, much too low for Wm to catch.

Mesmer nodded and turned to beckon a valet to bring up a chair, gesturing to Rosalie that she should turn her own chair round. They sat down facing one another, so close that Mesmer's knees enclosed hers. Wm could hear the rustle of her grey silk dress against the coarser material of his breeches, which were now visible as the purple robe fell open. Mesmer raised the palms of his hands and very slowly drew them down her body from the high sash just below her breasts all the way down to her thighs. Then he leant a little further forward so that his face was only a few inches from hers, and he passed his right hand behind her body, moving it with the utmost deliberation down from her shoulder blades to a point below her waist. There he paused. They sat frozen in this intimate proximity for what must have been a minute or more. Then he took his hand away and clambered out of his chair in a clumsy motion quite unlike the precise delicacy of his movements a few seconds before, as though he like his patients was emerging disorientated from an experience akin to a trance.

Then he bowed to her, but she seemed too overcome to respond and continued to sit in the posture in which he had placed her, her head lowered, her hands clasped in her lap, in a posture of utter submission like a servant being reprimanded by her mistress.

Wm was discomfited by this sight. He had never seen her other than ebullient and blooming with self-confidence and energy. But he could find no words to console her if consolation was what she needed. He looked at Mesmer in the hope that he might do something to restore her, but the doctor's burly figure had moved on and was already bowing to the next patient.

A spasm of indignation overtook Wm, putting to flight the amused scepticism he had sought to maintain ever since they had entered the rue Coq Heron and observed the pretentious torches blazing outside the doctor's mansion. Who was this fat charlatan to prey upon the sick and defenceless with his parlour tricks? Wm reckoned they had some pretty fancy customers back home, travelling wizards who sold poultices to cure cancers and oils that offered infallible protection against rattlesnakes. But this variety of deceit was altogether more double-dyed.

At last Rosalie made a sign to him that she wished to leave the seance – she still appeared incapable of speech – and he led her out into the dark hall, now more or less deserted. But it was not until the German porter had whistled up the coach and they were safely trotting back towards the rue de Seine that he dared to speak to her. 'What . . . what did you say to him?'

'Oh, nothing, nothing of any consequence,' she murmured in a distracted manner. 'I told him that I had a malady of the digestion, not at all grave.'

'And what happened?'

She opened her mouth, then checked as if uncertain what words to use, before continuing: 'It was very curious. His hands did not touch me at all, did not even touch against my dress, and yet there was a sensation of heat all the way down my body and down my back too when he placed his hand there.'

'Was it pleasant?'

'Neither pleasant nor unpleasant. The heat just travelled down me, as though someone was shining a torch on my bare skin but not even grazing it. It was a level, even heat, and afterwards I felt very tired, although I had not moved a muscle. I feel so ashamed of myself.'

She was near tears, but Wm thought she did not sound unhappy. Even her confession of shame sounded oddly formal, as though shame was the sentiment she knew she ought to feel whereas what she felt in fact was something quite different, such as relief or even happiness, which Wm could not understand at all. He even began to feel rather jealous that Dr Mesmer had declined to treat his backache seriously.

And when she dropped him off near the Ministère de la Marine, there was, no, not coolness between them but a little distance.

'William, did you manage to find the time yesterday to drop by for that book of d'Argenville's?'

'Ah, no, how forgetful of me.'

'No matter, no matter. I'll send Vendôme over this afternoon.'

'I would not dream of permitting such a thing, sir. I'll get it myself directly.'

Where in hell's name was it? Of course, he had left it propped under the bunk seat of the Duchess's coach. They had been so overwrought when they parted that he had forgotten about it. Who knew where on earth it was now?

He hailed a cab in the Champs-Elysées and was back in the rue de Seine within half an hour. With luck he could sneak through the side door into the stable yard and retrieve the cursed volume. Surely the coachman would not have been so punctilious as to clean out the carriage already.

But as he was sidling through the little colonnade, he was hailed by a hearty cry. 'Ah there you are, monsieur. We have been looking for you everywhere.'

'For me?' Wm stared agape at the servant. This was very bad. Was he already known to be a skulker round the back parts of the hotel?

'Yes indeed. His Grace will be so glad I caught you, he is most anxious to thank you.'

'Thank me?'

'Yes, monsieur. Please follow me.' Blushing and bewildered, Wm was led up the great marble staircase between the weary tritons holding up the balustrade with one hand and blowing their curly horns with the other. The *huissier* showed him into the library on the first floor, where the Duke sat surrounded by books covering every desk and bureau plat and spilling over the floor, some with tasselled markers, others kept open by their spines spreadeagled. At the Duke's side sat a neat man, his grey hair cropped close to his scalp and a look of extreme alertness on his face.

'You know Monsieur B-Bailly, the great astronomer?'

The neat man winced at this description and in the same moment rose briskly to take Wm's hand.

'Do s-sit down, my dear Mr Short,' the Duke said. 'I am so much in your debt. You should not have left my house without giving me a chance to thank Monsieur Jefferson for his generosity and you for your kindness in personally delivering this magnificent work. As it was, I had to deduce the identity of the messenger from the coachman's report that the handsome young American brought it – my dear Short, you should not blush at a compliment from a c-coachman.'

Now for the first time Wm spied the d'Argenville book in its red-and-gold binding lying on the table in the clutter of brown wrapping paper.

'If old Labiche had not written "for Mr Jefferson" on the parcel, we would not even have known whom to thank.'

The Duke smiled and Monsieur Bailly smiled too, by proxy as it were. Wm bowed in acknowledgement, desperately calculating whether he had time to reach Labiche's before the old brute put up his shutters and whether in any case he would have another copy to sell him, no doubt at the same extortionate price.

'Bailly has come here to discuss the municipal c-constitution for Paris. We hope to present our plans to our colleagues in a month's time. We have been taking a leaf out of the Virginian book, although the Commonwealth of Massachusetts also has much to teach us, do you not agree, Mr Short? I know you are a keen student of these matters. Mr Short was kind enough to speak well of my poor translations,' he added, turning to Bailly not without a smidgen of satisfaction.

'Yes, yes indeed.' Wm's mind was still on the damned book. Why couldn't people just lay out a garden and be done with it as they did back home without writing a whole pompous book on the subject and calling it an art when all it was was digging up the earth and stuffing it with horse manure?

'I am particularly anxious that some distinguished p-practitioners of natural science should join us on the committee for reform. Bailly has been kind enough to suggest some names from among those who recently served with him on the Academy's commission on mesmerism. You had mustered there, I believe, the flower of French science, not least its chairman.'

'Your Grace is too kind.' Monsieur Bailly inclined his head. 'I was most fortunate in my associates.'

'Let me see, there was the estimable Dr Guillotin. And the great ornament of our chemistry, he was one of your number too, was he not?'

'Monsieur Lavoisier, yes, and Dr Cabanis who is such a pioneer of the medicine of the mind, what we call psychophysiology. And your own Mr Franklin, sir, was good enough to serve, though he was in frail health and had to spend much of the summer at Passy, but with characteristic generosity he permitted us to use his house for some of our—'

'Experiments in animal m-magnetism,' the Duke cut in. He had a way of cutting in. He liked to finish other people's sentences for them, which was odd seeing that he had so much trouble with his own. 'I am sure that Mr Short will be anxious to hear a little more of your remarkable work.' The Duke leant forward and tapped Wm's knee, a glow of excitement suffusing his pale features. Was it fancy or was his scar beginning to pulsate? How strange it was that these dry matters should so animate this calm, sceptical man. Was he similarly animated when he and Rosalie – but Wm did not care to let his thoughts stray too far in that direction. All he wanted to do was get away and get another copy of that damned book for TJ.

'It was of course our principal duty,' Monsieur Bailly began, 'to discover whether this mysterious universal fluid of Dr Mesmer's actually existed. I instructed my fellow commissioners at the outset that we must limit ourselves to physical proofs. Could one smell or taste the *fluidum*, could its presence in the *baquet* be confirmed by means of an electrometer and so on? I need hardly add that we found no such evidence. We also thought it our duty to undergo magnetising ourselves. Not a single one of us felt the slightest effects. We were, it is true, all healthy men in no need of medical attention. When we made similar magnetic experiments upon diseased members of the lower orders, one or two of them did show some of the purported effects of animal magnetism, but we ascribed these violent symptoms to the excitation of the imagination and regarded them as more likely to prove harmful rather than healthy in the long run. For that reason we appended to our report some confidential observations concerning the moral aspects of Dr Mesmer's clinic.'

'Ah, that was what I wished to hear about most particularly,' the Duke put in.

'The magnetisers are invariably men, whereas the majority of their patients are women. Thus there exists always a danger that contact between them may unleash the power that nature has caused one sex to exert upon the other. Your Grace may not be aware that in certain private consultations, which take place in a darkened section of the doctor's surgery, the magnetiser and the patient sit face to face, with her knees tightly encircled by his. Accordingly his knees must be in immediate contact with the lower posterior part of her body. The magnetiser then touches the hypogastric region with his hands, sometimes as far as the ovarium, which is, as you know, the female's most sensitive region. He may then pass his hand behind her, bringing her into closer contact still.'

'No, do they so?' The Duke whistled. 'Can you imagine such a thing, Mr Short?'

'It is hard to credit, sir.'

'And that husbands should permit their wives to engage in such intimacies in the guise of medical science,' the Duke said. 'Well, I am sure your report will put an end to such d-dangerous nonsense.'

Bailly coughed. 'In strict honesty, sir, I ought to confess that our report was not entirely unanimous.'

'Not unanimous?' The Duke seemed as distressed by this news as though hearing that his favourite horse had gone lame.

'For reasons I do not fully understand, Monsieur de Jussieu the botanist insisted on writing a minority report, and a scandalous one it was too, which had much better have stayed in his head.'

'Oh dear,' the Duke said.

'He asserted that we had not investigated the causes behind Mesmer's cures thoroughly enough and that some secret must lie precisely in the way Mesmer and his assistants excited the imagination of their more impressionable patients. Jussieu argues that the combination of the imagination with the physical contacts, all the licentious touching and rubbing that goes on, produces what he calls "animal heat" and that this phenomenon may actually cure such physical ailments as paralysis and the flux.'

'I never heard of such a thing,' the Duke said, 'and such a distinguished b-botanist too. But come, Bailly, we must not waste the morning on these f-fairy tales. You had, I believe, some comments on the taxation bill that is to come before us next week. William, I fear my days may be much taken up with these matters over the next few months, and I shall be unable to devote as much time as I would have liked to showing Mr Jefferson and yourself the delights of Paris, but then I know that Mr Jefferson is an intrepid explorer on his own account. He walks everywhere,' the Duke said, turning to Bailly with a gesture of mild wonder, as though referring to some extraordinary and perhaps unnatural feat.

'You are most kind to show us such consideration,' Wm said in his best courtly manner.

'However, in your case, Mr Short, I have a plan. My dear wife is, I think, too much among p-persons of my generation who are prone to be wrapped up in their middle-aged concerns. I have often thought that she needed the company of people nearer her own age, though she would not dream of saying such a thing herself and is indeed genuinely interested in the causes close to my heart, such as the modernisation of our agricultural practices. She is devoted to my mother, her grandmother, and finds it hard to leave her side, whether in Paris or at La Roche. All the same, I know that Rosalie – you must not hesitate to call her Rosalie, everyone does – would be delighted to show you the sights of our capital and of the Ile-de-France. She has already spoken to me of the pleasure she takes in your company, as in that of Mr Jefferson of course. So I hope you will not take it as an imposition if I suggest to her that she might propose one or two excursions with you, though naturally she would seek out your own views and preferences.'

While the Duke was bringing this roundabout speech to its startling conclusion, Wm kept his head bowed in the modest posture of a schoolboy who has been summoned to his headmaster in the expectation of punishment only to find himself commended and who cannot believe his luck. He felt that if he dared to look the Duke in the face his tumbling emotions would show all too plainly. Something was falling into his lap, even if he did not like to define too precisely what that something might turn out to be; in fact, not defining it was part of the intense pleasure that flooded through him, as the Duke pursued his laborious way, suggesting how Rosalie might best convey her wishes to him and vice versa, while Monsieur Bailly drummed his fingers on the bureau plat, impatient to get back to business.

Wm could not afterwards recall how he managed to take his leave of the two serious men and how he clattered down the stairs and out into the courtyard and up the rue de Seine, walking a good three-quarters of a mile before he realised that he must retrace his steps to go back to the Palais-Royal and see if he could track down another copy of that damned book. One way and another, botanists seemed to be causing a good deal of trouble, although Wm could not help feeling that Monsieur de Jussieu's speculations might not be quite as baseless as Monsieur de Bailly made out. The imagination was a powerful organ, after all.

V

Follies

Mr Jefferson loved follies. His watery blue eyes took on a sparkle when he came upon the absurdest confections in stone and plaster, the most futile buildings in the shape of a pineapple or a sheaf of corn. He would laugh at architectural jokes with a heartiness that verbal jests never provoked in him.

By contrast Wm preferred gazing at a building that had some purpose to it: a fine row of stables perhaps, or a well-planned manufactory. But they joined in approving the gargantuan commercial development at the Palais-Royal undertaken by the Duc de Chartres (Duc d'Orléans since his father's death, an event hastened, according to some, by his despair at his son's debaucheries). In fact, TJ had suggested to Wm that they might themselves go into partnership and build a similar indoor mall in the centre of Richmond, Virginia. They had even agreed on a suitable site for the venture, Shockoe Hill, but nothing came of the project. The two Americans also liked to take a stroll from the legation to inspect Monsieur d'Orléans's frenetic building developments in their own neighbourhood, which were fast growing into a city within a city, another Nouvelle Orléans as Mr Jefferson wisecracked. Sometimes, too, they would saunter on beyond the dust of the building sites to Orléans's private park, the Parc Monceau as it had formerly been known after the old village that had stood there until the wilful Duke had swept it away and turfed out the luckless villagers (or those of them who were unwilling to become his workmen). The place was now known as the Folie de Chartres from the huge sums the Duke had spent on digging up the ground to impart a more picturesque 'English' aspect to the landscape.

'It is strange, is it not, William, that a man who is so sunk in debaucheries of the lowest kind and is so incapable of quitting them for business should have devised such a garden of delights.'

They were standing next to a sizeable artificial mound upon which a gang of sweating workmen were attempting to erect two large broken Ionic columns. A little further off, another dozen men were piling up giant fractured tufa boulders to compose the basis of a ruined grotto. At that moment a gardener in a green apron shouted at them to step aside so that he might wheel a handcart full of ferns and other bosky shrubs for the beds that were already being manured around the site of the proposed grotto.

'But is there not something a little absurd,' Wm ventured, 'about deliberately erecting all these ruins, while behind them the Duke is building a modern city that will transform the government and commerce of France?'

'My dear William, you are too solemn. Surely the spirit of commerce, admirable though it may be, needs now and then to be leavened with a soupçon of frivolity.'

They stood for some minutes watching two workmen hammer a flawless fluted cylinder of marble into a suitable ruined condition and then rope it with a block and tackle to begin hauling it into position on top of the shattered column. As the rope's squealing filled his ears, Wm suddenly had an idea. 'You recall, sir, Monsieur de La Rochefoucauld's suggestion that while he was so heavily engaged upon the new constitution, I might make myself useful as escort to his wife.'

Mr Jefferson recalled no such thing, for the very good reason that Wm had said nothing about it to him. However, he shared the amiable weakness of even the greatest men, viz., that of not caring to admit that he was ignorant of or had forgotten something that he was supposed to know about. 'Ah yes, yes. You are sure that this is a wise arrangement? You do not think that the Duke in his innocence of the ways of the world may have neglected to consider the dangers of gossip?'

'There is no question of gossip, sir. I shall make it entirely plain that the Duchess will be apprising me of the most modern developments in the city, so that I shall be better informed and better equipped to carry out my duties on behalf of the American people.'

'I see,' said Mr Jefferson doubtfully, not liking to stand in the way of the American people.

'And one particular subject, which I know will be dear to your own heart, sir, is the brilliant variety of pavilions, bagatelles and other architectural inventions that have sprung up in and around Paris within the past few years and which offer the best possible models to adorn the infant cities of America. I can think of no better way of making myself useful than to carry out a careful study of these monuments both for your own pleasure, sir, and for the utility of the nation we serve.'

For a moment Wm wondered whether he had pitched it a little too high, but he need not have worried. Mr Jefferson was never averse to solemnity. 'My word, that is a handsome scheme, Will. You might publish your observations in a book. But did I not hear you say that you did not care for bagatelles of this sort?'

'I must learn to love them, sir. Besides, there is surely advantage in a scrupulously critical eye being cast upon such things rather than a too indulgent fancy overlooking their defects.'

'You are quite right, Will. I am perhaps a little too indulgent myself in such matters. And, by the way, do I recollect that the Duchess has a gift for sketching?'

'So she has,' Wm agreed. 'I am sure that we shall co-operate very well and I hope that the day may come when you are proud to acknowledge your old secretary as a professor of follies.'

'A professor of follies, that's good, very good,' said TJ, coming as near as he could to a chuckle. But then a thought struck him and he cried with an almost prophetic force, 'You must go to the desert!'

'The desert? I must admit that I had thought of confining our studies to Paris, at first anyway, but . . .'

'No, the desert must be your first port of call. It is hard to find, but Vendôme knows the way, so you must take the embassy carriage.'

Wm stared at his master, wondering whether his overloaded brain had finally exploded into delirium. Where was this desert? Vendôme was a reliable pilot and the coach had been specially built to Jefferson's own design to withstand the buffeting of the French roads, but even so . . .

'It is possible, I suppose, to make the journey within an afternoon, but I counsel you rather to take the whole day.' Then, seeing that his protégé was still gaping at him, he interrupted himself: 'You have not heard of the Désert de Retz? Well, perhaps it does not yet enjoy the fame of the Bagatelle or the Temple of Philosophy at Ermenonville, but to my mind it outshines them all. I must surely have expounded its beauties to you.'

Well, perhaps he had, but Jefferson's forays into pillars and perspectives had a way of inducing Wm's thoughts to wander off into irrelevant topics like the surprising curve of Rosalie's breasts when she bent to step up into her carriage and the dark curls that wandered over the frill of her dress. But he had no objection to TJ's fussing if it was to lead to days in Rosalie's company that might otherwise have been spent on the tiresome details of the second Dutch loan on which he had spent so much time of late and Mr Jefferson so little.

And he was still blessing his luck as old Vendôme took them along the road that he had come to know so well. In his first days in Paris it had been the road to Lilite and the homely comforts of St Germain. How long ago it all seemed now, the lamb gigot and the irregular verbs and the stolen kiss on the landing.

'What a strange man your master must be. I never heard of an ambassador who instructed his secretary to make it his business to study follies.'

'There is no one like him. Sometimes I wish he were more like other people. But in this case I am grateful for his eccentricity.'

'Are you sure you would not rather be negotiating all those important loans?'

'Quite sure.'

'Someone has misinformed you, or Mr Jefferson. I am an architectural ignoramus.'

'Then we are equals. How delightful.'

As they approached the town of St Germain, Vendôme took a side road, not much more than a lane, off into the chestnut woods. In the shade of the trees they fell silent as though they had just entered a church. Wm sneaked a sidelong glance at her. She was wearing a jaunty little hat of peacock blue. Somehow the hat made her look sad, or perhaps it was only the coming and going of the light through the trees. He wanted to break into her reverie, to reassure her that there was nothing but happiness in prospect for both of them, but he could not quite think of the words.

Wm was grateful when the carriage jolted to a halt and turned sharply to the right. At first he thought Vendôme had lost his senses and was charging directly at the wall of rock that confronted them, but then he saw an open gate and – what was this? – a ruined grotto with ferns dripping in its mossy cracks. Twisting his neck out of the open carriage window, he saw on top of the rocks a strange capering figure brandishing something.

He knew this place. He had been here before.

This was the capering satyr who had lit their entrance. In the daylight he could see that it was only a flimsy simulacrum of tin. And there ahead of them where the trees thinned out was the weird broken column gleaming now in the shafts of sunlight. How strange and huge it looked even in daylight, fifty foot high at least and like no pillar Wm had ever seen in France or anywhere else.

And there, standing by the column as Vendôme reined in the horses, was another figure whom Wm recognised the moment he saw him and one not made of tin either.

'That must be Monsieur Racine de Monville,' the Duchess said. 'I had heard he was a handsome man and he does not disappoint.'

The Duchess skipped down the carriage steps and went over to greet the tallish man in the blue coat. Wm followed more slowly, trying to gain a grip on himself.

'And this is my friend Monsieur Short. He is Mr Jefferson's secretary, you know. In fact, he is practically the ambassador because Mr Jefferson has so many other pursuits to attend to.'

'Monsieur Short and I are already acquainted,' the man in the blue coat said with a smile. 'Good day, Monsieur S.'

'Good day, Monsieur R.'

'Ah, you already have pet names for each other, what fun.'

'Oh, it is only a silly joke. We met at, where was it?' Wm said desperately, appealing to Monsieur de Monville to help him out.

'At the Swedish embassy perhaps. Yes, I think it was the Swedish embassy. We had this fancy that after the revolution when all titles of nobility had been abolished we should be known only by our initials. I would be Monsieur R and Monsieur Short would be Monsieur S.'

He was as fluent as a mountain stream and Wm bowed his head in grateful acknowledgement.

'But you would be merely citizens, would you not? There would be no more monsieurs, only Citizen R and Citizen S.'

'You are right, of course, madame. We were not so far-sighted. But you must come inside and see my retreat from the world. I am like St Simeon Stylites, except that I live inside my column rather than on top of it.'

He beckoned them through an unsuspected door that led inside the weird column and then up the winding stair that threaded the middle of it. The place was surprisingly commodious. On the ground floor they peered inside an oval dining room and had a glimpse of a cabinet de toilette and a small bedchamber beyond. On the next floor they were shown more bedchambers and a studio, on the floor above that a scientific laboratory – 'for my little experiments,' Monville said with an air that suggested he was not far behind Lavoisier or Priestley in that department – and a salon large enough to accommodate a small billiard table. Monsieur de Monville encouraged his guests to peer out of one of the oval windows, and there it all was spread out before them: the lake and the stream, the Gothic ruin a little off to the left (by daylight no bigger than a dovecote) and the pyramid that had loomed so large in the darkness and now might have served as a plaything for children to slide down.

'That is my ice house. I thought that if the ancient Egyptians had used their pyramids to preserve their pharaohs, why should I not use mine to preserve my ice?'

And Wm recalled those glaciers of shattered ice piled high with oysters and lobsters and trianons of ice cream. He looked further down the slope and there in a little Chinese garden of its own was the Chinese palace, its gilded tassels and scarlet lattices shining in the afternoon light.

'There' – they followed his pointing arm – 'that is the Isle of Happiness with the Tartar Tent reflected in its waters and beyond it on the hill you can just see the Temple of Pan.'

'It is a veritable heaven you have created here, Monsieur R, if I may call you so.'

'I am glad to have my heavenly vision certified by such an angel.'

They bowed to each other, but all Wm could think of was Monsieur de Monville holding his glistening tool as he proceeded from one girl to the next and the little agonised yelp he gave when he could hold back no longer and sprawled, spent and panting, on the last but one of them with his Chinese coat settling over him like a counterpane, while Madame Sylvie stood leaning against the marble chimney-piece, negligently observing them as though she were watching her pet dogs frolic.

'Come, let us plunge into my wilderness.'

Monville tapped him on the shoulder, and Wm turned round to find his host miraculously transformed into an archer in a leather jerkin with a longbow in his hand and a quiver of arrows slung over his shoulder.

'Now then, walk in single file, as the Indians do,' he called to them when they were out in the open air. They followed him through the bushes, imitating his half-crouched posture. Every now and then he motioned them to a halt when he heard a rustling.

After a few minutes they passed an elegant white obelisk rearing on a slight eminence in a grove of polar saplings.

Monville tapped the obelisk and it gave off a hollow metallic sound. 'Tin,' he said, 'there's nothing like tin.'

A little further on they came to a gaudy pavilion of blue-and-gold stripes. 'Ah, my beloved Tartars' lair; touch it, please.'

They stroked the side of the tent, expecting their hands to be lost in the folds of heavy drapery. But their fingers encountered only cold metal.

Monsieur de Monville grinned to see them so discountenanced. Then suddenly he froze. 'Hist! Don't move.'

They heard only the zing of the bowstring and the thump of the arrow hitting its mark. Thirty yards away a cock pheasant toppled over in a whirl of feathers.

'I used to employ a local fellow as gamekeeper,' Monville said as he picked up the bird and briskly wrung its neck, 'but I came to the conclusion that I was a better shot than he was, so I taught him to paint in the Chinese manner and made him my decorator instead. You will see some of his daubs in my Chinese house.'

Wm did not particularly fancy a return visit to the Chinese house, but he could see no escape.

'How can you call this a desert, sir? It is surely rather a garden of delights,' said Rosalie, sensing that Will seemed reluctant to pull his weight in the conversation.

'Ah, I will tell you the story. When I first bought the old farm at Retz, this patch was marked on the map as "Essarts", the old-fashioned word for freshly cleared ground you know, but in fact the undergrowth had gone wild since the map was made and had to be cleared all over again, so I called it a 'dessart', you see.'

Wm did not quite see and did not want to see either. He was beginning to be disgusted by the entire spectacle. What a false, trumpery thing the whole thing was, this desert that wasn't a desert at all but a piece of old scrubland, with its pretended satyrs and obelisks and Tartar tents that were no more than tin toys for adults, and its Chinese palace that was painted by a French peasant who knew no more of China than he did of painting. And this Monsieur de Monville in his archer's costume looking like a fop at a masquerade, which was exactly what he was. The only real thing in this artificial tableau was the pheasant, and that was dead.

But Rosalie continued to be enchanted by everything that Monville showed her and she skipped up the bamboo staircase in the Chinese palace eager for the next sensation. William saw Monville following her with his eyes and admiring her upwardly mobile ankles, which were as slender as a pheasant's neck.

'And what,' she enquired lightly, 'exactly do you do in this delightful room?'

'Oh, madame, we make music.'

Wm thought that this must be as big a lie as their supposed meeting at the Swedish embassy, but there at the far end of the room where Madame Sylvie had sat and watched them now stood a gilded harp.

Without waiting for an invitation, Monville sat down at the instrument and began to ripple the strings. 'I used to accompany Jarnovitz, you know. Monsieur Gluck was kind enough to say that he could not decide which of us was the better player. Sit down, sit down, please. I think this is an afternoon for Lully. Do you know this courante? I transcribed it myself.'

And his fingers began to pluck the strings to more serious effect. Wm noticed to his annoyance that Monsieur de Monville's fingers were long and tapering like those of a Baroque saint.

Rosalie settled herself on the sofa by the fireplace. That surely was the one on which he and the dark girl had made hay until she cried out that he was hurting her and – no, perhaps it had been the rose-coloured divan opposite.

How earnest Rosalie looked, not like a duchess or anyone from that milieu, but like a young student whose only wish in all the world was to concentrate and not be distracted by anything resembling flirtation or frivolity.

'That was very beautiful,' she said when Monsieur de Monville had finished and looked up at them for their applause. And so, damn it, it was. Even Wm could tell that Monville had the most delicate of touches and an exquisite unhurried discrimination of tempo.

'I used to play that for Madame du Barry. I knew her when she was eighteen and the best model that Labille had in his house. It is amusing to reflect in view of what later passed between them but at that time the Queen always asked her to model the gowns that she was interested in, though they were not at all the same shape. Well, who was? La Barry's figure was so remarkable that no matter how modestly she dressed, artists would approach her and beg to paint her nude. But she was such a simple girl, no more than a peasant really, and so good-hearted.'

'She lives very quietly now, I hear.' Wm was pleased to note a tarter note in Rosalie's voice.

'Oh yes, I go over to Louveciennes once a week and try to divert her. We make plans for her garden, but since she was exiled from court she has so little money. I am afraid her mind is too much fixed on the old days. I prefer to live in the present and look to the future, madame.'

The gaze he fixed on Rosalie left little doubt what particular future he had in mind.

'You too, I think, Monsieur S, you are a man of action rather than of recollection.'

Wm realised that Monville must assume that he and Rosalie were already lovers, as they certainly would have been if Monville had been in his place.

It was unpleasantly hot and airless in this upper chamber, but there was to be no early release from it, because Monville took their enthusiasm as encouragement to play a piece by his admirer Monsieur Gluck, which in turn reminded him of a motet by Rameau that was not often heard these days and then an air by the incomparable young Mozart, which was heard everywhere and which errand boys whistled, like so, though it should more properly be played *ambulante*, like so.

By the time they descended the bamboo stairs again the sun was down behind the trees and in the shadowed light the Desert did seem deserted, even forlorn. Rosalie said that the reflections in the dark waters of the lake brought melancholy thoughts to her mind, and Monsieur de Monville said they brought melancholy thoughts to his mind too. In reading the reveries of the late Monsieur Rousseau he sometimes fancied that it was of his own Isle of Happiness rather than of the Ile de St-Pierre far away in Switzerland that Rousseau had been writing. And Rosalie exclaimed that there was a passage from the fifth of those reveries that had at that minute flown into her head.

'It is the place where he describes the pleasures of lying in his little boat and letting it drift across the lake until it fetches up on the little island and he lies there under the willows amid the clover and the thyme—'

'And the rabbits, madame, do not forget the rabbits. What a charming thought it was to bring the rabbits to the island so that they might multiply there in peace with no one to fear.'

'Oh, you know the passage. I find it so touching. Yes, the rabbits, I loved the rabbits.'

Wm wondered whether Monsieur de Monville intended to take his bow and arrow to this island of tranquillity and if so how long the rabbits would last. But he did not interrupt them, for he saw that Rosalie was much moved.

When they were back in the carriage and rumbling down the hill to the city in the dusk, Rosalie was pensive. Once or twice he thought she was about to speak but then – which was unlike her usual quick impulsive self – could not find exactly what she wished to say.

'It is strange, is it not – I mean, he is a strange man, do you not think so?'

'Monsieur de Monville?'

'Yes, he plays so beautifully and he has such an understanding of nature and such an imagination – he designed each of those buildings himself. Did you not hear him say so? Some visitors could not believe that a mere amateur of the art could display such skill and insisted that his friend Monsieur Ledoux must have helped him, but they were all his own work. And yet . . .'

'Yet what?'

'He is such a bad man. Well, he has such a bad reputation. They say he has slept with every royal mistress, Madame du Barry of course, perhaps not Madame de Pompadour, she would have been too old for him, but all the others.'

'All of them?' Wm queried.

'So I believe. And then with many married women too. I do not know all their names.'

She looked a little sunk by the thought as if the weight of so much infidelity had suddenly fallen on her slender shoulders. Wm realised that it was this serious innocence that had drawn him so powerfully to her. Somehow in the middle of all this paddling lechery, without being in the least pious, rather the reverse, she had kept the quality that children had. He was cast down by the thought. How could someone so, well, so stained as he was hope to win the deeper affections of one on whom the greasy world had left no visible mark? He did not wish to lie to her, yet he did not see how he could ever tell her the truth about himself.

She saw that she had depressed his spirits and she touched his hand. 'I did not intend to wax so melancholy. Monsieur Rousseau's reveries are catching, I fear. My grandmother is always telling me not to swallow him whole. After all, he was no saint himself, he left his children in an orphanage, you know.'

At that moment William Short, improbably but with every semblance of firmness, resolved thenceforth to lead an unsullied life. How Monsieur de Monville would have laughed to think that their visit to him had produced such a consequence. He certainly would not take up Monville's suggestion that they should visit his new house in Paris. There would be no more visits to the Green Dolphin either. He did not expect that this abstinence would win him Rosalie's love, for she would know nothing of it. No, he made the pledge so that he might himself feel clean and at ease with himself. And he remembered with a shudder Monville's Chinese robe rasping against his own sticky bare skin and the smell of rotten lime blossom that carried him further back again, to the back bedroom at Ma Scranton's and

Dolly crying out under him as she cried out half a dozen times a day under other men.

They said goodbye, each reassuring the other that the day had been entirely delightful. Yet the tarnished feeling had not gone away from either of them, and Wm was almost itching to get back to the Hôtel de Langeac and to converse with Mr Jefferson on any topic under the sun – the Dutch loan, the voting system under the new constitution – anything so long as it had nothing to do with Monsieur Racine de Monville and the sexual practices of *homo sapiens.*

To his surprise, as he came into the circular hall, there was the sound of laughter from the dining room, an alto girlish laugh. He had barely expected TJ to be returned from dining with Madame d'Enville. It was part of the bargain that had persuaded Rosalie to spend a whole day at the Desert, that her grandmother should have her hands so pleasantly full of Mr Jefferson, whom she liked as much as she admired. He had some earlier engagements with the Commissioner for Grain and the architects who had built the new Exchange, but these business acquaintances would scarcely have come on to take supper at the Hôtel de Langeac.

'My dear William, you have not, I think, had the pleasure of meeting Mrs Cosway. Pleasure is too tame a word, you will surely pluck a higher from your ample lexicon when you have come to know her better.'

The young woman – large liquid eyes, about thirty years old, a weighty crucifix dangling amid the ruches of her dress – rose still laughing and shook his hand.

'And Mr Cosway, the celebrated painter of miniatures, though I should add without wishing to provoke marital discord that his wife is almost as accomplished a painter. She studied with Mr Zoffany and Signor Batoni too, I believe.'

'Oh, I am only an amateur. People will forgive any blemish in a young woman's sketches.' She did not say 'pretty young woman'. She did not need to.

Richard Cosway reached across the table to take Wm's hand. He had nothing of the delicacy that might have been expected of a painter of such tiny exquisites, being somewhat square-jawed and with a smirking knowing look to him. If Wm had not been introduced, he might well have mistaken him for one of the Grain Commissioners, and a fly one at that.

Wm drew up an empty chair and noted with some astonishment the remains of supper. There had been no mention of any supper guests in the kitchen book and no mention at all of the Cosways. And what had become of Madame d'Enville?

'I fear I have been able to furnish only the barest apology for a supper. James has done his best but he will over-roast when he is flustered. I brought him with me from Monticello, Mrs Cosway, he is a bright boy. I sent him off to the Prince de Condé's to learn the finer points of cooking, but he is raw as yet.'

James Hemings was indeed a talented young slave who had picked up a good deal in the Condé kitchens. But he did need warning and this mysterious impromptu supper might well have taxed his fledgling powers.

'You know the old column at the corner of the corn market. That was were we met, quite by chance. I was walking with Mr Trumbull and he presented me to his fellow painters. I shall regard that spot as hallowed for ever. Indeed, I strongly suspect that the column was erected there in advance by a far-sighted Providence to mark the site of our first encounter.'

Wm noticed that Mr Jefferson had an unusual flush in his cheeks and was talking with an intensity quite unlike his habitual disjointed, sometimes distracted manner.

'Mr Jefferson insisted that we dine with him straight away at the Palais-Royal. We said that he must surely have a thousand other engagements, but he would have none of it and said he was only engaged to an old lady who would not mind in the least. I feel so badly that we should have led him astray.'

Mrs Cosway's large eyes implored Wm to share in her guilt. She spoke in a tearaway breathless style, which he could see might fascinate some men but not him, certainly not the new Wm in his puritan's habit.

'We dispatched lying messengers to every part of town,' TJ said cheerfully. 'My character is quite destroyed. I shall never be able to hold up my head in this city again. You will have to succeed me at the embassy, William.'

'I shall pray that you be forgiven, sir. I am sure it is but a venial sin.'

'She will too, you know,' Mr Cosway muttered in Wm's ear.

'Will what?'

'Pray, sir, pray. She is a very religious woman, more's the pity. You might not think it to look at her, but she became a nun as near as dammit.'

'Really? I would not have guessed.'

'Still wears a crucifix the size of a horseshoe between her bubbies,' Mr Cosway said, pointing a fork.

'Ah yes, I see,' murmured Wm, peering directly at the locus indicated.

'Tell me, Short, how long have you been in this fair city?'

'Oh, getting on for two years now.'

'Then you'll know your way about the place. Tell me, where do you go for a good fuck these days?'

'Well, ah, I do, er, happen to know of a place.'

'I knew you would, sir, I could see you were a knowing sort of fellow. If the Frenchwomen fuck half as well as the Italians, you must be a happy man. There's nothing to touch an Italian woman. I promised myself while I was there that I would never fuck an Englishwoman again if I could help it.'

'Tell me, Mr Cosway, if you will forgive me breaking in upon your learned discourse,' said Mr Jefferson from the far end of the table, 'would you esteem Titian as great an artist on canvas as Raphael or a greater?'

'Oh, I'll take the pair of them, sir,' said Mr Cosway, not at all discommoded by the change of subject thrust upon him. 'For colour there is no man to beat Titian, but for serenity of sentiment and perfection of design Raffaello is the master. There, sir, write down the particulars.' While continuing to converse with his host on the relative merits of the Old Masters, he thrust a pencil and an open sketchbook at Wm.

In the days that followed Mr Cosway was almost always of the party, showing no impatience at being separated from his easel, while Mr Jefferson showed Maria the sights of the city and its suburbs and environs. For Jefferson these days whirled by in a blur of happiness. All the loneliness and despondency of his widowerhood melted like morning mist. He experienced the full truth of Dr Johnson's dictum that there was no happiness on this earth like that of driving briskly in a post-chaise with a pretty woman. There was not a noted spot that they did not visit in those giddy days: the Bagatelle, that reckless folly of the Comte d'Artois, with its model of an American fort on the Indian frontier, the Château de Madrid in the Bois, the exquisite pavilion at Louveciennes, the great Machine at Marly, that hydraulic miracle which provided the millions of gallons needed to supply the fountains of Versailles, and of course the Désert de Retz.

How they had marvelled at the broken column, with what excitement they had skittered like schoolchildren up its ingenious spiral staircase, and with what sighs of pleasure they had wandered across the Chinese garden and rowed across Monsieur de Monville's lake to his Isle of Happiness. They had talked of Rousseau, of course, and Monsieur de Monville, an ever helpful and ever present guide, had drawn a most apt comparison between this island and the Ile de St-Pierre as described in Monsieur Rousseau's fifth reverie. Monsieur de Monville had told them about the rabbits too, and they had all exclaimed on the charming thought of the little colony multiplying undisturbed by the cruel world, though Mr Jefferson, his practical bent never quite obscured, could not help speculating whether the species might not degenerate through inbreeding if confined to so small an island. But in general he esteemed Monsieur de Monville a most ingenious and delightful fellow.

'And a great swordsman too, I understand,' said Mr Cosway, chewing a chicken leg, while they sat at table at Ruggieri's.

'Is that so?' said Mr Jefferson, leaning forward eagerly over his plate of macaroni.

'They say he has had every royal mistress of the last two reigns.'

'It is hard to credit,' said Mr Jefferson.

'The story goes that when the King, I mean the late King, complained to Madame d'Esparbes that she had slept with all his subjects, she demurred, fluttered her eyelashes and the King said, "Well, you have had the Duc de Choiseul," and she said, "But he is so strong." And the King said, "Then you had the Maréchal de Richelieu," and she said, "Oh but he is so witty," and the King said, "And you had Monville too," and she said, "But he has a beautiful leg" – though I wonder whether leg was the limb she really meant.'

Mr Jefferson laughed heartily, as he did at all Mr Cosway's scabrous anecdotes. True, TJ could never have been described as a prude, but he had always possessed a fine discrimination and where the free and easy shaded into the coarse he did not care to follow. Or had not, until the Cosways arrived. Indeed, Wm began to categorise his master's mental state into two eras: before Cosway and Anno Dominae.

In Paris they walked, how they walked. There were never such pedestrians, certainly none whose mileages were so lovingly tabulated. Mr Jefferson's pedometer played Cupid to their ramblings, and the day's accomplishment was recorded in his notebook and rehearsed that evening or the next day to gasps of amazement.

'Five miles and a quarter! My dear Mr Jefferson, I do not believe it. The milestones would have flown past if there had been any in that delightful lane up to what was the name of that dear little village, Montmartre, that was it.'

'Tomorrow I suggest that we might revisit the Tuileries. It will be your last opportunity to—'

'Oh, my friend, do not speak of last, I cannot abide last. Why cannot our walks continue for ever until we have girdled the globe? Why cannot the Duke of Orléans father more children for my husband to paint?'

'He is doing his best, even if they are not all his wife's.'

Wm preferred to absent himself from these excursions. He did not care to see Mr Jefferson in this spoony mood. Jefferson awkward, serious and somewhat out of kilter with the world, that was the Jefferson he loved. Jefferson flirtatious and sentimental, no.

So he was not of the party when the American ambassador escorted Mr and Mrs R. Cosway along the raised walk that divided the gardens of the Tuileries from the banks of the Seine. It was a fine September morning and the party's high spirits were only a little damped by the thought of the Cosways' impending return to London.

'Oh, how clumsy of me.'

Maria had dropped her reticule, an embroidered silk pouch so small it could scarcely have held so much as a handkerchief. It had fallen among the daisies in the rough grass the other side of a low trellis fence.

'Don't worry, my dear, I shall retrieve it.'

And going at it sideways, Mr Jefferson vaulted the insignificant obstacle, or attempted to. But his unpractised legs, shambling limbs at the best of times (not a patch on Monsieur de Monville's elegant shanks), failed to clear the top of the fence and he toppled over into the daisies, throwing out his hands to break his fall. He tumbled down in a sprawl and at once experienced an intense jarring pain in his right wrist, the most agonising sensation he could recall in his whole life. By chance one of the royal doctors happened to be walking nearby and instantly pronounced the wrist to be badly broken, though it needed no doctor to see the bone protruding from Mr Jefferson's pale flesh.

He was not a good patient. The pain remained excruciating, especially at night, so bad that the surgeon had to be sent for twice but had no remedy to offer beyond a sleeping draught, which had little effect. Wm's own work was doubled, since he now had to act as TJ's amanuensis and maintain his indefatigable correspondence as well as his own. He had to write such a quantity of stuff that he began to wonder whether the repetitive stress might not be doing some injury to his own right wrist.

There were all the letters to Mr Barclay about the Algiers business and an interminable letter to Mr Jay on that same subject, the text of the Treaty with Morocco, all twenty-five clauses of it; and then he must write to Monsieur de Langeac about the rent on the embassy; the American consular agents must be written a circular letter reminding them of the import duty on rice; Mr Bondfield's office had to be instructed on the procurement of powder and muskets for the State of Virginia; then they must respond to Lafayette's complaint that he (TJ) should not be importing harness from England rather than buying it from French saddlers and loriners; and perhaps most irksome of the lot, Wm must specify to Mr Macarty a fresh order of table china with detailed measurements of every dinner plate and salad bowl down to the last half-inch. All this dictated by Mr Jefferson in his rambling but unstoppable vein, then read over and endorsed with a few trembling squiggles from his unimpaired left hand.

For the first few weeks the pain was too bad for the patient to venture forth at all. So it was also Wm who must personate His Excellency at the important events of that crowded season, not least the unveiling of the bust of Monsieur de Lafayette at the old hôtel de ville amidst a host of notables, including Monsieur Houdon, the sculptor of the work in question, and the radiant Marquise de Lafayette. The great man himself was down in his native Auvergne, mending a few political fences before the forthcoming meeting of the Assembly of Notables. Perhaps, too, he did not care to have his own magnificence eclipsed by its marmoreal simulacrum. There is something demeaning about posing beside one's own likeness. But Adrienne was a brilliant substitute for her husband. She enjoyed the reflected glory of the ceremony so much that Wm wrote back to Virginia, 'I am persuaded that she did not receive more pleasure on the night of her marriage.'

Already the Virginia Assembly had commissioned Monsieur Houdon to carve a bust of Lafayette to stand in their own Capitol, but on further, even nobler thoughts they decided to commission a second bust to be presented to the city of Paris in honour of the nation from which the young Marquis had so gallantly sprung.

How Monsieur Houdon prospered. He already had two fine studios, one at the King's Library and another near the Foundry in the faubourg du Roule. And his busts were everywhere, in the Salon, of course, and in any self-respecting great hotel or chateau, not to mention the Commonwealth of Virginia for which he had done Franklin and Captain Paul Jones and General Washington at full length before he embarked on his first Lafayette. Gouverneur Morris, that wily one-legged tobacco agent from New York, had commissioned one of himself. It seemed as though the heroes of the age all had to be buffed and chiselled in marble, and by Jean Antoine Houdon and nobody else. For their part the La Rochefoucaulds had commissioned a splendid bust of their adored Monsieur de Condorcet, an unpromising subject, perhaps, but it was not the least part of Monsieur Houdon's genius that he could make the moral virtues of his subjects shine through, a double chin or a fleshy nose being no impediment. Every visitor to the rue de Seine felt compelled to admire the bust that stood upon the marble table in the salon: its lofty aspect, its piercing gaze, the sheer intelligence that glowed from the cold stone. Everyone agreed that this was the Condor to the life, no, better than life.

Mr Jefferson was sitting by the fire when Wm returned to the Hôtel de Langeac. He seemed broody and made only the most perfunctory enquiries as to how the ceremony had gone.

'Is the wrist painful?'

'Oh, it is nothing, I am scarcely aware of it. Are there no letters for me?'

'A note from Mr Stephens Smith about the printing press, he says it has been forwarded, but the harpsichord will be delayed until Dr Burney returns from the country.'

'Much use I shall have for a harpsichord with this wrist, though Patsy is in need of an instrument to practise on when she comes from the Abbey. Nothing else?'

'Nothing of note.'

'Nothing from Mrs Cosway?'

'No.'

'She is a woeful correspondent, she confesses it herself.'

Mr Jefferson looked into the fire with such an intensity as though he hoped its flames might have the power to douse his melancholy.

'Shall I send to her that you would greatly like to see her?'

'Oh, you must send to Mr Cosway as well.'

'Well then, to both of them?'

'No, no, it would not do, they will be too occupied in preparing for their departure.'

'Ah yes, tomorrow, is it not?'

'So Mr Cosway intends. He is impatient for London, which she detests. She hates the fogs, she says, and the bells tolling every five minutes as though one were perpetually at a funeral. She has a fine gift of expression, has she not, and she is as fluent in Italian as in English.'

Early the next morning Wm heard the tinkle of the handbell that Mr Jefferson had adopted to summon him during his indisposition. Wm came into his master's bedroom, which was also his study, to find TJ waving a paper at him.

'Pray dispatch this to Mrs Cosway.'

It was characteristic of Mr Jefferson that he forbore to fold even this tender billet, being contemptuous of all concealment. In any case it would have been a difficult manoeuvre to execute with only one good hand. So once out in the hall with the door closed behind him, Wm was able to digest the meagre contents almost at a single glance.

I have passed the night in so much pain that I have not closed my eyes. It is with infinite regret therefore that I must relinquish your charming company for that of the surgeon whom I have sent for to examine into the cause of this change. I am in hopes that it is only the having rattled a little too freely over the pavement yesterday. If you do not go to day I shall still have the pleasure of seeing you again. If you do, God bless you wherever you go. Present me in the most friendly terms to Mr Cosway and let me hear of your safe arrival in England. Addio Addio.

Let me know if you do not go to day.

Was ever a love letter so stilted and circumspect, so much to be read between the lines and yet so much felt? How poignant were the wavering lines of the script and the laborious almost childish forming of the letters. And how dejected the orphaned postscript straggling down towards the corner of the page. This was, so far as Wm knew, the first letter that Mr Jefferson had attempted with his left hand and it was a sorry sight.

But the Cosways did not go that day. Mr Cosway had unfinished business to attend to, whether artistic or of some less publishable nature, and it was a full week before they went. Mr Jefferson insisted on seeing them off at St Denis. When he returned to the embassy and Wm enquired after the farewell, he was too overcome to speak but went upstairs and shut himself in his bedroom. There he remained all that day and most of the next.

It was late afternoon when the handbell rang again. Mr Jefferson had taken to his bed and was sitting under the sheets bolt upright in his nightshirt. He looked pale but somehow relieved, like a feverish patient who has passed the crisis.

'Here, Will, take this vapid screed and fold it for me, would you?'

'Shall I dispatch it also for you?'

'Not under separate cover. I have a note for Trumbull here and you must enclose it with that.'

Perhaps TJ was no longer as innocent of the arts of concealment as he thought. After all, he had shown no compunction in making a mendacious excuse to Madame d'Enville whom he professed to worship.

'If you are quick about it, you might just catch the night coach.'

Wm hastened down to his own cubbyhole behind the stairs. As he was running down the stairs he was at the same time running his eye over the single sheet addressed to Trumbull.

> *. . . she promised to write to me. Be so good as to take charge of her letters, and to find private conveyances for them, or to put them under cover to Mr Grand Banker, rue neuve des Capuchins à Paris. Or she will do the last herself. All letters directed to me are read in the post offices both of London and Paris.*

And, he might have added, read too by my confidential secretary, Mr William Short. But then as an adoptive son, perhaps William scarcely counted as a distinct being, being little more than a pane of glass through whom Mr Jefferson perceived the world and communicated with it. It had, in fact, been William who had explained to his then innocent master that every word he wrote would be scrutinised in the post office if he sent it via the public mails and William too who had arranged for important letters to be sent via his bankers.

So, acting strictly in his official capacity as pane-of-glass-in-residence, Wm set about skimming the cream off this other epistle. It was a regular ten-miler of a letter. The three sheets, when folded up in the usual manner, amounted to twelve closely written pages, four or five thousand words in total, Wm hazarded. He would have to be quick if he was to catch the six o'clock mail. Meanwhile . . .

> *My dear Madam* [still so formal, but that was hardly surprising, Mr Jefferson was of the old school],
>
> *Having performed the last sad rites of handing you into your carriage at the Pavillon de St Denis and seen the wheels get actually into motion, I turned on my heel and walked, more dead than alive, to the opposite door where my own was waiting for me. We were crammed into the carriage, like recruits for the Bastille and not having soul enough to give orders to the coachman, he presumed Paris our destination, and drove off. After a considerable interval, silence was broken with a* 'je suis vraiment affligé du depart de ces bons gens'. *This was the sign for a mutual confession of distress. We began immediately to talk of Mr and Mrs Cosway, of their goodness, their talents, their* amabilité . . .

Amable indeed, but why bring Mr Cosway into it? Not only was he anything but *amable*, in Wm's eyes at least and he suspected perhaps in his wife's too, but the mention of such a coarse fellow detracted from the touching image of Mr Jefferson too close to tears to speak except of his beloved Maria. Wm began to wonder whether his employer had ever written a love letter in his life.

> . . . *Seated by my fireside, solitary and sad, the following dialogue took place between my Head and my Heart* . . .

Wm scanned on ahead and over the page. The whole letter appeared to be taken up with this infernal Socratic dialogue. First the Heart moans, 'I am indeed the most wretched of all earthly beings, overwhelmed with grief, every fibre of my frame beyond its natural power to bear etc. etc.' – which was admirable except that this lover's lament was immediately succeeded by a schoolmaster's report from the Head: 'These are the eternal consequences of your warmth and precipitation. This is one of the scrapes into which you are ever leading us.' Back comes the Heart in fine voice: 'Oh my friend! This is no moment to upbraid my foibles. I am rent into fragments by the force of my grief.' But the passion is instantly doused by the Head: 'Harsh therefore as the medicine may be, it is my office to administer it. You will be pleased to remember that I never ceased whispering to you that we had no occasion for new acquaintance.'

The Heart then scores a hit by pointing out that it was only the Head's concern with domes and arcades and other such architectural arcana that brought about the fateful meeting at the Halle aux Blés. Unabashed, the Head then digresses on to its plans to build a new public market in Richmond on the lines of Legrand and Molinos's corn exchange, with a noble bridge to be thrown across the Schuykill to improve access thereto (and this is a love letter? wondered William Short). Anyway, it was the Heart that caused the to-do by insisting that all previous plans for the day were to be cancelled. Unabashed in its turn, the Heart eggs on the Head to recount the transactions of that day, and then itself recalls those of the day they went to St Germain, to Marly, to the Bagatelle, to the Desert.

How grand the idea excited by the remains of such a column! The spiral staircase too was beautiful. Every moment was filled with something agreeable. The wheels of time moved on with a rapidity of which those of our carriage gave but a faint idea, and yet in the evening, when we took a retrospect of the day, what a mass of happiness had we travelled over!

How well Wm knew those feelings, how rapidly the wheels of time had spun when he and Rosalie had travelled the same route! TJ was an unexpectedly dab hand at the conjuring of romantic atmosphere. Yet here comes the Head again, reproving the Heart for 'imprudently engaging your affections under circumstances that must cost you a great deal of pain' – more especially if the lady had 'qualities and accomplishments belonging to her sex that might form a chapter apart for her, such as music, modesty, beauty and that softness of disposition which is the ornament of her sex and charm of ours'.

Then another thousand words of sententious philosophising before the Heart is allowed to return to happier topics '... the greater part of life is sunshine. I will recur for proof to the days we have lately passed. On these indeed the sun shone brightly! How gay did the face of nature appear! Hills, valleys, chateaux, gardens, rivers, every object wore its liveliest hue! Whence did they borrow it? From the presence of our charming companion. They were pleasing, because she seemed pleased.'

At last! After a good three thousand words of solemn academicising, a direct and unmistakable reference to the person of Maria in her own right, and with no yoking of the brutish Richard. Alas this romantic passage proves but a brief intermission. The Heart is the guilty party this time, swerving off into an improving homily on charity and the satisfactions of giving alms even to incorrigible beggars and worthless drunkards: 'tho we cannot relieve all the distressed we should relieve as many as we can ...'

The sound of horses' hooves in the courtyard reminded Wm that he must catch the mail and he hastened on to the conclusion of this strange enormity of an epistle.

As his eye sped down the final page, he caught sight of a few phrases that would do at a pinch in a love letter:

If your letters are as long as the Bible, they will appear short to me. Only let them be brim full of affection . . . my health is good except my hand which mends slowly, and my mind which mends not at all, but broods constantly over your departure.

No, thought Wm, as he carefully folded the sheets and folded them again, it is not that TJ is incapable of opening his heart, and certainly it is not that he lacks the art to set down his feelings – no man in America had a more expressive genius. But there is a mulish pride about him that insists on demonstrating, even in the extremities of passion, that reason is still in the driver's seat. That is what holds him back, his prizing the capacity for self-restraint above all other virtues that he possesses. Well, Wm concluded, he was ready to follow his master almost anywhere, but down that path he would not. For what was life without a loose rein and a full gallop now and then?

November was well advanced before TJ's right hand was back in action and, much to Wm's surprise, Mr Jefferson's spirits rose as fast as the pain subsided. He had not forgotten Mrs Cosway, certainly not, and he did write to her (Wm no longer had access to the contents but the sealed envelopes still passed through his hands). Yet their separation appeared to cause him no deep inconvenience.

Wm came to think that their affair, if it could be so called, was more in the nature of a liberation. It was just five years now since Martha Jefferson had died, though not yet two years since the death of little Lucy. Jefferson thought of them both every day, Wm was sure of that, but there were now respites from the grief when he could for an hour or more enjoy what the world had yet to offer. And it was Maria who had freed him from the sharpest, most unrelenting pangs, there was no doubt of it.

In fact, his friendship with Mrs Cosway now provoked him to seek and kindle friendship with other women who were not in the least like her. There was Madame de Tessé, for example, the enthusiastic pock-marked lady with a nervous tic that twisted her mouth into a grimace, whom Wm had met on his first visit to La Roche and who went into raptures over probability and who was celebrated for her reading parties, at which fashionable people dozed while she or some literary light read from *Tristram Shandy*. Wm was fond of this motherly personage and called her Aunt Tessé. She treated him like a scapegrace nephew and ticked him off about his friendship with Rosalie, in which reproof he was conceited enough to detect a hint of jealousy.

With Madame de Tessé and half a dozen more such ladies Mr Jefferson enjoyed conversation without commitment, friendship without passion. He seemed to ask no more of life than this. The Head appeared to have the Heart neatly harnessed up and the Heart, so far as Wm could see, was content with the arrangement.

Mr Jefferson was thus as free as he wished to be and no more. He unbent so far but his joints were not fashioned to bend further. When Patsy came back from the Abbey to visit her father, she was pleased to find a warmer welcome at the Hôtel de Langeac. But she was not long sitting with her father in the big oval room where he both worked and slept before he was quizzing her on her progress in mathematics and reproaching her for using a crib to construe Livy. Nor was her programme of education to be confined to the academic syllabus. She was soon to return to Virginia and learn needlework and other domestic skills, which would prove edifying distractions after she was married, for life on a plantation was seldom free of tedium.

Mr Jefferson did not, it seemed, envisage the free and easy life of the Paris salon as a suitable future for his own daughter. Patsy was annoyed that just as she was beginning to get the hang of French (she knew not a word when she arrived) and finding her feet at the Abbey, her father should be talking of plucking her away.

Wm admired his master still. Their old family ties were as unbreakable as Mr Jefferson's services to the nation were imperishable. Yet it could not be denied that TJ's views of his duties as Minister were elastic, to say the least. No sooner had the great Assembly of Notables opened at Versailles in a sludgy wet February than he decamped to the South of France on the pretext that he would bring back models of classical architecture to beautify the new capital of the young republic. This Assembly, the first such to be called in a century and a half, was the only hope of raising the revenue to meet France's steepling debts. So it was Wm who had to trudge down to the Hôtel des Menus Plaisirs to listen to this gathering of fogeys and popinjays denounce the Americans for costing them a fortune to liberate. Tax reform after tax reform was chewed over ad nauseam and then spat out, and there was TJ writing from the blue skies of Provence, seated with his sketchbook beside some picturesque classical remains, expressing his unbounded confidence that the Assembly was on the verge of achieving not only national solvency but a first-rate constitution on British lines (he was experiencing one of his periodic fits of enthusiasm for the institutions of his old enemy).

At the same time Mr Jefferson had not lost his faculty of disapproval: 'William, I have had occasion before to call into question the wisdom of your close acquaintance with madame de La Rochefoucauld, Rosalie as you call her. Madame de Tessé tells me that you were at the opera with her twice last week, and then once at the Italian comedy. We are of course on cordial terms with the La Rochefoucaulds, who are the most estimable people and of the most liberal views, and I am aware that the duke is content that his wife should show you the sights. All the same, I doubt whether it is wise for a secretary of legation to gain the reputation of a *cavaliere servente.*'

'Aunt Tessé only tells you all that in order to watch your disapproving face. She doesn't mind a bit herself.'

'I do not care to hear you refer to her so disrespectfully.'

'All the young Americans call her Aunt. I think she rather likes it, she's a sport.'

'Well, I don't care for it.'

If he had been like TJ and a loving friendship had been all he wished for – an *amitié amoureuse* as they called it over here, which sounded so much more languorous – then that summer with Rosalie would have come close to perfection. Mr Jefferson and Mrs Cosway were opposites, that was what struck the sparks between them. But with Wm and Rosalie there was no such *chiaroscuro.* Except in the colour of their hair, they were much the same in everything: both slender and slight, both twenty-eight years old, quick-witted but also reflective, so that their conversation was like a series of near-echoes, each reverberation returning the pleasure of the one before. And anyone who saw them out walking would have thought how well matched they were, this fine-boned miniature couple, and in that easygoing society would have assumed that they must be lovers.

But they were not, nowhere near it. And in a curious way their not being lovers was because they were so alike. Wm had kept his resolution to give up the pleasures of the Green Dolphin. There was in him a natural *pudeur* which coexisted with his healthy Virginian appetites, and if Rosalie was going to be his special girl, as they said back home, then she had to be the only one. But for her in her position that same modesty, which she possessed as fully as he did if not more so, meant that she could not admit even the thought of going beyond friendship. As the friendship became more intense, it was even more important to her that it should not stray by so much as an inch into forbidden territory.

When they first met, she would take his hand to lead him down one of the bosky paths in the shrubbery at La Roche and when he made her laugh, which he could, she laughed like no other woman he knew in Paris, full-throatedly, holding nothing back, and she would fall against him clasping his shoulder with both hands in mock fear that her hilarity had rendered her incapable of staying on her feet without assistance. And he remembered, too, how her little hand had pulled him up the last few steps of that chalky labyrinth to the fortress at La Roche.

But now she positively avoided physical contact with him, he was sure of it. If he put his hand on hers in a casual gesture of affection, she would with a soft unobtrusive movement remove her hand and find some object of interest that required her to take a few steps away from him. Often she would insist that her brother Charles should come with them. Charles and Wm had become friends just as Rosalie had hoped, not least because he was so like his sister in his quick wit, his mischief and occasional flashes of temper, which passed as quickly as a summer shower. If there had been no Rosalie in the world, Charles would have been a delightful consolation. But as it was, what was the French for gooseberry?

Wm could not see that she undertook these precautions because she feared that they were in too deep together and if she slackened her guard there would be no going back. He began to think that she might, *au fond*, be as frigid as duchesses were supposed to be and that, when it came down to it (and how was he supposed to keep it out of his mind?), he was her plaything and not much more.

They were reading together Monsieur Rousseau's great novel, *La Nouvelle Héloïse*, in the English translation to improve her English.

She knew the book almost by heart in the original and she hoped that her memory of it would prompt her when she was at a loss. William, who alone of all sentimental young men in Europe had not read it, was taking the part of Saint-Preux, the adoring and high-minded lover. She was sitting on a pile of logs. They had wandered deep in the Bois. Rosalie had promised that they would soon come out upon the river bank, but the trees seemed to go on for ever. So she sat down while he roamed up and down declaiming,

> *While I wandered in ecstasy through these obscure and lovely places, how were you occupied the while, my Julie? Had you forgotten your friend? But forget Julie? I could rather forget my own self, and how could I ever be alone for a moment, I who am nothing except through you? When I was sad, my soul took refuge with yours and sought consolations in those places where you were. When I was happy, I could not enjoy the pleasure alone and so I called you to my side to share it with you. I took you everywhere with me. I never admired a view without hastening to show it to you. All the trees I passed lent you their shade, every patch of grass was your resting place.*

'So you see, if I understand Monsieur Rousseau correctly, you need not actually be present for me to take a walk with you, though I am very glad that you are.'

'Oh, but I am not Julie, I am too faint a being for your imagination to summon me up.'

'On the contrary, my imagination is too feeble to do the summoning. In any case, I prefer flesh and blood.'

'But it is a beautiful passage, is it not?'

Wm agreed that it was but did not add that it was her influence that made him think so. Before he came to France he would have considered such fancies too high-flown for his taste, but now, here in these dappled glades with her there was room for the imagination to work its insidious magic. That was the key to it: the room, the space, the time, above all the time. America had physical space, miles and miles of it, endless untravelled acres, mountains and torrents every bit as picturesque – no, more so – but there was no time to enjoy them. They were there solely to be worked, tamed, exploited. That was what God had created Americans for, to do the working. If Wm had been back home in his backwoods in Surry, he would have ridden off straight away to enquire of the woodman why he had left those logs to moulder in the plantation instead of taking them down to the sawmill. But as it was . . .

'I think it is even more beautiful in English,' she said. 'But perhaps it is because I know the language so poorly, it sounds more mysterious and romantic.'

'How does the story turn out?' Wm asked.

'Oh, you must not run ahead. It will spoil the pleasure.'

'Please, I would love to hear you tell the story and then I can see if Monsieur Rousseau tells it as well as you do. But you must do it in English, that will be your test for today.'

'Well, if you insist.' She laughed. 'Then afterwards we shall change places and you will tell me an English story in French.'

She rose from the logs and began to stride up and down with big steps in imitation of him, turning to him now and then with her mischief-brimming smile. And he thought of the first time they had met, beside the canal at Versailles, where she had imitated the Condor. And he knew that he would never forget this moment either, her striding up and down with man's steps and him lying back on the logs feeling the sun on his face and the ridges of the bark through his shirt.

'Well,' she said, 'as you know, Julie and Monsieur Saint-Preux yield to their passion, but they are consumed with remorse because her father would never allow them to marry. He thinks of suicide but is saved by the offer of a place on the ship on which the Admiral Anson is about to begin to, how do you say, circumnavigate the world. While he is away, Julie obeys her father and marries Baron Wolmar. He is an elderly foreigner, twice her age almost, but he is kind and thoughtful, and she is not unhappy with him. Then when Saint-Preux returns after all those years at sea, the Baron invites him to stay with them, because, you see, he trusts that they will be loyal to him. And he makes Saint-Preux tutor to their children and they live together in virtue and contentment.'

'Except that he loves her still and she loves him as much as she ever did, am I not right?'

'Yes, but they struggle against their passions and they remain virtuous until she dies – is untimely the word? – an untimely death.'

'It is a tragedy then.'

'Well, it has a sad ending. But it is not really a tragedy because virtue triumphs and that is not what happens in a tragedy.'

'In her situation would you have behaved like Julie?'

'I could not imagine being in such a situation.'

'You do not think that—'

'I do not think anything, William. I know that I love my husband.'

'And you are not unhappy together. Is that enough, is that all you want, a husband who is kind and thoughtful and who makes you not unhappy?'

'You are presuming too far, monsieur. If you are my friend, you will leave this topic.' She shut the book with a frantic slamming as though to prevent something noxious escaping from its pages.

'I cannot leave it, Rosalie, you know I cannot without saying how much, how deeply I love you.'

'You are not to say such things, you know you must not. You must take me home.'

'If I have—'

'Take me home and do not say another word. You have ruined the day. If you understood one-tenth of what Rousseau understands about the human heart, you would never have talked so.'

She was on the verge of tears, hot and flushed in the face, and so magnificently angry that he was all the more in love with her. They plunged back through the coppices in search of the gate where they had left the horses. The saplings whipped at him as though they were in league with her anger. When they found the little gate and the horses quietly cropping, he gave her a leg-up into the side-saddle and she rode off without a word, scarcely gathering the reins before kicking the horse into a feverish trot. He followed, sitting morose and low in the saddle, wondering whether he really deserved to be compared so unfavourably to Jean-Jacques Rousseau who, as she herself had pointed out, had spawned several illegitimate children and abandoned them to the charity of an orphanage.

She did not turn round and throw him a word during the entire return journey. And when the gates of the Hôtel de La Rochefoucauld opened to receive her, she cantered through into the courtyard as though fleeing the attentions of a *bandito*.

*

The next morning there came a brief note for him:

> *After our conversation of yesterday I think it better if we do not meet again. I reproach myself for allowing such a misunderstanding to ruin our friendship. If I had read my dear Rousseau with more care, I would have realised the dangers that must inevitably arise in such a connection. Do not write to me. R.*

What a fool he had been, falling for a hopeless prospect like a French duchess. Anyone with a grain of sense could see how impossible it was that she should ever entertain any serious regard for him. He was no more than salon fodder, a useful bachelor to fill the last place at table, to hail the carriages and buy the ices while her husband was preoccupied with affairs of state. To her friends she probably spoke of him in pitying terms: 'my little American'. Madame de Tessé was right, Mr Jefferson was right, everyone could see it but William Short. His mooning after her must be the joke of the season.

He stumped out of the Hôtel de Langeac and marched along the new wall that girdled the whole of the inner city now, the 'farmers' wall', as they called it, though there were no crops or cattle anywhere near it, except what were impounded by the officials who manned the fancy pavilions that were set in the wall at every gate. They ran the biggest racket in history, these so-called farmers, had their grip on every indirect tax on the books: salt, tobacco, leather, ironware, soap. You name it, they controlled it. And as if they were not sure enough of their unconscionable profits, they had built this unconscionable wall so that nobody could smuggle anything in or out. *Le mur murant Paris rend Paris murmurant*, as the wags put it, 'the wall walling Paris makes Paris wail'. This infernal wall had Paris by the throat. Its stranglehold was ruining the health of the city's inhabitants by blocking out the country air, which alone could blow away the foul pestilences of the place. Millions of cubic feet of fresh air were stolen from the poor people who were thus in the pulmonary as well as the financial clutches of these bloodsuckers. Nor were visiting Americans entitled to feel detached from this hideous robbery, for it was the huge debts run up by the Americans in their war – more than a billion livres and almost all of it in loans – that had generated this frantic hunt for the last sou of revenue. The freedom of the Americans had been bought at the cost of enslaving the French.

The worst of it was that the bloodsuckers were not greasy lower-class villains like tax collectors in most other countries. On the contrary, some of the farmers lived the most elegant lives, were received in the best society and had their own houses crammed with pictures by Boucher and Fragonard, and ormolu furniture from the finest German *maître-ébénistes.* Lavoisier, the greatest profiteer of the lot, was the most famous scientist of the age, admired by one and all, and had just been painted amid a scene of domestic felicity by none other than Monsieur David.

As for the pavilions, they were built to the most ingenious modern designs by Monsieur Ledoux, each one different: one an undersized Parthenon, the next a rotunda modelled on the Pantheon in Rome, then a pastiche of the Little Trianon plumped down in the middle of the high road. Yet there was something about each of them that betrayed that they were built strictly for business rather than pleasure. The windows were small, like the windows of a prison or a barracks. There was a certain grim massiveness in miniature about the stonework, for they had to protect the little garrison in each pavilion against the potential indignation of the mob.

All the hot day long Wm relentlessly walked off his humiliation, striding past now the inside, now the outside of this bizarre circumvallation, noting, though grudgingly, the ingenuity of Monsieur Ledoux in building each of his fifty 'Propylaea of Paris' as he called them in a different shape and manner. The paint was still fresh on some of the window frames, and at the newest barriers there were workmen sanding the stone on the rusticated lower courses. They all seemed to be in a diabolical hurry to complete the work before – before what?

As the shadows of these fiscal fortifications lengthened, so Wm's disgust grew, not just at these monuments of greed but at the whole display of competitive extravagance that obsessed the nobility of this city. Was there really much difference between this necklace of pavilions and all those follies – those fake temples and pagodas and ruins and grottoes that he and Rosalie had visited? Pavilions and follies alike were built on the sweat of the labouring poor who could barely keep the roof on their own hovels while they tiled and thatched and slated these exquisite buildings that were intended to house nobody at all, except a countess or two who came to take tea with her coterie when the weather was dry.

Good God, who were these people who preened themselves on their progressive views and who threw away their fortunes on fripperies and regarded useful work as fit only for the bourgeoisie?

By the time Wm had circumnavigated Paris, his nostrils crammed with stone dust, he was as tired as Admiral Anson must have been after doing the same to the globe, and he was looking forward to a hot tub and a glass of claret. But as he came into the hall of the embassy, he was met by the chirruping of children and the sound of running feet.

'She is here, Will, here at last! Is it not a marvel to have both my little chickens under our roof?'

Mr Jefferson was standing at the foot of the stairs, half laughing, half crying as the two little girls ran in and out of the rooms, Patsy pointing out to Polly all the crannies and byways of the house. Behind them following rather uncertainly in their wake was a coloured girl, not much older than Patsy. She was clearly dog-tired after the journey and she was looking about her with big brown eyes, shy and bemused, as though waiting to be told if she were doing wrong.

'And this', said Mr Jefferson, 'is James's sister Sally. She has been looking after Polly on the voyage, though I must admit I had forgotten how young she was. How old are you, Sally?'

'Going on fifteen, sir.'

'The journey must have been very strange for you, too. You remember Sally from Monticello, don't you, Will, or was she too small to be noticed when you visited last?'

It was some time later that Mr Jefferson told him how Polly had been induced to cross the Atlantic. She and her cousins had taken an innocent-seeming excursion to visit a ship lying at anchor. The party had spent a fine couple of days romping on the ship's decks and playing hide-and-seek in the cabins until Poll seemed quite at home there. Then, when she had fallen sound asleep the cousins, acting under instructions, had crept away ashore. By the time Polly woke up, the ship had set sail for its five-week voyage. Mr Jefferson seemed to find nothing amiss in the stratagem and he made light of Polly's tears on the voyage, which had been copious. Her companion, Sally Hemings, had wept too, but she had no voice in the matter.

VI

Falls

William Short had seen a dead body before. He had seen his father lying stiff and small on the parlour table at Spring Garden before they took him off to the coffin maker. And as a child on the Tidewater he had seen through the tall reeds the body of a planter who had killed himself after the tobacco blight, but his nurse had pulled him away before he could get any closer.

The little huddle of blue rags outside the Hôtel de Langeac was worse somehow. At first he thought it was a bundle of some peasant's belongings that had fallen off a country cart, but then he saw the feet sticking out, swollen and purple, the heels just breaking the surface of an icy puddle. Wm stood there by the gate, staring, irresolute. A couple of young men scuttered past, muffled and hunched against the cold. One of them gestured at the corpse and the other turned his head, but only briefly. They did not stop.

Wm turned away to call for Vendôme the coachman. Vendôme would know what to do.

Everyone expected the winter to be a hard one, each winter nowadays seemed to be harder than the last, as though providence was testing how much they could endure. In July there had been hailstorms in the Beauce, stones so big they had killed partridges and hares, and withered the grapes along the Loire. The price of a loaf of bread had doubled, trebled in some places. But the worst famine was the cash famine. The beggars were everywhere, sleeping rough under the colonnades of the Palais-Royal, besieging the gates of the smartest hotels in the Marais, however fiercely the porters beat them off, a dirty great tide of misery that came back again and again in the hope of a crust or a couple of sous, which they might in the end get if the owners wanted to be rid of them before a dinner or a ball. But the beggars weren't the only ones. Half the aristocracy were mortgaged up to their eyebrows. And as for the royal debts, you would need one of Montgolfier's balloons to see how far they reached. The Assembly of Notables had dribbled into inanition in its last few weeks surviving only as a butt for the Paris wits. The Parliaments in Paris and most other places too would not countenance a single new tax worth having. The moment the King sat down to business, his ministers would besiege him with urgent requests, warnings, threats: it would be a calamity if the Queen bought Saint-Cloud, the two royal stables would have to be amalgamated, at least one pack of wolfhounds would have to be disbanded, not to mention the falconers, sixteen royal lodges and lesser chateaux would have to be auctioned off.

No wonder His Most Christian Majesty preferred to shut himself up in his workshop, hammering away at his locks and nautical instruments, before sitting down to another gut-swelling breakfast, then rushing out to hunt until dusk, anything to avoid the terrible insistent question: where was the cash to come from?

They were not in much better case in the American legation. Mr Jefferson had the devil's own business to persuade the Congress to disgorge his salary, let alone the thousand dollars per annum that was due to Mr Short and which TJ had so far met out of his own pocket. The Minister protested stoutly that his furniture, carriage and apparel were all plain, but plain was not exactly the word to describe the twenty-piece table silver that he had commissioned of Matthew Boulton or the silver-plated English harness to which Lafayette had taken such exception. Meanwhile the infant republic trembled as close to bankruptcy as the antique regime of France. Every message from across the ocean harped on the same string: how was the loan to be repaid, could not Mr Jefferson use his fabled powers to persuade the Dutch to ease the terms? And for Mr Jefferson read mostly Mr Short, who had perforce to become overnight an expert in finance. To his surprise he warmed to the work, when only a year or two previously he would have found it dry stuff.

But then he had few other consolations now. In the last months of that summer, the Hôtel de Langeac had been, all too briefly, a place of brightness and laughter. The two little girls rushed in and out of their father's room without ceremony. They skipped down the stairs to badger Wm in his cubbyhole, swinging on the new revolving bookcase of which he was so proud and generally making nuisances of themselves. If other amusements failed, they would rush off to flush the water closet until they exhausted the water tank, which provoked the most thunderous lecture from their father on the importance of water conservation and their duty as Americans to set an example of seemly conduct. And always behind them would be Polly's supposed keeper, the young coloured girl who seemed scarcely older than Patsy and much less sure of herself. She would hang at the door while the other two pestered Wm. When he caught sight of her round face, pale for a Virginia negress, and her big dark eyes staring at him, he would beckon her in and tell her not to be shy. But even then she would stand a little apart, her hands clasped behind her back, watching their antics with what emotion Wm could not decipher.

Down in the kitchens, though, Sally was more at her ease. She came into her own helping her brother stir his sauces and beat the butter and flour for the cakes and pastries he had made a speciality of the house. There, the roles were reversed. She would laugh with James and tease him about his lack of girlfriends, while Polly and Patsy sat on the cook's bench and watched them solemnly as though they were at a play. And Wm saw that this kitchen chatter was the nearest thing to home for the two motherless girls and thought how often they must have sat in the kitchens at Monticello and listened to James's and Sally's mother Betty as she prepared the simple Virginia dishes that Mr Jefferson liked then, though his tastes had amplified since coming to Paris.

Wm had heard the rumours that Sally, and perhaps James also, was the child of old John Wayles, Martha Jefferson's father, who had bequeathed the Hemings family plus a hundred and thirty other slaves to TJ when he died. Certainly she was pale, but then every light-skinned Negro was whispered to be his master's offspring. Mr Jefferson knew the rumour too, Wm was sure of that, but he never alluded to it. Was that because he believed it to be an absurd fabrication, or because he believed it to be true? Undoubtedly it would have been painful to him that one of his slaves should be his own sister-in-law. Yet would he have written those acerbic passages about the mental capacities of the Negro race if he knew (and might one day have publicly to acknowledge) that he was so closely allied to members of that race? Most probably he had put the rumour out of his mind five minutes after he had heard it and never recurred to it thereafter. TJ was good at that. He did not brood. He moved on. That was the secret of his greatness. And when it came to the point, he was not much incommoded by sentiment. When it was time to send Patsy back to the convent, this time accompanied by Polly and Sally too, he did not hesitate. 'You had not thought of engaging a tutor instead?' William asked.

'They will be better taught at the convent. And as for their spiritual education, there are as many Protestants as Catholics there and not a word is spoken in the classroom on the subject of religion.'

'No, it is just that they seem so happy here.'

'Happiness is not everything, William.'

Wm did not think to remind his master that the Declaration of Independence gave a different impression.

So the three girls went off to the rue de Grenelle and the Hôtel de Langeac was left to the widower and the bachelor. Only a month after that sad day Wm was alone in the rue de Berri, while Mr Jefferson decamped to the Rhineland in order to investigate the varieties of grape that might be transplanted to Virginia.

Before he went, though: 'I have had a letter, William, from Monsieur Brissot de Warville. He wishes me to join his new society, for the friends of the blacks.'

'Ah yes.'

'I have declined his invitation. The object is an admirable one, but I fear it would not be right for me to become a member, seeing that the nation I represent has not yet pronounced upon the matter.' Wm detected a certain extra convolution in Mr Jefferson's syntax, always an indication of some unease. 'I cannot see how it would help the cause in France and it might render me less able to serve it at home.'

'Er, would those considerations apply to me also? Only the thing is he asked me too and I have already accepted.'

'Have you now?' Mr Jefferson paused for thought. He did not seem best pleased. 'Your enthusiasm does you credit, William, though you might perhaps have consulted me first. Still, I do not see that it would matter greatly that a secretary in our legation should demonstrate that he possesses a liberal heart.'

Somehow this approval did not raise Wm's spirits. *A* secretary indeed.

'Besides,' Jefferson added, brightening somewhat, 'it would be useful that we should be kept aware of what this new society is about.'

'I cannot attend as a spy, sir.'

'My dear Will, the line between diplomacy and espionage is a fine one. But all I suggest is that you should keep in touch, that's the thing. It might be best, though, that James and Sally should not be made aware of your membership.'

'There is no reason that they should know anything of it, sir.'

This was not the first time that Mr Jefferson had shown a certain sensitivity in this connection. For if James and Sally had known the rules, they could have declared themselves liberated the moment they stepped ashore at Le Havre whether their master liked it or not. He stood to lose an excellent cook and a nursemaid who might still be a little green but who enjoyed the affection of Patsy and Polly and represented a precious link with Monticello. What they didn't know wouldn't hurt them.

So Wm went off by himself to the first meeting of the Société des Amis des Noirs. It was held in Madame de Tessé's drawing room in the rue de Varenne. He arrived early. Aunt Tessé herself had not yet come down. There was only one other person in the salon.

It was the Duke. He was seated at a rosewood *bonheur du jour*, his bony knees straddling the little desk like a jockey on an awkward nag. He was reading some documents with his habitual care, his big bony nose poking into them as though it was an auxiliary organ for classifying the material. He did not hear Wm come in through the half-open door but at the creak of his footsteps on the floor he turned and got up, half knocking over the desk in his anxiety to show the warmth of his welcome. 'Ah, my dear f-friend, Mr Short. William,' he added with the appearance of the christian name requiring some official endorsement before use. 'It is far too long since we met. This society will be most valuable if it enables us to keep our friendships in repair – although I do not of course mean that this should be its principal object.'

'No indeed, sir. I am delighted to see you here too.'

'If only R-Rosalie were here also. She would love to see more of you, you know. I had hoped that you might accompany her to this and that while I am so busy with the new constitution, but then you must be very busy too, now that Mr Jefferson is away again.'

'I am rather, but—'

'I tell you what, you must come on to dine with us when this is over. I am sure that Madame de Tessé won't mind a bit.'

Wm's heart beat so hard against his ribs that he could scarcely find the words to greet the other members of the new society as they straggled in – among them Lafayette, Condorcet and of course Brissot, bustling Brissot with his pamphlets and his travel books and his causes and his societies and his unstoppable tongue. Brissot had been all over the place. He had been jailed for debt in London, skipped in and out of trouble in Brussels and Boston and Berne. He was the son of a pastry cook, and he lived by his wits and seemed to be a perpetual-motion machine. His eager, bright little face popped up everywhere, his wet red lips never still.

When he took them through the agenda, it was more like the voyages of Jacques-Pierre Brissot. He seemed to know from personal experience every steamy tropical island and every plague-ridden jungle where slaves were groaning in their chains – *French* chains sanctioned, if not actively forged, by His Most Christian Majesty (though when it came to forging, the King was as dab a craftsman as any professional). How could it be right that there should be a single slave in France's colonies when there were none, by law and custom, in France itself?

William looked around the room and realised that he must be the only man there who had ever owned slaves. Plenty of those present had profited from that peculiar institution through investments in the plantations and in the sugar and tobacco they produced. But actually to have owned another human being, that was his fate alone, or rather had been his inheritance. He would always remember that strange feeling of his own liberation when he said goodbye to the last slave at Spring Garden, old Isaac, who was going to Mr Grant's but who died two weeks later before he could be transferred. He, William Short, was free even if his former slaves were not. Mr Jefferson by contrast still owned two hundred slaves at least, two of them being here with him in Paris. Looking round the eager faces in Madame de Tessé's salon, Wm began to think that Mr Jefferson had been right to decline membership after all. Even Wm himself could not escape moral taint. If he had told his personal history in this company, he could see how Brissot's supple lips would twist it and insinuate (as even dear Rosalie had) that he had merely sought to absolve himself by turning his slaves into cash. Was trafficking in human beings any lesser a crime than putting them to labour in the fields?

How he longed to be out of this conference and sitting opposite Rosalie again. She would not know, could not know, how bleak and long those nights had been, listening to the last carriages going home and the creaking of his narrow bed and the palpitations of his heart. In those comfortless hours there was no consolation he could grope for. He felt condemned to utter sterility, the cold sweat on his body like the foretaste of the grave. Towards dawn he sought relief in the old way and his prick bolted like a cabbage stalk and its sour juices spilled over him and he felt more desolate still.

There were other young Americans in Paris, idlers mostly, living off the backs of Boston or Philadelphia fortunes such as Tom Shippen and Johnny Rutledge. Wm enjoyed the occasional frisk with them but when they proposed to round off the evening at Madame Juppé's or that other place they went to down in the Marais he pleaded pressure of work and didn't care if they thought him a prude. They knew about Rosalie of course. Every fool straight off the boat seemed to know about his obsession with the little Duchess. But they did not see why that should inhibit him from taking his pleasures elsewhere too. This was Paris, after all, not Boston or Philadelphia. They could imagine (and envy) a young American enjoying a dalliance with a bored aristocrat, but what they could not figure out was that the young American might be so desperately in love that he had resolved to live as chastely as a medieval knight if he could not have her.

'My dear, I brought William Short home with me. I thought it was far too l-l-long since we had seen him. Madame de Tessé released him, though I have to say with rather an ill grace.'

She jumped up from her chair, white in the face. That was all he thought at first, how pale she was and frightened-looking. The paleness and the alarm made her more beautiful still. He had not remembered quite how beautiful she was, which he also thought was an odd thing to think because how could he have been in love with her, so constantly in love, if he had not thought her beautiful?

Then the colour came into her cheeks and the startlement left her eyes, and she managed to greet him more or less calmly as an old friend who had been out of touch for some tedious practical reason.

He knew now, in that moment, standing at the Duke's side a little apart from her, that he would never be free of her. He had suspicioned it before, but now he knew it. And he was pretty sure too that the same went for her. However it all turned out, happily or badly, together or apart, there would never be anything else like this for either of them.

They did not say much, hardly a thing. They did not have to, because the Duke had quite a deal to say.

'It was a r-remarkable day, my dear. I shall not easily forget it. The undertaking is such a noble one. Madame de Tessé's salon may become immortal for having given birth to it. We had d-difficulties of course. Should we call ourselves the Amis des Noirs or the Amis des Nègres? Which title would be the less offensive to those we were intending to help? We were most grateful to William for his assistance on this point.'

'I said *noirs* had more of a ring to it and *nègres* was a tad too close to nigger, which they don't much cotton to.'

'Then there was the question whether we should intend to achieve the abolition of the trade in slaves or of the condition of slavery itself in our colonies, or both, or if not both, which should come first. Young Brissot really is a remarkable fellow, he has been everywhere, you know.'

The Duke went on, and the afternoon light came in through the long windows, a dusky lemon light that softened everything and made the real world seem remote and powerless to touch them. The Duke paused and went over to the little bell on his desk to call for refreshments.

She came round the sofa and took his hands in hers. 'I am so glad you are here. It is stupid that we have not seen each other for so long.'

The Duke's back was not turned and there was nothing furtive about the way she spoke or held his hands. She could have done the same to an old general who had come to tea. But it was enough. 'It is so brave of you to join,' she said later when the lemonade had been brought. 'For my husband and his friends it is a gesture that costs nothing, but you may make enemies back home.'

'You know I have no slaves myself.'

'Yes, you sold them, but that will not stop your neighbours in Virginia thinking that you have, how shall I say, betrayed your class.'

'Oh, they won't find out and even if they do I'm not sure how much I care. They'll come round in time. Slavery cannot endure in the long run.'

'But while it does? Mr Jefferson is a little more cautious than you, I think.'

'Now then, you are not to provoke me into criticising my master.'

'I do not think that I can make you say anything that you do not wish to.' The Duke looked on their conversation with something like pride, as though he had trained these two players in the game. Had he any conception of their feelings, Wm wondered and thought not. In fact, he doubted whether La Rochefoucauld really understood very much about his wife. He admired her beauty, he swam happily in her affection and responded to the sharpness of her wit. But was she anything more to him than an engaging puppy who had come by arrangement to brighten his widowerhood? He seemed to overlook or actively to brush aside her deeper qualities – her lively apprehension of danger, for example, and her understanding that the ideals they all shared might be only tenuously connected to reality. But then that was too much to expect, perhaps, when he was twice her age and, being her uncle, had known her since she was a child.

All at once, as they stood there sipping their lemonade, which looked almost colourless in the hazy lemon light, Wm was overcome by a sensation that could only be described as dread, not so sharp as the dread when you put a horse at a stiff fence, no, this was a more insidious apprehension of uncertainty. Did they know, any of them, what they were letting themselves in for? The Duke moved across to the tall glass doors that gave on to the court and he pointed out to Wm the gravel walk and the little oblong parterre that Rosalie had laid out to relieve the severity of the yard: a criss-cross pattern of box and lavender bushes with slips of rose newly planted in the middle. The skimpy fledgling plants shivered a little in the breeze that had got up. Wm shivered too and she took his hand again. This time the Duke had his back to them.

William's time of solitude was over. But another kind of ordeal was only just beginning. They saw each other almost every day now and the intimacy between them ripened in every way except the most obvious, the most natural, the most fundamentally human.

She had spelled out the rules in a quick flurry of sentences, which he was sure afterwards she had rehearsed. It was the third time they had met since the breach between them had been repaired. They were walking along the cours la Reine, the little road between the Tuileries and the Seine where Mr Jefferson had taken his nasty tumble.

'You know how it must be between us, don't you? I am very fond of my husband and he I think of me, and I owe him so much and I would do nothing to hurt him or my grandmother for he is her son and we are everything to her. I want nothing more in the world than for the friendship between us to grow and grow deeper but there must always be limits to it, you do understand that, don't you? And I can trust you to observe those limits, observe is such a pompous word, it sounds like a legal edict, doesn't it, but you know what I mean. It is much to ask, do not think I do not know that, but you are the only person I have ever met whom I could ask it of.'

There was not much that he could say to all this, except what he did say, which was that he entirely understood and respected and admired her feelings, which were just what he would have expected of her, and he only hoped that he could prove himself worthy of those feelings. As he was making this speech, he reflected on the bright side, viz., he was now allowed to say how much he loved her so long as he did not trespass beyond the bodily frontiers, and she now allowed herself to respond in every way except the aforementioned. But God, how much had to be conceded in return. It was child's play to commit oneself to liberating every nigger in America, but how on earth could he hope to spend hour upon hour in her company without laying a finger on her, without so much as bussing the little dark curls behind her ear or stroking her cheek, let alone sliding his hand along the inside of her peachy thigh or – but anyway that was how it had to be . . . well, for the time being. She might imagine that they could go on indefinitely keeping company in this chaste twilight, like that milksop Saint-Preux and whatever her name was, but he had other ideas. You could not live your life like a character in a novel. Old Rousseau certainly had not, otherwise how come he had all those bastards? But the strain was certainly beginning to tell on him.

Even Johnny Rutledge noticed. 'How's your little Duchess then? She refusing you your oats? I'd say you looked a touch sickly. Don't you think he do look sickly, Tom?'

'He surely does, John. I think Mr Secretary needs a holiday. Why don't you come on with us down to the south and on to Italy? We can compare the wines and the women. We need your experienced eye.'

'Well, I don't know about that. I'm pretty much tied here in Paris.'

'She really has you all strung up then?'

The odd thing was that he didn't mind their coarse wisecracking. It was a relief from his afternoons with Rosalie. Each time he came away from the long room in the rue de Seine, he was more in love with her than ever, but more in despair. He began to fancy that the servants knew his secret and beneath their politeness were all laughing at him. Even the great marble bust of Condorcet on the buffet seemed to be sneering at him.

Mr Jefferson, too, the next coolest thing to a marble bust, had spotted something. 'You do not look well, William. I begin to wonder whether your train of life in Paris is entirely healthy. Perhaps I should dispatch you back to Virginia to look for a wife. Or you might find profit in exploring Europe a little.'

'I find Paris very much to my taste, sir.'

'Certainly its distractions are delightful. But all too often I fear they offer only moments of ecstasy amid days and months of restlessness and torment. Our native soil furnishes steadier pleasures, I think, because they are founded upon fidelity and modesty.'

Wm thought that he would not mind a few moments of ecstasy in exchange for the restlessness and torment that he was already suffering. What an irony it was that these none too subtle reproaches should be addressed from one monkish celibate to another.

'Besides,' TJ continued, 'I am conscious that my repeated absences have thrown the labours of Hercules upon your shoulders and that it is time I take my turn to mind the shop. There are so many questions that I failed to resolve during my excursion to the south. You would be able to fill up the gaps in my geography.'

'What exactly had you in mind, sir?'

'Whether the grapes of the Italian hills might be suitable for our own southern climate, and the rice too, which I understand is now the staple crop in the valley of the Po. I am allured, too, by the project of tasting macaroni at home such as we have delighted in at Ruggieri's and am eager to know the secrets of its manufacture. Then there are the architectural models of classical Rome, which we might build upon. Our new Capitol surely will have much to learn from the old one. It is a source of regret to me that I but tiptoed into Italy and failed to see the beauties of Rome or Florence or Venice.'

'But in these tumultuous times ought I not to remain here?'

'My dear William, you should not be so ready to believe old wives' tales. As yet the tumults have not cost a single life according to the most sober testimony we have been able to collect. Nine-tenths of Paris believe that two hundred were killed at Grenoble where there was in truth but one officer wounded. I am sure it will end in calling the States-General next year, in May or thereabouts. And that I think will secure the reformation of their constitution without bloodshed. I wrote to Johnny Rutledge to tell him so last night. It is a pity that Tom and he should already have gone off to the Netherlands. But I believe they still mean to go on to Italy later and you may make a rendezvous with them there. But even thus far you need not travel alone. The Paradises are off to visit their daughter at Bergamo.'

'Sir, I do not—'

'Mrs Paradise tells me that she and her husband would like nothing better than to have you as their companion.'

'Sir, I do not think that Mrs Paradise and I, in the close confines of a post-chaise, well, I do not think that we should get along.'

'William, I had expected better of you. Lucy Paradise may have her faults. She is a little volatile for some tastes but she has her troubles. John Paradise possesses a fertile mind. I derived much profit from my conversations with him in London. No man in Mayfair peppered his talk with more Greek phrases, but he is not an early riser, he attends to business fitfully and their debts have mounted. Lucy tells me that every hogshead of their tobacco that comes ashore at Wapping is mortgaged to their creditors and on poor terms. I am doing what I can to help her but—'

'Sir, you have not seen Mrs Paradise in her moods, she can be a virago.'

'William, she is a Ludwell from Williamsburg. We have obligations of kinship to her and if you object further to the proposal that you should travel together, then I shall be bound to conclude that you do not wish to leave Paris at all and I shall know the reason for it.'

On 17 September 1788 he set off with the Paradises in a post-chaise, with the aid of £35 10s borrowed from Mr Jefferson (who could ill afford it, being not much less indebted himself than the Paradises).

But first he had to tell Rosalie. 'Mr Jefferson insists that I should go. He wishes me to act as his scout.'

'Scout?'

'To study the Italian varieties of grapes and rice and architecture, for use back in Virginia, you understand.'

'I do not understand, William. Surely there are vines enough in Champagne and by the Loire. As for porticoes and colonnades you have only to look out of the window. Be honest with me, you are going because you wish to be as far away from me as possible. If you did not wish to go you would find a way of wheedling Mr Jefferson round to your point of view. He is very fond of you, I sometimes think that you do not understand how fond.'

'Oh, I know that well enough and will always be grateful for it in the depths of my heart.'

'But in the depths of your heart there is no room for me, that is what you wish to say, isn't it, but you do not quite dare. Well, I don't blame you. I have asked too much of you, I know I have. It was a stupid idea, that we could go on like this for ever. It was my fault entirely. I have been reading too many silly novels. Real life is not like that, real men are not like that. Why should they be? Perhaps if I had spent more time with people my own age, I would have learnt more of life.'

'Rosalie, you must not be so understanding. I would almost prefer it if you were angry. I do not think I can bear your forgiveness.'

'No, really, it is time I tried to be grown up for once. I have nothing to forgive you for. Anyway I am quite angry, or at any rate I am suffering from a severe case of injured pride, though why should I think I am the only woman in Paris who is entitled to have an admirer without giving him anything in return? Well, perhaps I am not the only one, or was not I should say. There may be other spoilt women like me. We could found a society like your society for the blacks, a Society for the Friends of Unsatisfied Lovers.'

He had not seen her cry before and he thought it did not come easy to her, her sobs were odd little convulsions, like miniature hiccoughs.

'No, listen,' he said. 'This is what I should have said to start with but when I am with you I always lose my place. It is not because I have fallen out of love with you that I am going abroad but because I am deeper in love than ever and I cannot stand it. I am not Saint-Preux but a regular run-of-the-mill Virginian who has fallen for a girl and can't get over it. So the only hope is to try a fresh tack. I know I'll feel the same way when I come back, I'll bet my last dollar on it, but will you? If you don't, then that will be the end of it and that will be the best thing for both of us. And if you do, feel the same I mean, then I'll ask you to – no, I'll damn well insist that you – come away with me, whatever you say to the contrary.'

He had no clue as to how she would react. He reflected, a little to his surprise, that he had not given much thought to that side of things. This showed how absurdly egotistical all lovers were when it came to the point, or perhaps it showed how his going away came out of his desperation. It was a cry from the heart not a calculated stratagem.

'Yes,' she said, after a long pause. 'I believe you. I have always believed you, believed what you said, I mean, since we first met.'

'Too dull to make it up, I suppose, that's me, probably most Americans.'

'Not at all. I have met several of your countrymen who can lie as well as we can. Mr Humphreys, for example, or Mr Morris, especially Mr Morris, he could pass for a Frenchman. Even Mr Jefferson may at least deceive himself from time to time though he would not stoop to an outright falsehood. But you are truthful.'

'Still sounds to me like a way of saying dull.'

'No, no, telling the truth is such a rare thing that it is, I don't know, startling. But perhaps sad too, yes I think sad. Fiction is after all the way we cheer ourselves up.'

He was not sure how much more he wanted to hear of this philosophising.

'So,' he said, 'what do you think?'

'You are right to call me back to the question of our relations. I was trying to get away from it – how unlike a woman, but then perhaps I am not a proper woman.'

'Well?'

'I have nothing to say, nothing worth saying, that is. You are going away and I am sad. When you have gone, I shall be sadder still. And that is how I shall remain until you return. Nothing else in life means as much to me as you do, nothing at all.'

She stopped but it was obvious that she was only gathering her strength to go on. 'Now,' she said very quickly, 'I will kiss you and turn away and you are not to follow me.' He felt her lips on his, as quick as a bee's sting, and then she was gone. He did not follow but through the long window he could see her in the yard stumbling over the little hedges she had planted and even through the window he could see she was crying.

'Marriage, do not talk to me of marriage. If the world only knew what our sex has to put up with, they would do away with marriage this afternoon. Why is it that only the least fitted males choose to marry, let alone remarry? There is Mr Jefferson, dear, dear Mr Jefferson, the kindest and most sensible of men, a widower and like to remain so, I'm sure. And William, I may call you William, mayn't I, since we are both from the Tidewater and we are to travel so far together, there *you* are, the next most sensible and dearest of mortals in Paris after Mr J and a confirmed bachelor, I can see. Why, by the time I was your age my daughters were almost grown up. And here I am yoked to the most impractical, inconsiderate and insensible human being in the universe. Mr Paradise has a great name in London as a scholar, he is a Fellow of the Royal Society and he speaks six languages but he has not a word of sense to utter in any of them and he is no more fit to manage his own affairs than a frog or a toad. I do not need to tell you, William, that I was born a Ludwell of Williamsburg and we expect our menfolk to carve out a name for themselves. Why, my father was President of Virginia and owned a good stretch of the north bank of the James river.'

'I remember that on a clear day we could see across to your land from the top field at Spring Garden.'

'Just so, and now if it were not for Mr Jefferson's kindness we should not be able to pay the maid or the coachman. But much *he* cares about such things.' Mrs Paradise gave her husband's knee a sharp rap with her tortoiseshell fan.

John Paradise FRS retained a negligent, defensive posture with his slim volume of Propertius held well up to his nose much as a pugilist maintains his guard. His knees, however, remained exposed and were accordingly subjected to a bastinado from the fan. Nonetheless, in such a confined space Mr Paradise made a magnificent show of being somewhere else entirely.

Lucy Paradise was pretty, nobody had ever denied that. She was thirty-eight but in her calmer moments looked a good deal less. Her neat features and her trim little figure were of the sort to show off a flirtatious manner and she certainly did not despise such traditional wiles when she was in dire need of a favour. The trouble was that she was so quick to fly into a passion and so reluctant to quit one that she never practised those wiles for five minutes together. They had met only four or five times since the Paradises had come over to Paris but Wm had noticed almost immediately the way she would start off wheedling and fluttering her eyelashes, usually in the quest for a loan of some sort, but halfway through this delicate operation she would lose her temper and burst out in a scalding philippic, usually against her husband or against the lawyers who managed their dwindling estates. William had decided that if they were to cross France without the carriage being shaken to pieces by her explosions he himself would have to take charge of the practical business – the horses, the innkeepers, above all the disposal of the cash. He had, he explained, been in France for nearly four years now and had a fair grasp of the language.

'Oh, as for language there's no French spoken to match Mr Paradise's. Mr Buffon said he had never heard such French in his life before. But my husband could no more order an egg to be boiled or a bed to be turned in French or any other language than he could fly to the moon. So we shall abandon ourselves entirely to your management, my dear William. I look upon the day you consented to join us as the first break in the clouds since that unhappy morning I threw in my wretched lot with Mr Paradise. At least I was the object of his affections then, was I not John [rap], but he has long since fallen out of love with me, have you not [rap]. I languish at the bottom of the ladder of his affections [rap]. He would rather any one of his blessed books than ten of me. I declare he thinks I cannot read, he thinks I am an illiterata, don't you [whack]. When he is talking with Dr Johnson or Dr Burney, he waves me away as though I were a wasp or a fly, do you not so?'

'Certainly I do not, my dear. Dr Burney spoke warmly of your singing voice.'

'He could do no other since he was dining at our house in Charles Street and you had compelled him to accompany me at the harpsichord. I nearly died of shame. As for Dr Johnson, I do not recall him addressing a civil word to me on that evening or any other.'

'Well, he does have a reputation as a bear, my dear.'

'Nonsense, he fawns upon that stupid Thrale woman. You had poisoned his mind against me, or rather told him that I was entirely mind*less* and unworthy of his attentions.'

'I would not dream of saying any such thing.'

'You never remember what you have said in company. You are so fuddled by the time the company assembles that I wonder you can say anything at all. William, I look to you to regulate my husband's drinking upon this voyage.'

'Lucy, I hardly think that Mr Short—'

'You will notice that he becomes remarkable lively when it comes to ordering the wine. If he were as diligent in attending to other business as he is to whether we should drink Rhenish or Burgundy, we would be rich beyond the dream of Midas.'

Mr Paradise gave a weary smile, which illuminated his long dark face. Either his mother or his father was Greek, he had said, Wm could not remember which; he had been brought up in Salonica and knocked around the world dispensing an unforced charm, which had made him welcome everywhere. He was unfailingly agreeable and he always knew as much about what people were talking of as they did themselves and made them feel that he felt just as they did on the question. His bona fides were unimpeached except by the occasional curmudgeon such as the old Scottish chemist who had growled when Paradise was elected by acclamation to the Royal Society, 'But what has the fellow *done*?'

'Well,' said William, 'I shall have my hands full with my principal business upon this tour, which is to keep a journal for Mr Jefferson. As always, he is abuzz with questions, which I am to satisfy.'

'A journal, William, how fascinating.'

'In the form of letters, you understand. For the first part of the tour I shall be comparing my notes with his own, but when I ride beyond Milan I shall be traversing ground untrodden by him. At all events I intend writing to him once a week.'

'How admirable,' she cried. 'Mr Paradise has not written me above three letters in the twenty years we have been married, have you?' But though she accompanied this last accusation with the usual thwack at his knees, she remained strangely pensive after Wm had disclosed the duty imposed on him. In fact, for the rest of that long day and the next, as the dusty post-chaise rumbled along the chalky roads through Burgundy, she was quiet, even docile, and made some show of civility towards her husband. Just beyond Auxerre, Mrs Paradise requested that the coach stop for a few minutes. She alighted and walked off behind a clump of bushes. It was a hot, sleepy afternoon but William became aware that John Paradise was wide awake watching him.

'That was a smart device, the letters.'

'What?'

'Even if you never write a line to Jefferson she will remain in mortal dread that you are writing a poor account of her to him.'

'I swear I had no such thought.'

'Well, you may count upon it she has. There is no one in the world she worships more or on whom she relies more, to bail us out you know. I fancy we may be in for a tolerable smooth ride.'

And so they were. Every now and then she fell into a doze and let her head loll against her husband's shoulder. In repose her little face looked like a girl's and you would not have guessed an ounce of malice in her. All the same, it was a long journey and Wm was not sorry when they reached Villefranche and found a decent inn. He climbed the creaking stair, his hand resting on the greasy banister. Down below he could hear Lucy, now revived and thinking herself out of earshot, haggling with the landlord over the cost of clean sheets. He intended to ask for a couple of chops to be sent up but he fell asleep as soon as he lay down on the rickety iron bedstead.

'William, William. The landlord says we must be off by eleven o'clock if we are to reach Lyons by nightfall. You must go straight to Mr Grand's otherwise we shall starve on the journey.' He stumbled off the bed, still dressed in yesterday's clothes, and shambled down the stair after her. 'The fifty guineas from Mr Jefferson's advance will not see us over the Alps and this is our last chance to draw on his credit. You would not wish our poor bones to be eaten by the wolves, I know you would not. I have a bill of our expenses here. I had to do it myself in a bad light, Mr Paradise being sound asleep. Our expenses are thirty-three guineas, which leaves us but seventeen. We shall never see Italy unless you make haste to the bankers.'

In the slow methodical way he had learnt as indispensable in any business, large or small, Wm tallied up the items she had scribbled in her wild girlish hand. 'You have written down last night's supper twice,' he said, 'and omitted your share of the horses from Auxerre. I make the total twenty-eight guineas.' He saw that she was about to expostulate but then thought better of it. Any parting on bad terms would surely find its way into the next letter to her dear Mr Jefferson.

There was no question but that they must draw the whole amount of the credit. As the clerk handed over the money, he said, 'You are Mr Short, are you not? This letter was sent on from Dijon. I fancy it has been galloping after you the whole way from Paris.'

He knew the hand, of course: neat, springy, rapid, just like the way she walked he remembered thinking the first time he received a note from her, to thank him for accompanying her to the comedy and for the ices they had stopped off for on the way back to the rue de Seine. Even writing her name in his little grey cloth notebook had given him a stab of pleasure – 'Ices, com. Ital., Mme de La Roche., 35 sous.'

He turned in the bright sunlight, meaning to go over to the quay and sit on the stone parapet to read the letter. But Lucy insisted on dragging him back to the hotel to say goodbye to Mr P who had not finished his toilette.

'You will come and stay with us in Bergamo, promise you will now. My daughter, little Lucy the Countess, Lucy Two we call her, is longing to meet you, she is starved of Virginian men, and Mr Paradise needs someone to talk to about Horace and Homer, because the Count's English is not very good except when he is discoursing about his wife's dowry. You will find the Italians very mercenary, I am afraid, William. It was quite a shock, I can tell you, for people like us who were raised to think it ill-bred to talk about money.'

It was not until the post-chaise had rattled out of the hotel yard with Lucy blowing kisses out of its window and even John Paradise waving a languid paw that Wm was able to break open the little envelope.

You were right to go away. It is easier to say goodbye at a distance. And that is all we have to say. I shall not forget our friendship but you must forget me.
R.

He looked up and saw a middle-aged man, weather-beaten with a friendly look on his face, standing a few yards away, politely waiting for him to finish reading.

It was Monsieur de l'Aye, the friend of Mr Jefferson's who was to show him how to make wine. They had met the day before, coming into the town.

'Not bad news, I hope.'

'Oh . . . no, only confirmation of news I had received earlier.'

'Good, good. My old rattletrap is waiting in the road when you are ready.'

They drove through meadows beside the Saône. Cows as white as unicorns were munching the long wispy grasses. On patches of waste-land reddened by dock leaves there were goats tethered to long ropes – they made the best goat's cheese in France, Monsieur de l'Aye said. This side of the river there were low blue hills, on the far side the tops were covered with snow. He was reminded of the country round Albemarle and Amherst, and resolved to tell Mr Jefferson so when he next wrote.

Monsieur de l'Aye swung the carriage up a long chalky track between vines, then stopped the horses and hopped down to pick a bunch of grapes, which he presented to Wm. 'Here, try these, they are much like the Volnay grapes whose wine you had last night.'

'They resemble the wild grapes that grow back home in Virginia and – yes – they taste absolutely the same. There is a vine at my father's that grows on an old oak tree, all by itself and in the full sun. My father tried his hand at making wine from it one year. It came out quite agreeable, very sweet, not at all like the Volnay.'

'Ah, that is the art, to keep out the sweetness without losing the bouquet.' Monsieur de l'Aye rubbed his fingers together in a gesture to express the subtlety demanded by the process. He was like an old peasant, Wm thought, though without an ounce of cantankerousness. The Château de l'Aye was a fine old house that had no pretension to it. The dining room was a plain sort of room, simply furnished just such as you might find in Albemarle rather than in a financier's mansion at Philadelphia. While they were dining on a rich mutton stew, at the other end of the room the women of the house were sewing and repairing a long tapestry rug together.

After dinner they sat by the fire and Monsieur de l'Aye talked of the harvest. Wm let his thoughts wander back to Surry County. He imagined a vineyard blooming with grapes, stretching all the way up from the home orchard to the old oak tree. They would make wine as easily as they now made cider. But who would 'they' be ?

In his bedroom he wrote to Mr Jefferson and told him of his smooth ride with the Paradises and their friendly parting, and of Monsieur de l'Aye's vineyards and a dozen other things that had caught his eye on the journey. And he ended with a message that he knew would be welcome: *'I have not time to tell you how certainly and with how much pleasure I experience that I can quit Paris without regret, notwithstanding what you think to the contrary. When I say I do not regret Paris I mean Paris without any person from America in it.'* It was a roundabout way of putting the matter, but he could not bear to mention her name, not yet, and anyway the mails were always read.

He looked on those next few weeks as a recuperation, like learning to walk unaided after an accident. He abandoned himself to all the sensations of travel – the gentle gliding of the water diligence down the Saône to Lyons, then the winding road up to Geneva, that dignified

Protestant city with its shimmering lake and the mountains beyond, then the slithering, soaking-wet, fog-sodden passage over Mont Cenis and at last the first sight – how long he had dreamed of it – of the orange roofs and steepling bell towers of Italy. In Turin he heard Lolli play, something by Haydn he fancied, but he was in such a daze he could scarce attend to the music. And as they were rattling through Piedmont he quite forgot to visit the rice mill at Novara, which Mr Jefferson had particularly asked him to do. He took up Lucy's invitation to call on them at Count Barziza's castello outside Bergamo. He even egged on Johnny Rutledge to meet him there. The whole of Italy lay before him and he intended to see every inch of it.

So it was without any back thoughts about the Paradises or their mercenary son-in-law that he clattered up the stony track to the Castello Barziza, a great dismal barracks of a place with the plaster cracking off its walls. And when he saw Mrs Paradise tripping down the grim outdoor staircase in the courtyard, he almost jumped from his bony hack to embrace a fellow countrywoman.

'Why, William, your cheek is glowing from your ride.' He did not care to say that on the contrary it was her cheek that was sweating and that a comprehensive aroma of wine, garlic and something else that he did not care to name filled his senses with such a potency that it was as though he had recovered his sense of smell after long deprivation of it. In fact, he had to admit that after walking up a further flight of steps to the Count's draughty salon he felt decidedly weak at the knees and was glad to sit down in one of the worm-eaten walnut chairs that were more or less all there was in the room except for a ragged tapestry flapping between the windows depicting a subject that was impossible to identify.

The Count was a low, rat-faced fellow, a striking exception to the claim he lost no time in pronouncing that the gentlemen of Lombardy were the most handsome in Italy. By contrast he entertained no such illusions about the state of his seat. 'This castle very bad,' he said. 'All good things, pictures, silver, all gone – my uncle take them. Then I marry American girl, I hope I am in Paradiso, ha ha.' He rammed home the jest by prodding William in the ribs with his clenched fists. 'But is hell. I expect the millione, I get the zero.' He made a zero with his thumb and forefinger and squinted through it.

'I am afraid that we have proved something of a disappointment to the Count,' said Mr Paradise with his charming smile.

'Nonsense, my dear. Mr Staphorst and Mr Anderson explained the whole matter of Lucy Two's portion. If the Count did not take it in, then he has only himself to blame. In any case he did not think fit to inform us that three-quarters of his estate was mortgaged.'

The wrangle warmed up. Wm gained the impression that it was liable to break out at regular intervals and that the actors knew their parts pretty well. He himself found it hard to concentrate, his head seemed to be floating off his shoulders and he had such an ache . . .

'Why, William, you are sick,' said Lucy Paradise, 'we must get him to bed this instant.'

It was a high fever, Mrs Paradise declared she had never seen a higher. The Count's view, instantly relayed to the patient, was that William was certain to die and that it was *mala fortuna* if a stranger died beneath one's battlements. Lucy pooh-poohed this, though she herself wrote to the Hôtel de Langeac to say that she was greatly afraid that Mr Short's constitution was not so strong as he himself thought it and that the physician had told her and Mr P that he believed that Mr Short was 'in a slow consumption', those had been his very words.

This greatly alarmed Mr Jefferson at first but then he reflected that he had never known Lucy Paradise to give an accurate report of anything. And it was not long before he had a letter from Wm himself saying that he was on the mend and fretting to be off to Milan with Johnny Rutledge rather than remain under the care of the Paradises more or less in perpetuity, as Lucy advised.

At the height of his fever Wm did think that he might well be dying. If so, he reflected, why could he not have some more uplifting accompaniment – monks chanting for the repose of his soul, perhaps – rather than the noise of the Paradises and the Barzizas quarrelling, all four of them fortissimo since Lucy Two was fully a match for her mother and the Count managed to provoke Mr Paradise out of his amiable torpor?

'Not a penny, not one penny do I receive. You stay here all these month and I meet you all the great *nobiltà* of Bergamo and you no *soldi*.'

'Now listen here, Count, it has been three weeks now and I haven't seen my Lucy wear her jewels once. It's my belief that you have pawned the lot. Where is that lovely diamond corsage that Aunt Hetty Ludwell gave her when she could have left it to her Skipwith cousins?'

'You dare speak of diamonds. The Barziza diamonds—'

The next day Wm felt better, very weak still, but clearer in the head and the terrible aching was gone. His recovery was not greatly assisted by a bedside visit from the Count. 'You not die, I am *certo*. I pray to Santa Ursula, she our *padrona*. When you are better we go to Venezia. Just boys.'

'What?'

'You, me, Paradiso and your friend Johnny. No ladies. We have good time.' Once again the thumb and index finger formed a circle. This time, though, he plunged his other index finger in and out of the 'O'.

'Oh, I see. Do you think Mrs Paradise will approve?'

Mrs Paradise did not approve. 'I declare this to be the vilest and most disgusting scheme that ever I heard of. To prance off whoring after women in the backstreets of that insanitary plague pit, well, I know Mr Paradise to be capable of anything and I would not be in the least surprised one of these fine days to find his corpse floating down some dirty canal, but I had thought better of you, William Short. I shall be charitable because I am a charitable person and assume that it is because of your mortal illness that you have been led astray by my son-in-law who has no more morals than an Arkansas polecat. If you had been in your right mind, you would not have consented to abandon us poor womenfolk with a baby teething and hare off after your own selfish pleasures.'

'My dear,' said Mr Paradise who had barely come into Wm's sick-room but remained hovering at the door, prepared for a swift exit, 'we had in mind merely to show William the beauties of the place, the Grand Canal and—' The carafe of water that had been on the bedside table smashed against the door with Mr Paradise safely on the other side of it. However, he was still skulking on the landing, perhaps to regain his breath, and Mrs Paradise ran out and dragged him back by the lapels. He stood there mute and unresisting while she pummelled him with her fierce little fists. 'You are not to go, do you hear me, you shall not go. You are a monster of selfishness. You. Shall. Not. Go.'

She was hitting him so hard it was a miracle he had any breath left in his body. William thought he ought to intervene if he was not to stand accused of being accessory to murder and he clambered gingerly out of bed and attempted to pinion the termagant. But Lucy whirled round and now began drumming on his chest with equal ferocity. Through his thin nightshirt each blow stung like the devil. It seemed as though the punishment would never end. Then abruptly she stopped.

'Get back to bed, you stupid boy. John, go and tell the Count this instant that you have not the smallest intention of going anywhere without your wife and he must say the same.'

'Yes, my dear heart, of course. I should have consulted you, I know I ought.' The Paradises withdrew.

In the beautiful quiet that succeeded their exeunt Wm quickly came to three conclusions: that he would never again travel anywhere with John and Lucy Paradise even if they paid him (a most unlikely contingency), that the sooner he left the Castello Barziza the better, and that he and Johnny Rutledge might pass a tolerably jolly time in Venice somewhat along the lines suggested by the Count. He was pondering how these excellent plans might be executed when Mrs Paradise came raging back into the room, bright red in the face, the strings of her bonnet flying like streamers behind her.

'You are a lying hypocrite, William Short. I had painted you as the innocent of the party but now the Count tells me that you were the author of it all along. I shall never believe another word you say.'

'I promise you, Lucy, I said only how agreeable it would be to make an excursion to Venice and the Count kindly offered to put us up at his palace.'

'Palace,' she snorted. 'I am sure that it is no better than a flea-bitten hovel to judge by what we have had to endure here. You shall not escape scot-free. I shall make sure that Mr Jefferson hears every particular of this shameful episode. When we return to Paris I shall paint everybody in their true colours, see if I do not. I can assure you that Mr Jefferson, that dear good man, will never again be so deceived in his secretary – secretary forsooth, whoremonger would be the *mot juste* I fancy.'

As it transpired, this return to Paris was to occur sooner than anyone thought. For while the trip to Venice was still being fought over, flattened, then resurrected with ladies included, there arrived letters from Mr Anderson, one of their bankers in London.

'No more *soldi*, they have not a penny left, zero,' ejaculated the Count, half furious, half triumphant. Again the thumb and forefinger circled, this time without any intrusion from the other forefinger. 'They must go back to Parigi.' And go they did, floated thither only via a loan of eighty pounds sterling, extracted from the unwilling Count who was reconciled to unbelting this tidy sum only by the thought that he would not have to see his parents-in-law for a long time, perhaps with luck never again.

William, restored to something close to health, set off with J. Rutledge. They ambled through the vines and mulberry trees round the shores of Lake Garda, then on to Verona and Padua whence they took a delightful creaky old barge down the River Brenta. In Vicenza, so he wrote Mr Jefferson, he had been tempted to buy Scamozzi's edition of Palladio in four fine folios, for he found he had got a thirst for classical architecture. There was a villa by Pisarro between some cypress trees halfway down the Brenta that had bowled him over, and he had formed the fancy of buying it and retiring there to grow wine and make silk. Johnny Rutledge wrote Mr Jefferson too, about the virtues of the olive tree, and later the beauties of the Tarpeian Rock and other estimable subjects.

Back in Paris enduring the coldest winter in living memory, and to tell the truth a little starved of company, Mr Jefferson thought of his boys with pride and pleasure. He wrote his protégé a long and thoughtful letter of advice. William could not hope to secure a permanent diplomatic post if he stayed in Europe because America handed out such offices on the knowledge of persons and not by the recommendation of others. Even the best appointments offered no chance of saving money, TJ assured his secretary from bitter experience, and afforded but a bare existence and a solitary one too, for a married man could not live on them.

> *A young man indeed may do without marriage in a great city. In the beginning it is pleasant enough; but take what course he will whether that of rambling, or of a fixed attachment, he will become miserable as he advances*

in years. It is then too that he will want the amusement and comfort of children. To take a middle course and pass the first half of your life in Europe and the latter in America is still worse. The attachments and habits formed here in your youth would render the evening of life more miserable still in America than it would be here. The only resource, then, for a durable happiness is to return to America . . . I think you will never wish to return to Europe. You will then be sensible that the happiness of your own country is more tranquil, more unmixed, more permanent.

Wm read these words with a tear brimming in his eye, not so much for the advice itself but for the feeling behind it. It was the thought of his master anxiously brooding on his future and taking such evident pleasure in his letters, seeing Italy through his eyes. Well, not seeing quite all of the Italy that he and Johnny were seeing.

'I make that nineteen women we have had between us since we left Bergamo, *amico mio*.'

'Are you counting that singer outside the Teatro Olimpico because . . .'

'No, she was *interrupta*, I don't score any but the full article. And believe me, she was no singer.'

Back in South Carolina Johnny had been nicknamed Rutter. In normal circumstances he was an easygoing, tolerant fellow, a little dull and stolid perhaps, always ready to fall in with anyone's plans, but when a woman under the age of sixty came within range he was a different person.

'When my prick says go, I go, like the centurion.'

'Centurion?'

'Don't they read you no Bible in Virginia? He says Go and I goeth.'

But Wm did not delude himself into thinking that it was Johnny who was leading him astray. He had his own urgencies pent up. Twice when he was with a woman during those delirious months, once in a calle behind the Arsenal and then in one of those curious little wooden shacks the far side of the Tiber, he had gone in so hard that she cried out, not from pleasure but from pain or fear. Was he making up for lost time or for lost contentment, or compensating for rejection? Certainly he had never thought of himself as violent. He surprised himself.

One morning in Naples, though: 'Johnny, my prick is on fire.'

'You're a lucky man.'

'No, it is the torture of the damned when I piss.'

'You are merely sore, *amico*, you have overdone it. You must learn moderation like me.'

'No, no, I am infected, I must find a doctor.'

'These Neapolitan quacks are more likely to kill you. Just slaver some ointment over the offending article and forget about it.'

The doctor, however, pronounced the case to be a *gonorrea indisputabile* and dosed him with mercury, which was almost as agonising as the complaint itself. This diagnosis proved more reliable than the slow consumption detected by the Barzizas' physician though no more welcome. Apart from the general debility and the local itching there was also the humiliation, not improved by Johnny's disposition to treat the matter with elephantine levity.

See Naples and die, the saying went, and Wm determined to fulfil at least the first half of the agenda at the risk of completing the second. They made their way slowly through the crowded streets, their dusty boots skidding on the rotten fruit, their travel-stained coats showered with more mud from the ridiculously high wheels of the carriages of the local *nobiltà* in their gay costumes who rattled past with a hoity-toity disregard for the ragged and noisy Neapolitans who filled the side gutters. In the foothills beyond the city the young Americans stumbled through almond orchards just coming into blossom and finally reached the last licks of the lava from the mountain and journeyed on through the sulphurous rocks and pools of the Phlegrean Fields. Everywhere they encountered the smell of decay and the unsightly scabs and eruptions of the earth, not to mention the no less unsightly scabs and eruptions in Wm's own groin. He felt like some strange creature of the underworld spewed up by these volcanic belches. Yet as they peered over the crater of Vesuvius and reeled back from the clouds of ash and pumice stone that were thrown in their faces, he was surprised by an unexpected sensation of cheerfulness.

The truth was that he had begun to weary of all this soulless fucking. The whole deceitful ritual sickened him: the false flirtation in the foyer, the stilted badinage, the chink of coin if required, then the rattling on the bedstead, the smell of bad fish and the quick throb of release – he had

had enough of it all. Even before he got the clap he had tried to say something of this to the Rutter, who remained magnificently impervious: 'Had enough, *amico*? All the more for me then.'

In the Corso Wm bought an iron macaroni mould and a treatise on the manufacture of silk, both items earnestly desired by Mr Jefferson. Then he walked down to Monsieur Grand's agents, Donat, Orsi et fils, at their offices by the quay. Funds were running low. He had already spent nearly all the £700 he had allowed for the whole tour. Mr Jefferson's letter of credit was looking decidedly dog-eared.

The walk took him quite some while. He had to proceed in a crab-like fashion with knees wide apart to stop his sores rubbing. Child beggars, some looking no more than six or seven years old, imitated his gait and tugged at his sleeve. One exposed his tiny genitals with a lewd gesture. Wm wondered what the urchin would do if he retaliated. Not much probably. He would have seen chancres and pustules like that every day of his life. The poverty and squalor in this city were really not picturesque at all.

There were two letters waiting for him at the bankers', one inside the other's envelope. When he had successfully obtained the money – Mr Jefferson's name had come up trumps once more – he rushed outside and stood on the pavement with the macaroni mould under his arm and tore open the smaller envelope first.

You are quite right, as you always are. It is my own fault. I implore you to forget me and you do me the kindness of doing so. What else did I expect? Yet this silence is too cold and painful to bear with so many hundreds of miles separating us. I know that it shows how weak is my nature but I would greatly value a few words from your hand if only to show that you bear me no ill will and that you still feel at least some small portion of that affection that I have felt for you and shall always feel. We must *be friends, do you not see that? I am sure you do, for otherwise there would be a false ending to a chapter that had nothing false in it.*

I heard that you were ill, even gravely ill. They did not mean me to hear it, at least I think they did not. But I overheard Mr Jefferson saying to Madame de Tessé that it was feared you might have contracted a slow consumption but that he personally believed it to be no more than a fever caught in crossing the Alps at that season. Mr Jefferson did not think to inform me directly of all this, which naturally I took badly, although I know he has only your best interests at heart. But when he next came to the rue de Seine, I was bold to presume on my prerogative as hostess and enquire of him how you did and he said you were quite well again to his great relief. I am not sure which of us blushed the more deeply. But after that I knew I had to hear from you directly or I would contract a fever myself. So I beg you to forgive this letter or if you cannot forgive it at least respond to it and let me know that you are as well as Mr Jefferson says you are. You cannot imagine the happiness that just a few lines in your hand would give your devoted R.

Good old Vendôme has volunteered to put my letter in with Mr Jefferson's for I had not your address but nobody must know of this.

Wm let the macaroni mould slip from under his arm. It clattered into the gutter from where it was retrieved by an alert urchin who immediately demanded *soldi* for his services. In his delight Wm gave him what must have been the equivalent of a week's wages.

The other letter, Mr Jefferson's, brought news from both continents. In America the elections had been held, the opposition to the constitution was growing feebler by the day, the new government would be beginning on Wednesday next, Mr Adams was generally expected to be the Vice-President. In France there had been a fray in Brittany. Only a few dead and things there were now quiet. The States-General were likely to meet under happy auspices. Great numbers of American vessels were now arriving in the ports of France with flour and wheat to remedy the famine caused by the terrible failure of the harvest. Altogether, in fact, things were going along pretty well and no evil was to be apprehended.

Wm smiled. It was hard sometimes not to smile at TJ's unquenchable optimism and hard, too, not to share in it and wish to be part of it. Great events were gathering pace, in the life of both nations and, who knew, in his own life too perhaps. He found a shabby albergo by the sea and ordered a glass of Lacrima Christi, the wine he had tasted on the slopes of Mount Vesuvius and taken a fancy to. And he wrote her a letter. He scarcely knew what he wrote – a weird mixture of apology and love and regret and hope, chaotic, tumbling out of him, nothing like his usual orderly progression from A to B. As he wrote with the February sunshine coming in through the grubby windows and the smell of the sea and the rotting dock smells coming in through the albergo's door that would not shut, he felt a happiness flooding through him that he was sure could never be equalled.

He must hurry back to Paris. That was the place where all his hopes were parcelled up together. They did not entirely curtail their Grand Tour. For once Johnny Rutledge dug in his heels and insisted that they complete pretty near the whole itinerary they had originally projected. But they certainly put on a spurt. Florence, Pisa, Leghorn, Lucca, Lerici, Monaco, Marseilles – all passed in a blur, accompanied by squawks and protestations from Johnny, who was as avid a notcher up of sights as he was of women.

'Hey, *amico*, we haven't seen the Campo Santo yet, the frescoes are supposed to be quite something.'

'Damaged beyond repair, my dear Johnny, not worth a minute of your time.'

In Nîmes they did make a pause in order to give a proper salutation to the Maison Carrée. Wm was pleased to confirm to Mr Jefferson that they agreed it to be 'the most perfect remains of antiquity which exist on earth', a judgement that pleased TJ hugely since by now William had seen three times as much Greek and Roman stuff as his master. And it was there too, sitting on the steps of that weathered old temple, that the two of them read Monsieur Necker's report convening at long last the long awaited States-General. They hugged each other.

'This is the moment, *amico*,' Johnny said. 'France is going to have her own revolution, just like ours only a darn sight better.'

'For once you may even be right,' said William Short, with a double rapture swilling around inside him.

They travelled by cabriolet and post horses all the way back to Paris. Even so they were a week too late to see the opening of the Estates-General, that gorgeous festival in which the last gasp of the past was to mingle with the insistent clamour of the new.

Mr Jefferson had not missed a minute of it. With the one-legged tobacco agent Gouverneur Morris stumping along beside him complaining of his sunburn, he saw the procession of the Holy Sacrament to the cathedral in Versailles: the King and the nobles wearing the most amazing specially designed hats in Henri Quatre style with the brim turned up in front, preceded by the royal falconers on horseback, each carrying a hooded raptor on his wrist, then the heralds blaring away on their silver trumpets with purple banners, and after all this garish pageantry the Third Estate dressed severely in black with white muslin cravats and not so much as a sword between them, looking like a congregation of Puritans that had strayed into a coronation procession.

The next day, the day of the opening session, Jefferson and Morris had left Paris at six in the morning to be in their seats by eight. As they arrived in the Salle des Menus Plaisirs (what an odd name for a room whose contribution to history was to be neither slight nor unmixedly pleasurable), there was a sense of utter disorder. Nobody seemed to have the least idea who was to go where or what was to happen next. Three thousand people were packed in between the Gobelins tapestries (a few of the more indecent scenes had been removed out of respect to the clergy), shoving and jostling, with only a dozen frantic ushers to find them their assigned seats. Which Estate was to sit with which and which separately had been at the heart of the argument from the start and should have been sorted out long ago.

The King, that clumsy, myopic little man, was of course incapable of giving a lead. He could not even get the business with the hat right. First he doffed his great plumed *chapeau* to the audience and the nobles took off their hats in the usual fashion but then some of the Third responded puckishly by putting their hats on and slowly removing them again, inducing the King to do the same, which the nobles did too. Then the Queen, rattling her fan in her irritation, could be heard whispering into his ear to put his hat back on. 'If the ceremonial requires these manoeuvres, then the troops are not properly drilled,' the sardonic Gouverneur murmured to Jefferson. Then Monsieur Necker spoke, for an eternity. He was inaudible. The King spoke. He was inaudible too, though the words 'much exaggerated desire for innovations' were faintly to be heard. 'I fear the King is insensible to the pang of greatness,' Gouverneur murmured.

But Mr Jefferson was not be cast down. 'On the whole, I thought it went off very well,' he reported back to Wm. 'And I am much encouraged by the progress of the debates in the Commons, as I call them. The meetings of the nobles are impassioned affairs, even our friends such as Monsieur de La Rochefoucauld find it hard to calm their tempers, but the Third Estate are always rational in debate. I have urged Lafayette to work out a compromise by which the three Estates would transform themselves into two, the lower house made up of the Commons and an upper comprising the nobility and clergy.'

'Like the English system you mean? But would the nobles stand for it?'

'It is the only way, Will. But they cannot do it without a constitution.'

'And how is all this to happen?' queried William.

'Why, I declare you are as much an unregenerate sceptic as that one-legged Yankee.'

Wm was not without respect for Gouverneur Morris (who had lost his leg in a carriage accident but did not demur when people assumed he must have lost it in the revolutionary wars), but he did not care to be lumped together with him and he persisted in asking Mr Jefferson how these high-flown ambition were to be realised.

'We are to go down to Versailles tomorrow and draw up the documents with Lafayette and Monsieur Rabaut de St Etienne to speak for the Third Estate. Rabaut has the right ideas but he needs bridling.'

'But we are Americans,' stammered Wm.

'Just so. We are the only people on this earth who have had the good fortune to throw off the tyrant's yoke and learn how to govern ourselves. Who better to advise the best men in France?'

'No, but I mean, our vocation is diplomacy. Surely we ought not to meddle in such ticklish business.'

'My dear Will, liberty is the business of every man whose soul is not dead. If we Americans cannot teach the world how to be free, what are we good for ? I have here a few preliminary notes. I should be glad if you would look over them for me.'

And so William Short, still catching his breath after the whirl of his grand tour, found himself the scrutineer of the first draft of the Declaration of the Rights of Man. At least his sores had healed, although there was a vestigial itching in his groin as he sat in his cubbyhole at the Hôtel de Langeac savouring the fine phrases that TJ could whip up as effortlessly as James Hemings could now spin sugar.

How odd it was, he thought, that a recently poxed Virginian still in his twenties should be charged with editing the text that was to guide the most powerful nation on earth.

Even Mr Jefferson was not without a qualm or two. As Wm handed him back the scribbled draft, the Minister said, tapping the paper with his long bony finger, 'Nobody is to know of this, mind. You are not to breathe a word of it to anyone in France. If anyone enquires as to the author, Lafayette is to have all the glory, which as you know he will not dislike in the least.'

When they set out the next morning, with the precious draft stowed in Wm's wallet, they went by a side road through the forest and Jefferson wore Vendôme's old driver's cloak to avoid attention. Wm had muffled himself up too in the travel-worn heavy coat he had crossed the Alps in. It was a glorious June morning and by the time they came out of the Bois he was dripping with sweat.

'Must we wear these coats the whole way? After all, there can really be no offence in two Americans taking a ride to Versailles to see the sport.'

'No breath of suspicion must attach to us, Will. The less our participation is known or guessed at, the more posterity will have to thank us for.'

In practice, though, as they trotted along the back roads Wm came to be grateful for their modest disguise. Beyond the city limits there were bands of men hanging around at the edge of the forest and in village squares, men with hollow eyes and filthy clothes. One or two of them waved sticks as they rode past. Mr Jefferson could not help acknowledging these salutations as though he were decked out in full ambassadorial fig, but Wm thought there was more menace than camaraderie in their waving. How mean and starved-looking they were up here in the north. Even the squalor of Naples was not so pinched and bitter.

The four of them met at an inconspicuous inn behind the royal stables well away from the tumult of the Salle des Menus Plaisirs. As Lafayette opened the window of the stuffy upstairs room, the noise of the crowd swilling around the palace gates came in but only faintly, like the noise of starlings in a distant wood.

Wm would always remember that quiet conclave in the bare room with the old wooden bed in the corner: Rabaut, the Protestant pastor with his grating voice, always trying to insert a denunciation of the nobles or another assertion of the unique sovereignty of the Third Estate ('the nobles don't even deserve to be citizens, they are cockroaches, vermin, leeches on the nation', at which point TJ broke in to ask if Wm could have some lemonade sent up); Lafayette, ever enthusiastic, contentious too but essentially good-humoured – 'Oh, that is a splendid phrase, I like that, that would sound fine' – and he would repeat the phrase listening to himself sounding fine – and his master who had brought him along on this vaunting business. How at ease Mr Jefferson was here, although his French was a little stiff, and now and then he had to turn to Wm for a word or to have one of Rabaut's intemperate splutters translated. All the awkwardness that disconcerted strangers on social occasions was absent from this intense drafting session. He calmed Rabaut, nudged Lafayette in the right direction and encouraged William to make his own contributions, deferring to him with great courtesy: 'That was how we did it in Virginia, was it not, William?' or, 'I seem to remember that in our Declaration we found it advisable to . . .' – *Our* Declaration, as though Wm had had a full hand in that glorious effusion and not been a sixteen-year-old schoolboy at the time. There were moments when Mr Jefferson's greatness was not to be questioned.

As the afternoon crept in, the distant tumult faded to insignificance. The only sound was the buzzing of some insect in the corner of the room and the scratching of Wm's pen as he took down the latest revisions.

'Well now, gentlemen,' said Lafayette. 'I think we have gone as far as we can. I suggest that we leave it to our American friends to put the finishing touches. Be in no doubt that when France has finally secured her place among the free nations she will always be grateful to both of you.' And he spread out his hands to them in a priestly benison. William found this little speech (delivered in Lafayette's squawky but serviceable English) very moving and he felt tears pricking behind his eyes, but he managed to hold them back. Wm could not help feeling that this sandy-faced, beaky-nosed show-off was a great man too and might yet save France.

Afterwards Wm was hard put to identify exactly what phrases he had himself contributed to the Declaration of the Rights of Man. Was it the bit about liberty consisting in the power of doing whatever does not injure another? Or the decision to call the rights of man 'imprescriptible' rather than TJ's preferred 'inalienable'? But whatever he had or had not added to or subtracted from the document, he had been there at the making of it, the first modern declaration of what it was to be a human being (it was to be a couple of years yet before Mr Jefferson succeeded in tagging on something of the sort to their own constitution).

As they rode back to the Hôtel de Langeac, Wm was seized with an irrepressible exhilaration. If he had not been with Mr Jefferson, he would have burst into song. Even the gangs of hollow-eyed men gathering in the village squares at dusk had no power to damp him off.

Mr Jefferson too was in high spirits. Wm heard him humming a tune as he passed his master's bedroom/study the next morning. He heard too the creaking of TJ's latest copying machine, a marvellous little contraption of wood and brass that could produce two copies together and dispensed with the drudgery that had tortured secretaries since the beginning of time. Then a mere quarter of an hour later Mr Jefferson called him to look over the final draft of the ten-point declaration and if he liked it to send the copies straight away to Rabaut and Lafayette. As Wm left the room, Mr J picked up his violin and (his wrist long since restored to its pristine wiry state) began to play the melody he had been humming.

Why should he not be cheerful? Patsy and Polly (and Sally) had come back from the Abbey in April while Wm was away and one of the upstairs bedrooms had been subdivided into two smaller rooms for them. Sally had to make do with a folding bed in the little vestiaire next to Wm's bedroom, which was itself by no means spacious, for the Hôtel de Langeac had been built as a pleasure house, a place for show, not a family home with all its ramifications. As TJ put it, it was like a Philadelphia melon, all shell and no flesh.

He had hauled his girls back from the Abbey, partly because he loved to have them with him – they were the consolations of his solitary state. He also was beginning to worry that the nuns were not stretching Patsy's sharp wits enough. But above all he had brought them back because in a month or so, just as soon as everything was ready, they were going home. Only for six months, for the official leave that TJ felt was his due, long overdue, in fact. The Jeffersons would return to Monticello, to the capacious bosom of their sprawling clan of cousins: the Wayleses and the Eppses, not to mention Uncle Field Jefferson and his larky quiverful of sons and grandsons. And trusty William, secretary par excellence, would mind the shop, which Wm did not mind so long as he was officially named chargé d'affaires, for he knew by now how much these things mattered in the great world.

So Mr Jefferson was in a fever of anticipation. His natural optimism had been reinforced by the prospect of seeing Monticello again. Each fresh twist of events in Paris only buoyed him up further. When the guards fired on the rioters at Monsieur Réveillon's wallpaper factory and killed a hundred or more, he wrote to Mr Madison that 'this execution has been universally approved'. Anyway, how could a revolution begin with wallpaper? Then, when the price of bread went sky-high after the dreadful harvest and the arctic winter, he reassured the nervous Monsieur Necker that the grain ships from America would remedy the situation in no time. And when the Third Estate took the country into its own hands and swore their famous oath in that shabby old tennis court behind the palace, he reproved the ever-sceptical Gouverneur for saying that the French were sure to overshoot the mark. On the contrary, he assured Mr Secretary Jay back in America that the crisis was over and he would not have anything interesting enough to trouble him with.

William could not resist the usual contagion of his master's enthusiasm. In any case, he was himself brimming with expectation. Not only was he on the verge of becoming a quasi-ambassador, he was also on the verge of acquiring the perquisite of every ambassador, a beautiful and high-born mistress. Of course he was an idealistic young Virginian and not a cynical Yankee like Gouverneur, so he did not express his hopes, even to himself, in quite such coarse terms. But there was no mistaking the feeling behind her last letter. That moment he had dreamed of so long could surely not be far off. And as he wandered idly amid the excited throng at the Palais-Royal and listened with an indulgent smile to the gesticulating orators outside the Café Foy (how ridiculously young they were, a couple of them no more than boys), she was always in his mind.

But she was in the country waiting on her grandmother who had not been well. She did not come up to Paris till June was over and the Estates-General had broken up in riotous enthusiasm because the King, as usual stubborn at first, had given way also as usual and allowed the Third Estate to call itself the National Assembly or whatever other fancy title they wished. For the King was in no state to care very much about anything, and the Queen even less so, because it was only three weeks since the little Dauphin had died. They said that it had turned Marie Antoinette's hair grey, or perhaps it was just easier to see what colour it was now that she let it fall over her shoulders like a citizeness (already they were calling each other by those cumbrous terms). And it was partly because of the dead Dauphin (only seven years old) and the grey hair that they shouted '*vive le roi*' and even, though not many of them, '*vive la reine*'.

But the troops were still massing – Hungarian hussars who spoke weird guttural French, gawky young guards from the Pas de Calais, rough German dragoons camping in huge numbers on the Champ de Mars and up on the Buttes de Montmartre – twenty-five, thirty thousand of them, nobody was sure how many. And standing nervously at street corners there were small detachments of the Paris garrison, with their officers looking anxiously up and down the boulevards, without a clue where the trouble would come from, their minds as bewildered and loyalties as torn as their men's.

He went on foot to meet her. It would have been crazy to risk the carriage with the mob on the lookout for anything to tip over and smash up. Down the first stretch of the Champs-Elysées it might have been any Sunday in July. There were families sitting under the trees. At the Rond-point he saw a man with a torn red shirt singing a patriotic ballad to a jovial little crowd. But as he came down towards the place Louis XV the crowd thickened and its mood was surlier. On the far side of the enormous space, beyond the dust and the commotion that filled most of it, he could see the German cavalry drawn up in lines sitting very still, only the horses now and then tossing their heads.

As he came up to the Tuileries, he was suddenly overrun by another crowd helter-skeltering down across the rue de Rivoli from the place

Vendôme. There were thousands of them shouting their lungs off. And now behind them came the clanging of bells, not from a single belfry but from half a dozen churches or more. And though the crowd were so noisy, the queer thing was that three-quarters of them were wearing black coats and hats, and were waving black banners. With the deafening clamour of the bells the whole procession was like some huge funeral cortège that had gone desperately wrong. Well, Wm thought, perhaps that was what it was, the funeral of the old regime.

Then he saw something that froze his blood. The ringleaders of the mob were carrying human heads stuck on long poles. The dead heads wobbled and juddered above the heads of the living, a terrible earnest of the bloodshed that might be to come.

Horrified yet fascinated, Wm ran to get a closer view of these grisly relics. Closer up, one of the heads bore a frightening resemblance to the flabby features of Monsieur Necker. It was only a couple of days since the King had dismissed him. What a hurtling fall from First Minister of France to a bloodstained head on a pole. And there, surely the other head could not be, yes it was, the dissipated Duke of Orléans. But how strange that these two should be the first victims, for they surely should be the darlings of the mob, not the most urgent targets of its anger.

Then, as the mob tumbled past him through the gates into the Tuileries, he saw that the heads were only waxworks. They must have been looted from Curtius's museum down the street in the Palais-Royal. These greasy busts were borne aloft as emblems of the people's cause, not as sacrifices to it.

He gaped at this curious spectacle, then shrugged his shoulders and navigated his way past the tail of the mob and on down the street. It was not his quarrel after all and he had other business, to him the most pressing business in the world.

It was past five o'clock in the afternoon as he crossed the river by the Pont-Royal. Looking back diagonally from the bridge as he stopped to buy some flowers for her, he could see the dark line of the cavalry at the end of the gardens and the mob surging round it. Even from this distance the noise was hellish and the bells now seemed to be ringing right across Paris. Then he saw the line of cavalry begin to move forward in an irregular wavering motion, like the shuffling of a giant caterpillar. He saw the puffs of smoke first. The noise of the shooting and the cries came to him an instant later. The fragrance of the roses in his arms was clouded by the tang of gunpowder.

It was quiet in the rue de Seine. As he went up the stairs by himself – he had assured the footman he knew the way – the silence seemed stifling. He could not help listening to his own steps, first creaking on the wooden floor, then muffled by the carpet, as though the sound had some ominous meaning to it.

She was sitting in the library in the same place as when they had said goodbye almost a year before. She stood up in that quick way of hers, looked at him for a moment, not long, then threw her arms round his neck, crushing the roses between them so that his nostrils were filled with their fragrance and he could feel the thorns through his light summer coat.

'It is so wonderful to see you, Weellyarm,' she exclaimed, resurrecting the mocking way she had said his name the first time they met.

'And I suppose I shall have to call you Rosalie though you know I don't care for it.'

'I suppose so,' she said, burying her dark head in the roses. 'Oh, these are such terrible times, I do not know what to think any more. My husband is at Versailles. I hope he is all right; the people are so inflamed though I cannot say I blame them, the winter has been so hard.'

'If it is any comfort, I think the scene of the action has shifted. I heard, well, I saw gunfire in the Tuileries as I came here.'

'How awful it all is, how fragile our hopes look now. It is so stupid to make plans when we cannot know what is going to happen from one moment to the next. Sometimes I am confident that our dreams will be realised in the end, though perhaps after terrible things have happened. Then I am simply fearful, and dread the slightest thing and cannot believe that any of us will ever be safe again.'

As she was speaking, the happiness that had flooded over her when he came into the room seemed to evaporate and he saw how tired and anxious she was.

'My grandmother is so frail now. I dare not leave her alone in the country for too long, yet someone must be here to see to this house and my husband is so utterly consumed. I do not think he has slept more than a couple of hours together since the States first met.'

And he saw that she too was consumed by her anxieties for the welfare of those she loved and for the survival of her whole world, and he wondered how much place there would be for him in it.

'Oh, but I have your friendship' (his face was easy enough to read), 'do not think that I do not value that and I am so sorry for the cruel misunderstanding, that was all my fault. I have behaved so childishly and I have no right to expect your forgiveness. But when you wrote back to me from Naples, it was the happiest day of my life.'

Well, this was the moment, there would not come a better one. He moved a step forward – how quiet the room was, even in that briefest instant he was conscious of his footfall – and he put his arms round her and kissed her with everything he had, but she twisted away.

'No, not now, you must see, I cannot, not now.'

'But surely, I thought – no, well, I suppose I had no right to anything.'

'Oh, you do, of course you do. But I cannot.'

He had meant to be gentle, was not so puffed up as to think that her resistance was sure to melt in the delirium of their meeting. He knew after all – how painfully he had won that knowledge – how much in herself she would have to put aside if she was to give way to him, what a cat's cradle of loyalty and affection she would have to disentangle herself from. He had even dared to imagine himself comforting her if she should feel pangs of guilt afterwards. But every inch of that pale distraught little figure told him now that there was to be no afterwards. All the hopes that he had been hugging during that breakneck ride to Paris were callow illusions. He was no nearer his ambition than he had been a year ago; further back, in fact, because he could see now that this was as far as she would ever go. Friendship she had said and friendship was what she meant, no less but certainly no more. He had been a fool from the very first moment he met her and misread her bright and charming way as directed at him especially and so had begun to think that she felt or might come to feel for him something she had never felt and would never feel for anyone else.

And so he lost it, that imperturbable coolness that he schooled himself so hard to maintain. It had never come naturally to him. His mother thought there had once been a touch of carrot about his sandy hair and at the age of ten or eleven he was easily provoked into wild rages. His Skipwith cousins would stir him up, dancing round him chorusing 'Short temper, Short temper'. These days his temper was to be seen in nothing worse than a fretful impatience when he was kept waiting or a servant made an annoying mistake.

But now he raged as he had not raged since he was half his age. It was as if the depth of his frustrations had called up from some forgotten zone of his being the old volcanic force. No accusation was too cruel, no language too vile. She had abused and exploited his feelings, treated him like a plaything, a dribbling lapdog. He should have expected it, of course, he should have known better. Beneath her absurd intellectual pretensions she had all the old stupid arrogance of her class. She talked of friendship, she had no more idea of friendship than a rabbit. As for love, her insipid twitterings were meaningless chaff from an empty heart. How could he have wasted all these years listening to her idle nonsense? She was a futile, spoilt, trivial character, what they called back home a cockchafer (he broke into English for this choice noun), but of course she would not know what such a word meant, even in French, because she was so well-bred, so refined, too damned refined to understand that other people, even people not of her own sort, common people, still had feelings and that their feelings could be hurt, as if she cared. And so on, until he ran out of breath.

She had collapsed sobbing in a heap on the sofa, incapable of uttering a word. He had no more to say and hurried out of the room, if anything boiling even hotter because he could hear himself saying all those shameful things and he was angrier still that she had made him say them.

The anger did not ease off as he strode along the river. He called in at a café, a gloomy deserted place by the bridge, and threw back a couple of brandies.

'I wouldn't cross the river if I were you,' the waiter said. 'There's fifty killed already by the Germans.'

'Frankly, I could not care less,' Wm said, ordering another brandy and gulping it down as he picked up his hat.

After he had crossed the Seine, he tried to skirt the trouble by keeping to the bank, past the scene of Mr Jefferson's mishap and along under the trees towards the next bridge. Even so, the shouting of the crowd came to him on the warm evening breeze, incoherent roars and wailings that rose and fell and rose again. The bells had stopped but there were other noises now, bangs and strange knocking tumbling sounds as though a series of walls were falling. As he came to the bridge he met a straggle of rioters running to cross the river with wild looks on their faces, of fear or exultation or both. Some had clothes ripped or smeared with dirt or blood, a few were carrying the tatters of the black banners now torn away from their poles, one or two still clutching their black hats, battered now and dusty and broken. As he threaded his way through them, he suffered an elbow across his windpipe and kicks and scuffs from the frantic fleeing rabble. A big dark fellow gave him a deliberate hack across his shins and Wm retaliated with a full-blooded kick at his lurching form.

This relieved his feelings a fraction and he pressed on, taking a loop to avoid the mob in the Champs-Elysées until the last turning before the rue de Berri. But in his distracted state he went on too far out to the west and found himself slap up against the great serpentine barrier of the farmers' wall, that monstrous invention of the bloodsuckers.

Here he found the explanation of the strange tumbling noises. For there were dozens of men hacking away at the wall with any tool they could lay their hands on, picks, spades, shovels, sticks, stones. One little old man was even belabouring the masonry with the flat of a rusty sword. As the more effective demolishers dislodged the stones, gangs of women, by now like the men covered in dust and dirt, were piling them up to serve as ammunition. Already there was a huge hole gaping in the enceinte between the Chaillot and the Longchamp gates (he had his bearings now), and little boys were jumping through the hole and sliding down the chute of debris on the far side.

It was a superb spectacle of chaos and Wm's rage responded to it and the honourable secretary to the American ministry picked up a couple of stones and chucked them with delirious abandon at the egregious monument to greed and oppression. The stones bounced back without inflicting any visible damage, but a stringy woman with a mottled face, who was standing, almost naked to the waist, by a wine barrel under the tree cheered him on and offered him a tin cup of harsh red wine, which he swallowed with a courtly bow.

'No more bowing,' she said, 'but I'll forgive you this time. I like your anger.' And she passed him another cupful as a reward.

He rushed on along the wall towards the Etoile gate, followed the whole way by the noise of the hammering as though he were being pursued by a flock of angry woodpeckers. The dust that fell on his clothes only added to his manic mood. It seemed like a kind of baptism.

Finally he reached the Champs-Elysées and cut across the swirling throng. It was growing dark now and the crowd was noisier, rougher, even less predictable. He saw to his relief that there were a couple of guards posted at the gates of the Hôtel de Langeac and through the railings he could see old Vendôme peering out anxiously.

'Thank heavens, monsieur, we had no idea where you had got to. They have already broken through the garden and stolen four of master's best candlesticks. This lot would skewer your guts for a sou.'

Inside it was cool and the noise of the crowd died away.

'Here, drink this, monsieur.' Vendôme had the brandy bottle ready and handed him a bumper ration, not out of a tin cup, of course, but from one of the brandy glasses Mr Jefferson had ordered from Bohemia and was pleased with, though he considered the stems too long. Wm drained the glass and ran up the stairs two at a time, thinking only of a hot bath and fresh clothes. But when he reached his little back bedroom overlooking the rue de Berri he realised how tired he was, lay down on his bed and, without intending it, went straight off into a doze.

He woke with a jump. He had no idea whether it was the middle of the night or just before dawn or even whether he was really awake at all and not still caught up in a violent disordered dream full of cries of pain and people running. Then suddenly the running feet had gone and he seemed to be in the middle of a quite different dream. There was a girl standing by his bed in a long white dress and she was beckoning to him, or perhaps beseeching him. He could not make out her face and her voice was too low for him to understand what she was saying, but she did appear to be appealing to him in some way.

'Sir, sir, it's me, Sally.'

'Who? Oh, Sally. What are you doing out of bed at . . . what time is it?'

'Mr Short, I'm so frightened. Patsy and Polly are asleep and I don't like to wake Mr Jefferson. But there's such a racket and a hollering outside and Mr Vendôme says they are pulling the wall down and they'll come and get us and cut our throats, I'm sure they will.'

Her voice was trembling and he put out his hand to her and he felt her body trembling too under the thin white nightshirt.

'I don't want the wall to come down, it was keeping us safe,' she moaned, and even in his half-drunk stupor William reflected that Sally must be the only person in Paris who actually liked the wall.

'Sally, it's all right, no harm will come to us here.' He put his arm round her and she curled up beside him on the bed as if this were the most natural place in the world to be. The white nightdress was all rucked up now and his hand found the bare curve of her hip. He could feel her heart beating against his ribs, as quick as a trapped bird's. It was she, or so he said to himself later, whose lips went towards his, as though seeking comfort from his mouth. But the first violent movement was his. He pulled the thin white material away from her body and felt down, and all the anger of the day came back with the desire of the night and there was no thought of her, only a cruel impatience as he tore open the dusty flap of his breeches and went at her as hard as brass. When she cried out the first time, he thought it was from surprise but the second time there was no mistaking her pain and he pulled out and she slipped away from under his tense arched body. She fled across the floor out to the little antechamber, rapid and silent like a white moth. He lay there still fuddled with sleep and drink, not too drowsy to feel the first flush of shame but not too ashamed to forget how beautiful she was in the half-light of the curtain chink.

The next morning she had already gone from the little vestiaire. She must be over the other side of the building with Patsy and Polly. Mr Jefferson had given orders that the girls were not to venture out that day, but TJ himself could not wait to see more of the action. All day long he ranged the streets, as far down as the Marais and up to see the troops encamped on the Buttes de Montmartre, clocking up record mileages on the pedometer. Sullen workmen piling stones to throw at the German hussars would look up and see the tall American with his shambling gait coming down the street with his curious watery blue eyes and his notebook. Back at the Hôtel de Langeac William was thankful to be deluged with panic-stricken requests for visas, imperative appeals for help from stranded Americans who just had to be on the next Havre boat, and letters and pamphlets from all the reformers of the Faubourg, the La Rochefoucaulds and the Lafayettes and a dozen hostesses and salonnières, all desperately seeking advice, encouragement, comfort and even cash from 'les Américains' who knew all about this business of revolution if ever anyone did.

All day the press of business distracted him from what had happened or not quite happened the night before. In the brief moment that it flicked through his mind, just as he was tending to the complicated needs of Mrs Van Fleet's nephew who had exhausted his letter of credit, he could almost imagine that it had not happened at all, that the whole thing had been brewed up in his fuddled dreams. When he went to bed that night, as tuckered out as an Alabama mule, he went past the little hooped doorway into the vestiaire without a second glance, after the first glance had told him that the door was shut.

At noon the next day news came that thirty thousand muskets had been looted from the Invalides. All they needed now was the powder and shot, and there was only one place for that. The garrison commander, Besenval, who wasn't quite as clever as he thought he was, had had all the city's powder moved down from the Arsenal to the Bastille. That sounded like a wise precaution, except that it had the effect of concentrating all minds on a single fortress, which was now both the grim embodiment of royal oppression and the biggest magazine in France.

'The girls must stay indoors again, William, and I fear I must ask you to continue as their jailer. I dare say you have enough business to attend to here in any case.'

'And you, sir?'

'I am bidden to dine at Mr de Corny's. He is leading a deputation of the volunteers to the Bastille. He hopes for a truce from the governor, though he doubts whether the crowd will be satisfied with a peaceful resolution of the matter.'

TJ seemed to be reserving all the excitement for himself. But Wm bit his lip and took his instructions, slipping into his master's chair at the bureau plat in the oval salon overlooking the garden, where the papers were all heaped up.

The morning had brought low cloud from the north, and the cloud had settled in bruised and glowering bolsters over the city. It was one of those steamy days that made Paris in July so uncomfortable. William took off his blue swallowtail coat and sat in his canary waistcoat with his shirt cuffs turned back, and tried to immerse himself in the sluggish sea of paper around him. After an hour or so he heard the rattle of gunfire on the far side of the long garden, and he sent Vendôme down to make sure that the looters had not climbed over the wall again. Stray crescendos of shouting came to his ears and then swiftly diminuendoed again. It was a stifling afternoon. He got up to pour himself a glass of water, then he opened the door into the great antechamber hoping for a cooller current of air from the hall below.

There was a scuttling noise like a mouse in the wainscoting and he saw the little hooped door into the vestiaire being closed, but carefully as though the person closing it wished to escape attention. He walked quickly to the door. It was not yet latched and he had only to push it.

She looked at him with big scared eyes, her fingers still clutching the latch. 'Oh, it's so hot, ain't it?'

All she had on was the long pink dress he had seen her wearing around the house. He was very quick and this time she did not cry out. Later he fucked her again but slower. She still had her eyes shut but she was smiling. Then a third time, and then he wished he were dead.

You could argue – and people did – about when exactly the old fortress could be said to have fallen. Was it when the white handkerchief was flown from the battlements, or when they poured in over the drawbridge? Anyway, give or take half an hour, it was at about the same time.

VII

Chargé

Among the sea stores packed in stout boxes that were sent ahead to Havre de Grace for the voyage back to Chesapeake (if Mr Jefferson could find a boat so late in the season that called as far south) were: six pounds of macaroni, eighteen pounds of Parmesan cheese, a pound of sweet almonds, five pounds of dates, ten pounds of raisins, two bottles of vinegar, ten bottles of oil and four canisters of tea. To wash down the victuals during the voyage Mr Jefferson had consigned twenty-four bottles of Meursault, a dozen of Sauterne, and a dozen each of Rochegude and Frontignac. Another selection of fine wines and delicacies filled Hamper No.1 labelled straight for Monticello. Hampers Nos 30 and 31 were destined for the President and the Secretary of State, and contained an even more refined selection of wine, viz. a dozen Montrachet – the best white Burgundy in TJ's view – a dozen non-sparkling champagne (which he hastened to assure Mr Secretary was the kind the French still preferred) plus the Rochegude and the Frontignac. All of them he boasted he had direct from the vignerons who made them and not from the merchants who always adulterated their wines even when they swore they hadn't. For Mr Madison instead of wine there was one of the half-dozen busts of Admiral Paul Jones, which filled crates Nos 33–35 and came freshly carved from Monsieur Houdon's assembly line. Box 24 contained two and a half cubic feet of books for the General-President, Box 28 contained ten cubic feet of ditto for Mr Franklin. Then there were thirteen trunks, cases, boots and portmanteaus stuffed with wearing apparel for the party. And there were the most bulky items, to wit, the phaeton and the chariot.

But that was not the end of it. For Mr Jefferson's luggage was not simply a collection of belongings. It was an orchard. No traveller in history had carried such a horticultural transplantation across so vast an ocean unless it were Sir Joseph Banks on his return from sailing with Captain James Cook. Mr Jefferson carried with him on the *Clermont*, two hundred and thirty tons, Captain Colley commanding (a ship fixed on after a good deal of havering, which had the disadvantage of putting in no nearer Paris than Cowes on the Isle of Wight, but it was late September and the other ships had sailed), the following shrubs and saplings *inter alia*: four melon apricots, an angelic fig, three sorts of rose bay, two cork oaks, buckthorn, pistachia terebinthus (which oozed a curious gum, much chewed by the natives), assorted mimosas, the double-blossomed peach, the globe buddleia, three Italian poplars, various other figs, and even such modest plants of the hedgerow as ivy and sweetbriar, for Mr Jefferson was no discriminator when it came to plants rather than wine.

They stood, all three girls, by the coach steps in the little odd-shaped courtyard of the hotel. Patsy and Polly were wearing the dark-blue cloaks they had worn at the convent. Sally wore the old grey mantle in which Patsy had crossed the Atlantic the other way. All three of them were weeping, or trying not to.

Patsy was the first to rush forward and kiss Wm on the cheek.

Then Polly followed suit. 'You must kiss Sally goodbye too,' she said. 'It isn't fair if you do not, because she's crying too.'

So he went across to Sally and kissed her. His lips brushed against the tears on her warm cheek. It was the first time he had touched her in two months.

She took his hand (they were half hidden from the others by the high coach wheels) and she clutched it fiercely.

'Do not forget me,' she said.

She had put up a fight against going, but of course nobody could think why. Look, they said, James is going back home, and don't you want to see your mama and all your folks, and anyway you came to look after Polly and Patsy and are you not fond of them? Yes, I am, mighty fond, she said mulishly, but I want to stay in Paris.

'I wonder if someone has been stuffing her with notions of getting her freedom if she stays over here,' Mr Jefferson said. 'Alas, I fear it is a poor lookout for a young coloured girl on her own in Paris. Anyway, I have told them both that they can have it when they are twenty-one.'

'Have you, sir? That was good of you,' Wm said, somewhat taken aback. TJ was not a great liberator of his own slaves, despite his principles. Perhaps he was making an exception for the Hemingses because he thought them his late wife's kin.

'Or it may be,' Mr Jefferson said, a rare mirthful gleam stealing into his watering blue eyes, 'that Sally has grown sweet on you, William.'

'I hardly think that likely, sir.'

He had fabricated a mask of frigid indifference. At first, when they passed one another in the narrow passages around the top of the stairs (the hotel's upper reaches were a warren of zigzags because of it being built on a corner wedge site), she would slip him a sly grin that pierced him so sharp he was hard put to maintain the distance he had fixed on. When he was sitting with Mr Jefferson in the big oval study and she brought in the hot chocolate in that fine silver urn that TJ himself had designed, he did not look up from his papers. But these precautions failed to keep her out of his mind: the way her strong brown legs began to move in time with his, the quick sobbing that overtook her and the sweetness of her languor afterwards, which was somehow different because she was still so shy. The thought of her beauty kept swimming through him as he was totting up the figures for the importation of rice through Lorient, which TJ was anxious to have settled before he left, being resolved to demonstrate that it was a better port for the purpose than Havre de Grace. Sally, Sally, he murmured to himself, as though repeating her name would somehow expel her from his thoughts.

He could not, would not, become one of those hard-boiled Virginia squires who always kept the youngest prettiest slave in the house. How dared they prate of liberty and the rights of humanity when they were fucking the most fuckable fifteen-year-old on the plantation and then packing her off down to the sheds when they had had enough of her?

Doing it here in Paris was no better, worse in fact, especially when he was the American nation's unofficial representative on the Société des Amis des Noirs. Could he ever again sit in Madame de Tessé's salon listening to those high-minded dukes gassing on about the dire conditions in Sainte Domingue or Haiti when all he was thinking about was Sally – and how she clenched him . . . why did it make him think of a tulip?

'This figure, for the kingdom of Sardinia, it seems somewhat high.'

'What, sir? I was distracted.'

'The importation of rice from Sardinia, 41,363 quintals, I had not thought they could produce so much.'

'It does seem high,' said Wm, struggling to find his place.

He managed the business, but he knew how cruel it was to her. He saw her lovely oval face with its serene moon-look tighten first into uncertainty and then into the certainty that he had rejected her.

For several days she threw him piteous smiles. Then, as he passed the little hooped door on the way to change his clothes for dinner at Aunt Tessé's, she came out and stood in front of him, four-square. 'Will you not speak to me? What have I done wrong?'

'It is I who have done wrong, Sally.'

'I do not think so, sir, and if I do not—'

'I cannot stop to explain now, I must go, I am late,' he said, turning away hurriedly. But she just stood there as though she were modelling for a monument to sadness.

He knew he had to do more to make matters plain. The next morning he found her leaning over the balustrade that surrounded the skylight from the hall below. For a moment he was seized by the terrible fear that she was about to climb over and throw herself down. But her staring seemed too listless and vacant for any action so violent. He stood beside her and looked down into the hall as though they were a couple of tourists gazing upon some celebrated view.

'Sally, what I did to you was wrong and I am very sorry and it must not happen again.'

'I did it too,' she said, not without a flicker of pride.

'Well,' he said, 'but I should not have initiated it.'

'I don't know about nishying but if we love each other, then it's natural.'

'Oh Sally, I do not think we can talk of love.'

'Why not?'

'For a start, you are so young.'

'Jane Quilt weren't above fifteen when she took up with Mr Baines and they been living together ever since, and my mother—'

'I just do not think—' he said harshly, interrupting, and there he stopped, for what *did* he think that was not calculating and selfish? That he could not become an ambassador if he had a black mistress? That he would be the scorn of liberal Paris if it became known that he had abused a slave?

'Sally, we must agree to end our' (our what? There was no word that covered both her tenderness and his coldness) 'our – we just cannot, you know, it has to stop.'

'But it only just started, sir.'

'Don't call me sir.'

'What else am I to call you then?'

'I fear I have nothing more to say, that must be the end of it,' he said and he walked away.

But every morning as he and Mr Jefferson set off to roam the streets, no matter how early they started, there she was, standing by the little hooped door, silent now, just looking at him with her huge eyes. Sometimes she would try a smile, but it was a smile that had no hope in it, nothing like that brimful loving smile she had once given him, full of all the pleasure in the world.

Together he and his master saw all the sights of those tumultuous months. They watched the citizens, sixty thousand of them in every shape and size, the lucky ones with the muskets they had prised out of the Invalides and the Bastille, the others with pikes, scythes, pruning hooks, sticks, anything they could lay their hands on, following the King's carriage all the way to the hôtel de ville, with Lafayette riding behind on his white horse, at once the King's protector and the people's general, his beaky nose sniffing the summer air, loving every minute. And standing on the steps of the town hall, they saw their friend Bailly the astronomer, now transformed into civic dignitary, stick the red-white-and-blue cockade into the King's hat and prompt the poor stultified monarch with a few appropriate words, which of course he muffed. They saw the crowds scavenging the boulevards and the alleys, battering at the doors of bakeries shut against them because the terrified bakers had no more bread. They saw the Bastille being pulled down stone by stone, the most joyful demolition site in history. They checked the wilder totals given for the casualties of the tumults and reckoned that the corpses were to be tallied in dozens rather than in the rumoured thousands and tens of thousands. And then on top of all that they had to busy themselves with the many preparations for Mr Jefferson's going on leave and Wm's stepping into his shoes.

Yet however late he came to his room, footsore if he had been out, for the streets were still unsafe for carriages, and his head abuzz with bills of lading and letters of credit if he had been all day in the office, there she would be, leaning over the banister as he came up the stairs or sitting at the door of her room, for all the world as if she were sheltering from the midday sun on the veranda at Monticello. At these evening encounters she would bob to him, as though she were a servant he hardly knew. He suspected some mockery in the curtsy, but could see no sign of it in her face. He slept badly and wondered whether she did too. He wondered also whether others in the household had any inkling, but their wing of the hotel was remote from the main part and he never ventured now into the kitchens where she spent much of the day with her brother and the girls.

'You seem distracted, Will.'

'There is much to do before you go, sir.'

'I fear that there is. You will find it delightfully peaceful when we are gone. I am reluctant to leave Paris in such interesting times.'

This was humbug, Wm thought. TJ was itching to go home and had been in a great fret until he had received his official *congé*. His concern with the progress of the revolution in French affairs had visibly ebbed. He turned his mind to other topics: the fusil muskets he had promised Mr Madison, the design for the new candlesticks to replace the stolen ones, Tom Paine's ingenious design for an iron bridge to be erected in pre-cast segments. France had no further need of his counsel. TJ had in fact persuaded himself (and there was no greater master in the art of self-persuasion) that her affairs were now largely under control and no longer demanded his intimate supervision. He wrote to his correspondents in England and Geneva to tell them that 'tranquillity is perfectly established at Paris and pretty generally so thro' the whole kingdom'. He himself had slept as quietly through the whole commotion as ever he had in his life. He had the highest confidence that the National Assembly would use their power justly. Indeed, he would agree to be stoned as a false prophet if all did not end well in this country. This was but the first chapter of the history of European liberty.

And he himself had played his part in it, had he not, a part no less brilliant than he had played in the revolution of his own country. It was he who had drafted the declaration that had grounded the new National Assembly and he who had touched up the second declaration that Lafayette presented only a couple of days before the Bastille was taken. Besides, any fool could see that the language and sentiments of it were as to nine-tenths filched from America's own declaration of independence, and who was the author of that? In his spare moments he had also to say a good deal to Mr Madison on the terms of the new Bill of Rights that was to be tagged on to America's constitution. So that made a round total of four declarations on two continents, each of which schoolchildren would be condemned to learn by heart for all eternity. Time enough to take a holiday.

The girls were flitting around the back of the coach like a little flock of finches, trying to stuff some last articles into a yellow wooden trunk. Then they turned, or Patsy and Polly did, to run and greet their father who came through the grey doors of the hotel and across the yard with that inimitable shambling gait that gave the impression that he had not yet fixed on his final destination. The girls danced alongside him tugging at his long bony hands. Suddenly Wm had a plummeting feeling in his stomach that he would never see any of them again.

'Well, William, as you know, I find farewells painful. Let us comfort ourselves with the thought that we shall all meet again in April.'

'Till April, sir.'

They clasped hands. William wished he had the courage to embrace his master but he feared to encounter a repulse. Instead he looked into Mr Jefferson's watering blue eyes with a long and loving gaze. Perhaps he had never done such a thing before, certainly not with such intensity. Virginia gentlemen did not as a rule stare at one another. At any rate he was startled by what he found. In the depths of those eyes there was a terrible coldness. Their blue was the blue of an iceberg in the Arctic Ocean.

'Come on, Papa, come on.'

Mr Jefferson hoisted his angular frame into the coach and slammed the door in that abrupt way he had with doors. The dull clop of hooves on the gravel, the jingling of the English harness that Lafayette so disapproved of, the slow scrunch of the carriage wheels. Hands waving at the window. Was that a light-brown hand among the others? Then they were lost in the bustle of the rue de Berri, and the courtyard was silent and empty.

As he walked across the yard, Wm felt bereft, but he also had to admit to certain sensations of relief that he knew were not to his credit though he tried to give them decent covering. It was better for Sally that she should be away from him; he could bring her nothing but distress and he hoped that she would not take amiss the lacquered box containing ten louis d'or that he had given Polly to give her, on strict condition that she, Polly, swore not to tell a living soul of it. Even as he comforted his *amour propre* with these thoughts, other thoughts came back to him, thoughts of her long legs and the slow, slow – but he managed to swerve away from all that by concentrating his reflections on Mr Jefferson.

The icy look in those blue eyes suddenly reminded him of another scene, a very recent one, which had greatly disquieted him at the time but had dropped out of his head with all the hubbub of TJ's departure.

Ten days before TJ had left Paris, Monsieur de Condorcet had invited Jefferson and Wm to a farewell dinner at the Mint, where he was now one of the two Inspectors General and enjoyed an apartment of heroic dimensions.

He was in great heart now, the cadaverous Condor. To everyone's amazement he had swooped down and carried off the beautiful and brilliant Sophie de Grouchy who was half his age. Gossips claimed that the Duc de La Rochefoucauld, still besotted with the savant, had tipped him a dowry of five thousand livres a year, because Sophie had none of her own. But in truth Condorcet was, for the first time in his life, rolling. He had five thousand livres a year from the Mint, three thousand as perpetual secretary of the Academy, eleven thousand from his uncle's estate, two thousand from his father's. He could do without the Duke's charity, if ever it had in fact been offered.

So there he was in his finery that September evening, standing to welcome them on the steps of the great Hôtel des Monnaies on the quai Conti with its freshly minted statues and gleaming Ionic columns. And at his side La Belle Grouchette with her big black eyes and her retroussé nose and saucy smile and tumbling hair, not to mention her gently swelling stomach. A Condor chick was due the following spring.

'People say,' Monsieur de Condorcet remarked in his weak, grating voice, after passing on this remarkable news, 'that women should be denied the right to vote because they are liable to become pregnant or because every month they are subject to passing indispositions, but we do not deny men the vote on the grounds that they may suffer from gout or catch cold in the winter.'

'No, indeed, that is very true.'

'And as for the supposed ignorance of the sex, if we were to permit only men of high intelligence to take part in public affairs, our parliaments would be but ill frequented, would they not?'

'Quite so,' said Wm, joining in the dry snigger that Condorcet was wont to emit after a remark he considered especially cutting, a noise not unlike the rustle of dead leaves on a pavement.

'Shall we go in, my dear?' said La Belle Grouchette, gazing up at him with adoration.

Wm followed his host up the great marble stair to the piano nobile. Condorcet's head was still hunched into his neck and he still drew his cloak about him as a great vulture gathers his wings, but there was a spring in his gawky legs and a general sense of potency that Wm had not noticed before.

Despite Condorcet's new magnificence, Wm in his Virginian innocence had still expected his table to be a plain one, as befitted a high-minded philosopher and economist. So he was dazzled to find himself in a huge dining room, a good forty feet long, lit by a thousand candles and filled with a glittering throng all talking at a giddy rate. He recognised only a few faces: Mr Bache, Franklin's grandson; Dr Cabanis the brilliant doctor of psychophysiology who had married Sophie's sister; the playwright Beaumarchais who had written those wicked comedies that had made the court uncomfortable and who was now collaborating with Condorcet on bringing out the complete works of Voltaire. If there was anywhere in Paris that you could call the intellectual centre of the city – well, to be frank, the centre of the world, because where else was there? – then this was it. Wm braced himself for the inexorable brilliance of the conversation and scoured his head for something to say to his neighbour at table, a handsome, slightly plump woman in her thirties, with an unnerving beady look in her eye.

'She is very beautiful, is she not, Madame de Condorcet. I had not seen her before,' he lamely offered, conscious of how far below the required standard he had begun.

'Who? Oh, La Grouchette. She is pretty enough, I grant you, if you like that vapid sort of face, but she has no more brains than a flea, and as for tact . . .'

'Oh, really?'

'When the two of them became engaged, she had the impudence to suggest that if anything should happen to Monsieur Suard – he was not well at the time – we should share Condorcet between us.'

'How very strange.'

'Not as strange as all that,' she said tartly. 'Surely you must know that there was a time when Condorcet was head over heels in love with me. But I could not think of abandoning Suard, that was when I was still in love with him of course. Later on I told Suard I had fallen quite out of love with him. Oh, he said, don't worry, your love will come back. But I love another, I said. Oh, he said, that will pass. The conceit of men! That's him over there, look.' She pointed to an elderly fellow with a long nose and a sly expression who was telling a joke with every sign of enjoying it.

'So that is Monsieur Suard, the editor?'

'The hack, you mean,' his wife said merrily. 'He'll write anything to keep the roof over our heads. He even agreed to edit the *Official Gazette* though Choiseul had given him strict instructions that it was not to be the slightest bit amusing. He was dying of boredom when luckily Choiseul was thrown out.'

'So were you distressed when Monsieur de Condorcet got married?'

'You're a nosy one,' she said with a laugh. 'Yes, I certainly was, wept buckets, in fact. I thought he still loved only me, but the truth is that he prefers them young. Ugly men often do, I don't know why. When he was lodging with us, he even dared to run away with my niece though she was barely eighteen and her mother had just died. We had to move heaven and earth to get her back, but at least she did love him, the silly goose. I am afraid the Grouchette is just in love with his fame.'

'Are you sure? They seem very happy.'

'I think I know a little bit more about the situation than you do.'

'Of course, madame.'

Madame Suard had a sharp tongue but she seemed a genial sort and instructed him to call her Amélie, everyone did and they were not at court now. It was not hard to see how the Condor could have been in love with her, but how could she ever have cared for him?

Though he was some way down the table, Wm could still pick up snatches of that strange voice which, now that he had taken a glass or two, sounded more like a saw sawing wet timber.

'Yes, these are Breton sardines, I would countenance no other. And the pike comes from the Loire or to be exact from a tributary that I do not expect you to have heard of, I shall keep it as my secret, no, not the Cher. There is a mill on this modest stream that for some reason leaks corn into the millpond and fattens up the smaller fish that the pike feed on, giving them, I think you will agree, a remarkable sweetness and removing that muddy quality which may otherwise creep into even the best-made quenelles. And the wine, Mr Jefferson, I am sure you will guess.'

'Oh, from the Loire too, I do not doubt.'

'Ah, what pleasure it is to entertain a true savant,' Condorcet cackled. The Inspector of the Royal Mint was leaning back in his chair now, the candles shining on his beaky nose and giving it a peculiar translucence. 'Yes, it is a Pouilly, the unsmoked kind, always to be preferred with any fish worth eating, the other sort drowns the taste so.'

'How lucky Condorcet is,' grumbled Madame Suard, 'he eats like a pig and drinks like a fish but he never gets fat. Look, see how your master is falling for La Grouchette. You Americans have no taste at all.'

Mr Jefferson, being a minister plenipotentiary, was seated next to his hostess. His face too shone in the candlelight as he bent forward to talk to her, his head a little to one side as was his way when making up to a pretty woman.

'He is probably discussing constitutions, he usually does when he meets a woman for the first time. It's his way of breaking the ice.'

'Oh, then he will surely find his way to her heart. She is quite a bluestocking. She tells me that she intends to help her husband with his speeches in the Assembly, ha.' There was satisfaction as well as bitterness in her laugh at the thought of Condorcet, who was notoriously fussy about his prose, fending off his wife's interpolations.

'Will you tell us, please, Monsieur Condorcet' – it was Franklin's grandson, young Bache, asking in his slow French the sort of question that Americans always asked – 'what does the Assembly intend to do about titles of nobility?'

'It will abolish them of course,' said the Inspector with some asperity, this being a subject he had not himself chosen to introduce into the conversation.

'I can assure you, sir, that this news will give a fair deal of satisfaction to the good folks back home. We'll all be right behind you there.'

'That is most agreeable to hear,' said Condorcet, not sounding agreeable at all.

'So you yourself will, pardon me for asking, you will no longer be the Marquis de Condorcet but plain Mr, sorry, Citizen, that's right isn't it, Citizen Carabas ?'

'Caritat. In fact no.'

'No, sir?'

'We have no intention of forcing persons to abandon the names by which they have become known. So long as there is no question of asserting any seigneurial distinction, one may continue to use any name one chooses on one's seal or the livery of one's servants. To avoid embarrassment or confusion I shall continue to call myself Condorcet, since it is the name under which I have, I fancy, achieved some modest renown as a mathematician and philosopher.'

'Really, is that so? Thank you, sir, that is most illuminating,' said young Mr Bache, his last words dwindling to a whisper as he retired in confusion.

On the other side of the table, three or four chairs beyond Wm, there was a minor commotion as a skinny young man struggled to his feet. He was struggling because old Suard, still with a foxy grin on his face, was trying to hold him down in his seat.

'No, we must do it, I insist,' the skinny young man spluttered. Suard gave up trying to suppress him and sat back in his seat with an amused shrug.

'We must all drink a toast,' the skinny young man shouted. 'Down with tyrants!'

Most of the guests in his region of the table shuffled to their feet and obediently drank, mumbling 'Down with tyrants', some of them barely bothering to raise their glasses as though used to this kind of thing.

William looked up the table to where Mr Jefferson sat. Unlike his neighbours his master was standing stiffly to attention and raising his glass in a high solemn fashion.

The skinny young man – he could not have been more than twenty-two – looked along the table with a hunted glance as though expecting, perhaps inviting, a reprimand. Then, seeing no reproachful looks, he tapped his glass with his fruit knife and shouted in a much louder voice, 'Down with kings!'

Again most of the company, with four or five exceptions, rose to their feet and made a show of draining their glasses, although by this stage quite a few of the glasses were already empty. Mr Jefferson was not among the exceptions. Although his glass too was empty, he raised it to his lips, after clearly enunciating the three words called for.

William stared at his master, astonished and not a little horrified. He knew that Mr Jefferson had no time for kings and in private conversation delighted to dwell upon the deplorable effects they had upon the moral tone of a nation, showing no hesitation in offering the character of His present Majesty as an example. According to TJ, Louis XVI was too small a man for the great role that history had thrust upon him: easily panicked, not over-bright in the head, inconstant, muddled, he could hardly have been a worse choice. The French nation would have done better to have gone out into the street and whistled up the first coachman and made him king instead.

Yet never had Mr Jefferson uttered a syllable of such views in any public forum. And here, after all, they were sitting in the King's Mint at the table of his Inspector. It would surely be all over Paris before breakfast that the American Ambassador had drunk to the downfall of the court to which he was accredited. Was this the way to steady the ship in such stormy times?

But there was TJ, sitting as happy as a frog in a pond, whispering to La Belle Grouchette nothings that seemed to be growing sweeter by the minute, to judge by the way she tossed her tumbled hair and rapped Mr Jefferson's knuckles with her fan.

Then Wm understood. TJ no longer cared, he did not give a damn, these were not his people, they could not vote him in or out, and he was going home to his own people who could and who might be tickled rather than annoyed if they should chance to hear that their man had drunk confusion to all kings. It was from that moment that Wm began to form the conclusion that not only was Mr Jefferson going home, he was not coming back.

And Wm was suddenly angry. This nonchalance was, well, it was too selfish, too preening. He did not fancy himself as a diplomatic personage, he had no training for it, he knew only what he had picked up as he went along. But surely there had to be some restraint.

He felt a tug at his sleeve. It was the Duke. He had come in late to dine and William had seen him, but they had not yet spoken.

'Mr Short, William, I am so glad to see you. That was a stupid b-business, was it not. I would not wish you to think that it meant anything at all. I saw that you did not d-drink.'

'Oh, the toast.'

'Piece of n-nonsense, yes, but Condorcet should not have allowed it.'

'As far as I could see, he had little choice in the matter.'

'No, no, but it should not have happened. Did he drink himself; did you see whether he drank?'

'No,' Wm lied in the hope of calming the Duke. In fact, he had seen Condorcet knock back his glass with a gay cackle.

'And Mr Jefferson? Did he drink? I am sure he did not.'

'I think he was too much preoccupied with Madame Condorcet.' Another lie and just as white a lie too. The Duke began to look less agitated, though his scar seemed still to throb in the candlelight.

'Oh, Sophie, she is such a good person. We have known her since she was a little girl, you know. My m-mother is not best pleased with the match, she does not like her fledglings to spread their wings, though the Condor is rather too old a bird to be called a fledgling.' He laughed in an agitated way, pleased to have made a joke without setting out to make one. 'You must c-come to La Roche, it has been far too long. It will be our d-duty to console you after Mr Jefferson has gone.'

'I fear I shall be—'

'Very busy, yes, of course you will be. All the same, P-Paris is such a hothouse, one cannot think straight with all this going on. Besides, Rosalie would never forgive me if I f-failed to make you promise to come.'

The wound of rejection was still raw, yet the thought of going to La Roche again, the thought of her, was never quite out of his mind all that strange lonely autumn and winter, when nobody knew which way anything would turn out and the highest hopes were twined with the worst fears. Wm devoted himself to his work. He became a monk. Sitting at the desk TJ had left behind in the oval room, he toiled over his dispatches long into the night, resolving that his account of these tumultuous and tangled events should be as clear and dispassionate, yet as vivid and true to life, as any human being could make it. Nobody would be able to say in years to come that the American government was not furnished with the most accurate record. He would be the modern Thucydides.

He hoped against hope that the enslaved people of France – that was how Mr Jefferson thought of them and so did he – would somehow achieve the free government that was their right. He had hugged Johnny Rutledge for joy in the Roman ruins and he did not repent of that hug. When they dragged the King from Versailles to Paris and stuck Lafayette's new red-white-and-blue cockade in the King's hat, Wm's heart was touched and he walked the length of the rue de Rivoli with that great hobbledehoy procession.

He was a witness to history. He had better things to do than run after a spoilt girl who wouldn't know what the real thing was in a million years. If he took up that stammering old fool's open invitation, she would think that she had him back on the string.

But then he thought again and knew there was nobody he would rather see in the world, whatever she thought of him now. Several times he began to write a little note to the Duke, then he tore it up. Once he began a note to her, then he remembered exactly what he had said to her on the day the Bastille fell and he tore that up too.

It was not until the first week in April that he found himself trotting along the old road by the Seine to La Roche-Guyon. Even then he felt that he was being drawn there against his will by some implacable mesmerist. To his embarrassment there was no stammering duke to greet him (he had to stay in Paris to battle with the Assembly over the Budget). There was only Rosalie standing at the gate of the courtyard and jumping up and down like a schoolgirl when she saw him come round the corner out of the village.

He had no idea what to expect from her. Yet from the moment they clasped hands he knew that it was going to be all right. It was as though all the intervening separations and misunderstanding and coolnesses had disappeared like morning dew and they were carrying on something that had started quite naturally from the time they first met.

And this was all the more intoxicating because La Roche-Guyon was in other ways oddly transformed, so that their broken, halting relationship now seemed like the one continuing thread. For one thing, Madame d'Enville was no longer in active charge. She was frailer now, kept to her room for longer periods of the day and went to bed earlier. When she did come down she no longer conducted the orchestra with her old imperious twinkle, but sat in her high-winged chair listening to rather than guiding the talk. And William, paying his first visit for a year or so, could not help noticing that the freedom they had once talked of in such high theoretical terms had now come to roost in little crannies of life at the chateau. He heard the servants gossiping among themselves as they brought in the dishes, something unthinkable before. One sunny morning he watched one of the old gardeners sitting on a bench at the end of the terrace munching his bread and cheese without a care for who might see him. Madame d'Enville's guests too were less circumspect. There was an old Abbé he remembered from earlier visits who now sat out on the attic parapet to shave himself in the delicious spring air.

And Rosalie? The sense of release seemed to touch her too, though it was hard to say how exactly. After all, her grandmother had always loved to see her run about, more in the manner of a granddaughter than a daughter-in-law.

They went haymaking together in the meadows a little upstream where the cliffs began to fall away from the river. Pierre went on ahead with the hay cart while they walked behind, carrying their pitchforks on their shoulders. Manual labour was all the fashion now. Marie Antoinette had never actually milked the cows or the goats at her model farm, but the King was helping to clear the stones off the Champs de

Mars to make a level playing field for the festival to mark the first anniversary of the Revolution. His Most Christian Majesty only turned a sod or two, though, but Rosalie was serious. Wm watched her compress her lips with the effort as she piled up her haycock. She paused only to wipe the dew of sweat off her forehead and to admire Wm's deft turn of the fork. Half an hour later she removed her little lilac broderie waistcoat and her bosom heaved so delightfully that he had to stop and lean on his fork.

'Ah, monsieur, slacking again.' This was Pierre with his melon grin coming past with the cider flagon for the rest of the workers. Wm had never heard him utter a word before. Now here he was, the village wag.

'Are we not to have any of that cider?'

'No, madame, this is reserved for the real workers.'

He passed on, chuckling, while she shook her fist at him in mock indignation.

'I still love you, you know. More than ever,' Wm said after Pierre had gone on down to the corner of the field where the rest of them were sitting in the shade of a chestnut tree.

'You can't, not after the way I have behaved. In any case it is impossible, as you know.'

'I do, that's all there is to be said and you cannot make me unsay it.'

He squinted into the sun at her and could not quite make out her expression. Was she perplexed or upset or what?

'We'd better go back to the house,' she said.

They shouldered their pitchforks and walked off to the gate in the hedge, moving rather quickly as though they were escaping from a bull in the field but trying not to look frightened.

When they were on the other side of the hedge he kissed her and she kissed him back, losing control of her fork so that it clanged against his and they both had to jump out of the way as it fell. He put his fork down too and they embraced, standing between the two forks like a couple performing some traditional country dance.

'This is no good, you know,' she said. 'You cannot mean it.'

'I do and you know I do.'

She bussed him, but this time lightly on the cheek as though congratulating him for some minor achievement, like winning a medal in her cousin Liancourt's agricultural show.

That was the end of it for that day. She seemed rather solemn all through till the evening, not downcast but thoughtful. When he came into the salon as they were lighting the candles, he saw her sitting beside her grandmother at the end of the room and she looked up at him with that same perplexed, solemn look.

The next day she insisted they take the canoes out on the millpond beyond the meadows.

'But the first thing I ever told you was that I know nothing about canoes. I am not a Canadian.'

'And the first time you saw me was when we were making such fools of ourselves in that canoe, Ariane and I. So it is high time we both learnt.'

Pierre drove them upstream with the canoes on the cart, three or four miles from the house. The little blue canoes slid into the water through the straggles of white duckweed. Several young boys were already paddling around in the middle of the pond and splashing each other with their paddles.

William and Rosalie floated sedately around the side of the pond, now and then bending their heads to avoid the overhanging willow branches. The splashing and the cries of the boys out in the middle made their own gliding side by side seem all the more silent and graceful.

'I feel like a swan,' Rosalie said.

'You don't look much like a swan.'

'What do I look like, then?'

'More like a moorhen, a very pretty moorhen.'

'A moorhen is not a pretty bird.'

'These days you would be much better off as a moorhen. Swans who have renounced their titles probably turn into moorhens anyway.'

'No, I shall be Citizeness Swan,' she said and dug in her paddle with a thrust that sent her shooting past him out into the middle of the pond. He followed, watching the neat flub-flub of her paddle. Just then the cries of the boys suddenly changed into a shrill cry for assistance. Wm turned and saw a red canoe floating towards the weir with the boy in it desperately beating the water with his hands, having lost his paddle. Wm rowed as close to the boy as he dared, then dived into the water, his clothes billowing as he sank into the duckweed. He could see the red canoe only a few yards from him, and swimming frantically managed to grab hold of its rim and tow it back out of the current. The other boys seized the red canoe and pulled it away toward the shore, keeping hold of the boy who was shivering with fright. But as Wm started to swim after them the weight of his clothes began to drag at him and he found himself being pulled back into the faster current. In an instant he was plummeting head down in eight or nine feet of water, paralysed by cramp or fear. For a few seconds he felt utterly lost, almost reconciled to drowning, then his will came back to him and he began to kick his way out of the millrace and struggled into slower water again and so laboriously to shore, where he lay face down exhausted in the chalky mud.

With the help of one of the boys Rosalie turned him over to regard him daubed like a clayey Lazarus but breathing and spouting like a whale. She began to scrape the mud and weed off him as best she could. He felt her little hands scrabbling all over his body, much like Gulliver being swarmed over by the Lilliputians. When he finally staggered to his feet, water sluiced off him in torrents. As he squeezed out his shirt-tails, he was not too sodden to notice that this was the first time she had touched him so intimately.

At dinner in fresh clothes, fortified by great draughts of Malmsey wine, he was the hero of the hour and she was licensed to look at him with open admiration because everyone else was looking at him too, including the old Abbé who had formerly been surly towards him, as old guests often are to new guests who they fear may supplant them. After supper, at Madame d'Enville's order, he played chess with the old Abbé and beat him inside a dozen moves.

The next day he had to go back to Paris and she cried as he left but tried to hide it, because she could hear Madame d'Enville hobbling up behind her. Her grandmother found Paris a frightening city now and she expected Rosalie to stay at La Roche. So he wrote to her there, renewing his love in the clearest and tenderest words he could think of. She wrote back the day she received his letter:

I received your letter as soon as I awoke. It was my first task of the morning and I shall spend part of the evening answering it, so you see that my whole day is devoted to you. I have had such pleasure in knowing that you are thinking of me and you know how much I love to have the proof that you are, but how can I possibly reply to all the nice flattering things you say about me? I can think of a thousand reasons to prevent my heart responding to yours, and you surely cannot blame me for seeking to prevent feelings arising in me which will be dangerous for both of us. Use your reason, which exists to have some control over us, to consider how much you risk making yourself unhappy in giving yourself over to your attachment if it really is a deep one. Think what your fate must be and how strongly the natural order of things must stop you from forming an attachment in this country without compromising your happiness. Besides, I care too much about what might happen to you to ignore the clouds. If your own interest by itself is not enough to make you pay attention to what I am saying, then think a little about my situation, and about what we would both be exposing ourselves to if I let myself be carried away by feelings that would have to be destroyed and broken at the very moment when it would be most painful. You know the way I think and how the ordinary tenor of my life has been removed from any constraint or falseness. So you must believe that I could only obtain any tranquillity by never deviating from the duties that are prescribed for me. I know that this language is very different from yours. All the same, I think I owe it to you to speak like this, because of the concern for you that you have inspired in me. Forgive me if this letter causes you pain.

It caused him no pain at all. On the contrary, it was the first letter he had had from her that betrayed how strongly she felt about him. Behind those graceful formal sentences (like Racine's alexandrines, he thought) he could sense the flutterings of her heart.

Even so, he had not expected to hear so soon that she was coming up to Paris after all. Only the thought of seeing him, she wrote, could bring her to enter those grim walls and suffer the stifling heat of the streets and the sullen crowds swirling round the Tuileries. She did not tell him the exact day of her coming (perhaps she did not know it herself yet) and he was out at the Assembly when another note was delivered to the Hôtel de Langeac: why had he not come to see her? How could she survive another day of this wretched stay in Paris without seeing him? It was a brief scrawl, nothing like Racine at all, this one.

In the event, she came to him (for once Monsieur de La Rochefoucauld was at home), to the big oval room at the Hôtel de Langeac and sat in the upright chair opposite him as though she were applying for a passport. He said again how much he loved her and there was no purpose in him not saying so. He was not sure afterwards which of them it was who rose first. But somehow there they were sitting side by side on the little chaise longue which Mr Jefferson had bought from Reisener's shop and nearly taken back to Monticello with him.

'No,' she said at the same time as she lay down with him, 'no, we cannot.'

But she let him stroke her there, and then she reached out to him and found the buttons of his breeches and rubbed him with a fierceness that finished him off in less time than he thought possible. Her white skirts thrown up and his fingers inside her and her fingers curled round him and milking him dry – with all that was to come he would never forget a moment of it.

'There,' she said, holding up her hand with the little creamy cupful she had gathered, '*vous êtes tellement chargé, monsieur le chargé.*' And she laughed at her joke before he understood it. *Chargé* – what was that? Oh, loaded, yes, the Rutter had said something when he couldn't perform – in Naples was it? – about his musket not being loaded and the girl had been angry.

They lay silent side by side, as silent as figures on a tomb.

'Are you . . . were you fearful of having a child?' he asked.

'No, no,' she said. 'There is nothing I want more. But it has not happened. Didn't you understand why I wished so much to go to Dr Mesmer's?'

'No, I did not.'

'I pretended it was for a joke, but I hoped it might work somehow, perhaps through the soul rather than the body. It was my last hope.'

'What did he say when he spoke to you privately?'

'He said there was no reason why I should not become pregnant, but it would need a longer course of treatment.'

'Hm.'

'You are sceptical. Perhaps you are right, but I wanted so much to believe him.'

'And your husband, does he long for a child too?'

'Of course, it is only natural.'

'But that is why you would not, just now, because of him?'

'Yes.'

The next day he went to the rue de Seine and they sat in the garden behind the stables in the shade of the trees that kept out the noise of the street. It was four in the afternoon. The servants were asleep in their attics. The Duke was somewhere between the National Assembly and the Paris Directory of which he was President. He was in meetings all day, she said, he came home hoarse and white in the face.

There was a small round pool to one side of the trees, not more than six feet across. He got up from the stone bench with its feet in the shape of some classical beast and went over to the pool and splashed his face with water. Then he came back to her and gently stroked her warm cheek with his wet hand. 'Wait there,' he said.

He went round the pool to the thickest of the lime trees, took out his penknife and began to carve their initials on the tree. He was only halfway through the R when she got up to see what he was doing. No, he said, wait there till I have finished. When he had rounded off the W with a flourish on the final stroke, he beckoned her over and she laughed when she saw.

'It's what we do in Virginia, lovers do, I mean,' he said, suddenly embarrassed.

'Oh, they do it here too in the villages, it is so sweet.'

She put her lips to the W and kissed it. 'Perhaps I shall turn into a tree, like Daphne.'

'That would be sad. I would not want to spend my life embracing a tree trunk.'

'Oh, I am sure you will carve many more initials. I expect there are already forests in America with the whole alphabet on them.'

'Not one, I promise you.'

'Come.'

She seized his hand and went on ahead of him through the little door that led up the back staircase to her private apartments. He had not been that way before. At the top of the stairs there was a side door into a small cabinet, a sewing room for the staff by the look of it – there were coats in the La Rochefoucauld livery heaped up on an ironing table and a pile of crumpled linen in a big wicker basket. She took him to the shabby *toile-de-jouy* sofa by the fireplace and pulled him down towards her. Yes, now, she said. He saw her white thighs for an instant and the dark hair – or perhaps he did not see all that, or not then, for she was so quick in everything and in this too. She told him what to do, he had not expected that. He had not imagined how much she would desire him. Do I please you, she said, do you like my body, except she did not say body. He certainly had not expected that. He told her he loved every inch of her.

'You are shy, I think, after all, William.'

He had not thought of himself as shy and did not know why she should choose this moment to say so, but he did not care. They lay in a moony languor, all tangled up together, his breeches caught somewhere in her shift, with the afternoon sun slinging dusty beams across them and the noise of the small birds outside and the acrid smell of the starch the housekeeper used for the shirts, and mixed in with it the fragrance of rotten lime blossom from the trees outside or perhaps it was from their own bodies – Apollo and Daphne were probably just as confused. Perhaps Daphne had asked whether Apollo liked her cunt, or . . . but by then he was dozing off and she had to wake him because the servants might be coming down about now.

La Roche-Guyon, seven o'clock in the evening

It is just at the moment when I would probably be seeing you if I were in Paris that I want to write to you and fill the same moments with the same subject. I am very sad to have left you and my first feeling when I woke up this morning before leaving was very painful when I thought that in half an hour's time I was going to go away from you. The only pleasure my journey offered me was to leave me free to think of you the whole time without being interrupted. Madame de Postulard was alternately reading or sleeping and left me in peace to my reflections, which went to and fro, for sometimes I let myself jog along in the sweetness of loving and being loved (for the movements of the carriage reminded me of it) and other times I foresaw a tragic future caused by the very same sentiment. I'm not telling you this to torture you but just to communicate all my thoughts. It is too pleasurable to open my soul to you not to hope that you will not despise the way my mind was going. I hope that you have thought of me a little since my departure and that I will soon have news of you. My God, should I be rejoicing or lamenting that I ever met you? In the bottom of my heart I cannot regret it. I have had so much happiness and it grows whenever I think that you feel the same.

The next day he went to the town hall, where he reassured Mayor Bailly about the American grain shipments and Bailly reassured him that the disturbances in the Tuileries were under control at last. Going home he fell in with Gouverneur Morris stumping along towards the Louvre.

'Ah, Short, I am just about to call on Madame de Flahaut. Are you on the same mission? I fancy I have seen you sniffing around her skirts before.'

'Certainly not, I hardly know her.'

'I am glad to hear it. The list of her admirers is quite long enough already. We have not sacrificed to the Cyprian Queen for a full week and I fear she may make other arrangements if I do not attend to my duty.'

'Ah, you . . . ?'

'We fuck like donkeys,' Mr Morris said. 'It is extraordinary to think what a bother I had to persuade her to come up to the scratch in the first place. She told me that she was married in all but name to Monsieur de Talleyrand and I believed her. But it seems the good bishop cannot celebrate Mass at her altar often enough to satisfy her.'

'I always knew no woman could resist you in the end,' said Wm.

'My dear William, you are too kind. But I fear that I cannot ascribe my little successes in the Paphian mode to my personal qualities. It is the temper of the times. Love is in the air. We have much to thank the Revolution for, you know. The moment the Bastille surrendered, so did every woman in Paris. Take me and La Belle Adèle: 12 July we discuss art and philosophy; 13 July we swoon over something by Monsieur Rousseau; 14 July we discuss Monsieur de Lafayette's declaration of human rights; 15 July, boom, boom. She'd have gone on all night if I'd been capable, I promise you. Since then we've done the needful everywhere you can think of, in my carriage, in her apartment while her husband was dressing across the corridor. We even did it in the waiting room at the convent when we went to pay a call on her old governess.'

The big New Yorker's face was gleaming with carnal recollection. His fleshy lips sucked and pursed as though at that very moment engaged on some amorous exercise. 'Ah, what bliss it is to be an American in Paris just now,' he said.

VIII

Soot and Eggs

At first he thought the clanking must come from the milk churns that woke him in the mornings. The carts trundled in from the dairies just before dawn and the churns chinked against each other as they went over the cobbles. But it was broad daylight now, ten o'clock, no, nearer eleven, much too late for milk. He got up to see what it was. The windows in his room were over the gloomy little garden, so he had to go to the landing and squint through the round window that looked out onto the street.

He saw below him a little procession of handcarts, the sort tradesmen employed to shift their wares about without the bother of harnessing up. It was the cans and buckets stowed in these that were clanking, less like churns, he thought now, more like cowbells when the cows were moving across a meadow. Every now and then the procession would stop and one of their number – who looked like a respectable bourgeois – would unload a long brush and dip it in one of the buckets, then go over to an inn sign or shopkeeper's board or street sign and smear it with whatever was in the bucket, some sticky black stuff by the look of it.

The King had fled in the night and Wm was writing to tell Mr Jefferson, but even in the midst of such great events he could not tear his eyes from the procession. It moved along the street with a methodical dignity as though it were a time-honoured ritual. The letter to TJ could wait until they had reliable knowledge of where the King had gone. Wm went out into the sunny June morning and at once he understood. The sign outside the saddler's where Vendôme took the harness to be repaired had said Sellerie du Roy in flowery script. Now it just said Sellerie. The Epicerie Louis XVI had been smeared into anonymity, the sooty muck still dripping from the board, the Boulangerie de la Reine was blacked out too, ditto the little wooden street sign for the rue du Dauphin. Down the side street two youths were trying to bring down a wine merchant's sign which had the King's ample profile cut out in painted gold. They were slamming at the shivering monarch with long wooden poles. Even this desecration was performed with some formality, as though they were beating the bounds according to ancient precedent.

If the King had decided to forget Paris, well then, Paris would lose no time in forgetting the King. Wm wondered how this extraordinary wiping out had come to pass. Nobody could have foreknown that at midnight the King would slip out of his palace dressed as the valet Durand, with the Queen disguised as the governess. It had happened by some spontaneous energy, some mysterious expression of the general will – perhaps their beloved Rousseau would have been able to explain it.

'Soot and axle grease. Some of us is using oil, but I say the grease sticks better.'

'What?'

'I saw you was looking at my bucket. I started mixing her the minute I heard. The fat bastard, why couldn't he see it out like the rest of us? But I'm not surprised, I always knew he'd hop the coop. He'll be in Austria by now.'

The man with the brush was a quiet-looking fellow, in his early forties, with watery eyes. He spoke without venom, if anything in a tone of disappointment. Like the rest of them he seemed to be engaged not in an impassioned act of defilement but rather in the business of clearing something up.

In the side street the two youths had finally managed to detach the monarch's profile from its rusty hinges and the sign fell to the pavement with a twanging clatter.

'Take it inside to old Poix, lads,' the man with the brush called out. 'It's his property, after all, though I don't know what use it can be to him now.'

But the youths paid him no attention and started battering at the golden head with their poles, banging in time to a raucous chant which

Wm soon recognised as *Ca Ira.* The noise sawed through his head (he had a headache anyway from the second bottle of Mr Jefferson's wine he had punished at his solitary dinner the night before) and suddenly the scene took on a brutish, menacing aspect.

Ca ira, ça ira, les aristocrates à la lanterne,
Ca ira, ça ira, les aristocrates on les pendra.

Something had happened, something decisive, and everyone knew it. The King knew it, as they brought him back, and so did the silent, sullen crowds who refused to take off their hats to him. The grim politeness was almost the worst – those posters all along the route: 'Anyone who applauds the king will be beaten, anyone who insults him will be hanged.' It was like the instructions to visitors at animal menageries. That was, after all, just what the King was now, a caged beast, and in future the cage bars would need to be stronger.

The politicians too knew that something had changed, and changed for good, but none of them wanted to be the first to explain what it was. In particular, none of them wanted to be the first to use the word beginning with 'R'. By his flight the King had thrown his crown into the gutter and fresh arrangements would have to be made, but for the moment a studied vagueness as to what those arrangements might be was the way to play the game. What, after all, was a Republic, mused Robespierre, gnawing at his fingernails with that smirk stuck on his face? Did not France already enjoy the best of both worlds under its new constitution, being in effect a Republic with a monarch?

But there was one public figure who lacked these arts of equivocation and blurring, a man who once he had an idea in his head, then out it popped like a cork out of a bottle: Condorcet. He might be a giant in geometry, an adornment to the differential calculus, but he was so poor a politician that he had ignominiously failed to get elected to the Constituent Assembly, when every third-rate lawyer and provincial hack had breezed in.

In these tremulous summer days when apprehension hangs so heavy in the air that you can feel it brush your cheek, what does Condorcet do? He gives a public lecture on why France needs a republic. There is the announcement bold as brass in *La Bouche de Fer*: 'Next Friday, at the Cercle Social of the Amis de la Vérité, Condorcet will talk about the Republic.'

So on 8 July two thousand Friends of Truth – doctors, duchesses, journalists, all-purpose rabble-rousers, pickpockets, the usual Palais-Royal crowd – pile into the new subterranean circus at the Duke of Orléans's palace of pleasure. That irrepressible showman has dug out this huge underground cavern beneath the lime avenues as a venue for equestrian displays. On a hot July evening the atmosphere is thick with the smell of horse. The venue is also inordinately long, as a classical circus has to be if the horses are to have room to prance and caracole without running full tilt into the pillared galleries that surround the arena.

So it may be that only the front few rows hear every word of Condorcet's broaching of the great forbidden subject. His frail, rasping voice never carries far. He does not speak for long, not more than half an hour and his delivery is always slow. What he has to say is very simple. Even those who only hear half of it and are not asphyxiated by the ordure probably get the drift.

It is time, he says, to abandon this impious superstition, which transforms an ordinary mortal into a sort of god. If a republic in France should fail, there is no danger that a new Caesar would arise from its ruins, because a free France will never enslave other nations or permit itself to be enslaved. We should not be teaching the Dauphin how to be a good king, we should be teaching him how to want not to be a king at all.

They hear Condorcet in complete silence to the end, then he is drowned in applause. The Assembly instantly asks for a text and sends him a vote of thanks before they have even read it. The last of the *Encyclopaedia* men has spoken, the friend of Voltaire has pronounced, the Condor has left his perch and soared.

La Belle Grouchette's eyes are wet with tears. Has she not helped her husband translate Tom Paine's *Rights of Man*? What does she care, what does either of them care if he has kissed farewell to the Royal Mint and those five thousand livres per annum, to say nothing of his chances of being appointed tutor to the Dauphin, for which he is the hot favourite? What do they care if the Lafayettes and the La

Rochefoucaulds never speak to them again? They are yesterday's men. Friendship is too frail a plant to survive the tramp of history. Omelettes cannot be made without – but we need not labour the point.

A few days later a modest crowd of patriots gathered on the Champ de Mars to sign a petition calling for the King to be put on trial. It was a steamy Sunday morning and a queue of patriotic men and women had formed up to the Altar of the Patrie. Alas, two low fellows had spotted an opening beneath the dazzling cloths that draped the Altar. If they squeezed in under, they might have a brilliant viewpoint for looking up patriotic skirts. In their excitement, though, they failed to calculate that their feet were sticking out and were instantly spotted by the sentries. The voyeurs were dragged out before they had glimpsed so much as a frilly garter and were slaughtered on the spot, not for their intended offence but on suspicion of planting mines to massacre the patriots. Even while their bleeding corpses still lay on the ground lately levelled by the spadework of His Most Christian Majesty, martial law was declared and Lafayette, escorted by the city council with Bailly the astronomer at their head, called out the National Guard. These were great days for the cause of the natural sciences. Who better to teach the nation the virtues of a republic than a mathematician? Who more suited to quell a riot than France's leading stargazer?

By now the steamy clouds had cleared, there were blue skies along the Seine and the temperature had risen to twenty-one degrees, as the new revolutionary system computed it. So several thousand Sunday strollers had gathered, more to take the air than to sign up to the Republic, among them Sophie de Condorcet and the Condor chick, the enchanting Eliza, now aged fourteen months and taking, thank heavens, after her mother in looks.

The troops were greeted with jeers. Stones were thrown. A shot was fired, nobody knew by whom or at whom, and a dragoon was hit in the thigh, only a flesh wound. Or the crowd disobeyed Lafayette's orders, or something else happened or did not happen. Anyway, the Guard opened fire and in a few minutes dozens of people lay dead on this martial field, which had only the year before been rededicated to peace. Or perhaps hundreds lay dead, but dozens were enough to be going on with. Enough, anyway, for Condorcet to speak ever after with scorn and loathing of Lafayette who had so nearly murdered his wife and daughter on their Sunday afternoon stroll.

There was a note waiting for him from Rosalie: '*Come tomorrow. M. de La R. will be in Paris for seven or eight days. My grandmother expects you.*'

He had thought that it would be just the three of them. La Roche-Guyon half asleep under its white cliff. The cuckoos in the woods above and the nightjars churring at dusk. The late butterflies fluttering up from the English garden and losing themselves in the cool arches of the loggia. Madame d'Enville sitting over the silver chocolate pot, smiling at them in that sly bright way of hers. And Rosalie.

But when he came past the musty old guardroom and climbed the winding stair to the salon, he was taken aback to hear male voices and surely, no, it could not be but yes it was, one voice in particular. There he was, Citizen Condorcet, no longer the marquis but otherwise not much changed, drawing his coat-tails round him and darting his beaky head out of his hunched shoulders as his harsh voice keened on remorselessly: 'My dear lady, there can be no doubt of it, this is the logical moment. Even the most uninstructed in political science must see that if France does not adopt the republican form of government by the end of the year she is lost. I am on my way to my local assembly at Mantes to explain the matter to them in person, and I could not pass this way without calling in to present myself to my earliest friend and patronne.'

'And the King? What is to become of the King?'

If the Condor was much the same as the first time Wm had heard him discourse on oysters and proportional representation – how long was it now? Five or six years – Madame d'Enville was utterly different. Her amused relaxed mien had gone. She sat hunched in her great chair, her frail hands clutching its tasselled arms, with an expression of dread and distaste on her face, quite unlike any time he had seen her before.

'Oh, we shall have to make special arrangements,' Condorcet said airily. 'In the next Assembly, in which I hope to play a modest part, there will be some form of examination, a judicial process of sorts, the details remain to be agreed.'

'A trial, you mean? You intend to try the King?' Madame d'Enville enquired, trembling with fury.

'Well, that will be for the new members to decide. As you know, the new Assembly is to contain none who were members of the old one. The fresh blood will take a much more intelligent view of the matter.'

'Blood, you talk of blood,' muttered the old Duchess, wilfully misunderstanding.

'I fancy,' continued Condorcet, paying no attention, 'that the Constituent Assembly was too respectful of the mumbo-jumbo that surrounds royalty. The new legislators will be able to see the futility and wickedness of maintaining at the public expense these families whose heredity is no guarantee of either talent or virtue. They may even find some merit in the suggestion put forward by a young mechanic in the latest number of *The Republican*, that we should replace the flesh-and-blood royal family by a collection of automata, built on the model of Kempel's automatic chess player. Such a mechanical monarch would be able to carry out all the functions that royalty at present exercises, it would pose no danger to liberty, it would cost much less and, if carefully repaired, I may add, it could last for ever.'

Since the 'young mechanic' was in fact Condorcet under a nom de plume, it was not surprising that he paused for a chuckle at the waggish brilliance of the notion.

A hiss of venomous intensity came from the neighbourhood of Madame d'Enville's chair. Swivelling his gaze in that direction, Wm was taken aback to see the Duke standing by his mother with a look of unbounded loathing on his pale face. His long bony hand rested on her frail freckled wrist, to comfort her or to restrain her, Wm could not tell which.

'If we seize this moment to plant the republic in good parliamentary soil, then it will grow straight and strong, if not—'

'B-by the way, C-Condorcet,' the Duke broke in, 'my g-gardener has a new method of planting espaliers, for the p-pear trees in particular. I must show them to you. Monsieur l'Abbé, perhaps you too would find it of interest.'

And taking the tubby little Abbé by the arm – Morellet or Chalut was it, Wm could not remember though he had certainly seen him before – he guided him so that the two of them encircled Condorcet and propelled him towards the door as neatly as a press gang picking up an unwilling tar. Even after they were out of the salon and halfway down the stairs, Wm could still hear the two voices in counterpoint rather than harmony, the Duke stammering about pruning techniques while Condorcet continued to descant upon the iniquities of hereditary government.

'I could not turn him out,' the old Duchess said miserably after the babble had died down. 'He has been coming here for twenty years, since he was a gawky young man and could barely open his mouth in company. I used to think of him as a second son and he, well, he has said many times that this is his second home, his only home come to that, at least it was until that silly girl turned his head. I blame her for a lot of this nonsense. I don't mean that these are her ideas, she is not intelligent enough for that, but she eggs him on so. A bride should sometimes be a bridle on her husband's tongue, do you not think so, Monsieur Short? Oh, I do wish he had not come. Rosalie will not stay in the same room with him any more. You must go and find her and tell her that the coast is clear. You know the way.'

He took his leave of her and hurried down the back stairs that led to the old part of the castle and the little corner room where they liked to watch the sun come over the chalk cliff and splash its morning light over the bend in the river.

'Oh, I am so happy, really happy to see you. I thought I would die when the door opened and I thought it was you and that horrid monster came in. How can he say such things at such a time? I know the King is a weak man and he listened too much to his brothers and would never listen to my cousin Liancourt who was the only one who knew what was happening. But even the King's advisers would be better than Condorcet who thinks that politics is just like a quadratic equation and who is mostly interested in having the glory of solving it.'

'Monsieur de La R. has taken him down to the orchard to show him how to graft pears.'

'I am sorry I said that my husband would not be here but the old Assembly finished early and he rushed down here because he is as worried as I am about Maman. Oh, I have had my fill of politics, I only wish—' then she stopped and looked at him and said, 'Well, you know what I wish.'

'Where . . .'

'If they have gone down, then we must go up.'

She took his hand and led him out of the little coffee room down the dank passage that passed by the dusty chapel to where the staircase in the cliff began.

He was a little giddy before they started up, giddy with delight and desire, and they had not climbed beyond the first two or three turns before he panted 'mercy, mercy' and she stopped by the open bay window, and turned to him laughing and not the least out of breath herself. He took her in his arms and pressed her against the chalk wall. As he pulled up her skirts, he could see behind her the sun shining on the river far below. They did it as quickly and lightly as a couple of birds on a branch, and the little cry she gave at the finish was like the cheep of a wren in the hedge. And when he put his head down to her she ruffled his hair as birds do with each other's feathers.

'Oh yes, yes. I am out of breath too now,' she murmured, 'but it was not a fair way to make me, you know.'

'It was the fairest way I could think of,' he said.

There was a narrow stone ledge below the window. They sat there side by side and let the cool breeze dry the sweat off them. She brushed his shoulders with her hand to wipe off the chalk dust and he did the same to her.

'We are like ghosts.'

'Do ghosts make love?'

'No, that is why they come back to haunt us, out of jealousy.'

They dragged themselves up the last few turns in the stair and came out blinking into the air at the top with only the blue sky above them.

'I must carve your name here too. I must carve it everywhere we have loved.'

'Oh, we must not leave such a trail. I am already worried about the one in the rue de Seine. I could blame it on the servants, but none of their names begins with W, though it looks quite like an N, I suppose, and there is a boy called Nicolas who works in the stables, but I would not wish to get him into trouble.'

She looked like a schoolgirl whose jape has gone wrong and Wm was so enchanted that he could hardly speak.

There was a pond in the hazelwood by the ruins of the old fortress, not much bigger than the pool in Paris where he had carved their initials. They splashed water over their faces and took off their shoes and stockings and paddled their bare legs. Then they lay in the sun to dry.

'It's too hot here. Let's go into the shade.'

They lay down in the shade of the bushes and he turned to her and she said yes, or perhaps she did not say it but only smiled assent to the question he had not asked and he slipped inside her and this time they were not at all like birds skittering on a branch but were long and slow at it. She said afterwards that she felt there was nothing else in the world but the two of them and he said he felt so too.

Slowly they came back down the chalk staircase, turning and turning in the sleepy afternoon as though they were performing some semi-aerial dance. When they halted at the embrasures to look out over the vast hazy landscape, they might have been planing across it in one of Montgolfier's balloons, their legs beneath so giddy with fucking and their heads empty of everything but pleasure.

As they came out of the long passage into main gallery, they almost collided with two, no, three servants staggering under some heavy load that Wm could not immediately identify.

'What's that you're carrying?' Rosalie asked rather sharply, startled by the near-collision.

'It's the marble, madame. You know, the big one from the table in the salon in Paris. Madame had us bring it down here, so we can put it up in the attics, didn't say why. It's the devil of a weight, madame, that I can tell you.'

In the half-light of the corridor the Condor's features looked sulky and full of menace. Monsieur Houdon had never meant his bust to be seen in such a light.

Even now their meetings were snatched and shadowed by impending departures: his to Antwerp, Brussels, Amsterdam, anywhere there were bankers with deep enough pockets to help refloat the struggling USA; hers to Paris with the Duke, the pale anxious Duke (was it Wm's fancy or was he paler still now that he had another anxiety close to home, or was he as trusting as ever?), then back to La Roche-Guyon to see to her grandmother/mother-in-law, leaving William in a delirious fret to wait for letters from Mr Jefferson, which never came, and from her, which did:

No, I shall never be able to express the delicious tenderness which your letter awoke in me. How you have found the road to my heart! I cannot and must not hold back the deepest of my feelings for you and I willingly subscribe to your demand never to hide from you anything that is passing through my heart where the image and memory of you are present every moment of the day, softening the darkness which melancholy reflections often bring to it. I cannot describe the pleasure I find in writing to you, in telling you everything I feel and think.

Monsieur de La R. has spent twenty-four hours here and has just gone. The post will be following close behind him. The purpose of his visit was to talk to my grandmother to persuade her to write a letter breaking off with Monsieur de Condorcet. This unhappy letter has finally been written and is ready to be sent. The effort has cost her a great deal and she is really suffering from it. He is to come here no more.

I will address this letter to Amsterdam where you will be when it arrives. Perhaps when I am in Paris I will not be able to write to you so often, because I won't have so many ways of getting letters to the post. But I will write to you at least once a week and you must not write to me more often, because I have to receive your letters in front of everybody and they could make remarks which would embarrass me. Please be careful about the address and put 'Madame' in big letters, so that the footman doesn't make a mistake and give it to my husband. You cannot imagine how much these little precautions cost me and how little they suit my character and my feelings for you, which I would like to tell everyone about and enjoy openly.

When you go to Brussels, you will surely see my relations and you will be able to tell them all sorts of things about us, which can hardly be put in letters. I would especially like you to talk to my brother Charles, because his absence gives me much pain, it is our longest separation since we were born. You know that Charles has taken on a challenge, which I am delighted about. He has asked the King for permission to enlist in the new guard as an ordinary soldier. That will protect him from having to serve in the army, which would be horrible if it meant fighting against his friends and even his family.

William had never had such letters before. Girls in Virginia did not pour out their souls in prose alexandrines. But it was not simply her outpouring of love that touched him, it was the anxiety she felt for all who were close to her in this ravaging time: for her grand Rohan aunts and cousins, now mere émigrés like half their class, sitting numb and bewildered in drab lodgings somewhere behind the Grand Place in Brussels, for her brother Charles, that bold, sweet boy whom she loved more than any man in the world except Wm, for her poor grandmother who was almost as fond of Wm as she was of her son and grandson and then, no, not least, for the Duke still trying to navigate through the vicious currents with the noise of the terrible weir growing louder all the time.

Sitting in Amsterdam looking out over the stagnant canals and fretting to be so long separated from Rosalie and growing more anxious for her safety by the day, William relieved his feeling by writing a letter to Mr Jefferson:

> *I should not be surprised to hear of the present leaders being hung by the people. Such has been the march of this revolution from the beginning. The people have gone faster than their leaders. The new tribunals were supposed to protect the accused from immediate massacre by the mob. But Robespierre and others of that atrocious and cruel cast compose the tribunal. We may expect therefore to hear of such proceedings under the cloak of* égalité *and patriotism as would disgrace the most inflamed assembly. Humanity shudders at the idea.*

But Mr Jefferson did not shudder. In fact, he did not reply to this or any of the other warnings that Wm had sent him since he left Paris. When TJ wrote at all, his anxieties were reserved for the packing of articles he had left behind. Every one of his books was to be wrapped singly in paper. Delorme was to be employed for the specialist packing work – the clocks, busts and marble pedestals. The chairs were to be lapped one into the other, according to Mrs Adams's method, the silk seats being previously covered with coarse linen. Ditto for the bodies of the chariot and the new cabriolet. The gilt frames of all pictures and looking-glasses to be covered with slips of oilcloth, for the gilt would fall off if the least damp got to them. The cotton bed-curtains to be washed before packing, because they washed so much better in the Parisian laundries.

And that was only the packing up. There was also the shopping. In the months since he had arrived back in America Mr Jefferson's ingenious mind had begun to fill with afterthoughts of all the stuffs and volumes and objets d'art and de vertu that he had neglected to buy while he was in Paris: rouleaux of wallpaper of every colour and pattern in the book – sky-blue, pea-green, plain crimson, brick, latticed – all to be got from Arthur's on the boulevards now that the luckless Réveillon's manufactory had been burnt in the opening days of the Revolution. There was the little clock with obelisks that had been stolen and must be replaced as near the original as possible. Two more sky-blue silk screens to be fitted up like those he already had and an oval glass to be the exact fellow to the one which was broken in Polly's and Patsy's room, he suspected by Sally though she never confessed to it. A set of the works of Tacitus, and of Buffon and the King of Prussia. And the missing volumes of the *Encyclopédie.*

Then there was the livestock. When Petit the valet came over, he was to bring with him on the ship two or three pair bantam fowls, a pair of Angora cats, ditto of Angora goats (only to be had from the King's own stock), and as many red-legged partridge and skylarks as he could manage. Then a dozen or so plants of the Buree pear, red and white alpine strawberries, and several botanical afterthoughts to add to the sizeable collection Mr Jefferson had taken back with him. There was no end to his interests.

Well, in fact there was. What he was not much interested in any more was William Short Esquire, his anxieties, interests and above all his prospects. The adoptive son had been relegated to the margin of Thomas Jefferson's otherwise inexhaustible mind. Was Wm to be made up to full minister at Paris, as all his friends and admirers there hoped and expected? Or was he to be relegated to some lesser capital, The Hague perhaps, or sent in some junior capacity to London or Madrid? Again and again Wm wrote to his adoptive father. He did not scruple to expatiate on the merits he knew he had and any successor might lack: his knowledge of France and the French language, his unique experience of these tumultuous years, his financial experience unrivalled by anyone in the public service, save perhaps Mr Hamilton. He wrote so often that when Mr J did finally write him a letter he had wearily to acknowledge the receipt of half a dozen of Wm's.

And when he finally got down to the subject of Wm's future, his tone was frigid. All he would say was that a minister would be appointed and from among the veterans on the public stage, to judge by the names mentioned, which obviously ruled out W. Short. TJ wrote as if he had only the remotest connection with public affairs, but he was Secretary of State for heaven's sake, and one whom the President had had to drag almost forcibly to accept the post. Surely he could nominate pretty much whomever he liked.

I had fondly flattered myself, Wm wrote back in anguish, *that I should be employed here because I was known to you, that this would give me an opportunity of being known to my country in such a manner as to be employed by it at home at a future period. But I find too late that it is the illusion of a misplaced vanity and that I must endeavour to wipe it off as soon as possible and take precautions against such illusions in future* . . . and so on and on for pages in his neat hand. The wonder is that the writing was not obscured by the tears of chagrin spurting from his eyes.

It was some time before TJ condescended to reply to this outburst, and he took the opportunity to enquire what had become of the clock and of the *President's wine.* These last two words were written in cipher, as it would not have done for the spies and censors who generally passed their squinty eyes over such letters to know that the President was no flincher from the glass. The second half of the letter was in cipher too:

> *I have thought it better to let your claim ripen itself in silence. Delay is in your favour. I have done what little I could towards getting an appointment rather to please than to serve you. For I see fully that the leading interests of your life are lost if you do not come home ere long and take possession of the high ground so open to you.*
>
> *I am with great and constant esteem, Dear Sir, Your sincere friend and servant,*
>
> *Th. Jefferson*

Ripen in silence! Only TJ could announce so blithely that he was not prepared to lift a finger and make it sound like a noble action. In his desperation Wm even consulted Gouverneur Morris.

The wily one-legged tobacco agent was as full of himself as ever. 'So you think Condorcet's a scoundrel now, do you? I could have told you that straight away, you only had to look at the fellow. As for La Rochefoucauld, you express surprise that he is so terribly puzzled about the tax question. That is always the case with these men who bring metaphysical ideas into business. The only people who know how to govern are those who have been used to it all their lives and such men have rarely either time or inclination to write about it. So the books on the subject contain only Utopian ideas which influence the next generation of metaphysical men and so the world wags on to its doom. *Quod erat demonstrandum.* Heard anything yet from Jefferson? Depend upon it, we shall all of us get what we least expect. I would bet two to one against my being appointed anywhere. These ministerial seats resemble electrical charges, which give every occupant a kick in the breeches.'

All the same, Gouverneur encouraged Wm not to give up hope. It was coming close now to the time when Congress must at last, after endless deliberations and delays, agree the final list of ministerial appointments and Wm himself had caught a whisper a week or two earlier that had encouraged his hopes. He had even confided to Gouverneur that he was thinking of employing a maître d'hôtel and buying some plate.

It was only ten days later that he wished from the pit of his being that he had never uttered such words. In fact, he wished he had never been born.

At long last Congress had advised on and consented to the old General's list of appointments. Mr Short was appointed to The Hague, by fifteen votes to eleven. And appointed to France, after more than two weeks of ill-tempered discussion, by a similar margin (sixteen to eleven), was . . . Gouverneur Morris.

Everyone thought it a terrible choice. Mr Jefferson worried that Gouverneur had been poisoning the President's mind with his sarcastic private letters. But nobody thought it a more dreadful appointment than William Short. He bit his lip, congratulated his supplanter, presented him to the new foreign minister. But all the time he was going through these rigmaroles he was thinking: they are all laughing at me, the whole of Paris is laughing at me. There is no American anywhere who knows this country better, who has followed the twists and turns of its fortunes for seven years with more unremitting attention, and they have rejected me in favour of a one-legged tobacco merchant who has no more knowledge of diplomacy than a turnip and whose acquaintance with public affairs comes solely from sharing Talleyrand's mistress.

How everyone had marvelled at the intimacy between Mr Jefferson and his protégé, what a superb partnership of minister and secretary they had seemed. Now it was revealed as a sham. TJ had no more real interest in his secretary than he had in his valet; rather less, in fact, since Mr Jefferson's letters had devoted more space to the difficulty of luring the admirable Adrien Petit to act as maître d'hôtel at Monticello than to the question of Wm's future.

In that trembling spring, when the war that had been so long budding finally blasted through and what few restraints that remained snapped with a terrifying noise, Wm felt he was more desperately unlucky, more callously betrayed, his talents more ignominiously ignored than any man in or out of America. Yet when she put her head round the door of his study or she led him across the garden to the little summer house, he knew he was also the luckiest man alive. And these two extremes were surely linked together. For he had given up his worldly ambition for the sake of love, had he not? If he had followed Mr J's advice, he would be back in Richmond by now, grubbing around for votes to succeed Mr Lee in the Congress, chewing tobacco with the dull squires of the Tidewater.

'Ah no, dearest, not – not so hard. Ah, ah.'

'How I love you, you must forgive me, I would not hurt you for the world.'

He spun out his departure as long as he could.

By the time he set off for The Hague, French troops were already singing the thrilling new anthem that had just come up from Marseilles as they marched off to the eastern frontier. He left behind an adoring household. They had all come to regard him as the rightful emissary of the American nation. Madame d'Enville was not too frail or disheartened by Condorcet's defection to write to TJ scolding him for his failure to have Wm appointed in his place. And then there were the letters from Rosalie, the first dated the day after his departure:

Ever since you left, my whole family has been thinking of you, they regard you almost as a child of theirs, which is a great jouissance *for me. I really suffered the other day when I had to go in to my grandmother just after leaving you. I had a real struggle to collect myself and recover my calm, but luckily the dim light of the salon, which I managed to keep out of by staying in the shadow, allowed me to escape the gaze of the curious . . .*

We often speak of you and you are even more often in my thoughts. Almost every day I go to see the tree by the fountain in the garden, those carved initials give me the greatest pleasure, it is the most precious monument in Paris . . .

And then the next Sunday from La Roche-Guyon:

I am writing to you from my little house on the island, where I have come by myself and shut the gate of the bridge, and so I am shut up in this pretty pleasaunce, which is now full of the loveliest flowers you can think of. But I would rather talk about you and me, and remind you of our sweet memories. It is haymaking time now, two years ago exactly since we worked side by side piling up the stooks. It was all hope then, we were cheerful and almost happy. How far we are from all that now!

There's no news from Paris. Things follow their ordinary course. We are very quiet here and we are staying here. Today is the village festival and I promise you there is no hint of the Revolution, people dance and play and laugh as if no one in the world were suffering . . .

We went walking last night until nine in the evening across to the island and into the meadow, under the brightest moon you can imagine. The walk made us even sadder that you were not with us, but at least we had the pleasure of talking about you and saying how well you and the evening would have gone together.

How remote their little household felt from the worsening riot and bloodshed, and from the early disasters on the battlefield. They had with them now Madame d'Astorg, the friend who had been rowing with Rosalie that first day at Versailles (her husband, an army officer, had emigrated two years earlier) and Monsieur Patricolas who was teaching Rosalie English, besides several old associates of the Duke who needed a bolthole now. The Duke himself had resigned. He had lost control. What use was there carrying on as President of the Paris Directory when he was scarcely presiding over and nowhere near directing the affairs of the city?

The house was full of regrets, all the more piercing because they did not care to acknowledge them. They were yesterday's men now, mere spectators at a tragedy that had scarcely begun.

The first blow fell in the heat of mid-August.

> *The same evening that I last wrote to you, I learnt that my poor brother Charles has been arrested, interrogated at the Assembly and taken from there to the Abbaye prison.*

It was hot, every day was hot now. The King and Queen went to Mass in the Tuileries chapel with Madame Elizabeth and Marie Thérèse. The royal ladies never lifted their eyes from their missals. Everyone knew that the attack was coming that night. Armed men were all over the city.

Rosalie's cousin François was at a matinée at the Comédie when he heard the rumour. He was the elder of the two Liancourt boys who had preferred to go partridge shooting and miss the Condor's lecture. Both of them, François and Alex, had no truck with the new ideas of their father. Liancourt could not understand it and said, with a smile, that his sons were a throwback. He gave them an enlightened education, sent them to England to learn about modern farming and parliamentary democracy. But both of them remained resolutely counter-revolutionary even before there was a revolution to counter. Rosalie and Charles had teased their heavy cousins and thought them too stupid to understand how the world was going. But now Rosalie was disenchanted and fearful, and even Charles had lost his ideals (or illusions) and come to rejoin the King.

And to rejoin the King was François's first thought too. He rushed out of the foyer of the Comédie like a man fleeing a fire in the theatre and ran, casting his officer's dignity to the winds, down the rue de Vaugirard (where the Comédie had shifted for the season) and across the river to the Tuileries where he found a crazy scene. Gone were all the precedence and ceremony of the King's couchee. The whole court had crowded into the King's bedchamber, sitting higgledy-piggledy wherever they could find a space, on the floor, on the royal commode, on Monsieur Carlin's beautiful ormolu consoles, with some piffling marquis vainly trying to remind them that they must not be seated in the Presence, while the King himself, still in his purple coat with his wig awry and the powder splashed all over his shoulders, wandered around, red in the face, near tears, looking like an actor who had just been booed off the stage.

They got no sleep that night, lying wide-eyed on sofas listening to the raucous sound of the tocsin. Already before dawn broke red and bloody – *rouge matin, gros chagrin* – there were reckoned to be five thousand men pressing towards the Tuileries.

At about five in the morning François accompanied the King, corpse-pale now, on a tour of his guards.

Quick now, what next? Stay or go? How long could the National Guard hold out? The National Assembly was just across the yard in the old Riding School. Shelter there? They spoke in broken whispers, plans and projects no sooner muttered than abandoned.

By eight o'clock the Queen was decided and she decided the King. 'I am going to the Assembly,' he said. '*Marchons*' – a strange echo of that wild song that had come up from Marseilles.

So they went through the west garden door across the courtyard. Madame de Lamballe said, 'We shall never come back.' Marie Antoinette broke down once, and then again, and then again. François took her arm and found that she was trembling.

The Dauphin kicked at the pile of leaves that the gardeners had piled up in the corner. The King looked at the leaves as though he had never seen leaves before. 'What a lot of leaves,' he said, 'they are falling early this year.'

Inside the Riding School they were led into the little box behind the President's chair reserved for the Assembly reporters, the logographie as it had been portentously labelled. The logographie was a hole of a place, no more than ten feet square, with a grille at the back that was open to the full glare of the sun. The stenographers could not endure shifts in the box longer than a couple of hours before demanding to be relieved. All day long the King and his ladies sat and sweltered while the scattered delegates debated their fate. Out in the streets the dreadful tally of the night before was being totted up. Corpses everywhere, on the streets, in cellars and stables and churches that had been smashed open.

One member of the new Assembly was not in the Chamber to see the King and Queen sweat the day out. Citizen Condorcet was busy, desperately busy, along the corridor in the Commission of Twenty-one drawing up the indictment against the King. Never were his matchless skills as an editor more urgently needed. He boasted afterwards that it took him no more than half an hour to knock out a decree suspending His Majesty and setting up a provisional ministry to be elected by the Assembly, to be followed by the calling of a National Convention. While the Assembly was digesting all this – not without angry protestations, they wanted the King dethroned not merely suspended – Condorcet moved on to work up a proclamation designed to calm the citizens of Paris and to inform them that the members of the Assembly had sworn to uphold liberty and equality or die at their posts. That took another thirty minutes or so.

The Twenty-one had also to choose who was to lead this provisional ministry, who was to take the helm in this whirlwind? Condorcet did not hesitate. They needed a man who had the confidence of the people whose fury had just toppled the throne, a man who could somehow contain the explosive energies of the masses, who by his oratory, his strength of character, would not disgrace the ministry or the Assembly that he would have to confront and dominate. Citizen Danton alone filled the bill. 'I chose him and I do not repent of it in the least,' Condorcet said later. He did not add, as he might have done, 'We need a man with a voice like a cathedral organ, a man with the carriage of a bull and a cock like a maypole, a man of passion and instinct, while I am only a mathematician.'

All day long Condorcet laboured, while thousands died outside and Louis and Marie Antoinette sweltered in the box. By the evening the Queen's fichu was wet with sweat and her handkerchief was soaked with tears. Cousin François had squeezed into the box too and she asked if she could borrow his handkerchief. But he could not lend it to her, because it was wet with the blood of the Vicomte de Maille. He went out to borrow another handkerchief from one of the guards and never spoke to her again.

Night was falling now and the Condor was coming to the end of his heroic day's labour. He went to relieve Vergniaud in the President's chair. And there he sat till three in the morning. Behind him in the stale dark air the King sat in his box looking out with his lorgnette at this strangest of all plays, for it was about his own fate.

There was a little corridor leading to the logographie where the

King's shrunken guard had gathered to protect him if they could. François went out to see if his cousin Charles was there, not just to say hello but to try to soothe Charles's choleric impulses, which he knew all too well.

As he came into the ill-lit foul-smelling passage, Charles was coming on duty to relieve a guard who was going off to dine. Just as François had feared, Charles was in a violent rage, stamping his foot, his hands twitching. 'When that fucker Condorcet comes past, I'm going to spit in his face if I don't break his neck.'

But all they could see through the little window in the corridor was the imperturbable back of Citizen Condorcet's head, and all they could catch was the stray remark of the Acting President as he guided the Assembly through the script he had devised for its dying hours.

'Spitting won't help,' François said, taking his cousin's arm, but Charles shook him off and went to report to the captain of the guard. François too went off, in search of whatever supper he could find. A good soldier always seized an opportunity to refuel.

When he came back, it was nearly eleven o'clock. He peered into the Assembly where only twenty or thirty members were left. He could hear Condorcet's harsh quaver rejecting some new amendment.

Then he saw a figure lying asleep on a bench just in front of the King's box. François peered closer and saw it was Charles. He looked like a little boy sleeping. His eyelashes were as long as his sister Rosalie's.

How close they all were in the grey hours of the night: the King and Queen in their box, Condorcet in his President's chair, Charles stretched out on his bench – a counterpane would have covered the lot of them.

Later still that night, after François had gone, Charles was woken up and arrested and taken to the Abbaye prison, on suspicion of what who knew – for plotting, for falling asleep, for neglecting his duty, for sticking by the King? The Abbaye was full of such bewildered angry people.

The party of refugees at La Roche-Guyon had gone to take the waters at Forges-les-Eaux, a quiet little spa town a day's drive away in the rolling Bray country. Forges had few attractions: a down-at-heel convent, a royal hunting box (disused) and the mineralised waters that spouted from the strange geological formation known as the Button of Bray. They went for a change of air in a place that was not too far from home. Perhaps the waters might help Madame d'Enville's aches and pains. They needed to take a deeper refuge from the storm, to retreat into anonymity for a while, away from the proud chateau against the cliff that was so indelibly associated with their name.

Every morning the Duke took his mother's arm and they processed slowly down the street from their lodgings towards the little pavilion that sheltered the spring. Behind them followed the half-dozen friends and supporters who had followed the Duke into this deep refuge: the Breton La Bourdonnay, Dolomieu the mineralogist, and of course the faithful Madame d'Astorg and Monsieur Patricot. A chair was brought for the old Duchess, so that she could sit down while the attendant held the silver-gilt cup against the burbling fountain. Rosalie sometimes stayed behind in her room, pleading a migraine, to use the leisure and solitude to allow her thoughts to flow more freely in her letters to Wm.

Charles was well, she said, he was sharing a room with two other royal guards who had been arrested at the same time. The room was large so that they did not get on top of each other (she might have been writing about a new boy at boarding school who was settling in well). Dear old Patricot had permission to go and see Charles every day and get him anything he needed. His only complaint was the lack of exercise. As there was no evidence against him, she was beginning to hope that he might be freed in a couple of days (two of his fellow prisoners had already been released). Next week they would return to La Roche. The sooner the better in fact. Forges had turned out to be a dismal hole, with nothing to be said for it. Poor little brother, he had caused them so much pain, but the happiness of seeing him again would cancel it all out.

She had reckoned without the man of passion. This was Danton's hour. The same day that Rosalie was confiding her hopes to paper in her musty lodgings at Forges, the Minister of Justice was calling the nation to arms. The *patrie* would be saved, the people would defend her frontiers and her cities against her enemies whether they came from without or within. The tocsin that would sound was not a signal of dread but a summons to charge against the enemies of the fatherland. 'To vanquish them, messieurs, we need boldness, boldness unremitting, boldness for ever and France will be saved.'

Boldness was to begin at home, in the Minister's own backyard. The Inspector of Prisons had warned him that the prisoners were at dire risk from the mob. The Minister's response was magnificent: 'I don't give a fuck about the prisoners, they can fend for themselves.'

So there was no one to stop the crowd that poured into the Abbaye, armed with the usual assorted weaponry – knives, axes, hatchets, sabres and various other butcher's tools. Within an hour two dozen prisoners were slaughtered. Not as many as the hundred and fifty priests who were shot or hacked to death at the Carmelite convent that was being used as a holding centre. But having discovered how easy it was, the executioners made numerous return visits to the Abbaye (because they were being paid on piecework, so much per execution). By the end of the grisly business nearly half the prisoners in Paris had been killed, in the Carmelite and the Abbaye more than four-fifths of them, including Rosalie's Charles. The Minister of Justice was well satisfied. The executions were an indispensable sacrifice to appease the people of Paris. The voice of the people was, after all, the voice of God.

Only two days after she had written to Wm in such high hopes, she wrote again on 3 September:

> *I received your letter and thank you for the pleasure it gave me. I was sure that you would share my sorrows, they are so cruel, so hard to bear. Maman is keeping her courage up. She is less broken than I feared, but happiness is finished for her and for me. One never recovers from such misfortunes. From now on I shall live only in my memories.*

And she added, even in her overwhelming grief not forgetting the need to be discreet, *Adieu, write to me through the different channels that I told you about.*

She put down her pen and began desultorily to pack her things for the return to La Roche. Madame Postulard had gone for one last walk in the woods. Madame d'Astorg was taking a nap in her attic room. Anyway, these days Rosalie liked to do things for herself. Even folding the few dresses she had brought with her gave her the feeling that she might yet develop the strength to weather their misfortunes. She was standing idly in the middle of the room wondering whether the tight-waisted blue silk might be a little too hot for the journey when she heard the noise of running feet in the street. Like the rest of Forges, the street was usually quiet – on a Sunday afternoon it was like the grave – so she went over to the window.

Below her she could see the tumbled fair thatch of Pierre's head and she could hear him ringing the bell furiously. She met him halfway down the stairs with Raffron, the maid who had let him in. He was wide-eyed and gasping for breath. 'Madame, they are coming for us.'

'Who, Pierre, who's coming?'

'The commissioners, madame, and there's hundreds of feds with them on their way to the war, ugly brutes they are and most of them drunk.'

'From Marseilles, are they? We saw some of them at Paris, they did terrible things.'

'No, this lot are from Brittany, but they're just as bad. I know for a fact—' There was a fierce hammering at the door and three or four men in tousled uniforms burst in, looking more like the hunted than the hunters.

Through the open door behind them Rosalie could see a crowd of peasants stretching halfway down the street. They were carrying the usual staves and pitchforks and rusty old swords.

'Where is he, where is he, La Roche-fou-cauld?'

'He is out to lunch,' Rosalie said with a calm that surprised her though she could feel her knees knocking. No less than the truth. The Duke was seeing his old friend Madame de Tracy who was taking the waters too.

'Where, where?' they shouted. And the people at the back took up the cry: 'Where is he?'

Rosalie could see now that the commissioner who had spoken was trembling almost as badly as she was. He seemed propelled by the people behind, rather than leading them. She was wondering what sort of lie to tell next when the Duke saved her the trouble by coming in from the street and pushing between the commissioners with an almost apologetic courtesy as though slipping between two guests at a party. 'Here,' he said.

'Citizen La Rochefoucauld, you are under arrest.'

'Very g-good, and what exactly is the ch-charge?'

'Aiding and abetting priests and émigrés.'

'How strange, I am usually accused of being an enemy to both.'

'Now then, this is neither the time nor place. You'll have a chance to answer to the proper authorities. Officer, put guards on all the rooms and seal any documents. You are to come with us instantly.'

'Please, let me speak to my mother first.'

'It is not permitted to pass information to third parties.' The commissioner was gaining confidence as his instructions came back to him.

'May I at least kiss my wife?'

'That is certainly permitted, citizen, we are not monsters.'

The commissioner supervised with an almost fatherly indulgence the kiss that the Duke planted on Rosalie's cheek.

They marched the Duke off to the town hall.

After they had satisfied their *amour propre* and conformed to the regulations as they saw them, the guards let the women into the old lady's room but then insisted on staying while Rosalie explained what had happened.

'If we had remained at La Roche,' Madame d'Enville said reflectively, 'at least we would have been murdered in our own beds.'

At nightfall they brought him back. He was ghost-pale.

'You must be ready at four o'clock,' the commissioner said. 'We have to start before dawn for Vernon. It is for your own protection.'

They sat together in Madame d'Enville's large sitting room at the back of the house. The three guards had brought in extra chairs and sat in a line in front of them, yawning and then gossiping *sotto voce* a little, then falling asleep and jerking awake again.

The Duke looked at his fob watch by the light of the candle on the dresser. 'Time to go,' he said.

But the commissioners still had their hands full with other business in the neighbourhood, so the prisoners sat in their travelling cloaks watching the blanched light angle in through the cracks in the shutters. When it was fully light, the maid, Mademoiselle Raffron, undid the shutters and Rosalie looked at her sad companions sitting on the bed side by side, each of them thinking that this would be the last day they would see dawn together.

Raffron brought up coffee and brioche from the kitchen, and they eked out the morning, talking in whispers as low as their guards', both parties embarrassed to be so long in each other's company. It was not till three in the afternoon that the commissioners returned and hustled them into the carriage, grumbling at them as though the delay had been all their fault.

They were not alone on the road. A large company of gendarmes – twenty or thirty of them, Rosalie thought – marched alongside the coach, not to mention twice as many *fédérés* who looked every bit as rough as their reputation, and behind them a ragged tail of idlers, urchins and drunks.

They were close pressed in the carriage with the chief commissioner, Rosalie and the Duke, Madame d'Enville and Madame d'Astorg. Following on was a cabriolet containing Raffron and some of the luggage, and a very tall thin gentleman who was never introduced but seemed intimately connected to their arrest. It was nearly midnight before they reached the little town of Gournay.

The women were not guarded that night, but again they were told to be ready to move off at four o'clock, this time to avoid the dangerous commotion of Gournay market. Once more the commissioners were delayed and did not appear until eight o'clock, and they did not start until nine. The delay allowed time for a huge cortège to gather, determined to accompany them all the way to Gisors.

They reached Gisors at around noon, in the midst of a huge, steaming, thirsty mob of *fédérés* shouting threats and insults as they milled around the carriage. Even with the gendarmes smacking them with the butts of their muskets, it was a struggle to get down from the carriage and escape into the inn.

'Citizen, I think you had better show yourself at the window, just so they know we haven't spirited you away.'

'Is that wise?'

'They'll burn the house down if you don't.'

The Duke walked to the window, which was already open, and gingerly put his head out. His tall stooping figure remained poised there for a moment. There was something tentative and enquiring about his posture, as though he were testing the weather. But the horrible cries drove him back inside and he turned towards his wife and his mother with a stricken look.

'We've got the city guard coming, citizeness,' the commissioner said, trying to sound controlled, 'but if we don't look sharp about it we're all dead men. Look, I'll take him on ahead on foot so they can see we've got him and that will give you time to get back in the carriage while they're looking the other way.'

So the men trooped down the rickety stair of the Ange d'Or, the nearest thing Gisors had to a decent inn: the Duke, the commissioner and the tall thin gentleman who had not been introduced. Rosalie began to count out seven minutes as the commissioner had recommended, but before she had got to three, the shouts and curses from the street were so loud that she could not hear herself.

She gave the signal and they ran down together and found the carriage drawn up outside the door of the inn, with the coachman ready to move as soon as they had pushed Madame d'Enville into her seat (the old lady almost lost her footing as they dragged her inside).

They clattered off down the street, pursued by the hideous noise of the crowd. Rosalie and her grandmother huddled together into the depths of the carriage, keeping their faces turned away from the window.

A few minutes later there was a huge whoop of delight from behind them and Madame d'Astorg put her head out of the carriage. 'We've done him, lads,' she heard them cry and a minute later there was a whole crowd of them running past the carriage with three or four them carrying the Duke's body as they ran. She saw blood gushing from his temple all over his long pale face and down his buff waistcoat, and she could see too his dark tripes spilling out over his breeches, then she was deafened by the song she had heard the feds from Marseilles singing when they came down the rue Faubourg-Saint-Honoré a few weeks earlier.

She turned back into the carriage and realised instantly that the other three (Rosalie's maid Raffron was there too) had seen nothing of what happened. She was unable to speak and sat white and upright as the coach rattled on out of the town.

Then somehow the moment had passed at which she could say what she had seen. When they were out of the town and in the hot dusty countryside they had to stop to water the horses in a small village (she could not remember the name of it) and there they began to talk again, but very cautiously as though the slightest false word could bring out the news they dreaded most.

'Where do you think they will take him?'

'Oh, Vernon I should think. Yes, Vernon.'

'And will they try him there?'

'I should think so, yes,' said Madame d'Astorg vaguely.

It was only the following morning that Madame d'Astorg ventured to say, in slow broken sentences, what she had seen, prefacing and ending her account with the proviso that she could not be sure, although in truth she was as sure of it as of anything in her whole life. Poor loyal Madame d'Astorg (she was as poor as she was loyal and loyal because she was poor ever since her husband had left her with two small children) feared that they might reproach her for not speaking out straight away, at a time when they might have thought that something could yet have been done to save him (but what?) and indeed she reproached herself. But they had no energy for reproaches, they were sunk too deep in shock and grief.

William sat in the gathering gloom (it was the last week in October by the time he had Madame d'Astorg's letter and the leaves were already gathering in grubby swirls at the corners of the canals) and thought of the scene as she described it in her sprawling hand, so unlike Rosalie's neat exemplary script: that long broken body with the guts spilling out of the buff waistcoat he always wore and the blood from the temple spouting over those sad beaky features, with Rosalie and her mother shrinking into the recesses of the carriage to avoid the shouts and curses, and only Madame d'Astorg looking resolutely out of the window and seeing the laughing murderers carrying the body past her with no more care than if they were carrying a bag of rotten apples to the dung heap.

How odd, he thought, that he could now write to Rosalie as openly as he liked. All those elaborate precautions were as dead as, well, as dead as the Duke was. Then he blushed to think that he had thought such a thing and devoted a moment or two to praying for the soul of his kindly stammering host, who had never thought a callous thought and who had always striven – how earnestly and, yes it had to be said, how blindly – to do the right thing. And he thought too how strange it was that he who thought so little of religion should be praying for a man who might be best remembered for dethroning the Catholic Church from its privileged position. Each letter from Rosalie clutched more fiercely at his heart and made him long to see her that minute.

My health is not too bad, but my ordeals have struck at my nerves so that I cannot bear the slightest unexpected noise without extreme terror. My head is aching all the time and my memory often fails me, but the memory of those I have loved and those I love still will always remain in my heart. One day I hope we shall all be back together, and if you are ever free you will see how my family considers you as one of their closest friends. You already were that and would have been even more so if only my poor Charles . . . dear child, with what pleasure I watched the friendship between you two and how sure I was that it would grow closer still! Always cherish his memory, love him for himself, love him for me, in your mind think of him in our midst!

Was it from tact that she spoke so little of her husband? Perhaps there was little she could say, to Wm anyway. She might prefer to keep private from him the real affection and respect he knew she had had for the Duke. He could not blame her.

He asked her to describe how she spent the day so that he could think of her at each moment. She got up at half past eight, wrote and did her domestic duties until eleven or half past, then went in to see her grandmother for an hour or an hour and a half. Maman talked incessantly of her son and her grandson. She blamed herself for encouraging both of them in their radical ways, she blamed herself above all for encouraging Condorcet. He it was who had uncaged these cannibals. How foolish she had been to be led astray by the brilliance of his mind, not to see that he had no heart and, what was just as bad, no common sense. Sometimes Rosalie feared that her grandmother was becoming distracted by age and grief. Then at other times she seemed the firmest of them all.

They dined at three. Then they sat together until seven working at their little tasks. Rosalie was knitting waistcoats and vests for the children on the estate, which she liked doing because it did not tax her powers of concentration. The great rooms had all been shut up. They sat in her grandmother's sitting room and ate in her bedroom with no one serving at table. Rosalie's own rooms were too remote, so she had moved her things into a little lodging just above the library, which suited her much better.

It was the middle of December before all the business in The Hague was settled and William had his *congé* and could go back to France en route to Madrid, or rather Aranjuez where the Spanish court was and which was to be his new posting. Every minute of his journey across that mournful, muddy landscape, clattering through icy puddles and rumbling over the rutted old bridges, he pictured to himself the sad little group sitting round the sewing table or talking in hushed voices as they played cards while the old servant came in to draw the heavy curtains. Yet his spirits did not sink at the thought of intruding upon a household so lapped in grief. On the contrary, he longed to join with them in their sadness and demonstrate the depths of his love, like a pilgrim to some dolorous shrine. Right at the end of the journey, as his coach swung round the bend in the village street, he experienced an overwhelming, almost shameful sense of exhilaration, as though none of the horrors had really happened and he was as he had been before, a lover who had nothing more complicated in mind than to see his girl.

'Oh, but you look so well; you said you had grey hair and had become an old man.'

She had clutched him to her without hesitation or thought of propriety while the coachman was still unloading his baggage. It was dusk now and there was a light rain falling in the darkening courtyard, and her hand wiped away the raindrops when she caressed his cheek as though she were wiping away tears.

She took him up to her grandmother's sitting room where the little party was already assembled. He was taken aback by how warmly they all greeted him: Dolomieu the mineralogist whom he hardly knew and the Breton military man whom he did not know at all and whose name he did not catch, and the old Abbé, the one who liked to shave in the open air on the parapet and who was much aged. And Madame d'Enville, also much aged as Rosalie had warned, but still with something of the old bright look in her eye as she held out her hands to him from the high-winged chair that had been moved from its place in the salon.

'Oh Monsieur Short, how could they take you away from us? I have written to Monsieur Jefferson to reproach him, it is such a mistake for your country and such a tragedy for us. Mr Morris is not a patch on you, everyone says so. And now I hear that you are to be on your travels again. You must stay as long as you can. We shall not let you go until the last possible moment.'

He took her hand and kissed it, just as on the first occasion they had met, when this Frenchified habit had so irked Mr Jefferson. Then he looked around at the little group. They had welcomed him as a party marooned on a South Sea island might welcome a mariner who had strayed on to their shores. And he had a weird feeling that these were in some sense his true family in a way that all the Shorts and Skipwiths and Eppses back in Virginia were not.

After supper Madame d'Astorg read to the company from the *Travels of Young Anacharsis in Greece.* She read coldly without expression as though she would rather be somewhere else. Indeed, of the whole company she, who had been so bright and merry on their first meeting with the canoes, was the only one to show reserve, even hostility. Wm remembered that Rosalie had twice complained of this coldness in her letters to him. Ariane seemed not to appreciate the depth of Rosalie's grief or at any rate she was unable to respond to it, and Rosalie felt betrayed, for surely it was the touchstone of friendship to know how to comfort someone in the depths of their affliction.

'Did you not notice it? Do you see what I mean?' Rosalie said as he escorted her through the library.

'Oh, you do not think that she is perhaps still too shocked by . . . she was after all the only one who witnessed the . . .'

But Rosalie was having none of it. Madame d'Astorg had lost no one in her own family, unless you counted her runaway husband and she was well rid of him. Wm was glad to see the spark flare.

'No,' she said at the top of the little stairs when she thought he might be turning to go back down again, though he had no such intention, 'now you are here you must never leave me for an instant.'

As he had been jolting over the dykes and swamps of the Low Countries, he had wondered about this moment, whether he ought to go carefully or she might shy away, whether it would be too unfeeling to make love directly without first leading her through her sadness into a calmer, freer state of mind. But they had been through so much and said so many things to each other in their letters. And now all she had in her was a kind of wildness, a hungry desperation. Even before she was finished she was convulsed with a sobbing that would not stop but she wanted to stop so that she could tell him that all the terrible things that had happened had never shaken her love for him. The opposite, in fact, he was all she had in the world now and he was ten times as precious to her as he had been before.

He slept for a couple of hours, he could have slept for twelve he was so tired, then she woke him and he had never known such pleasure, had never been carried so deep. Her grief had been swept up in her desire. In an unholy way, it was as if they were doing it for Charles's sake. And just at the last moment he could not help thinking what Gouverneur would think of this fancy. His supplanter probably had some coarse axiom ready minted – the time to fuck a woman is when she has just lost her husband – and yet even this grossness seemed consumed by their love, the way the bright flames burn away the vilest rubbish.

They had only eight days together. On the sixth day he did what he knew he had to do, what he had resolved to do even before he left The Hague. He chose to do it just after the ladies had returned from Mass on Christmas Day. The rest of the party were falling upon a japanned box of preserved fruit that Liancourt had sent them from exile in Boston.

He led her away from her grandmother's room through the dark and shuttered salon with the dust sheets draped over the furniture. They came out on to the loggia and looked out over the wintry valley, the Seine scarcely visible for the mist still clinging to its waters. It was quiet and chilly, no sign of movement anywhere.

'You know what—?'

'What you are going to ask?' And for a moment he was strangely reminded of her husband's vexing habit of finishing your sentences for you. She did not do it so often, but in her it was always beguiling. 'Yes, I think I know, though it is presumptuous of me to think so.'

'You must let me ask it all the same.'

'Oh, I shall, though I cannot pretend it won't make me tremble.'

'Will you marry me, please will you marry me?' The words came out in a rush because he was so nervous and he was afraid they sounded mechanical, not coming from the heart. But she did not seem to think anything of the sort because she threw her arms at him more than round him and kissed him and burst into tears all in the same moment, or so it seemed to him.

'Oh, you are kind, you are the best, but you see I cannot, you must know I could not think of any such thing at present. You have seen the state Maman is in. She cannot possibly manage without me. I could not dream of leaving her now and going even to Spain, let alone to America. It would be like running away.'

He persisted but with increasing gentleness and she said, with a smile that was all the more bewitching because it started out serious and broke into a touch of mischief, that she could not prevent him and she could not deny that his proposing it gave her the most intense pleasure, as though he were making love to her at that minute in broad daylight – and she reddened, realising that she had said more than she meant. She was wearing her black widow's dress and a little black hat for going to Mass in.

When he left two days later, she clung to him as though she was drowning. Later as he drowsed in the coach, he fancied he could still feel the impress of her body grinding against his and hear her quick breath in his ear. But then as he finally fell asleep, he seemed to be in another coach altogether with Madame d'Astorg's plump cold face peering out alongside his own and men running alongside carrying a hideous bloody object, and he was turning away in disgust but Madame d'Astorg was saying, no, no, you must look, you must always look.

There was blossom on the orange trees at Aranjuez and he liked to take his morning chocolate in the little walled garden at the back of the Minister's lodgings. In among the official diplomatic correspondence he came upon the hand he knew best in the world after Rosalie's.

It was the first he had heard from Mr Jefferson for months. He had expected for some time now to receive further instructions on how to pursue with the Spanish authorities the matter of the Spanish claim to the territory of the Creek Indians. But Mr Jefferson had nothing to say about the Creek Indians. All of a sudden he had decided to return to the question of France, that question which he had shown such reluctance to address, ever since he skipped off from that country almost the minute the Bastille fell. Now he returned to the subject with a vengeance:

> *The tone of your letters had for some time given me pain, on account of the extreme warmth with which they censured the proceedings of the Jacobins in France. In the struggle which was necessary, many guilty persons fell without the forms of trial, and with them some innocent. These I deplore as much as anybody, and shall deplore some of them until the day of my death. But I deplore them as I should have done had they fallen in battle. It was necessary to use the arm of the people, a machine not quite so blind as balls and bombs, but blind to a certain degree. A few of their cordial friends met at their hands the fate of enemies. But time and truth will rescue and embalm their memories, while their posterity will be enjoying that very liberty for which they would never have hesitated to offer up their lives. The liberty of the whole earth was depending on the issue of the contest, and was ever a prize won with so little innocent blood? My own affections have been deeply wounded by some of the martyrs to this cause, but, rather than that it should have failed, I would have seen half the earth desolated; were there but an Adam and Eve left in every country, and left free, it would be better than it now is.*
>
> *I have expressed to you my sentiments because they are really those of ninety-nine in an hundred of our citizens. The feasts and rejoicings which have lately been had on account of the successes of the French showed the genuine effusions of their hearts. You have been wounded by the sufferings of your friends, and have by this circumstance been hurried into a temper of mind which would be extremely disrelished if known to your countrymen.*

And, Mr J did not shrink from adding, *was* extremely disrelished by the foremost of those countrymen, to wit the President, who had pretty much given up on young Mr Short as a consequence.

How could TJ say such things? Did he have the faintest conception of just how much innocent blood had been shed in France and was still being shed, and how much bloodshed was yet to come? Would he really prefer to see half the earth desolate than that the cause should fail? Sitting on his little hilltop in Virginia, did Mr J have any concrete understanding of what desolation meant, or what misery would have to be plumbed to create such a tabula rasa for this new Adam and Eve to delight in their liberty?

He did not reply. There was no profit in attempting to correct the incorrigible. But he knew there was worse to come. And he could at least shelter Rosalie. His years of patient dealing with Van Staphorst, Willink and Hubbard could now be turned to advantage. He told Rosalie to transfer as much of her personal property as she could into his name at the bankers. He was relieved, and flattered too, that she did not hesitate. In all, at least three million francs were transferred into his account, as a secret, interest-free loan. It was in contemplation of a forthcoming marriage between the two of them, he told the pig-eyed bankers to calm their suspicions of the subterfuge. That was in truth what he hoped for, but, marriage or no marriage, no regime that he had come across, however chaotic and bloodthirsty, ever dared to invade the private deposits of a Dutch banker.

Duchesses, though, were fair game. Had not their sons and husbands and brothers already experienced the justice of the people? Why should the brood mares be exempt? Their cousins and parents were already condemned as émigrés. How could those who remained behind be anything other than subversive agents of a foreign power?

In November, Rosalie and her grandmother were arrested. They were taken to the Convent of the English Augustinians in the rue des Fossés-Saint-Victor, which had been turned into a jail but continued to be run by the nuns, who were still known as the English nuns although the supply of English novices had dried up since the Revolution.

William sat in his orange grove, the last of the season's fruits now rotting on the sandy ground, writing minutes on the negotiations with the faraway Creek Indians. In his solitude and sorrow his mind unwound the whole ravelled record of his time in Europe, and in particular that first summer at La Roche-Guyon.

How far scattered they all were now. Charles murdered; now the Duke murdered; the other Duke in exile, in Philadelphia apparently; his son Alex in the West Indies managing his wife's plantations; François fighting on the other side for the Princes; Jefferson far away dreaming of his Adams and Eves; Lafayette in jail somewhere, Prussia was the latest report; and now Rosalie and her maman walled up in a convent from which they might never come out alive. Not one of that blithe, hopeful band left at liberty in France. Ah yes, there was one survivor: Monsieur de Condorcet. The only one of them not dead or disgraced, or in prison or exile.

Condorcet was dog-tired, he had been suffering from shakes and shivers for months – only to be expected in these feverish times. He had been working flat out for days and nights on end, dashing off draft laws and proclamations and committee reports, not to mention editing the *Chronique de Paris* and writing most of it himself. He had become a writing machine, not unlike the automaton monarch that he had suggested should rule France. But unlike the machine he was wearing out fast. One of the deputies strolling into the legislation committee room found the great man fast asleep under the bench, perhaps the same bench that Charles had been found sleeping on top of. Most of the time there he was, sitting in the President's chair, the angry sheep as white in the face now as an old *mouton*.

Yet throughout all those bloody days when the Prussians were besieging Verdun and the mob was rampaging through Paris he was curiously silent. He did not intervene in the debates or launch any of his brilliant polemics, except to welcome the Assembly's vote to allow divorce and 'end the long centuries of servitude for the other half of the human race', as he put it in the *Chronique*. But what did he have to say about the September massacres, when defenceless prisoners were being butchered in their hundreds? For the first twenty-four hours he said nothing at all and then he wrote in the *Chronique*, 'We shall draw the curtain on events of which it would be too difficult at this moment to estimate the number and calculate the consequences. What an unfortunate and terrible situation it is when the character of a people who are naturally good and generous is constrained to commit such acts of vengeance.'

So it wasn't really their fault then. How his old hero Voltaire would have minced that line of argument. And what did Condorcet think of the murder of his old friend and patron in front of his wife and mother? That he blamed on the poisonous journalists who had whipped the mob into a frenzy (as though he himself had never been near a newspaper). And in a sense too, or so he explained in a long letter to Mr Jefferson, it was Lafayette's fault as well, the vain and devious Lafayette who had led the poor simple Duke by the nose. Everyone's fault except his – but was it not Condorcet who had boasted of bringing Danton to the helm, and was it not Danton's thrilling exhortations that had unleashed the blood tide?

And Condorcet himself was swimming in that tide, elected by no less than five departments to the new Convention (only one in ten electors dared to vote but the successful candidates cared little for that), and then elected vice-president and first secretary of the Convention.

When it was all over, he did regret the slaughter in the Abbaye and claimed to Madame Suard that he had done everything a man could to have Charles released but these misfortunes were inseparable from the Revolution and such things were bound to happen in a nation at war. He remained passionately opposed to the death penalty and when he was called on that pale January morning to vote for the death of the King he refused. But this flicker of liberal principle aside, he was floating along with the current.

Who knows, perhaps he would have succeeded in staying afloat if it had not been for one thing that cut him to the quick. At long last his beloved draft Constitution came before the Convention, that precious confection on which he had laboured so long, with its delicate balances and counter-balances, its sub-clauses, its appendices – it took all day to read the thing through.

And they laughed at it, or rather they yawned at it. Instead, inside a week, some hack knocked out a cheap version a third the length and the Convention waved it through without reading even half of it.

For Condorcet this rejection was unforgivable. Maddened, exhausted, humiliated, he launched into a fatal retaliation. In denouncing the gimcrack, puny so-called Constitution that the Convention was now being asked to approve, he denounced all those men who ceaselessly flattered the people, to lure them into acts of violence. Such demagogues defiled the freedom of the press with an audacity the old despotism never dreamed of. Then, reckless to the last, he tossed in the worst accusation of the lot: that with this appalling Constitution these demagogues were preparing the way for the return of the monarchy. He published this denunciation anonymously but everyone knew instantly who had written it and everyone knew who he was aiming at.

It did not take long for Robespierre to hit back. There was not much quibbling about finding Condorcet guilty of conspiracy and issuing a decree of arrest against him. They were voting half a dozen such decrees a day now, the deputies were giddy with voting them, those few who dared to turn up and the even fewer who dared to vote, each fearing that it might be his turn next.

And unlike the old regime they could move quickly too. An hour after the Committee of Public Safety had the order signed and sealed, the local commissars were knocking on the door of Condorcet's Paris apartment, at 505 rue de Lille. The concierge told them that Condorcet was out at his country place at Auteuil. The commissars stopped the Paris earth by sealing up No. 505 and the adjoining flat inhabited by Condorcet's secretary. Two other commissars were sent hotfoot to Auteuil, rousing the mayor, who was so deplorably leisurely about putting on his sash and breeches that by the time they reached the Condorcet house the alarm had clearly been raised. Madame Condorcet was there with her brother-in-law, that wily Dr Cabanis who also happened to be a municipal officer in Auteuil. The commissars were given to understand that Condorcet was at that minute over at his friend Debry's. When they got to Debry's lodgings, they were told that Debry was at home but that he was ill in bed. The local procureur, the only man there in the commissars' opinion who was worthy of the people, insisted on going upstairs. The bed was made, no Debry. Back to Condorcet's, where the gardener said his master had been a few minutes earlier. But Madame C said her husband was in Paris and she did not know whether he was returning that day or not.

By this time Condorcet was well clear of Auteuil and was soon being hidden by two of Cabanis's medical students in their lodgings with the widowed Madame Vernet near the Luxembourg Gardens, 21 rue des Fossoyeurs. And here a real heroine enters the story.

When the medical students asked Madame Vernet: 'Would you give shelter to a wanted man?' she asked only one question: 'Is he a good man?' Yes, they said. Let him come, she said, and she took him in without asking his name. She did not think of changing her mind when the students told her who he was.

From that frantic day of his flight in July to the end of March the following year, Condorcet never left No. 21 rue des Fossoyeurs.

Madame Vernet lived by letting out rooms. She never accepted a penny from Condorcet or from Sophie. There were other lodgers, Madame Vernet's cousin, a professor of geometry called Sarret with whom Condorcet practised Latin conversation, and an old professor of mathematics who also happened to be a deputy in the Convention, and one of extreme views too. None of them gave him away. In that narrow lodging house Condorcet often shivered from the cold and trembled for fear of discovery, but he never lacked for friends.

And there, hidden away in the heart of Paris, pursued by Robespierre's implacable fury, Condorcet found a strange freedom. His goods had been seized. Sophie was penniless and had begun to scrape a living painting miniatures in a room over a lingerie shop in the rue Saint-Honoré – everyone wanted miniatures now to remember their nearest and dearest in these times when the next day they might disappear for years or for ever. Condorcet's own disappearance made people think that he too must have emigrated, perhaps to Switzerland. The plight of an émigré's family was worse even than that of the family of a man who had an arrest warrant out against him.

Condorcet was torn apart with guilt, worrying himself every time Sophie trudged from 352 rue Saint-Honoré to the rue des Fossoyeurs to bring him fresh linen and a few such luxuries as Paris still afforded. She dressed down as a peasant and took a different zigzag route each time, sometimes melting into the crowd who were off to see the guillotine (Dr Guillotin's invaluable device had been transferred from the Tuileries, where its operation might upset the deputies, to the place de la Révolution, formerly place Louis XV, later place de la Concorde, where it gave nothing but pleasure). She wrote to him, too, as often as she could, imploring him not to think he was harming those whom he loved: *Enjoy the little happiness I have been able to give you in return for what you have given me. I am sending stockings, shoes and trousers and I would like to send you also all the tender things your little Eliza says about your absence – she asks people who are leaving to please ask you to come and have supper with her. Adieu! Live for happiness.*

And he wrote back to her a cack-handed little ode to celebrate the seventh anniversary of their marriage:

I served my land, your love deigns me to bless
I shan't have lived not tasting happiness.

As the winter deepened, Sophie was driven to the extremest measure of all but the only one that offered any prospect of protecting her and little Eliza: divorce, though she could not bring herself to mention the word. *'This apparent separation, while my attachment to you and the bonds which unite us are indissoluble, is for me the worst misery of all.'* Condorcet responded immediately and offered to put his consent to the divorce in writing. Then she changed her mind and would not accept it. But on 14 January 1794 (or 25 Nivose An II, as it said on the document) the divorce petition was lodged in Auteuil. When he had voted for divorce as a humane remedy for couples who had fallen out of love, Condorcet can scarcely have imagined that for him its use would be to save the lives of his wife and daughter.

All through that winter he wrote his great work, the only work that anyone would remember him for, *A Sketch of a Historical Portrait of the Progress of the Human Spirit.* It was Sophie's doing really, Sophie with her heart still as full of love for the Republic and for her husband. She told him that he should not waste his energies in fruitless polemics and apologias, he must use this precious time of solitude and reflection to compose the book that would resound down the ages as a vade-mecum for the march of humanity.

So he wrote it all out, with a flow and vivacity and confidence that no other human being had so far surpassed: stage by stage, he described how our species had raised itself out of the mud and slime, had passed through the ages of ignorance and despotism and had eventually stumbled, not without brutalities and backslidings, into the age of progress and perfection. Nobody had ever written anything quite like that before, nobody would muster the confidence to write anything so blithe again. And it was all done by a shivering, hunted man whose blood was freezing in his veins and who was shortly, by a decree of 13 March 1794 to be precise, to be declared an outlaw. And who better to frame such a decree than the ingenious, fiery young Louis-Antoine de Saint-Just who at half Condorcet's age had himself written a glowing description of the ideal republic. Saint-Just who had noticed something nobody else had quite put into words: that happiness was a new idea in Europe, *the* new idea in fact. That, after all, was what united everyone: Condorcet and Sophie, Mr Jefferson and Mrs Cosway, William and Rosalie too. *Le bonheur* was the one thing worth having, the only cause worth striving for.

But before the reign of universal happiness could begin, the ground had to be cleared and the work must not be shirked or skimped out of mistaken notions of charity. The beauty of Saint-Just's decree was that it swept away any need to plough through the list of attainted citizens. Article VIII of the Decree of 13 March (23 Ventose An II) simply affirmed that 'all those indicted with conspiracy against the Republic who have evaded judicial examination are hereby declared outlaws'. And Article XI stated that 'anyone who conceals an outlaw at home or elsewhere shall hereby be considered and punished as their accomplice'. As soon as Condorcet's identity was established he could be executed without trial. The same fate awaited Madame Vernet if he were caught.

Already there were strange visitors to No. 21. On 24 March a man called, saying he was a dealer in saltpetre and wanted to see a room that was to let, repeating several times that if one had something precious one should take good care of it because visitors were not always people one could rely on. Condorcet overheard the conversation from the adjoining room. The next day he had word that the premises were going to be searched on suspicion that there were fugitives from the south hiding there.

Madame Vernet would not let him go. He had already given her his last will and testament. Two months earlier he had sent Sophie his wishes for Eliza's education. He wanted her to learn English. If she went to England, he commended her to Lord Stanhope; in America to Mr Jefferson and to Franklin's grandson, Mr Bache. He wished also that Eliza should be brought up in the love of liberty and equality, and that she should be kept remote from any thought of personal vengeance. *Tell her I never felt any myself.*

Then he put all his papers – his algebraic calculations, his notes for a universal philosophical language (the last thing he was working on) and the manuscript of his precious *Sketch* into a canvas sack and gave it to his fellow mathematician, Sarret, saying, 'Here are some papers, do what you like with them.'

He took no baggage with him, but he stuffed into his pockets his razor, a knife with a horn handle, a little pair of scissors, a silver pencil case, a pocket Horace (a present from Madame Suard) and a small purse containing two of his wife's miniatures, and locks of her hair and Eliza's.

Then he went down to the ground floor to find Sarret. Madame Vernet was standing there, an anxious look on her round face.

'Salve.'

'Salve, domine.'

'Imus subiter.'

'Imus subiter,' Sarret replied.

Madame Vernet had no Latin.

'Oh madame, could you be so kind as to fetch my tobacco pouch from my chamber. I have my hands full with these wretched papers.'

Madame Vernet, always so quick and eager, was up the stairs in no time but could not find any pouch. She was down the stairs again in time to hear the cry of horror from her maid as Condorcet rushed out of the door followed by Sarret who slammed it behind him. By the time she had the door open again, they were round the corner and out of sight. With her quick mind she saw in a flash that to chase after them would only draw attention to all three of them. She closed the door quietly and collapsed into the maid's arms.

It was a beautiful spring morning. The pale sun shone on them as they walked out of the city. In half an hour they were past the Maine gate and more or less in the country. The by-lanes were sprinkled with blackthorn blossom.

Cordorcet could not go back to his brother-in-law in Auteuil, let alone seek refuge with any of his friends in Paris. His only hope was to throw himself on the mercy of his oldest friends of all, the Suards.

They had a big place out at Fontenay-aux-Roses, only a few miles beyond the Maine gate, nothing to an average walker. But Condorcet, cooped up at No. 21 for nearly a year, with his terrible circulation, could scarcely walk at all. He hobbled along beside Sarret who kept on having to slow down to keep pace with him. Every half-hour he had to stop for a rest. When they reached the Montrouge plain it was midday and the sun was hot on Condorcet's pale flaky face. Sarret embraced him warmly and went back to Madame Vernet, whose response was to leave her door unlocked for the next eight days in the hope of his returning, as one might leave a chink for a runaway cat.

It was well into the afternoon by the time Condorcet limped into Fontenay. He had been five hours on the road. The Suards were not there. They had gone to Paris. He dared not give the servant his name, still less wait there till they came back. He was too exhausted to return to Madame Vernet's and in any case he could not have passed through the Maine gate again without Sarret's help.

So he trudged back to Montrouge and lay down under a hedge, shivering uncontrollably as the night descended. Under his short carmagnole jacket he had only his green-and-grey striped silk waistcoat, thin grey trousers and cotton stockings.

The next morning, Sunday, he returned to the Suards. They were still away.

He spent the day prowling in the woods, keeping well away from the string of villages along the plain. That night he slept in a disused quarry, gathering grass and bracken to soften his bed of stones.

The next morning at nine o'clock an alarmed servant rushed into Amélie Suard's room. 'There's a wild man with a beard just called. I've taken him in to monsieur.'

Madame Suard waited for what seemed like an age but in reality was no more than a few moments. Then her husband entered. There was a desperate look on his usually imperturbable face.

'Give me your keys, darling – the ones for the wine and the sideboard. I'll tell you everything later but stay here and don't move.'

It was less than half an hour later that Suard came back to her room. As he entered she could see through the open door a man going downstairs, a man with hunched shoulders and an air of the deepest dejection. As the man descended, he searched one pocket, then the other for something it seemed he could not find.

'That was Condorcet, my dear.'

'Is he going away?'

'Yes, he is going away now. It is better.'

'Yes.'

'I have asked him to come back after dark when Jacques has gone home. Then he can stay the night and we'll find somewhere safer for him.'

'Yes.'

'I'll go back to Paris and speak to Cabanis, perhaps he can get him a false passport. Please make sure that the door in the garden is opened for him. He has left his tobacco pouch behind.'

'Yes. I'll see to the garden door.'

Condorcet was desperately hungry. Suard had been so keen to get rid of him that he had had only a few moments to wolf down some bread and wine. By two o'clock in the afternoon he was famished. He had reached Clamart, a couple of miles from Fontenay. He saw an old inn sign at the crossroads. He did not resist.

'Yes, citizen?'

'I'd like an omelette. Could you make me an omelette?'

'Of course, citizen. How many eggs?'

'Oh.' He paused. How many eggs did one have in an omelette? 'A dozen.'

They were the last words he spoke as a free man.

A dishevelled customer with four days' growth of beard who thought you needed a dozen eggs to make an omelette for one person had to be an aristo on the run. And besides, the innkeeper happened to be the commander of the Clamart republican militia. Also present in the inn was the president of the local popular association, a fire-breathing troublemaker who spent most of his time in the pub working up accusations against citizens he had it in for.

They took no time at all to see through Condorcet's carefully prepared alias: Pierre Simon, native of Ribemont in the Aisne, fifty years old, valet de chambre. So why no papers, why no cockade? He was taken by the police to Bourg-la-Reine. They took him in a cart because he could no longer walk. He was put into a cell in the local lock-up still claiming to be Pierre Simon, valet de chambre, former soldier, residing at 505 rue de Lille (well known to be the residence of one Citizen Condorcet). They emptied his pockets, leaving him with enough cash to pay the turnkey for his board and lodging.

The next morning the said turnkey, Antoine Chevenu, found him in his cell stretched on the ground, face downwards, arms by his sides, stiff and dead.

There were two theories. That he had died of an apoplexy – there was blood coming out of his nostrils and his circulation was notoriously bad. Or he could have taken poison to cheat the executioner. A few months earlier Dr Cabanis had given several of his friends the poison which he called 'brother's bread'. It was a lethal mixture of opium and stramontium. History would remember this pioneer in the medicine of the soul mostly for the terminal remedies he gave his friends for the afflictions of the body.

On the other hand, the prisoner had been thoroughly searched. Where could he have secreted the little pillbox or phial? Condorcet was a clumsy man at the end of his tether, not likely to be adept at concealment.

Madame Vernet, who had trusted Condorcet so utterly before she had seen him or knew who he was, did not trust Madame Suard's version of events. The week after Condorcet had been found dead she took the trouble to go down to Fontenay. There she inspected the only door into the Suards' garden and found a pile of turf wedged against it so tightly that it could not be opened from the outside. The turf had not been disturbed for months.

IX

Downriver

They woke early when they slept at all. Madame d'Enville thought herself lucky if she had two or three hours a night. The high windows of their room had no curtains. The nuns had needed none, having to be up before dawn to say their office. The convent of the Filles-Anglaises was a shabby old building in a side street behind the Bastille. For centuries it had provided a refuge for English girls with a vocation that they could not pursue in their own country. The girls came mostly from Lancashire. One or two had gone home when the Bastille fell (they heard the firing and the shouts all day, and then the remorseless hammering for days afterwards), a few more when France declared war on England, but most of them stayed, unmoved as were most of their French sisters by the Constituent Assembly's decrees against nunneries. The monks by contrast unfrocked themselves in droves when the State seized their premises and no longer recognised their vows. Clairvaux and Cluny became lovely ghosts of their former selves. But the English girls went quietly about their business. 'Girls' was not really the word; by now most of them were middle-aged because the supply of novices had dried up. As they spoke English only to one another, they had kept their raw Lancashire accent, which Rosalie found difficult to follow, though she had determined to make the most of this enforced opportunity to perfect her English.

'Eh, thou looks a mite peakish today, ma'am,' Sister Gregory said as she plunged two bowls of soup and a plateful of crusty bread on their table. Sister Gregory had a brick-red face and a bony jaw with protruding upper teeth. She had been born Jenny Holroyd in a village high up in the Pennines where they had burnt witches until quite recently and which she had not been sorry to say goodbye to.

'Peakish, please, what is peakish?'

'Eh, sickly like.'

'I am quite well, thank you,' Madame d'Enville said.

Though the convent had been commandeered as a place of internment, its rules were tolerably relaxed. The irreproachable character of the nuns reassured even the zealots of the Committee of Public Safety. The gendarmes who came now and then to inspect the place were polite and even tactful by the rough standards of the moment, and outside visitors were not frowned on. Monsieur Patricot came up twice a week from La Roche-Guyon with cheese and eggs from the farm, fresh linen and lavender water, and books from the library. On Wm's instructions, Gouverneur Morris called in to make sure that they were all right. When they had been at liberty, Rosalie had boasted to Wm in her letters of how cold they had been to the man who had usurped his rightful place. But now they were prisoners and any voice from the outside world was welcome. Anyway, Gouverneur was charming, as he could be, especially to women, when the mood was on him.

'Well, it's not a bad place you have here, ladies, all things considered. And those gawky girls see to you properly, do they?'

'They are good creatures, though one cannot say they are elegant,' Madame d'Enville sighed.

'No, I dare say not. If they were, they wouldn't be in here.'

'No indeed.' Madame d'Enville smiled. As a child of the Enlightenment she had little more sympathy for the monastic ideal than the sceptical New Yorker, though of course she had always been meticulous in her acts of charity to the local convent at La Roche.

'That's a fine waistcoat you are knitting there,' said Gouverneur, gesturing at the dove-grey gilet that Rosalie was halfway through.

'I am so grateful to my grandmother for teaching me when I was a girl. It is such a soothing occupation when one's mind is overwhelmed with grief.'

'Or with revenge, madam. When I see those old hags clacking away beside the scaffold, I often wonder what they would do if their hands were not occupied with their knitting. Tear the prisoners limb from limb, I expect – but I am sorry, these are not thoughts fit for this company.'

'On the contrary, Mr Morris. We must confront the worst that men – and women too – are capable of or we shall be swept away.'

'I am glad to find you so dauntless, madam.'

'I do not feel in the least dauntless, but these simple women make one ashamed of one's fear. It cannot be easy for them in a foreign country, pressed into service as jailers, knowing that at any moment they may be massacred as so many of their sisters have been.'

'These are terrible times and I am conscious that I am a woefully inadequate substitute for Mr Short. It is a great pity that he should be called away so long at such a time. I can at least assure you that your loans to him are now set down in his name at the bank and I have power of attorney to draw on the funds whenever you wish. I only wish it were as easy to call back Mr Short as it will be to call on his bank balance.'

Rosalie felt Gouverneur's greedy eyes on her and did her best to look impervious.

How pale she was now, too pale for his tastes and too thin – his own fickle countess was an armful – but he could not deny she made a fine figure in her close-fitting widow's weeds with her head bent over her knitting. He began to feel comfortable in this plain whitewashed room with its few sticks of furniture and the bright light streaming down from the high window on the roughly carved wooden crucifix nailed to the wall. He almost felt envious of this plainness, this still and quiet existence, while he had to stump about Paris ten hours a day (and his stump had been painful of late, the doctor could not tell him why), watching the sullen crowds, listening to the rattle of the carts carrying the accused to and from the prisons – at times it seemed that half the public buildings in the city had been turned into prisons – struggling through interminable financial negotiations with jumped-up ministers who knew nothing about money and would scarcely last above a month or two in office before they too were chopped down, then snatching an hour of fretful pleasure with his Adelaide, who was not his at all, or not exclusively since she was trying out half a dozen other suitors and had even had her eye on Mr Short before he was packed off to Madrid. How appeasing to the spirit it would be to sit here a while with only a glass of wine for company and the charming—

'You are in a trance, monsieur. You must find our company very tedious after all the excitements of the moment,' said Madame d'Enville with a touch of her old spirit.

'I beg a thousand pardons, madam. The truth is that I have been bustling around the city too much and my wits are wandering. I have seen too many horrors, madam, though none to touch those you have endured. And there is one more horror to add to the list. Condorcet is dead. Dead by his own hand, according to some. Of an apoplexy, say others. At all events, he has cheated the guillotine, for Saint-Just had him outlawed and as soon as they picked him up, out in the country it was, near Bourg-la-Reine, he was a dead man.'

As he told the story, the two women listened so intently they might have been jurors listening to some crucial passage of evidence that would either hang the accused or set him free.

'Well,' said Madame d'Enville, 'I have lived long enough to know that there is no justice in this world, but there is revenge. I believe that Condorcet could have saved my son, I know that he could have saved my grandson. I cannot now pretend that I am sorry he could not save himself.'

There was no note of satisfaction in her voice. She might have been some official of the court deputed to read out a judgment written by others.

'I never thought much of the man,' Gouverneur said.

'I thought the world of him, as you know. That is my sin, which I must carry with me to my grave, which fortunately will not be long coming. It was my own folly to be seduced by his eloquence, his confidence that he and he alone could unlock the secrets of the universe. It was I who promoted him, persuaded my family to worship him and hang on his every word. I cannot forget Charles sitting by the fire at La Roche, he can't have been more than sixteen at the time, and listening open-eyed as Condorcet went on about some foolishness or other. How could I have been taken in by him, how could I have misconstrued his selfishness as idealism? Oh, I—'

'Maman, do not reproach yourself, he was very persuasive.'

'But I should have seen through him, and I thought I was so wise and enlightened, such a woman of the world.'

'Madam, it has been a duping age and it has come to a bad end. I must take my leave.'

All of a sudden he wanted to be out of the room. He was discomposed by the figure of the old Duchess, her frail body shaken with these convulsions of guilt but her face hard set with no suspicion of a tear. Rosalie rose to say goodbye. His hand brushed against the cold knitting needles she was carrying and he trembled as though the needles carried some electrical charge.

'Oh,' he said just as he was turning towards the door, his curiosity never entirely subdued by the most tragic circumstance, 'that bust you had, the one that Houdon did of him. I heard that you had your servants throw it on the dunghill.'

'That is a vulgar calumny, monsieur. I had them wrap it in straw and carry it up to the attic. It may be that the straw is the cause of your misconception. I would never treat any work of Monsieur Houdon's with less than the greatest respect.'

'No matter what the subject?'

'No matter what the subject.'

Shortly afterwards Mr Morris left Paris, under something of a cloud, and he never saw either of them again.

The unworldly Lancashire women who served as jailers felt no safer from the Commune's whim than the sophisticated ladies they were guarding in this strange prison. While the sisters said their office *mormorando*, as though fearful that their voices might percolate through the crumbling old walls and stir up the fury of the local collective, their prisoners, many of them elderly and shaky like Madame d'Enville, sat on the cheap wooden chairs that had been dragged out from the cells into the passage and strove to pick out the familiar words floating through the grille in the rough English accents: '*Ave Maria, gratia plena, ora pro nobis nunc et in hora mortis nostrae . . .*'

Other internees came and went, several of them old friends from their own milieu. Rosalie had been delighted to see the Malesherbes girls, Marguerite and Louise, who shared a cell further along the corridor. Each morning she would knock on their door bearing some delicacy that Monsieur Patricot had brought up and they would sit down on the truckle bed huddled together and share their sorrows and their fears.

But the morning came when Rosalie knocked on the low door of the girls' cell and Sister Gregory opened it with a folded blanket over her arm. 'They've been taken away, madame.'

'Oh, not—'

'No, the Committee of Public Safety is sending the lasses to be put together with their mother and their menfolk over at Port-Libre. So there's some little spark of decency left in these monsters after all. They'll be better off over there, they do say they hold concerts and dances.'

'Oh, that is good news.'

In Port-Libre (what a mockery of a name) the prisoners did indeed keep up a plucky imitation of their old life. The place was full of officials and financiers who had figured prominently in the old regime, including Lavoisier the great chemist and greater tax collector, together with their wives and children. In the evenings they listened to Vigée recite his latest verses and actors from the Comédie rehearse from memory favourite scenes from Racine and Molière. Those who preferred to remain in their cells could hear the melancholy dwellings of Witterbach's viola d'amore. The satisfactions of keeping up such stoic gaiety were enhanced when the latest batch of discredited revolutionaries were dragged in, whimpering and half sick with fear, knowing all too well what was in store since they had helped to draw up the rules. There were two dozen of the toughest Jacobins dumped there, shivering and shitting themselves before they were taken away to be shaved (the sort of slang they delighted in when it was their victims who were in the barber's chair).

But those who remained at Port-Libre enjoyed only a short reprieve. The tribunals made it a point of honour now to root out entire families with counter-revolutionary connections, as though the contagion might linger in and spread from the slightest drop of blood that was spared. The Malesherbes girls had a month or so together with their father and their husbands before the whole lot of them were carted off. They shared a tumbril with the Duchesse de Châtelet whom they had never much cared for, the Duchesse de Grammont who was fearfully grand, and the man who drew up the map of the new departments whose name they never quite caught (there was not much introducing in the carts and no chance to choose one's travelling companions).

'At least they all died together,' Madame d'Enville said.

'Well, Maman, it cannot be long now before our turn comes. Sister Gregory says there were five hundred and nine people executed during Prairial. I don't know how she knows the figures so exactly.'

'I am sure Condorcet devised some system for recording the numbers. Prairial indeed. No, it cannot be long now, my dear.'

Even the short summer nights were unendurable. Rosalie looked out at the deep blue night and thought of Condorcet lying low all winter only a few streets away. How strange to think of them both confined to a single room all that time, with nothing to do but recollect a past that was irreparably lost. And then him breaking out and stumbling down the street into the country, his gangling legs hobbling over the stony plain, utterly alone with only his mathematical visions to console him under the stars.

She dreamed of Wm too, but not of their fucking or even of their first passionate declarations of love. Sorrow had chastened her. All thought of desire or its fulfilment had been bleached from her mind. Only the quieter recollections came to her now – of Wm standing at the edge of the lake at Versailles, that slight fair figure, so neat beside the lanky figures of her husband and Mr Jefferson; William sitting beside her grandmother in the little salon reading Voltaire's *Zadig* in his pure French and pausing now and then to smile across at her; William in his canary vest tossing the hay into the stooks and singing some old Negro song that she did not understand.

In the long silences of the night and in the afternoon when her grandmother had gone to sleep, Rosalie sometimes fancied that the world had stopped, as though the burden of sorrow it was carrying was so great that it had simply ceased to spin.

Then, when she heard steps coming along the passage, she would sit up with a shudder. Sooner or later, probably sooner, those steps would be coming to tell her to get ready. It would be a consolation then to have her grandmother to look after. That might help her to make a brave end, though what use was a brave end? Her brother and her husband had been torn apart by savages without a moment's warning. Why should she wish for anything better? She thought that she ought to have a farewell letter to William prepared, but then she did not wish to leave anything for their executioners to spit on. Wm would know what she felt. She had told him often enough.

Sometimes she was angry and raged at the world's unkindness. At other times she felt weirdly removed, as though she were in a mesmeric trance, looking down at these terrible events from a great distance and wondering that God could allow them to happen, wondering if they had happened at all. At any moment Charles might come in from the terrace, stepping through the long windows, fanning himself with his peasant's straw hat and shouting, 'How do you keep so cool, Ro-Ro? I swear you must be sitting on a block of ice.' Or her husband would look up from his papers and smile over his spectacles: 'Ah, there you are, my dear, is Maman down yet?' And then she would lurch back into reality and the hard outline of despair that no daydream could dispel.

She was tired to the point of extinction. At first she could not understand this. What, after all, did she have to do all day except sit and knit and talk to her grandmother? Maman explained that it is only hope that refreshes us and gives us energy to continue life. Without hope they must reconcile themselves to a life in the shadows. 'We are ghosts, my darling, you and I, part of the living dead. There are whole regiments of us in France now. Perhaps there always were. We just never noticed when we ourselves were full of the joy of living. Now we can feel their presence everywhere.'

It was hot again. Even their cells, so cool from November to May, had become unbearable. Sister Gregory tried to open the windows with her long pole, but they had sealed them tight at the outbreak of the Revolution (after all, the Bastille was only three hundred yards away) and now the catches had rusted.

'Pouf, I am stifling.' Madame d'Enville sighed. 'Perhaps the heat will finish me off before the list reaches us.'

There was a clatter of steps outside, too loud and fast for one of the sisters. This must be the time. Rosalie's heart beat as fast as a trapped bird's.

But it was after all Sister Gregory who burst in, her red face dripping with sweat and her blue eyes shining with a watery gleam. 'Bloody heck, ma'am, pardon my language, but they've done him.'

'Who?'

'The little fellow, Robespierre. Chopped him this morning, though they say he were already half dead from having tried to top himself last night. All covered with blood he were before they put him on the plank.'

'There may be worse to come, all the same. Men who are capable of killing such a man must be even more desperate than he.'

'No, ma'am, there ain't no worse. Take my word for it, this be the end of it.'

Rosalie and her grandmother stared at Sister Gregory's gleaming face, her great red hands clasping and unclasping in her delight. And somehow they believed her.

It took several months from that day in Thermidor, to the beginning of Brumaire in their case, before the authorities felt confident enough to release the more harmless prisoners. Even then Rosalie and her grandmother were ordered to stay at La Roche and not to wander about the country, which they had not the least wish to do. They were thankful to see the Seine again and the chateau rising out of the mist and half the village standing at the gate to welcome them – and in turn to receive their thanks for the petition the commune had sent to Paris which had hastened their release.

The second day after they had come home she wrote to Wm who was still bowed down by business in Aranjuez:

My dear and tender friend, the length of our separation distresses me beyond words, I see no end to it. Misfortune seems to weigh down my sad days. After having lost almost all my family, most of them by the assassin's blade, having endured ten and a half months of captivity and seen my companions in misfortune taken from me and a hundred times expected the same fate myself, my courage was sustained by the feelings that united us, by the certainty of your love, by the hope that heaven would bring together two hearts to love one another. The memory of you was my only strength, the picture of you and the hope of seeing you again my only consolations.

When I was set free, I experienced the joy which is natural on the return of something so necessary to existence, but after those first moments of pleasure in seeing the people and places I thought I would never see again, I felt once more the emptiness that your absence causes me. I write you this letter out of my need to think about you and talk to you, though I have no idea if it will ever reach you. Dreams are my only comfort now that reality has nothing more to offer me.

I kept all your letters – they were my most precious possession – but they were then burnt, not by me, at a moment when this seemed necessary. I only discovered this some time afterwards and I was deeply pained to discover it. I have now only the last one that I received in prison and two others that reached me before I was arrested. I have carefully preserved some books you gave me – the works of Pope in very small print and Lyttleton's History of England. *For the past two years I have never failed to wear the little gold ring in links (the one you had our two initials engraved on). It is very dear to me, for it always recalls our love and the happier days when you gave it to me. I have also the lock of your hair, which I cut off when I gave you mine just before you left for Holland.*

Take care of yourself [here for the first time in all the years they have been writing to one another, she *tutoyers* him], *keep your heart safe for me, it is my only treasure, you gave it to me and you will never regret it. My darling, I am not unhappy, since you love me and since neither time nor distance can destroy these feelings.*

All the places in the countryside here where you showed those feelings to me are dearer than anywhere else in the world. I seek them out and they mean more to me than I can tell you. That meadow where I received the first overtures of your heart, the hillside where you renewed them the next day, the embarrassment and perplexity they caused me, although I now think that those reactions were already the beginnings of love, to judge by the pleasure I now take in recalling them.

And do you think that I have forgotten that day when we were sitting together by the pond in the garden in Paris and you suddenly got up to go and carve our initials on the bark of a tree without telling me what you were doing and you begged me not to come nearer until you had finished? And when I was allowed to look at your work, the only way I could express what I felt was to press my lips on the initials and you did the same.

For almost two years the heartless fate which is opposed to our happiness has kept us apart. Neither fear nor even the threat of impending death ever made me forget you. On the contrary, the shadow of death inspired me with a desire to die worthy of you. In the end heaven has ordered things differently, but in snatching me from death, has it done so only to leave me to drag out a miserable existence far from everything I love? No, I prefer to believe that life was not restored to me in vain. This is the second time I have escaped death when I thought it inevitable. It is the will of providence that I shall find my beloved again and that his tenderness will comfort me in my sorrows. At any rate I cannot stop hoping for this and surrendering myself to such sweet delusions, which will perhaps not be delusions for ever.

She had never before written him so long a letter, nor one that moved him so much. And it came to him at the worst time in his life, at least that was how he thought of it. Before he read more than the first page, he had to sit down in the wicker chair in his glassed-in loggia to recover his calm. And when he had finished reading and looked out at the dry bony mountains beyond the plains of Castile, he found that his eyes were watering.

Only two days earlier the worst of the rumours had been confirmed. He was not to return to Paris and nor (vainest of vain hopes) was Mr Jefferson. James Monroe, his fellow alumnus from Virginia, was to replace Gouverneur. That he already had wind of, and that was bad enough. But he was not even to stay in Madrid. The Queen's favourite, that sly army officer, Manuel Godoy, had complained to General Washington of him. Senor Short lacked the stature, the circumspection to negotiate with the Spanish court on so ticklish a matter as navigation rights on the Mississippi and the southern boundary of the United States. A plenipotentiary of greater weight was required. Wm had already had it out with the slimy Godoy, who of course denied that he had made any such complaint. But the damage was done and Mr Pinckney in London was already packing his bags for Madrid.

Wm fired off letters to all and sundry, even to TJ with whom he had become virtually incommunicado. Washington's treatment of him would embitter and perplex him for the rest of his life, he said; he would of course resign from the public service since his own services were so little appreciated. It was small comfort to him that he had been proved right in everything he touched. He had forecast the terrible course that events would take in France, he had faced down the Dutch bankers and secured the finances of the US for years to come, and as for the Spanish-American treaty that Mr Pinckney was to have the glory of signing, that would be pretty much on the terms that he had already mapped out. But none of this counted in the eyes of muddle-headed presidents and secretaries of state and a braying Congress. To them William Short was dispensable, little better than a dead man walking.

When he had finished writing, he saddled his diminutive Spanish mare (more like a mule than a horse) and rode out into the stony pampas behind his lodging. There was a biting wind off the mountains and it was bitter cold despite the clear sky. The wind kept his eyes watering but his self-pity was changing into defiance. Crawling for office was no way for a man to live. Godoy was a miserable creature, more to be pitied than envied. You could detect his shifts and shuffles a mile off. Wm would do his duty and guide Pinckney in the right direction. Then he would be off, to live the life of a free man, which was above all to love and be loved.

They would marry, perhaps not immediately. There was still Madame d'Enville to be thought of. But they would marry and sail to America and make a home in Virginia. They would build their own Philadelphia where there would be no slaves but only free men employed. Who knew, perhaps his example might persuade Mr Jefferson to free his slaves at Monticello and so the movement for liberation would spread throughout Virginia until even the dullest Tidewater squire followed the fashion. As he trotted through the bushes at the edge of the plain, he caught the faint winter scent of thyme and sage and began to dream of Rosalie weeding in their potager beside the banks of the James river and of the little pavilion on the hill above the swamp oaks which he would design himself and where they would take coffee – it would be on the lines of Madame du Barry's tea house at Louveciennes but smaller (even in his daydreams he could not shake off his American suspicion of grandeur). And perhaps if his neighbours approached him, he might consent to run for the Senate in the room of Mr Lee, or perhaps for Governor – how Rosalie would grace the Governor's mansion with her irresistible French accent and her elegant French style. Or if not, then so be it. He was content to let his achievements speak for him, while he felt the wind on his cheek and thought of her just as he knew she had never ceased to think of him.

*

So when Pinckney arrived at Madrid (taking his time about it), Wm was able to greet him without any show of rancour and stand at his elbow, just as President Washington had asked him.

'You're not sorry, then?'

'Sorry?'

'To be leaving the foreign service.'

'I was never happier in my life.'

Pinckney was startled by Wm's vehemence, but he was telling the truth, for this was surely a godsent opportunity to carry out the greatest mission of all, which was to live for love, sincerely and without simulation or artifice just as Rousseau had prescribed, to live as no other generation of humanity had lived, finding the truest satisfaction in the eyes of the Other. For the troubadours of old Provence love had been only a game, for the Christians (and William was pretty sure he was not a Christian) it had been a confused emotion to be poured out upon a Being who was at best indifferent and probably did not exist at all, in short to waste your energies upon a delusion. But to love Rosalie as he did, that was the least delusive vocation in the world, it was the passport to the ultimate reality, for everything he loved in her was real, not just her mischief-brimming black eyes, her white apple-breasts and her soft thighs grinding against him, but also her deep unshakeable affections, the sharpness of her wit, her quick apprehension of danger, her surprising perseverance, her tenacious hold on life, even when or perhaps precisely when she said that her sorrows had ended all possibility of hope. And her faults, these were real too and he loved them just as much, not only because she owned up to them so sweetly but because they made him so aware of the blood coursing in her veins: her quick temper like her brother Charles's, her flashes of childish snobbery, her refusal to forgive.

My God! How delighted I was to hear news of you from Paris this morning. I could not believe that you could be so close to us. Come and see us as soon as you can. Maman will be overjoyed to see you. What pleasure I shall have, how many things I shall have to tell you that have piled up since you left us. Three years gone, and what years! It could be as many centuries.

Three years they had been apart and in the two years before that, when their affair had burst into flame, they had snatched only a week here and there together and always in conditions that demanded concealment, and were flushed with embarrassment and guilt. Even that final fortnight at Christmas three years earlier when they were first free to sleep together she had been in mourning – he remembered the slither of the crêpe as he unhooked her skirt.

'You will find Maman sadly downed,' she said to him after they had kissed out of sight of the coachman unloading the bags.

He dreaded to find those bright old eyes dim and unseeing. Perhaps she would not even recognise him. But Madame d'Enville held out her arms as though welcoming a child that had only just learnt to walk. 'Ah, Monsieur Short, it is an eternity since we have seen you.'

It was only later on, when they had drawn the heavy brocade curtains, so frayed and dusty now, that she began to wander a little. 'Is Monsieur Jefferson coming? Have you brought him with you?'

'Maman, Monsieur Jefferson is in America.'

'So he is, I forget. I have written to him, you know, to tell him that you must be the next minister.'

'That is very kind of you, madame.'

'But I do not think he has answered yet. Rosalie, have we had a reply from Monsieur Jefferson?'

'Not yet, Maman.'

'My son must write to him too. Monsieur Jefferson thinks very highly of him, does he not, Monsieur Short?'

'I cannot think of anyone in France he esteems more highly.'

And so this evening passed by the fire, as other evenings were to pass, in the exchange of soft half-truths and consoling glances. Madame d'Enville liked to take both their hands and hold them in a surprisingly firm grip, as though she were a priest joining them in marriage.

In the mornings her mind's grip too would be surprisingly firm. 'I talked a great deal of nonsense last night, I fear. Rosalie, you must tell me when I am talking nonsense or I shall become insufferable.'

'On the contrary, madame, you are becoming more lovable by the day.'

'William, you are much too flirtatious for an American. I suspect your mother must have been Italian.'

When the old Duchess called him by his first name, a curious sensation overcame him, which he could not quite analyse: affection for the old lady certainly, but it was also a kind of awkwardness, even shamefacedness, as though she were welcoming him into an intimacy to which he had no right. She knew what they were about, he was certain of that, had known it perhaps before they were quite sure of it themselves, might even have assumed they were making love upstairs when in fact they were still shyly sounding out each other's feelings. She came, after all, from a generation that took such arrangements for granted. Yet he wondered whether she might be less tolerant if she knew how deep and all-consuming their love was, how they now lived only for each other. Perhaps that was the one thing that might shock her. The Duke was, after all, her son.

Wm's uncertainty, his awkwardness, did not entirely disappear when he and Rosalie were alone together. And she noticed how hesitant he was.

'I do not want you to be gentle; that might show that you love me less. When we were let out of prison, it is true that I was almost as fragile as Maman. I could not think of such things, it was as though being in a convent so long had turned me into a nun. For a time my monthlies stopped and I was nervous even to touch my own body, but I have had a year's convalescence and now – yes, like that, oh yes.'

He waited a day, then another day, and even then he was hesitant to ask. 'You will say it is too soon, I am sure you will, but you know what I wish to ask you.'

'It is not too early for you to ask, your asking gives me more pleasure than you can dream of, but it is too early for me to answer. You have seen the state Maman is in and I must tell you that she makes a great effort in front of you. When we are alone together her condition is much worse.'

'Is it then – this I certainly have no right to ask – but is it the case that she will always, I do not say come between us because you know how fond of her I am, but will she always postpone your answering?'

'You must assume so, I am afraid.'

'But one day you will come back to America with me?'

'Yes. I will,' she said.

'And seeing how respectable we Americans are, you know what that would mean?'

'I do and that would be the best of all possible reasons for crossing the Atlantic, but you must not try to trap me into giving an answer which it is not now in my power to give, even for the dearest of motives.'

Sometimes, when he fucked her in the afternoon, she cried out like an animal in pain and he felt that they had gone back in time so far they were scarcely human. Then at night when he crept into her bed from his cold bachelor quarters down the passage, they made love like an old married couple, like two stately ships rocking at anchor.

'As soon as I receive my official letters of recall, you know I must go to America and repair my fortune.'

'Oh, I am sure you can repair it here,' she said, lazily playing with him. 'Look, it is repaired already.'

The letters came. After eleven years of public service he was officially a private citizen again. She was sitting in her arbour on the little island, bent over a book. He could see the pale blob of her straw hat through the rambling roses that had now swamped the pergola. He remembered seeing the workmen hammering the stripped logs together to construct it ten years ago, on his first visit.

She heard the click of the gate and got up to come and greet him, ducking her head under the bosomy roses.

'I am a free man at last,' he said, waving Mr Jay's letter.

'Free? Not free of me, I hope,' she said, laughing because he was laughing, but not hiding the apprehension that flooded up inside her.

'No, on the contrary, we are free to follow our own fancy together. Never again will I be dispatched at my master's whim to fry in Madrid or freeze at The Hague.'

'That is wonderful,' she said dully.

He saw how upset she was and cursed himself for having run down to the arbour like a child who cannot wait to show off a new toy. He should have waited, pondered the matter and explained to Rosalie what he had in mind. But then that ought to be the glory of their new life, that there need be no pondering in it. So he kissed her neck, or rather the dear little nook just inside the collarbone that she told him the French called *la salière*, the salt cellar, and he said they called it that too in English. Then he murmured some foolishness about Rosalie among the roses and she slid her warm hand inside his shirt and caressed him, very tenderly as though he had a bruise there that needed massaging.

'So,' she said, 'you are going to go away. That is what you intend, isn't it?'

'I only wish to be with you, to live with you, for us to be married – I know you told me not to say that word but I cannot help it because it is the only thing I really want in the world.'

'But in America, only in America, that is what you really want. You must surely love me enough to tell me the truth.'

'You said once, no, more than once, that you longed to go with me to my own country.'

'Oh, and I meant it, Will, you cannot imagine how sincerely I meant it. All the time I was learning those strange English pronunciations, how "cough" and "through" end the same way but you say them so differently, all the time I was dreaming of you and me over there, how we would plant the vines below that oak tree you told me about, a whole new life together. But you must see that it cannot begin now. We have only just started to recover from our horrors. No, recover is not the word, we cannot recover, certainly Maman cannot, we are barely alive, she and I, but I have you to revive me. If I lose you now, I shall sink into the shadows, it will be the end of me.'

'You will never lose me. Have I loved you so feebly that you cannot be sure of that? But I have to go back to America, only for a little time and then I will return and we can plan the rest of our life together.'

'But you have only just come back to me. I cannot endure another separation. You would be away for months and months, six months at the very least and then the double sea voyages and you are such a bad sailor.'

'Rosalie, I am desperate to settle my affairs. My brother Peyton is off to buy half of Kentucky with our share of father's estate. Colonel Skipwith is snapping up military warrants as fast as Peyton is accumulating western land certificates. Neither of them has the first idea what he is doing and they may very well find themselves saddled with reams of worthless paper. Mr Jefferson who has charge of the income from my investments in Virginia has put nine thousand dollars of my money into his nail factory at Monticello and his flour mill at Milton, and even if any profits ever come out of either, I doubt if Mr J has the nous to keep separate accounts of our dealings. Last year he bought on my behalf for four thousand seven hundred dollars thirteen hundred acres of Albemarle County, at a place called Indian Camp next to Mr Monroe's, and I have not had a penny out of it though he declares the land is good and I can expect to double my money if I should sell. I cannot presume for ever on Mr Jefferson's kindness in looking after my funds, even if I were convinced of his acumen in such matters, which alas I am not. Then I have just entered into partnership with the Willinks and old Van Staphorst to buy a large tract of western New York that belonged to Mr Robert Morris before he went bankrupt despite Gouverneur slaving for him on his tobacco interests though they were no kin. The Dutchmen have taken upwards of a thousand square miles, reaching from Lake Erie to the Genesee river. I have eleven thousand dollars' worth of the syndicate and they have invited me to stand as their agent, since they must have an American figurehead if they are to secure their rights. So you see, I cannot hope to manage all these ticklish matters at a distance of three thousand miles.'

He stopped for breath and was suddenly overtaken by embarrassment and did not know how to go on.

Rosalie froze too. The little hand which was still nestling inside his shirt turned to marble. She withdrew it. 'You certainly have a large number of interests, William, I had not known you possessed so many.'

'When I was in Spain, I filled the desolate hours with a great quantity of business correspondence,' he said lamely.

'These are the concerns closest to your heart, I can see that. Maman and I cannot expect to occupy more than a small corner of your attention. It was foolish of me to imagine anything other. I shall always be grateful to you for preserving my fortune. Will it be safe for me to have the money placed back in my own name quite soon, do you think?'

'Quite soon, I hope, if the Directory can find enough troops to maintain law and order, which they say they can. But you are welcome to leave the money in my name as long as you wish.'

'I remember Lafayette saying to my husband once that the Americans were only interested in business. They may pretend to care for love or art or politics, they may have such exquisite manners as to put ours to shame, but really they are truly happy only in the counting house. My husband protested that such was not his experience, but for once Monsieur de Lafayette was the more perceptive, I think.'

'Rosalie, you must forgive me, I was overexcited by the news of my official release, or I would not have run on so.'

'On the contrary, monsieur, I am grateful to you for disclosing to me the true priorities of your heart. I must go and attend to Maman, she will be down by now and she needs me to help with her medicines, she gets so confused.'

Rosalie got up from the rustic wooden seat they had been sitting on (he remembered the woodmen sawing and hammering that too) and left him. There was a dignity in her walk that he could not help admiring.

And yet, he thought as he sat down again, what right did she have to be so high and mighty? If some of her family had shown a little enterprise they might have been able to feed their people better and would not have come to such bad ends themselves. America was going to be a country, damn it, was a great country already, the greatest the world had yet seen, even if they did have to borrow from the Dutch at four and a half per cent, and the reason America was so great was because Americans believed in tomorrow and were ready to back it with their own money. He had never been west of the Genesee himself, but he was prepared to make a wager on a tract of land he had never seen. That was an act of faith and though he was no sort of religious man himself (he went along with TJ in thinking that the teaching of Jesus had been encumbered with a whole bunch of superstitious fabrications), he believed that without faith, rational faith, *homo sapiens* would never amount to much. If Rosalie was going to take that kind of attitude, he was not so sure that she would transplant to the other side of the Atlantic.

He walked across the island and glared into the river as though this gentle backwater had done him a personal injury. The sun was beating on the water. The dragonflies were hovering over its shimmering surface looking like they might expire at any minute. William felt the sweat trickling down his neck. His anger had set his blood pumping.

He took off his shoes and stockings and paddled in the muddy shallows. The water was deliciously cool. He waded back to the shore, stripped naked and ran splashing back into the water, ducking his head beneath the surface with a gasp of pleasure. He swam a couple of strokes but then let the current carry him round into the dappled pool. With a modest effort he could float there without being carried downstream and so he lay lazily kicking his feet against the current when he needed to and watching his cock and bush twirling like pondweed in the bright water.

How ridiculous that he should be so het up – he was as absurd as she was, as all men and women were when they took themselves too seriously. One should love them all, just because they were so absurd, that was the thing to understand.

'Willi*am*!'

He turned in the water to see a frantic little figure wading out towards him, holding up her skirts as she splashed through the shallows. He rose in naked majesty and went towards her.

'Oh, thank, thank heaven,' she panted. 'When I saw your clothes, I thought, oh, the worst.'

'You didn't.' He could not help laughing.

'And then when I saw you floating, I thought you were already—'

He hugged her to his bare body. A shower of drops fell over her muslin dress and he was carried back to the days of their innocence – the canoeing and the boy who had nearly been carried over the weir and Rosalie running everywhere. He realised that it would be madness to leave her now. She was right, they had earned a respite from the brutal rush of history. Against all the odds she had been reprieved. He must help her to make the most of it.

For the rest of that year he did not write a line to his bankers, nor to Mr Jefferson. At Christmas Jan Willink wrote discreetly enquiring after his health. Wm did not bother to reply. He had taken new lodgings in Paris, at 8 rue de Matignon, but he scarcely used them.

Much of the time they lay by the log fire at La Roche (he cut the logs and brought them in himself) and read the *Arabian Nights* in French or made idle conversation of that meandering kind that they could hardly remember which of them was talking or what they were talking about.

'We have turned into vegetables.'

'The only question is whether to be a carrot or a cabbage.'

'A carrot, I think, one of those white carrots with delicate fronds that only grow in France.'

'You or me?'

'Both of us. A fine matched pair, we shall win prizes at the Liancourt show.'

In English he recited,

> *'My vegetable love should grow*
> *Vaster than empires and more slow.'*

'Did you invent that ?'

'No, it was an old poet called Marvell – Merveille to you.'

'You are my Monsieur Marvell.'

'Even if I do think of nothing but money?'

'Money and me – what else is there to think about?'

The second week in January it snowed for three days. He found some planks in the sawmill and knocked them together into a rough sleigh. Beyond the chateau there was a meadow that sloped down to the river at a tolerable angle and they tobogganed down it through the hissing snow, throwing themselves off before they hit the hawthorn hedge at the bottom. He had never seen her cheeks so pink. Perhaps she would do in America after all.

The fancy revived in her too and in her pale leather drawing book she began to sketch her idea of the house they would build together. 'Mr Jefferson will be green with jealousy. It will be twice the size of Monticello.'

'In that case I will abolish the stable wing. I should not like to upset Mr Jefferson.'

But then the thaw came and the restlessness began again. In March there was a letter from Peyton and another letter from the Willinks. If he did not return to the United States soon he would lose everything – the land titles, the agency beyond the Genesee, any hope of a political career. If he dawdled in France any longer he would not simply be a forgotten man, he would be a bankrupt.

Without letting slip a word to Rosalie he began to make preparations. He instructed the Willinks to switch his Paris investments to their

American agent. He wrote (swallowing hard) to tell Mr Jefferson that he would be setting sail for Virginia in May. He booked his berth on the *Siren* and even paid his passage money in advance to cement his intention. Then he told her.

'It will only be for a short time. Think of the separations we have already endured when I was in Holland and Spain. We came through those and our love was stronger than ever.'

'That is why I cannot endure another. When you threatened to go after you were released from your foreign service I nearly died, do you not remember? I could not go through another such agony.'

'Listen, my darling. I shall only be three days in New York at the most, then a brief visit with Willinks' man to view the Lake Erie tract, let us say no more than a week. Then I shall go straight across country to Virginia – another week, perhaps less. I trust that Peyton and TJ will have the papers ready and we should have finished our business in one week more. Then there will be a choice of boats from Norfolk. At worst I shall be a month in America, well, perhaps six weeks. If I am not back by Christmas, you may burn my effigy at the stake.'

But she was sobbing too violently to listen to his calculations. For several days her frenzy prevented any conversation between them. She raged through the little kneehole desk she had allotted him, hoping to find and destroy the receipt for the passage money, thinking that then they would not let him on board. But he kept the receipt safe in his wallet to remind him of his resolve, which was not nearly as strong as he pretended. For they were glorious, these early spring days at La Roche-Guyon and his eyes grew misty at the thought that he would not this year see the pale green corn turn to tawny gold and ripple across the chalky fields. When she was calmer, though no more reconciled to his going, they wandered side by side along the hedges where the hawthorn blossom had already grown dusty and the first scarlet poppies were showing through the grass. She held his hand very tight as though she feared he might make a run for it that very minute across the field and jump into a waiting carriage.

'The corsairs will have you, I know they will. The *Mercure* says they have never been so bad as they are this year.'

'They will not attack an American boat.'

'You cannot know that. I am sure they are too savage to know the difference. And the ice, it is floating further south than ever, Madame d'Astorg told me yesterday. I am sure you will hit an ice mountain.'

'Rosalie, there is more danger of the coach overturning on the road to Rouen than of running into an iceberg.'

At night she made love to him with a passion that seemed unappeasable, as though she were doing it for the last time on earth. In the morning he was so sore he could hardly move.

Even as he was halfway into the coach she still clung to him. 'I cannot bear it, you know I cannot. I shall never see you again. Even if you come back, I shall be dead.'

But that was not what happened.

She had delayed him at La Roche a day longer than he meant to remain and then there had been confusion over the change of horses at Rouen, so that he had less than two hours to spare when he finally reached Le Havre. He had not much luggage since he planned to return so soon. Even so he was fretting to get it all aboard before the *Siren* weighed anchor. So he was curt to the man who pulled at his sleeve and stammered, 'Monsieur Short, beg pardon, sir.'

'Yes, yes, what is it, can't you see I am trying to get aboard before the confounded ship sails?'

'Sir, sir, I am s-sorry.' The man was filthy dusty from the road and so out of breath he could hardly utter. 'But I have a message from Madame la Duchesse. She is dead, sir, that is what I am to tell you.'

Wm stared in amazement and horror. What was this nonsense? How could she – but perhaps the message was meant to say that she was going to take her own life. Was there no end to her play-acting?

'The old lady, sir,' the breathless messenger wheezed, 'she went on Sunday, very sudden, it was a proper shock though she were so old.'

'Madame d'Enville is dead?'

'Yes, sir, and madame says you're to please come back home, because she can't carry on by herself. She would have written a note but there weren't time.'

'Madame d'Enville is dead and I am to go back,' Wm repeated in a trance-like way, as if repeating instructions from Dr Mesmer.

'Yes, please, sir, I know madame will be ever so happy if you oblige.'

He recognised the man now. It was Pierre, one of the wagon men who had brought Rosalie's canoe on the cart that very first day. Not the sort of fellow you would normally send off on a breakneck ride across country to deliver a crucial message with his slow speech and his sleepy grin. But there he was at the bottom of the gangway, clutching his dusty cap in his big red hands, looking as though his own fate as well as his mistress's depended on William's answer.

He did not hesitate.

Madame d'Enville had been eighty-one years old. She had survived the deaths of her son and her grandson but her heart and lungs had been failing before those two blows within a month of each other broke her spirit. Every winter they had wondered whether she would get through the pneumonia that always gripped her. In the summer heat her palpitations kept her to her room, except for a short walk along the terrace in the early evening. There was nothing less surprising than her death and it came peacefully enough in the early hours of a Sunday morning, just before the bell began to ring for Mass (another sign of the new relaxations). She felt no need to cling to life any longer and had said so at regular intervals.

To Rosalie the death of Maman was the end of her close family. The rest were all dead or scattered far away. None of them had lived with her through the worst times. As grandmother and mother-in-law combined, Madame d'Enville had been more of a mother, and for much longer, than her actual mother.

He knew he must wait. Even as he urged his weary horse over the hills of Bray, he knew that the urgency was all on his side. She was tired, not simply from shock and grief and from the long months of caring for her grandmother, smoothing over the times when she repeated herself or lost her bearings in the conversation and, most difficult of all, trying to keep amused an old lady who had always been impatient and had counted on the best minds in France to divert her.

'I am here and I love you, that is all I have to say. Tell me what to do, think of me as your factotum, your Figaro. I won't ask anything more.'

'As long as you promise not to sing. That would be, what do you call it, "the last straw",' she finished in English.

He treated her as an invalid, as though she had simply replaced Maman as the centre of all their concerns. When she felt a little better he drove her in the cabriole down the sandy track by the river. He never allowed the horse to get out of a walk, so they had time to watch the ducks diving and the moorhens lead their broods through the overhanging willow branches. She had taken over the old green straw hat that Maman used to wear in the summer. He could scarcely see her face under its droopy brim. And he remembered how he had adopted his father's battered old farmer's felt hat after his father died. There was some primitive comfort to be had from putting on something that belonged to the person you were mourning.

'We must go away,' she said suddenly. 'I must break the chain of memories.'

'We could go to your house in the Auvergne, I should love to see it. I remember Lafayette telling me that it was the most beautiful part of France but perhaps he was biased because that was where he came from.'

'No, no, he was right. There is nowhere like the country round Verteuil, but that has many sad memories too. No, I think we should go to Vichy.'

'But I thought you hated spas and after all it was at Forges-les-Eaux—'

'Forges was a wretched place but Vichy is different. I remember as a child my parents taking me there after I had nearly died from the whooping cough.'

He did not care for the idea, but it was his firm conviction that she should be contradicted in nothing until she was well again, well enough, that is, to say 'yes'.

They had not reserved lodgings in advance. The best they could find was a miserable second-floor set in a gloomy house at the edge of the old town where the carriages turned to go on to the thermal springs. There was a gaming house in the woods beyond the springs and the local blades were in the habit of going on there after the assembly rooms closed and not coming back until two or three o'clock in the morning. Wm was always a bad sleeper and it was just at the moment when he was finally dozing off that the carriages would return to the town, creaking and rumbling at the sharp corner and the tipsy gallants and their women whooping with pretended panic at the lurching.

Then he would lie awake staring at the blotches of damp on the cheap wallpaper, a pattern of pink shepherds and shepherdesses capering endlessly across a scrubby arcadia. Beside him he could hear Rosalie's gentle breathing. He imagined her flushed and frightened with the whooping cough and her parents hanging over her in a rented bedroom like this. She had grown thinner since being imprisoned and somehow this made her look younger still, like one of those pale serious little girls he had seen in their white dresses outside the church waiting for their first Communion.

In the morning they trudged along beside the shallow scummy river, following the other patients towards the springs.

'Do we look as bad-tempered as that?' said Wm, pointing to a crapulous man of about seventy who was bursting out of his clothes and looked scarcely on speaking terms with his vinegary wife whose nose was screwed up in disdain as though she could already inhale the bad-eggs smell of the springs.

'Worse, I should think. Oh, look, there's Madame de Maupertuis.'

'Will you allow me a moment to jump in the river and drown myself?'

'You must say good morning to her first and then she can tell everyone that she was the last person you spoke to before the tragic event. You know how she loves to be part of a drama.'

'Oh God, and there's the man with the terrible warts, the Comte de something.'

'Durance,' Rosalie prompted him. 'He told me with pride that his doctor said he was the most bilious patient he had ever examined. He's been coming here for years.'

'Does any of them ever get better?' William sighed as he surveyed the sickly yellow and purple complexions of the visitors moving slowly towards the little pavilions that housed the springs.

'Ah, and there is Madame de Durance. I had heard she was bedridden, with a palsy I think, though she said it was some disease I had never heard of and certainly could not spell.'

'In Virginia we would call this swampland and only the slaves would live there, which is why they all catch the fever.'

A light rain began to fall, more like mist. The green hills surrounding the spa seemed to close in on them.

Madame de Maupertuis did not say good morning to them but bowed in a distant fashion.

'Do you think she disapproves of us?'

'I hope so,' Wm said.

'Couldn't we tell her that we are living together as man and wife?'

'Is that what we are doing?' he enquired.

'Well, man and would-be wife.'

'But I haven't even asked you, at least not since I came back from Le Havre.'

'I thought the last time you asked still counted, like a passport that is valid for several journeys. Was I wrong?'

He did not answer but hugged her and whirled her round like a Russian dancer. Out of the corner of his eye he could see Madame de Maupertuis staring at them.

The rain was heavier now and their faces were wet with tears as well as rain.

'Why should we cry when we are so happy?'

'Rousseau says somewhere that all profound feelings express themselves in tears.'

'I don't care what Rousseau says.'

'You will come to America with me then?'

'Of course I will but not yet, there is so much to settle, we must not run before we have learnt to walk.'

He did not press the question. It was enough to have asked it and for her to have said 'yes'. More than enough, he thought, as he whirled her round again, his hands slipping on the wet silk of her dress. A gaggle of visitors with their umbrellas up had to step aside from the path to get past them.

'Look,' Rosalie said, 'we have made them smile.'

'We must plant a tree to mark the event.'

Standing there, out of breath with his arm round her waist, he thought he had never been so happy. The steamy green hills that had seemed so oppressive only a few minutes earlier were now an enveloping blur of bliss. The visitors carrying their personal silver-gilt cups to the springs were like a procession of the blessed in a medieval painting.

All the same, he could not wait for ever, not now that he had her answer.

'This letter from Peyton says that I am sure to be made bankrupt if I do not return. I know he is inclined to take fright easily, my poor brother, but even so—'

He did not need to remind her how he had rescued her from the same fate by guarding her fortune through the Terror, nor how many of her friends had not been so lucky and were now skimping miserable existences in places like this or in seaside lodgings in England or Belgium.

'It will only be for a short time now,' he said. 'I shall be back by the spring.'

She nodded without speaking.

'Elbridge Gerry is travelling home on the same boat,' he said. 'He is a fine fellow and he will repair the gaps in my knowledge of American affairs.'

'I can see you are looking forward to the voyage already and you used to be so frightened of the sea.'

'Well, it has to be done,' he said lamely.

He secretly thought that in the end she might decide to come with him. Perhaps they could marry on board. A ship's master was licensed to perform the ceremony.

But as the day of his leaving grew closer he could see that she had no such intention, so he didn't mention it.

They said goodbye in her little house in the rue Faubourg-Saint-Honoré (she had sold the great hotel in the rue de Seine three years earlier, just after the Terror had ended).

'The sooner you go, the sooner you'll be back. That is what I keep saying to myself, but I don't really believe it.'

'Well, it's true,' he said.

'I won't be able to endure it, you know.'

'You have endured separations much longer than this.'

'But I was younger then,' she said. 'I had friends and family. Now I have no one but you.'

'You have hundreds of friends who would be only too glad to keep you company at La Roche.'

'Oh, I shan't go to La Roche, I should die in a week rattling around there. I'll go to Acosta, to Adelaide's. It's close enough to home and they are always so kind.'

'You will be in good hands there, the best in fact.'

He thought with affectionate recollection of that long low chateau a few miles down the Seine from La Roche-Guyon, where Rosalie's cousin Adelaide de Castellane had so often entertained them. In his mind he could feel the boards of the long gallery under his bare feet as he crept from his room in one of the pavilions to hers in the main block, and he remembered the mist from the river curling in through the open window and cooling their naked limbs. And in the morning he would listen with that sweet drained feeling throughout his body while his host discoursed on freedom of religion, a subject on which he had made quite a name for himself in the Assembly, and little Boni de Castellane crawled in and out of the table legs, unreproved by his father who was a fervent follower of Rousseau's educational methods. During the Terror Monsieur de Castellane had lived quietly among his tenantry but Robespierre had not forgotten him and the day before the Ninth of Thermidor had him thrown into the Conciergerie. But it was Robespierre who finished up on the scaffold while the amiable and popular Castellane was released a few weeks later, like Rosalie and Maman, after an appeal from the local commune. Yes, Rosalie would be looked after well at Acosta.

He slipped off early the next morning while she was still asleep to his apartment in the rue Matignon where he had his bags packed. He left a short note behind. Her reply was waiting for him when he broke his journey at Rouen.

Paris, 9 a.m., 9 Thermidor

After a restless night, my dear sweet friend, I have just woken up to find your tender note. As I was waking I thought I held you in my arms for a minute but alas it is only your thoughts that surround me. I foresaw last night that our sad farewells would not be renewed this morning. I did not insist on it, because I feared I might make it worse for you, but it would have been douce *to see you once more.*

Let us think of the future and annihilate the present and shorten the distance that is going to separate us by thinking only of each other and of our plans and our most cherished desires. It is to my dear husband that I am writing, my husband whom important business is carrying far away from me but only for a moment. Imagine that this is the last disappointment we shall experience between us, in a few months we shall meet again, never to be separated. This letter will arrive at Le Havre almost at the same time you do. Keep loving your wife, whether absent or present. I will be travelling with you to Le Havre and you will follow me to Acosta. Goodbye until tomorrow, gather up my tenderest kisses, my darling friend, my heart is all yours and for life.

He could not stop the tears pouring down his cheeks as he read the final sentences of the letter, remembering how they had read together in *La Nouvelle Héloïse* that same fancy of the lovers being always present to one another, wherever they might be physically.

The next day she wrote from Acosta,

We went for a walk this evening, the night was calm and mild, but a year ago I walked the same way with my lover and now I am without him. I secretly hoped that I would not be given the room I had last year and given yours instead. I don't know if they guessed, or if it was by chance but here I am. What pleasure it gives me. I sit in the same chair as you did, I sleep in your bed and I am surrounded by everything of yours that I could collect: your little portrait is on the desk and the note you left behind and I kiss them all . . .

Goodbye and think of your wife, your dear wife, let us love each other for ever. Let us number our letters, so that we know if they have gone astray. This is number 2 and I hope you will have received the one I wrote yesterday an hour after you left

Every day she wrote, numbers 3, 4, 5, 6 from Acosta where Adelaide and Monsieur de Castellane were being infinitely kind and understanding. In number 5 (13 Thermidor) she regretted bitterly that he was going at all:

Oh God, how I wish we could cancel this cruel separation, how I would use every influence I have over you to keep you with me, yes, even to demand in the name of our love that you sacrifice this terrible voyage for my sake and begin from this very moment to secure our happiness. Ah, how miserable I am to be the cause of your grief! How I repent of not having settled our destiny last year!

She returned to Paris where she wrote him numbers 7, 8, 9, 10 and 11, again and again rehearsing her love for him, her agony that they should be separated and her passionate desire that he should cancel his passage on the *Sophia* and come back to her.

I think I never knew quite how much I loved you [this was number 11]. *Is there really no way for us to come together again and to abandon this sad voyage and begin this very moment to enjoy our happiness and our union? You are the only person in the world for me, the rest are nothing beside you. Every day I go through torment not knowing whether you have embarked since the letter I have just received from you and whether you are at this moment enduring the hurricane we have just endured here.*

William was in fact on the point of leaving Le Havre, but not by sea.

'Not sailing? My dear Short, this is a very sudden change of plan.'

'Unfortunately some letters I have received make it impossible for me to travel.'

'Well, I confess I am deucedly sorry to hear it. I had much looked forward to our being shipmates.'

'So had I, Mr Gerry. I hope that we may correspond and keep up our acquaintance that way.'

'Nothing could be more agreeable to me, sir. But not sailing, well! You have no complaint of the *Sophia*, I trust?'

'She looks very well found. It is just that I have unavoidable business in Paris. Thank you, my bags are already ashore.'

Mr Gerry waved him goodbye from the gunwale, staring at him as at some rare species previously thought extinct. There was a letter waiting for him at his lodgings on the harbour front.

I am only writing to you, my dear friend, in case you have not left already. I hope that tomorrow you will be starting back towards me. I am waiting for you with a pleasure and an impatience equal to the profound misery I have been enduring till now. I spent the whole day in a profound agitation, which

I cannot describe. At last I shall see you again and I shall be happy. Goodbye, but it is only a short goodbye before we see each other again and never separate, no, never.

'You are my Scheherazade.'

'Your Sche – I do not think I like the comparison. Because then you must be the cruel sultan who puts his wives to death.'

'No, no, for us the death would be to be separated and every time you put off the evil hour by telling me a story.'

'A story! I do not much care for that either. You think that when I wrote you all those letters I was inventing my despair just to keep you on a string.'

'No, no, those were true stories that you told me and the tighter the string binds us together, the happier I shall be.' He could see that she was not angry exactly but fretful, as though the drift of their talk was uncovering feelings which she did not wish to admit to herself or did not like to see surfacing in him too, however indignantly he might deny them.

'Next year we really must go, you know.'

'Ah, next year.' She spoke dreamily as if speaking of a date so remote as to be scarcely imaginable.

'Mr Jefferson writes that he has a great longing to see us, he sends you many fond messages.'

'I am sure that Mr Jefferson can barely remember which one I am from a cloud of duchesses, all equally worthless in his eyes.'

'No, no, I assure you, he formed a particular attachment to you, he has told me so many times.'

'It is you to whom he is particularly attached. I have seen his eyes light up when you come into the room, you are the son he never had, you have told me so yourself. Besides, I do not think he cares much for women, except silly women like Madame Cosway who flatter him.'

'You would love Albemarle County, it is very much like the Auvergne, though the hills are not so big.'

'Ah, well then, why should we travel so many thousands of miles if it is only to find another Auvergne with smaller hills?'

'Oh Rosalie, at any rate let us get married. We can go to America at our leisure.'

'I do not think I wish to be married "at any rate". You make it sound like a mere *convenance* so that we shall be respectable and be received in the best society in your beloved Albemarle County.'

'You know I meant no such thing.'

'In the Auvergne we need have no such worries. People are not always asking whether one is married or not married.'

They spent the summer in the Auvergne, surrounded by the hills that were so much bigger than the hills in Virginia. They did not lack for company. Old friends had trickled back. Lafayette had returned to his huge estates, bruised by the knocks he had taken but not dejected. Madame de Tessé came to stay, as caustic as ever. William played billiards with florid Auvergnat squires, while Rosalie sat at cards with the ladies.

'Don't you ever get bored with whist?'

'Oh William, you are so serious. Can one not amuse oneself when it is raining?'

'It seems to rain a great deal in the Auvergne.'

'Well, perhaps you had better go back to Albemarle County and count your slaves.'

'Oh Rosalie, let us get married.'

'You think that would make us quarrel less? That is not my experience of married couples. But perhaps they are different in America, everything is so much better there.'

In the autumn they went back to La Roche-Guyon.

'Oh, this house is so big, I cannot see the point of hanging on here since I have no children. I must hand it over to my cousin Liancourt.'

'And then . . .'

'But I cannot while he is still in exile. It is my duty to stay here until he returns. I must continue to play the chatelaine.' She struck an ironic attitude of grandeur. But his heart sank.

The next year Liancourt came back, with Talleyrand's secret encouragement. Things were easier now. Liancourt busied himself with an account of the splendid prisons he had seen in the United States. He also began importing from England large consignments of Mr Jenner's vaccine against the smallpox. He set up dispensaries to distribute the miraculous medicine to the poor. Down at Liancourt before he left for exile he had built a cotton mill with twenty-four of the latest spinning machines, the Jeannettes, which could turn out fifty pounds of cotton a day. On his return he found that the business had pretty well come to a halt. So he sold the Jeannettes and imported the latest Spinning Jennies from England. By the time production was in full swing, the Liancourt mills were turning out two hundred and fifty pounds of cotton per diem and employing a hundred and nineteen workers, none of them earning less than twelve hundred francs a year. Then there was his wool factory, which treated four thousand fleeces and employed another four hundred and forty workers with four hundred children working alongside their parents.

'I fear that cousin Liancourt is too busy to think of taking over La Roche-Guyon just yet. He is a veritable electric shock, my cousin.'

'And I am not?'

'Oh, do not be so prickly, Will. You know I could not live without you.'

But he began to chafe. It was bad enough to be separated by three thousand miles from all his affairs and to receive such irregular and alarming tidings of how they were faring. He trusted none of his agents; Peyton and Colonel Skipwith because they were not hard-headed enough, Van Staphorst and the Willinks because they were so hard in the head they might knock him out entirely if he was not on hand. And Mr Jefferson? Well, Mr Jefferson was about to become President of the United States and his head for business, always on the shaky side, was liable to be distracted by other matters than the rent from Indian Camp or the bookkeeping at the nail factory.

Then there were his many French acquaintances. When he had been chargé d'affaires, he had been the coming man, in formal terms the first American in Paris. Later on, when he was passing through the city as Minister to The Hague or Madrid, he was negotiating the business of two continents and still only in his early thirties. But now he was merely a private citizen adrift in a foreign country like so many others who had been left behind by the fortunes of war and revolution. And he was – what was the phrase he had sworn to avoid even in his innermost thoughts, but the phrase that could no longer be avoided? – he was dancing attendance, he was a *cavaliere servente,* almost a *cicisbeo.* There was one way and one way only to restore his position and his self-esteem.

'Rosalie, I must talk to you.'

'My darling, we never stop talking. We chatter like starlings to one another.'

'No, seriously, we cannot delay—'

'You will come with me to look at Reuil, will you not? Everyone says it is just the place for me, in pretty country and half the size of La Roche.'

'Rosalie, we must get married.'

'Indeed we shall and then we shall go to America.' She spoke like a child repeating a lesson, making no effort to pretend that she meant it.

'But—'

'But not today, today we must go and inspect this delightful residence at Reuil. I really think that quite soon either François or Alex will be thinking about moving in here while their father stays on at Liancourt. You know Alex's wife is a cousin of Madame Bonaparte's and is probably going to be her *dame d'honneur*, and I was thinking that I might offer my services too. Her first husband, Madame Bonaparte's I mean, was a poor relation of my husband's and used to spend his leave here when he was a young officer, so we are quite closely connected.'

William gaped in amazement. Any thought of pursuing the marriage question fled from his mind. 'You would work for that little Corsican bandit?'

'For his wife. In any case he is not much shorter than you are and I am no giantess myself.'

He looked at her, still astonished as though she had been spirited away and replaced by a complete stranger. 'Well, I do not think your husband would have approved,' he said.

'I do not think I would wish to be your wife if that is going to be your attitude. Are you coming to see Reuil or not?'

'Another time, another time,' he said.

It grew upon him quite slowly, this conviction that he was no more set upon the marriage than she was. Most of the time he loved her still. They always made it up after the bickering. And he renewed his proposal whenever he saw an opening. But now when she deflected him with some charming irrelevance or some fresh practical objection, he became aware that he was experiencing a new sensation and that sensation was relief.

But he lingered. In those queer, uneasy days after the Directory had been chased out and the little Corsican was spreading his wings, Paris was still delicious. There was a gaiety which might be febrile but was also irresistible as they greeted old friends and resumed old pleasures. And in the Auvergne it did not always rain. He began to delight in country pleasures too – the boar hunts in the scrubby woods at the head of the valley, driving in Rosalie's gig at high speed over the stony country tracks, stalking the partridges across the stubble at the end of the summer. When he came back to Verteuil as the sun was going behind the green hills and tossed his straw hat on the old walnut table in the hall and shouted up to Rosalie that he was back, he forgot his restlessness and felt that he was at home. And in winter when he stamped the mud off his boots and warmed his hands at the great fire in the salon at La Roche (for the Liancourts were still being slow about taking over the place), he could fancy himself the French squire.

But then one day at the end of May, quite soon after they had moved down to Verteuil for the summer, he was walking through the market in the local town, a backwoods place with one decent saddler's where he planned to buy a new driving whip. As he passed through the crowd of idlers under the arcade, he heard an old man say, 'Oh, him, that's madame's little American. They say she can't wait for him to go back home.'

He said nothing to her that night. But the next day he told her he had to go to Paris to talk to his bankers.

Which was true. He transferred all his assets in France to his agents in America and engaged passage on the next convenient boat, which was the *Activité*, bound for Norfolk out of Le Havre at the beginning of July.

She was in tears all that day and most of the next. But then the following day, when he was to depart, she was strangely quiet, seeming almost detached from what was happening. And he felt the same. It was as though, quite suddenly and by mutual consent, although not a word was spoken to that effect, they had come to an end. Not the end of their physical love – he fucked her tenderly that last night and she clung to him as tightly as she had ever clung to him – but to the end of the conviction they had shared so long that their love was the only thing in the world that mattered.

He even had an odd sensation – he reassured himself that it was probably no more than a fancy consequent upon his disordered state of mind – that they were not the only ones who had come to this terminus. It was as though, all over the world, the conviction that love was all that mattered had, by some brusque dictate of providence, become impossible to sustain. Some heartening light, some warming glow, had disappeared and everything was left cold and grey, and the only sound in the universe was a voice whispering that it was all an illusion, each man (each woman too) was alone in this world, always had been, always would be.

And her letters that he kept so carefully in the cherrywood writing box his father had given him when he graduated, what earthly use were they? Posterity would marvel that grown men and women should write such stuff and spoon over it for years afterwards. He should have burnt them, just as that unknown person had, quite rightly, burnt most of the nonsense he had written to her. Ashes to ashes, that was the right way. Why should only our illusions survive when the rest of us was gone?

They said goodbye in a sober loving fashion almost as if they had in fact been married all the time and there was nothing to fuss about.

'And, after all, you will be back so soon,' she said.

'You know I will,' he said and he wondered which of them believed it less.

In two days' time he stood on the deck of the *Activité* – what a strange name for a boat, how it mocked his frittering of these last four years. He had lolled too long on the foredeck of that pleasure yacht, the *Inactivité*. And his mind turned with a remorseless slow curl, like the curl of the ship's rope slipping from its capstan, to the reproving words that Mr Jefferson had written to him thirteen years before when he was scampering back to Paris from his Grand Tour:

A young man indeed may do without marriage in a great city. In the beginning it is pleasant enough; but take what course he will, whether that of a rambling or a fixed attachment, he will become miserable as he advances in years. The only recourse then for durable happiness is to return to America.

After he had gone, she began to weep again, all that day and half the night off and on. She slept for half an hour at most and woke red-eyed, not caring who saw her in such a ravaged state. She stumbled across to the window and looked down into the street. Usually the clatter of the rue Faubourg-Saint-Honoré was enough to shake her out of a gloom but now the heedless comings and goings only reminded her of her desolation. How quickly William had come back from Le Havre when Maman had died, so that she should not have to pass more than a few hours without the comfort of someone who loved her more than anyone else in the world. Now – but she was shaken with such sobbings that she could not think.

For days she was lapped in misery, unable to go out or to give the simplest command to her maid or to the cook, who had to guess at what simple soup or junket she might be able to swallow. The whole apartment was in mourning. Monsieur had gone and it was somehow universally understood that he was not coming back.

Yet there was one regret that she did not have, one thought that never occurred to her. She never wished that she had gone with him. Over and over again she wished that he had been made Minister to Paris, and then they could have been married and as happy as they deserved to be after waiting so long and suffering so much. To please him she had toyed with the idea of the charming *villino* they would build together within hailing distance of Monticello, of the vines they would plant and the cotton they would spin (she liked the project of building her own cotton mill as her cousin Liancourt had done), but though she did not care to admit it to herself it was all play-acting. She could not leave Europe, she could not abandon the only world she knew.

The first sharp grief faded into a duller misery. Then one morning – it must have been three or four weeks after William had gone – she woke up and felt that she could begin to . . . no, not live again, for if life was to include any real hope of happiness her life had ended the day William went. What she felt was that she could carry on, that she had to carry on just to show that she could, to spit in the face of fate. So she put on the gown of green sprigged muslin that Wm had admired (though what was that to her now?) and she went to call on her cousin Adelaide.

Strictly speaking, Adelaide was not her cousin, being only the wife of her cousin Alex. But Adelaide genuinely was a cousin of someone rather more to the point, namely Josephine de Beauharnais. They had both belonged to that raggle-taggle planter society out in those steamy islands whose wealth was so relentlessly squeezed out of the cane stalks, the Taschers and the Pyvarts and the La Pageries, families of mixed morals and some said mixed blood, sprawling across the French islands, Martinique, Santo Domingo, anywhere the sugar would grow. The difference between Josephine Tascher de La Pagerie and Adelaide Pyvart was that Josephine was penniless and had nothing to recommend her except ringlets, a pretty face and a delicate touch on the guitar, whereas Adelaide was sole heiress to some useful acres on Santo Domingo and – although short, verging on the plain and with a curious stoop – had accordingly netted Alex, the younger of the Liancourt boys.

But now the tables were turned, rather violently. Josephine was married to the First Consul, while Alex who had fled France in '92 to manage his wife's plantations was now back (some said he never got the hang of sugar) and looking for employment. And so was his wife.

How delicious, then, for Josephine to be able to take on a duchess as her *dame d'honneur* and to murmur to that duchess, 'Ah, my dear cousin, would you be so kind as to . . .' And if one duchess, why not two?

At the start, though, the family name proved a hindrance rather than a help.

'Who shall I say, madame?'

'The Duchesse, I mean Citoyenne La Rochefoucauld.'

'No, no, madame, I meant: who shall I say you are.'

'Citoyenne La Rochefoucauld.'

'You can't be, she's here already.'

'I'm her cousin.'

And then in a minute she was enveloped by warm plump arms and an overwhelming fragrance of patchouli and garlic, and the Citoyenne Bonaparte was laughing into her ear. 'Oh, it's too funny, you cannot expect poor Roger to cope with two duchesses at once. Come in, my dear, Adelaide has told me so much about you. And we have such a great deal in common, you and I. After all, both our first husbands were murdered, though I'm sure yours was a better lot than mine.'

Rosalie was captivated. Everything about Josephine was so different, her breezy candour, her casual extravagance, the litter of discarded clothes all over her apartment and the little dogs pawing them, the card tables set up with the cards scattered across them.

'Adelaide is so brilliant at telling our fortunes. She learnt the art from an old Creole woman we knew when we were girls and she is as good at it as Madame Le Normand who is positively the best clairvoyant in Paris and who promises to write my biography some day because she understands me so well. Tell me, Addie dear, how is the Consul this morning? It is the most extraordinary thing, you know, the last time he had a stomach-ache she told me the exact moment it started, two days before his letter arrived and he was hundreds of miles away at the time.'

The little figure was bent over the cards, so stooped that she seemed almost to be knocking her head against the green baize.

'Oh, this is a bad morning, the queen of hearts is next to the ace of spades. I fear that the Consul has met with an accident.'

'An accident, how dreadful, what sort of accident?'

'An accident that no doctor can cure, for it is an accident of the heart.'

'You mean, it is a new mistress, please do not say so, Addie, it cannot be, he was so loving when he left for the front.'

Rosalie watched, scarcely able to hide her astonishment as Madame Bonaparte greedily lapped up the gloomy runes. Adelaide (whom she had previously thought rather commonplace) looked so menacing as her bent little body twisted from the cards to Josephine and back again, piling on the dismal prognostications. How could people believe such stuff? What must the Consul think? For all his vulgarity, he was a man of the Enlightenment.

Yet she could not help liking Josephine and she felt that to be part of this ramshackle entourage might be a distraction that no watering place could match.

'Oh yes, my dear, Addie mentioned something of the sort and it would be so nice to see more of you. I tell you what, would you care to be my Mistress of the Wardrobe? This whole place is such a mess and my maids are dear girls but quite hopeless and I have so many new gowns ordered for when the General, I mean the Consul, returns; he never likes to see me in the same dress twice. Oh, look at that wretched dog, I can't imagine why Roger thought he was house-trained. Roger, where's the coffee, we are dying of thirst, and do bring a cloth when you come.'

Well, it would not be like discussing philosophy with Condorcet and Jefferson, but it would be a breath of life.

He stepped out of the heat of the August afternoon. It was cool in the passage. He paused to look at himself in the long oval-topped mirror that TJ had brought back from the Hôtel de Langeac. His hair had flopped across his face after the weary ride over from Richmond. He smoothed it back and straightened his white stock. A few grey strands around the ears, perhaps a little plumper in the cheeks, but otherwise he thought the seventeen years since he was last at Monticello had not done too much damage.

The third President of the United States was sitting out on the terrace in a lounging chair of his own devising. He was wearing a straw hat, which he threw off with unfeigned joy as he caught sight of Wm coming through the open French windows.

'Oh, my dear boy, how long I have waited for this moment.'

No, they were not to be separated, not by wide oceans nor by differences of opinion that were wider yet. It was – how long? – thirteen years since they had last set eyes on each other and their letters had become sparse and reproachful. Yet their clumsy embrace, like the clash of turtles mating, had nothing but love in it.

'And she has not come after all, your friend?' TJ enquired. Even now he could not quite manage to refer to her by name.

'Not on this visit. I thought it best to confine this trip to business, but I hope to spy out the land where we may settle together. She sends her best regards to you and cannot contain her impatience to see you again.' How fluently he lied now, as fluently as he had when he told her that this temporary separation would only strengthen their love. Anyway, with one part of his mind he still half believed it himself.

'Well, well, I am sure you could build her a fine *villino* out at Indian Camp. Or if that site should not please her, I am reliably informed that you could sell it tomorrow for double what you paid.'

'I am deeply troubled that you should have had to expend so much time on my poor affairs when you have a whole nation to attend to and my prime purpose now is to relieve you of those cares. I cannot tell you how grateful I am.'

'Well, that is good of you, sir. I confess that the burden of them has come to weigh on me since I have been dragged back into the public arena. I only hope that you will find that I have been a tolerable steward.'

'Oh, my dear sir, you may be sure that I shall never forget what you have done for me.'

Which was true enough, though not entirely in the amiable sense that his tone conveyed. For it turned out that TJ had made a pretty fair tangle of Wm's affairs. He had informally lent himself nine thousand dollars from Wm's account, which money he had invested in two of his admirable projects – the nail factory at Monticello and the flour mill out at Milton – but the third President was now forced to confess that he had miscalculated the profits, though he claimed to keep such exact accounts. Totting up the whole ledger, including accumulated interest, it was clear that he now owed Wm fifteen thousand dollars and there was nowhere near enough coming in to pay off the loan. One of the farms had been idle for seven years for want of tenants and the Shadwell property was leased out in such small units that the tenants could barely feed themselves, let alone keep up with the rent.

Yet how sweet the prospect was from the veranda, with the newly planted vines and orchards slipping away down the hill and the tobacco fields beyond, and then the blue hills. The tribulations of Mammon had left no mark on the President's long face. To Wm he looked just as when he had first seen him thirty years earlier. The God in whom he only half believed had dowered him with a serenity that was certainly not to be shaken by a few financial hiccoughs, let alone by the unsavoury effluvia of politics, that black art for which TJ had such a surprising inclination, being a dab hand at the kind of intriguing and horse-trading that you might have thought beneath him.

'You will stop a few days, will you not? I have Lee and Pinckney and a few of the other fellows coming over. It will be good for you to pick up the threads.'

'I would like nothing better,' Wm said firmly, 'but I fear I must take ship for New York to meet my bankers. I have a passage booked out of Richmond tomorrow.'

'That is very sad. I shall take it greatly amiss if you do not come back immediately and take a journey with me to see all the improvements that are going forward at Poplar Forest. Besides, you must greet all our friends from Paris, Polly and Patsy of course, and Petit, who has settled down splendidly over here, and James who is now in my poor judgement the best cook in Virginia, and then you will remember little Sally who is little no more and has become a most admirable *mère de famille*.'

William could scarcely trust himself to speak, he was blushing red enough as it was, but if he did not say something he knew that TJ in his remorseless rambling way would continue to give news of Sally's progress, which was the last thing on earth he wanted. He had planned that his visit should be short to the point of abruptness, so as to reduce the chances of having to see her. So he said now in a rushing effusive fashion, which he feared must sound as false to the President as it did to himself, 'There is nothing I look forward to more earnestly than to see them all again, but now, I know it is unmannerly and the pleasure of seeing you again, sir, I cannot say how profoundly I feel . . .'

'Nor can I, my dear William, I have missed you greatly and I look forward to our next meeting with the greatest *empressement*.'

Wm could not say afterwards how he managed to take his leave, he retained only the most blurred recollection of the President waving him off with his straw hat as he made his escape through the French windows.

As he stumbled along the brick path towards the stables where his hired horse was being fed and watered, he passed the slave quarters that Mr Jefferson had just rebuilt in brick of a pleasant mellow tint. Two or three boys were tossing stones at each other and looked up at him curiously as he passed. By the last dwelling there was a brick well-head with an iron hoop for the drawing rope. Two women were talking there, one leaning against the hoop, making a dreamy gesture with her hand. Their faces were turned away from him. But something about the gesture – no, surely that was fanciful, after thirteen years you could not recognise someone by a gesture.

Then the woman who had made the dreamy gesture called out to the boys and they ambled across as boys do when their mother calls. The taller boy must have been eleven or twelve by the look of him.

Wm visited Monticello once or twice more but always on business and for the briefest possible period. That winter he spent in New York City. He took the opportunity to refit his wardrobe for his new life. He had Rich and Disbrow make him breeches of black Dutch cashmere, a waistcoat of striped Florentine silk and flannel drawers for the cold weather. The next year he moved down to Philadelphia to take up residence in the St Francis Hotel. He had his tailor there make him a pair of black cashmere pantaloons (the coming thing), a French napped coat and a velvet surtout. He was becoming a financier.

He reckoned that on his return he possessed a total of thirty-nine thousand dollars in liquid funds in the United States, all held by Daniel Ludlow, Van Staphorst's man in New York. Then Mr Jefferson had invested nearly forty-seven thousand dollars for him, mainly in US bonds, which were cheap just then because the Peace of Amiens had forced the wartime speculators to sell up. Then there were the thirty-three shares he held in the James River Canal Company, worth a cool ten thou, as they said in New York. Not a bad haul but one that became a good deal larger when Wm started reinvesting it. He took four hundred shares in the Manhattan Company Bank and another tranche in the Bank of Pennsylvania. Most of the rest he put into New York real estate at seven per cent, which he fancied would provide the best security if the United States became embroiled in Napoleon's wars and destroyed its funds. He became known as a long-headed sort, 'a warm man', well launched on the way to becoming that once unimaginable being, a millionary, or as they were beginning to call it now 'millionaire', which sounded more expansive yet with that swaggering final 'aire'.

And did he think of her? Yes he did, every day. He took the cherrywood box on his business trips and on lonely nights in grubby upstate inns he would take out her letters and read them with meticulous care as though he feared he had missed something. He thought of her too as he was being paddled in a canoe across one of the Finger Lakes to inspect a stretch of timber that he was interested in. The drops of water cascading from the paddle as it came out of the water brought back that first day on the lake at Versailles when he could not believe that she was the Duke's wife and had mistaken poor Madame d'Astorg for the Duchess.

Then, when the native guide was showing him the stacks of timber that had already been felled, the sawdust and the fresh scars on the logs reminded him of their walks up in the hazelwoods at La Roche-Guyon and the time when she had accused him of playing the simple woodman.

He looked away from the stacked timber to the standing trees stretching over the hillside. It was cool, almost chilly in their shadow, though the sky overhead was a deep blue-violet. His eyes ached following the bare trunks upwards to the firmament. How mean and insignificant they were, this little group – himself, the guide and the agent – haggling about what price these noble sentinels would fetch after they had been cut down and trimmed and sledded over the pass and floated down the river to some depot far off in Canada. What right had they, in preference to all other species in the universe, to expect to enjoy some sort of perpetual happiness?

Too much was asked of love. It could not always be bright and all-consuming. Love wore on, as even the best of days did, and the most you had a right to was the memory of how fresh the dawn had been. As for happiness, perhaps that was not the same thing at all. Nobody could live for ever at the peak. Happiness was what you found when you came lower down into the trees – a cooler, quieter place where a man could breathe. Is that what Mr J had meant by the pursuit of happiness? But then he remembered that same day at Versailles when the third-President-to-be had seemed a little foggy about exactly what he had meant.

'They are asking three thousand dollars including the island. That seems a bit steep to me. I'd better have Daniel's agent do a proper valuation. He is a fine judge of timber.'

He went to visit his sister Jenny in Lexington, Kentucky, and told her that he still meant to marry Rosalie. Jenny was the one in the family he had always liked best and he did not wish to disappoint her.

She wanted to see him happy and settled as she herself was and she was indignant that anyone should be so heartless as to refuse to marry her charming brother. She fussed over his clothes because he had no woman to look after them. He had put on weight and she let out the seam of his favourite cream-and-gold waistcoat that Rosalie had embroidered for him. Rembrandt Peale painted him wearing it, and when the portrait was finished Wm gave it to Jenny as a surprise present because she had been kind to him in his solitude.

'Oh, it is so like. What's that in the background?'

'It's the temple of Paestum, Jenny. I saw it when I went to Naples with Johnny Rutledge.'

'I think it would have been better if he had painted that chateau, what's its name, that she came into, you know, the one in the Auvergne.'

'It would be rather presumptuous to put it in a portrait of me, it's scarcely my property.'

'Well, it surely ought to be. I don't know who she thinks she is, keeping you on a string like that all these years.'

'Jenny, to me Rosalie is everything that's good and clever.'

'Well, she could prove it by making you a good old-fashioned wife.'

'One day I'm sure she will,' he answered weakly.

'One day,' she snorted. 'Listen here, William Short, if you really are going back to her, nothing will reconcile me to her but she marries you the day you step off the boat in Paris.'

'Boats don't go up to Paris, sister,' he said.

All the same, he began to convince himself that it might still be possible. They would each of them have tasted solitude and, busy as he made himself, he had to confess that the taste of it could sometimes be bitter. When he came back to his hotel and pulled off his boots in his first-floor room with its view over the park, he began to muse on their days together driving over the stony tracks of the Auvergne or reading in her little island garden at La Roche-Guyon or sitting in the early evening by the pool beyond the parterre at the rue de Seine, and he started to imagine that all these things were part of his future as well as of his past. How could such sweet days not come again?

This hope flickered and faded again to dwindle into the faintest ghost of a chance on the farthest horizon and he had almost given up on it altogether when he received a letter, out of the blue, from Mr Jefferson. The third President intended to send him to Moscow. It was part of his latest grand design, to encircle and so isolate the overweening British. Tsar Alexander was the hope of liberal spirits everywhere. The Tartars and Muscovites were to be brought in to redress the balance of the old world.

Secrecy had grown upon Jefferson as he grew older and it now gripped him with an obsessive power. He warned Wm that his mission *must be suspected by no mortal until it is arrived at St Petersburg. I write you this now before our minds are all made up, that you may begin to huddle up your affairs and to give out that you shall without delay return to France.* By the time the Senate knew of the mission, Wm would be in Paris. In theory, he could have travelled directly to St Petersburg, but it was the end of September and the ice was already closing in, and the Baltic sea lanes were no place for neutral shipping. So he was to proceed swiftly and without fanfare to France and thence overland to the Russian court. He took only his French valet and his polygraph for making copies of his dispatches. His covering story was that he was going to supervise his investments in Europe.

'Not changed, even a little? It is six years, you know.'

'No, you are lovelier than ever, just as I dreamed you would be, all my lonely nights in strange hotels.'

'You have come back more of a flatterer than ever. The ladies of Moscow will be bowled off their feet.'

'No, no, you must not mock me, I am so overwhelmed to see you again and to know that you have not forgotten me.'

'Can't you see that I am in the same case? When I heard that you were here my heart stopped, and now I can hardly form my words.'

'I would have forewarned you, I had no wish to take you by surprise, but there was no time. Besides, I dared not break Mr J's oath of secrecy, though the Senate will have to know soon enough.'

'Oh, let them wait, let the whole world wait.'

They kissed and he began to unhook her lilac dress. He was impatient and rough, and his fingers had trouble with the hooks. She stepped away from him and unfastened the dress herself. He pushed her back on the sofa and threw up her petticoats. He had not had a woman for six months and then it had been a streetwalker in a small Canadian timber station when he was sheltering after a thunderstorm.

'You are not . . . disappointed?'

She flexed her knees wide to make it easier for him.

'Rosalie, you know how happy you make me. After, let us not say how many years, we cannot expect instantly . . .'

'No, of course not, it will take time, and then it will be as it was for us before you went away.'

But as he kissed her hot cheek, he had to admit that he was dismayed. It had been a quick dry humping, there was even something – no, ugly could not be the word – impersonal about it. As he caressed her apple breasts he felt like a customer rubbing the merchandise between finger and thumb. And he found himself thinking of the Canadian girl – she had been pretty, with long legs and she cried out as if she meant it. Rosalie tried to rub him into life and he hardened but it was a mechanical response, he felt as though it was nothing to do with him. They did it again and they both knew that it would be the last time.

'You must meet the Empress. I am so fond of her, I cannot understand why people say these unkind things about her and of course the Emperor has been so cruel. She has such a good heart and she is much cleverer than they say. I am sure she will be very helpful to your mission.'

'I am sure she will.'

But his mission could progress no further until the Senate had confirmed him. And so he resumed his former life among old friends, Madame de Tessé, Madame d'Astorg, Lafayette, even old *Mère* Postulard who had fallen asleep beside Rosalie in the carriage when she was going home just after they had first made love and the jolting of the carriage had reminded her of it. They went again as they had in the old days to stay with her cousin Boni de Castellane whose wife had just died, and to her country house at Reuil, now well established, and on down to the green hills of the Auvergne that were so much bigger than the hills of Albemarle County. But now they kissed each other goodnight and went their separate ways down the passage like old married couples who find it too uncomfortable to share a bed but who are still fond.

France had not lost her enchantments – the little Corsican could not take those away. In fact, in his quick greedy way he wanted to make them his own. But Paris was sadly changed. It was a brash, trumpery sort of town now. William's friends from before the Revolution seemed like fish gasping for air. He supposed that conquerors always wanted to leave their mark, but there was an unutterable crudity about the monuments that Bonaparte was erecting to celebrate his victories, that heavy great triumphal arch with the bronze horses he had stolen from Venice stuck on top of it, and that half-finished Temple of Glory, which was to have been a church until a greater Saviour came along, and then, as if the message still needed rubbing in, the even bigger triumphal arch he was building at the top of the Champs-Elysées, still only finished up to knee height. The little Emperor flew into a rage when he heard that it could not be made ready in time for the procession through it to welcome the new Empress. To placate him they were hurriedly throwing up a painted canvas replica on the site, though as yet only the wooden scaffolding for the replica was in place. Paint and canvas – that was all it was, the entire mad adventure. In a couple of years it would all be broken down and Europe would be left to mourn her dead. He had no wish to be there to see it.

William became impatient to be off to Moscow, though he did not dream of admitting it. He waited in a fever for each day's post, but when the blow fell he was quite unprepared for it. In fact, he was flabbergasted.

'They've refused to confirm me.'

'Refused? How can that be? If the President says—'

'Rosalie, you understand nothing of American politics. But then nor, I am coming to suspect, does Mr Jefferson. If the President hatches a secret plan, the Senate will do its damnedest to frustrate it.'

'How spiteful.'

'Not one of them voted for me, not a single one. If only the President had gone about his business openly I might have made a better showing. As it is, I am the biggest fool in Christendom.'

He had thought himself past the age of disappointment. He had put behind him the humiliations of his earlier diplomatic career. But then it had still seemed the springtime of his life and he had Rosalie to look forward to. Now he had no prospect, only retrospect. Once again

TJ had failed him and the rest was bitterness. It turned out to be Jefferson's last act as President and his successor Mr Madison was never one to lift a finger on Wm's behalf. A month later the new President nominated John Quincy Adams in Wm's place and after an initial rebuff (and that not half as humiliating as Wm's) Mr Adams was confirmed by a handsome majority of nineteen to seven. Madison cruelly told Adams that the unanimous vote against Wm's nomination had been not against the mission but against the man.

After a decent interval to show that he was not leaving with his tail between his legs, Wm left Paris and took a boat to England from Dieppe because there was no boat due to sail to America until later in the year. He did not warn Rosalie he was going.

At Dieppe he found a letter from her waiting for him.

> *It is hard to express what I felt this morning at five o'clock when I received your note. I have been unable to stop crying for the past two days. Oh, my dear friend, how unfair you would be if you ever doubted my total devotion to you. Do not leave me without hope of seeing you return to a country where you have so many friends and one in particular who will be a friend to her last day and will be the same in all the different situations of life. Never stop loving someone who loves you to the bottom of her heart.*

Well, he thought, can any man ever have received so many love letters while waiting to board ship?

Six days later she married the widowed Monsieur de Castellane.

He did not move back to Philadelphia directly but put up until the autumn across the river at Morrisville, New Jersey, to avoid the sickly season in the metropolis. When he crossed back after the first frost, he took rooms at the United States Hotel, but he soon found that the new boarding houses springing up along Walnut and Locust Streets suited him better. He switched from one to the next as soon as he began to weary of the company at table. He still possessed seven hundred acres out at Indian Camp, down the road from Monticello, but he found the rents hard to collect. At least that was what he said, but the truth was that he did not care to live too near Mr Jefferson or his household. In the end he was happy to sell Indian Camp for a small profit. 'I like city life,' he told Daniel Ludlow, who had now become his man of business. 'I like to see things moving, so you see I am becoming a true American again.'

He had been an early enthusiast for canals, but he went and talked to the few qualified civil engineers then to be found in the US, and he decided that canals had had their day, so he sold most of his stock, apart from the Chesapeake. He had great hopes of a young engineer, Moncure Robinson, and he took a slice of the railroad Robinson was building, the Pittsville and Dansville, which he wagered was only the foretaste of things to come. By the time Robinson had built the Petersburg and Richmond and, after that, the Richmond, Fredericksburg and Potomac lines, Mr Short was drawing ten per cent a year from them, and that was before he started raising capital from some of his London friends to build steam locomotives. He had every confidence in steam because he had already done pretty well out of Robert Fulton's steamboat company down at Natchez.

But property was the sure-fire thing. It took him fifteen years to build up his stake in the Macomb tract on the Niagara but by the end he had the lion's share, sixteen thousand acres out of twenty-five thousand, more than his partners had put together. Still they all made a packet that time. In those years any American who kept his wits about him could pile up a tolerable fortune. And the satisfactions were not to be reckoned in dollars only. There was gratification to be found in carving farmland out of virgin forest and transforming swamp and scrub into homes and villages. William relished nothing more than his journeys upstate to visit that electric German, George Scriba, who had taken a small tribe of Dutchmen to settle on land he had bought from the Holland Land Company (William had shares in that too). He lent Scriba money secured on the tracts of land that were soon to be adorned with settlements bearing homely names like Rotterdam and Harlem, but were then known only as Number Seventeen or Number Twenty. William smiled to think how much time he had spent in France viewing the artificial wildernesses that the *ancien régime* had delighted in, and how he liked nothing better now than to see the loggers and the road builders carving their way through the real wildernesses of his native land.

One morning as he was setting out on his promenade down Walnut

Street, he was hailed by a woman in her later years, on the stout side but with a bright look about her. 'Mr Short, I can see that you do not recognise me.' She had a French accent but spoke in quick, confident English.

'Ah, yes, of course, madam . . .' he said vaguely, raising his hat to her.

'It was a long time ago. Condorcet's grand banquet at the Mint. We drank confusion to all kings, but we met quite often after that.'

'My goodness me, Madame Suard, you must forgive me, my memory has gone.'

'Amélie,' she corrected him.

'How amazing.' He looked at her with delight, remembering how sportive she had been and he could see that she had not lost her malicious twinkle. 'And your English is so perfect.'

'Ah well, we made our living as translators, you must remember. When my husband died I could not stand Paris a moment longer, not with that little man there, so I came to Philadelphia. And *voilà*, I am a landlady.'

'A landlady? ' He was not sure she had the right word.

'I have a French boarding house at 70 Walnut Street. The *Inquirer* was good enough to describe it as the finest in the city.'

'You must forgive me again. I have been away travelling in New York State.'

'I know, because naturally I sought you out as soon as I was established here.'

They stood chatting on the sidewalk in the bright sunlight and William was enchanted. He dined with her at No. 70 and found the company agreeable, by Philadelphia standards almost sparkling. It was a matter of days only before he decamped there as a permanent resident, securing the suite of rooms on the second floor front, lately vacated by a Mr Frost who had been called away to Boston.

He must have been at Mrs Suard's about a year when he had a letter from Rosalie, the first in a long time:

> *I am taking advantage of an opportunity offered by my dear friend Mr Worden to send you the famous bust of Condorcet, which has so long lain addressed to*

you and which was even sent seven years ago to Cherbourg from where it could not continue the journey and was ultimately sent back to me until a better means of transport could be found. I hope that this shipment will be more fortunate.

As to the bust, I value it less than I am sure your compatriots will. I am far from regarding the subject as a great man. He is no doubt celebrated in the eyes of the public. For those who knew him as I did, he remains a mean spirit whose heart was never animated by any generous impulse and who was moved only by resentment and vengeance. In spite of my justifiable dislike of this man, I believe that you will appreciate possessing a marble bust of a famous person whom you have known and who will surely be viewed with great curiosity by your fellow countrymen. I am delighted to present it to you, my dear friend.

He read the rest of her letter with only half an eye, partly because it was full of the comings and goings of her numerous relatives, but also because his mind was seized by the sad fate of the noble bust that he remembered so well thirty years earlier occupying pride of place in the salon at the rue de Seine: first smothered in straw and exiled to the attic for a decade and more, then stuffed into a crate and sent off to Cherbourg, only to be returned in ignominy to the attic still muffled in its crate, and now at last being buffeted on the high seas, no doubt sliding from side to side in some greasy hold, rejected by its own people. How like the last days of Condorcet himself, confined to a dismal attic in a backstreet for months, then wandering the streets out into the country rejected at every port of call, or every port of call but one.

Several times that day after they had unwrapped the bust his thoughts returned to Condorcet. He had come to a dismal end and had nobody to blame but himself. Those who ran with the mob must expect to be trampled by the mob. He had less common sense than a sparrow and at tight moments he had scarcely shown exemplary courage. William could not blame Rosalie for her indignation. She had every right never to forgive him for his cowardly failure to defend her husband and her brother.

And yet. Was she right to say that he had never shown a generous impulse? And was he so incapable of love? He had surely loved Sophie with all his heart, and he had stood up for liberty and the poor, and for the rights of women and even of the blacks at a time when Mr Jefferson, for example, preferred to lie low. The day might yet come when that silly, squawking condor might be remembered better than any of them.

After all, they had all been in it together at the start, the first great conspiracy to make men happy. They had dreamed of a world irradiated by *le bonheur*. They had dreamed too much, of course, and expected too much – he himself had seen that soon enough, sooner than most. He had always been pretty good at telling how things would pan out. People didn't necessarily want to know, though, that was the trouble. But even he could not help being caught up in the pursuit of love, happiness, call it what you like. Yet the chase could not last for ever. What was that line he had just read somewhere – 'the heart must pause to breathe and love itself have rest'.

He had been right about one thing at least, the thing he had told his first girl, Louisa, that sticky afternoon in the back bedroom on 4th Street: that he would end his days a rich frontier bachelor with a broken heart.

That evening just before supper there was a knock at the door of his sitting room.

'Amélie, I am glad to see you up and about. I heard you were taken poorly. To tell the truth, you still look mortal pale. The shock of seeing our old friend again after so long, even clad in marble, so to speak . . .'

'You are always so quick to understand things, William.'

'Much good it has done me,' he said with that little moue of his downturned mouth which had become a habit with him.

'It is a very fine bust,' she said.

'So it is indeed. They say Houdon idealises his subjects but to my eye that is the Condor to the life.'

'I could not agree more. And that is precisely why I must ask you a favour.'

'Anything, anything, my dear.'

'Would you be very much distressed if you found some other resting place for it? I must confess – it is a weakness I freely admit – that I am not entirely comfortable with it in my house. Its presence stirs sad memories. I am too old to see ghosts in my parlour.'

'Oh, my dear, I could have saved you any anxiety on that score, but I did not wish to disturb you while you were not well. The moment I saw it I knew it was too big for an ordinary house, not that your house is ordinary in anything but size. It is purely a question of size, you understand. The Philosophical Society will be very glad to have it. As soon as I have made the necessary arrangements, Simmon can take it over in the cart. I instructed him to keep the crate so that we may use it again.'

'You are so kind as always. The bust will be much appreciated over there, I am sure.' She began to recover her colour. 'What a terrible thought it is that if only he had come back to me that night, he might be with us here today.'

'An honoured guest of the President, I dare say,' William hazarded.

'The Terror had only another three months to run. If he could have found shelter somewhere . . .'

'Yes, yes, quite so.' He was imagining the Condor in Washington, talking in his harsh quavery voice to Mr Monroe, Wm's old friend from William and Mary days. Who would have guessed when they were in the Flat Hat Society together that it would be Jimmy Monroe who would . . . but there was no use going down that track.

'I opened the garden door, you know.'

'Yes, so you told me. It was all a great pity.'

Gilligan's Hotel

We stopped for gas. There was nothing between the gas station and the desert except a straggly hedge of aloes. The other side of the gas station there was a motel with a sign that flashed 'Rooms' and 'Casino' alternately in red-and-green lights. There was no other building in sight.

'Stayed there one time,' the big man said. 'Dropped a bundle. Didn't have a cent left, limped into Vegas with the gauge on empty.'

Behind the motel you could see the mountains, mauve and golden in the afternoon light. It was strange to feel the desert under your feet, like crunching lumps of sugar.

The big man was not fat, just burly, an athlete who had thickened up. He had been a quarterback for Michigan State before he did his knee in. He came out West to work for Boeing, but they let him go in the recession, which he didn't resent at all, he preferred the nomadic life. He had made a study of the Native American culture and he reckoned some of it had sunk in. There was a wife in Phoenix and a daughter in Salt Lake but he was on the road most of the year delivering Winnebagos.

'So what brings you on this bus?'

'Got a pick-up in Gilligan. There's hundreds of 'em there. They come down from Wisconsin in the fall, after the first snow, and spend the winter in the desert. Gilligan folk call them the Snow Geese.'

'But don't they need the Winnebago to go back to Canada in?'

'Sure they do, if they go back. But some of the girl croupiers are darned pretty and anyway, did you ever spend six months in a stationary

Winnebago with your partner? They say the divorce rate in that mobile-home park is the highest in the USA.'

He cackled at the thought, and so did the woman with the fair pony-tail.

'I seen plenty of them,' she said. 'When they're winning they think every woman is the answer to their prayers. I roomed with a girl once, when I was first working at the Bellagio, she regularly got engaged to one of the players, about once a week on average. None of 'em ever stuck, though.'

The driver beckoned us back on to the bus and the woman with the ponytail scrunched out her cigarette with her heel. It was a shock to come in out of the stifling heat.

'Las Vegas here we come,' the woman said as the driver started the engine.

'I'm getting off at Gilligan,' I said.

'Never heard of English folks stopping at Gilligan. They mostly go on to Vegas.'

'I'm going to a wedding. My god-daughter.'

'How cute. They've got such a darling wedding chapel, the Little Chapel in the Moonlight, you'll just love it. They have these beautiful painted statues.'

I had not thought much about the ceremony. I assumed that Jane would be one for a civil wedding. Certainly her mother never had any truck with God, and the same went for Franco, not that he deserved much say, seeing that he had left Polly when Jane was less than a year old. Well, 'left' was an old-fashioned way of putting it. The only vow they had taken seriously was the vow not to stand in the way if either of them wanted to be with someone else. They had to remain on friendly terms and this rule they kept to religiously. Franco was paying for the wedding.

'She a Catholic, your god-daughter?' the woman with the ponytail asked.

'No, I don't think she's religious at all. In fact, I'm not a proper godfather, just a friend of her parents. When she was at school, the other girls all had godfathers, so they asked me.'

'How cute,' the woman said doubtfully. 'What she do for a living?'

'She works for a bank, but she's really a gambler.'

'I like gamblers.'

Jane had inherited her mother's mathematical brain but not her sense of duty. She worked in asset management because it was the only part of the City that still kept civilised hours and left her plenty of time to sharpen her skills at bridge, blackjack and backgammon, from which she reckoned to double her salary in a good year. How could I have bred such a child, her mother wailed. Polly was coming up to retirement but still worked ten hours a day as chief exec of a health authority in south London.

'Hope she wins enough to pay for the wedding. It's a great place to get married, Gilligan.'

'Yes,' I said, though I was beginning to have doubts. She was marrying Jonty, a tall quiet boy who worked in Systems. Apparently he didn't like gambling much, but he thought he might be able to fit in some birdwatching, further up the valley in the high sierra.

But it was not on Jonty's account that a little dread was leaking into my thoughts. It was the prospect of seeing them all again and being cooped up together in the hotel. Wizz and I wrote to each other, these days e-mailed, once or twice a year. But Franco I had not run into for ten, no, nearer twenty, years and as for Polly we met now and then, but only briefly at weddings and funerals, more often funerals.

'Isn't it odd,' she had said at the last one, 'when we were young, we thought we'd got away from all this.'

'All what?' I could not quite interpret the discreet spread of her fingers as if she was shaking a fan at the mourners now trooping towards the graveside under their umbrellas. I remembered that gesture and the little flip of the wrist that came with it and it touched my heart, as did any jolt from the past now. That was all part of getting on, the way your hold on the present weakened while the tug of the old days tightened, like one of those dog leads that reels itself in.

'Occasions like this, rites of passage. Now they're the highlights.'

'Speak for yourself,' I said, groping for the old familiarity.

'I always do,' she said. 'Nobody else is going to.'

Partly what I was dreading was Jane and Jonty watching us the whole time, imagining that we were still each other's best friends.

'Over there right by the mountains there was a Hopi village once but they moved back to north-eastern Arizona with the rest of the tribe. I saw them do their snake dance once but now they don't let the public in, frightened we might get the wrong idea.' The big man chuckled. 'Still,' he added, 'I expect our tribal rituals must seem peculiar to them.'

'Just what I was thinking.'

The golden light had gone behind the mountains and the desert floor was a dull dead colour, and the only thing to look at was the ribbon of oncoming headlights curling away to the horizon.

'Only ten minutes to Gilligan now,' the big man said. 'The Greyhound coming through used to be a pretty big deal. The old man would come out to welcome us in his cowboy get-up and he'd fire his forty-five in the air as we parked.'

'The old man?'

'George G. Gilligan. When he came out here, it was nothing but a couple of shacks at the river crossing, but that old riverboat gambler had the genius to see that some folks would be so eager to get rid of their money that they'd tumble out of their vehicles as soon as they crossed the state line – and the rest is history. There, you can see the lights.'

Far in the distance the ribbon exploded in a blaze in the darkness. Quite soon I could make out GILLIGAN'S in flaming lights. The gradient steepened down into the valley and I could see the sullen sheen of the river snaking through the rocks. As we came off the highway into the hotel driveway, the desert wind was swooshing through the line of palm trees. We got out and felt the heat of the night. There were sprinklers playing on the grass and the wind carried the spray on to my face. Beyond the hotel there was another hotel and then nothing but the mountains.

'Welcome to Gilligan City,' the big man said, 'and *bonne chance.*'

Under the vast hotel awning, there was Wizz eternally neat in a lightweight suit somewhere between magnolia and mayonnaise in colour. Self-contained and assured as ever, he might have been the hotel greeter. My heart skipped. It was marvellous to see him in such trim. But when I came closer and we embraced, I felt how thin he was around the ribs and saw how worn-looking his face was, all the more so because he still had that boyish look.

'You're allowed one stare,' he said. 'But you mustn't ask, it's so boring. Most of the time I feel OK. Let's go see Franco, he's in the library.'

'Library?' I queried, waving goodbye to the big man who had got his suitcase out of the Greyhound and was wheeling it back up the driveway towards the mobile homes that stretched along the opposite hillside, pale blobs in the gathering dark.

Beyond the foyer, double doors with gilt swirls all over them led into a huge room lined with gleaming bookshelves. Sunk in a leather armchair by a fire as big as a bonfire, desperately shrunk-looking in this oversized salon, was Franco. He sprang out of the chair with all his old monkey energy and came towards us, waving the book he had been reading in his prehensile paw, his finger still marking his place.

'Amazing, it's a first edition of Lucasta Mynors. Even Bodley hasn't got one.'

Wizz used to accuse Franco of sitting in a chair curled up like a chimp protecting his banana. Now he didn't uncurl even when he was upright, which made his arms hang down by his sides even more than they used to.

'See, now we're both bent,' Wizz said.

'Godawful poet, Lucasta, easily the least talented of the Hesperides, apparently a fantastic lay, though,' said Franco, paying no attention to Wizz – at least that had not changed.

'Polly's still freshening up, I think,' said Wizz, paying no attention to Franco.

But she wasn't, because at that moment in she came. She was wearing a sky-blue silk shirt and the stylish sort of jeans that all the women in the foyer had been wearing. To us she looked wonderful. If you had never known her, I suppose you would have seen a tall, rather severe elderly woman with a pale lemony skin and a daunting expression on her face.

'Oh, it *is* a library, how funny,' she said. 'I didn't believe it when they said that was where you were.' She smiled at the thought of not believing it. I could see that Franco was instantly captivated, partly, I suppose, because I was captivated too. They embraced, for the first time in I don't know how many years, not awkwardly but carefully, as if one of them might have a lesion or fracture that had not yet been identified by a qualified practitioner.

It must have been a difficult life bringing up Jane on her own. There had been other lovers. She kept Wizz up to date on them and he would pass on news of the latest to me, explaining what was going wrong. Sometimes he would sound exasperated with her and complain that she seemed to be deliberately avoiding any long-term commitment, though what business was it of his? Perhaps the life suited her. She liked to do things her own way. Difficulty interested her, and why shouldn't it? Most of the time she was worrying about Jane. In her letter telling me about the engagement, she said how she adored Jonty almost as much as Jane did.

'They've gone to talk to the minister at the Little Chapel in the Moonlight. Apparently the best time to have the wedding is at twilight when you get this fantastic effect through the windows because you're so high up.'

'What, is it up in the mountains?'

'No, it's on the thirty-eighth floor. You go out on this amazing terrace afterwards and have your champagne or whatever looking at the sunset.'

'When do we get to eat?' Franco pestered. 'I'm ravening.'

'You mean ravenous.'

'Ravening's better, dear, especially if the service is slow, reminds them of wolves.'

'I think it's through there, I saw a sign.'

'What about Jane and Jonty?'

'I told them to follow us in if they were held up. The restaurant's called the Condor's Nest.'

Wizz and I exchanged glances. 'My, this must be *meant*,' he said.

I had sent him the typescript months earlier and was surprised – in fact, hurt – to receive back nothing more than a note saying that the package had arrived and that he was looking forward to reading it. The research, after all, had taken up more years of my life than I could spare and Wizz was my prime audience – indeed, the only begetter of the project. If it had not been for him I would never have heard of any of them – the Condor, the little Duchess, William Short himself. I wanted desperately to know what he thought of the whole thing and could only assume – with a dreadful sinking feeling – that he did not think much.

The four of us walked out of the gloomy splendour of the library into a broad carpeted mall that seemed endless. It was lined with clusters of slot machines, whirring, clicking and jingling. The slots sounded cheerful and animated compared with their silent, rapt acolytes.

'You didn't like it,' I said.

'I loved it,' he said. 'It's the best thing you've done.'

'You didn't like it.'

'No, honestly, it's utterly fantastic. It's just that—'

'You see, I knew.'

We had to pause to let a party all decked out in ten-gallon hats and leather chaps cross our path. Either side of us stretched two more malls, equally broad but these ones filled with green baize tables and busty girl croupiers in glittering tuxedos. Above us soared a blue dome pierced with stars. It was like standing at the crossing in a great cathedral.

'No, no, I really mean it,' he said. 'It's just that I wasn't quite sure how to express my reactions on paper without giving you the wrong impression, which is exactly what I'm doing now.'

'You didn't like the way I approached the subject, the narrative was perhaps too—'

'No, no, it's the story, it's not your fault.'

'The story?'

'I thought the story was going to be so beautiful and it's, well, so sad.'

'It could be beautiful and sad at the same time,' I said tetchily.

'It could have been, but in fact it's just sad. The thing is I was finishing up selling my little business to Hellman Drax while I was reading it and I was expecting to be so happy. There I was, getting out in a blaze of dollars after thirty years of boutique broking and I was looking forward to reading the great American love story. But reading your stuff just got me down. As I say, it's not your fault. It makes you think that nothing really lasts, least of all love.'

'Well, that's the *truth* of how it all ended,' I said. 'I thought you knew.'

'I did, I suppose. But I thought it wouldn't matter, that it would be enough for it to have lasted as long as it did. But it isn't. Franco was right. Love was just a passing phase in history. It ought to have dates after it like the Industrial Revolution or the Hundred Years War.'

We trudged on down the mall. The carpet seemed to be getting thicker. I couldn't think of anything more to say.

Jane and Jonty were sitting beside each other at the big round black-jack table in the corner. When she caught sight of us she waved a thick wodge of purple chips in the air and scampered over.

'Oh darling, shouldn't you cash those in before you lose them?'

'We're going back in after dinner and playing until we've got enough for the deposit on our flat,' Jane said gaily. She looked like Franco, with a merry monkey face, and she could not keep still for a minute.

'Poor Jonty,' said Polly.

'Rich Jonty. We're on a roll, Mum, and we don't need any lectures from Gamblers Anonymous. Anyway, Jonty's loving it, aren't you?'

Her fiancé gave a shy smile. He looked the sort of person who smiles shyly a lot of the time and leads a largely interior life. I had read somewhere that moles only come above ground when they need to mate. That might well be the case with Jonty too.

Jane insisted on ordering Dom Pérignon with one of her purple fish, which turned out to be legal tender in the Condor's Nest. Her parents blossomed. They behaved like a long-married couple who had been briefly separated and were overjoyed to be back together round the same table. They seemed to be sharing a run of private family jokes with Jane, or perhaps it was the same joke that bubbled up again every time someone thought of a fresh angle. Wizz joined in too, but he still seemed depleted. It was clear that he was put out by our conversation, though surely I had more reason to be. After all it wasn't my fault the story ended the way it did. Or perhaps his annoyance was not just to do with what I had written. Did it date back to when his friend Glen had died? Had my condolences hit the wrong note? One way or another, I got the feeling I had failed him.

'. . . hire a jeep.' I came round from my perplexed reverie to discover that Jonty who was next to me had just volunteered something.

'I'm sorry,' I said. 'I didn't quite . . .'

'I was just saying, if you don't fancy sitting at the tables all day, I'm hiring a 4x4 tomorrow and going up-country to look at some birds, and if you felt like coming with me . . .' Contrary to what I expected, his voice was decisive, rather clear and attractive as though he was accustomed to explaining things to strangers and winning them over.

'That would be great,' I said.

'Wizz, would you like to come along?'

'You are kind,' said Wizz. 'But I think I'd better rest up for the wedding. I run out of puff so quickly these days.'

Well, I thought, I have been too harsh. He was just not well.

Jonty was waiting for me outside, standing by the hire vehicle, a rugged workhorse the colour of wet sand.

'Isn't the air wonderful?' he said. 'Like champagne they always say, except I don't like the taste of champagne, couldn't stick that stuff we had last night.' He looked pale, almost ethereal in the bright morning light. I noted again that he had definite views about things.

'Jane's fast asleep, she didn't come up to our room till half past four,' he said proudly.

'How did she do?'

'She's up eighteen thousand dollars. I said, isn't it time to cash in, but she told me not to be so wimpish. I expect she'll lose the lot today.'

'You don't mind?'

'People must do what they want to do, don't you think? She told me she had just bumped into Franco coming out of Polly's room. At four in the morning. He's amazing, isn't he? Now I see where Jane gets her energy from.'

We had left the highway and were zigzagging up a stony track, so my head was in danger of hitting the roof anyway.

'He said they had so much to catch up on that they lost track of the time talking. And Jane said, only talking, how sad. And he said, well, a bit more than talking, so she hugged him and said he mustn't feel he had to go back to his own room on her account, and he said, no, it wasn't that, he always preferred to sleep alone. Amazing, isn't it, after all that time.'

'Amazing.'

'I shouldn't think my parents have ever spent a night apart except when he was on night duty. He's a cardiologist. In Sandwich. Look, there's a tanager, it must be the western, the others are red all over.'

The brilliant scarlet bird darted into the aspens by the creek, then flitted off into the rocks the far side. The rocks themselves were almost blood-red, shading into pink where the sun caught them. Now that Jonty had turned off the engine we could hear the water running over the stones.

'The guide says that if we follow the track up to the trailhead we might see a golden eagle.'

'Or a condor?'

'Very unlikely, there are only half a dozen in the whole state. The rest are in southern California.'

The track came to an end in a grassy clearing sprinkled with bright orange flowers like tasselled marigolds. I asked Jonty what they were, but he didn't know, he wasn't interested in flowers. He had his glasses fixed on a little brown bird in the brushwood, which I could hardly see. I wandered off and stared up at the mountains above us, great fractured spires of rock all jumbled together like that cathedral in Barcelona which had taken the whole century to build and was not finished yet. Jonty had not noticed that I had gone.

Probably everyone needs an obsession, or at least a focus. You can't shamble through life gazing idly on whatever catches your eye. And you don't really need anyone to share your obsession. At this moment Franco would be telling Polly about Lucasta Mynors's sonnets or whatever it was she wrote and Polly would not be listening, not really, just as he would not be listening to her explain how frustrated she was that she couldn't get two of her hospitals to share a path lab. But that had not stopped them getting together again.

Far above us a huge bird with black-and-white wings was soaring in a lazy orbit.

'Could that be a condor?'

'No,' he said without even putting up his glasses. 'It's a turkey vulture, they're pretty common everywhere though they go south in the winter. I said, you won't see a condor today.'

I wondered if Jane had taken in what Jonty was really like. Perhaps she had and this definiteness was what she particularly liked about him. As the day wore on, he seemed to become less conscious of my presence. He was like someone you were sharing an office with but who didn't think of it as a relationship.

'Shouldn't we be getting back?' I said. 'I mean, you've got to change and so on.'

'Oh, there's no hurry,' he said. It might have been me getting married rather than him.

'Well,' I said, 'you can say you saw a what was it on your wedding day.'

'A green-tailed towhee. Actually I saw one yesterday too, just above the caravan park.'

'Ah.'

'He's dying, isn't he, Wizz?'

'I'm afraid he's a lot iller than I expected.'

'I wouldn't mind going like that, dying of something dramatic.'

'Would you really?'

'People will always remember how he died. I mean, I know it's a horrible death but—'

'Please, would you mind very much not talking about it?'

'I like facing up to things. I don't know why, perhaps it's because nobody else in my family does.'

'Look, I really think we ought to be getting back,' I said.

The sun was just beginning to flick the tops of the mountains and the golden light of the desert was turning to a dusty mauve. The rest of the wedding party was standing in the narrow slice of empty foyer before the endless ranks of slots began. Jonty was unfazed by our being late. So were the rest of them, as it turned out, because they had something else on their minds.

'You'll never guess.'

'Not in a million years, my dear,' said Wizz.

I guessed instantly. Admittedly Polly and Franco holding hands was a clue. I knew enough, though, to let them make their own announcement.

'It's going to be a double wedding. Polly and I are following Jane and Jonty's lead. They don't seem to mind us horning in on their party.'

'*No!*' I said.

'It is rather sudden, I suppose,' Polly said. Her severity had melted away. In the glow of the foyer she seemed abstracted, almost dreamy.

'At our age, who wants to wait?' Franco said. 'Anyway, I have a sabbatical in London coming up and I need some place to stay.'

'Insensitive English prof from wrong side of tracks seeks capable Brit female, must have GSOH and spare room and share love of minor eighteenth-century women writers.'

'Oh, I don't think we share anything except a past,' said Polly.

'And me,' Jane chirruped.

'You're part of our past, darling.'

'Look, we'd better hurry up to the chapel if we're going to squeeze two weddings into the same slot.'

'You have to take the Skyride elevator. The others don't go to thirty-eight.'

We squeezed into the transparent hexagonal capsule and began to glide upwards on the outside of the building, very slowly like a fly across a window-pane. Soon the turquoise glimmer of the floodlit pools and the green twirls of the palm trees began to look dwarfish and unreal like an architect's model and Gilligan City seemed no more than a forlorn oasis in the endless desert. The mountains were changing colour again, from mauve to a dull umber as the light slunk away behind them.

'God, it makes you feel dizzy.'

'And so exposed.'

'As though it might break away any minute.'

'Like in *The Towering Inferno.*'

The minister was waiting for us. It was a shock to see him dressed in black with a white surplice like at a normal wedding.

'Welcome to the Little Chapel in the Moonlight, Jane and Jonathan and the rest of you good folks.'

'Reverend, I know this is rather short notice, but could you possibly fit us in too? We're Jane's parents, but we never got around to, you know, tying the knot.' Even Franco came as near as he was capable of to blushing as he delivered this abbreviated version of events.

'Why, this is wonderful news, sir. You would like to share your vows with your daughter and her young man?'

'Yes, if that's possible.'

'Nothing would give more pleasure to the good Lord and to all of us here at the Little Chapel in the Moonlight. We pride ourselves on maximising customer satisfaction. There is, however, one small problem which I have to share with you. Your daughter and Jonathan here have given the forty-eight-hour notice required by state law, but so far as I am aware, you yourselves—'

'Oh dear, can't we—'

'But there is one exception to this rule. His honour the mayor has authority to conduct a marriage in an emergency twenty-four seven, no notice required.'

'Would he, do you think—'

'I am sure he would be just tickled pink by your predicament, sir.'

'So how do we get hold of him?'

'Why, we only have to call his penthouse and he'll be here in two shakes if he isn't otherwise occupied.'

'He actually lives here?'

'He surely does. Why wouldn't he? It's his hotel.'

'You mean, he . . .'

'Why, yes, Mr Gilligan has been mayor of the city ever since we got incorporated. I'll go call him right away.'

We sat on little purple benches in the waiting room. Jane and Jonty were solemn and silent, but Polly and Franco were giggling together, her pale face nestled into his shoulder. The place reminded me of a hospital. We might have been waiting for news of a difficult operation. Well, I suppose we were.

'That'll be just fine. Mr Gilligan is quite thrilled. He'll only take a few minutes to get dressed. He likes to do things properly.'

This time the wait seemed so long that I was dozing off and gave a jump as the lift door opened and a wheelchair appeared with a little old man sitting very upright in it. He was dressed in a black coat and black striped trousers and a winged collar, and he was being pushed by a big strawberry blonde half his age wearing a strapless gold lamé dress.

'May I have the honour to present Mayor George G. Gilligan and Mrs Gilligan.'

'Hi,' said the mayor. He had a rugged old face, which had once been ruddy, and a thatch of white hair. 'Great you all could make it, it's always a pleasure to greet folks from Great Britain. I took my wife on honeymoon to London last fall, though I can't say we saw too much of the city.'

'Oh George,' Mrs Gilligan said.

'So you're only just married yourself, sir,' said Franco.

'Sixth time of asking, sir, just beginning to get the hang of the business,' said the mayor. 'There was a time, it was in my thirties I guess, when I was up and down that aisle like a whore's drawers. But I'm sure you folks don't want to wait around all night listening to my marital career, so let's get the show on the road.'

He rapped the arm of the wheelchair and Mrs Gilligan pushed him through the pair of automatic doors at the end of the waiting room. As the doors opened, a hidden organ began to play Mendelssohn's 'Wedding March'. The air inside the chapel was heavy with the fragrance of white flowers and shimmering with the light of candles. The brightly painted statues standing well forward of their Gothic niches looked less like ornamental saints than members of a built-in congregation, installed perhaps because so many weddings here must be on impulse (as indeed one of these was) and might otherwise seem friendless occasions.

'Do you have any special vows prepared?' the mayor said, as he began hunting up his place in a handsome scarlet book with gilt toolings all over it.

'Special vows?'

'Well, you know, some folks these days like to customise their vows. As a matter of fact, we have a Rent-a-Troth facility right here at the hotel. But if you're happy, I'll just give you my own take on the service. I call it the Gilligan Authorised Version.'

'I'm sure that'll be fine by us.'

They shuffled into position in front of the altar, the two couples ranged side by side before the mayor in his wheelchair, with Mrs Gilligan standing behind him and the priest behind her, not unlike the three persons of the Trinity in a medieval painting.

The mayor looked up from his book. 'Hey,' he said, 'it is just the two weddings, isn't it? You sure you two guys don't want to make it a threesome, because our great state would be quite comfortable with that scenario.'

'No,' I said.

'No, thank you,' Wizz said.

'Just kidding,' said the mayor with an impish grin. 'OK, Charlie, let's take it from the top.'

My mind drifted from the scarlet book the mayor was holding in his freckled old hands to the scarlet birds flitting through the cottonwoods by the creek. So I paid little attention to the minister's easy drone as he took us through the preliminaries. Now and then familiar phrases floated past me: honourable estate . . . brute beasts that have no understanding . . . if any man can show any just cause . . .

'Right, Charlie, hold it there, this is where I come in.'

The minister moved to one side and allowed the mayor to wheel himself up to the two couples.

'Will you – that's both of you – have these women to live together according to the laws of this state for as long as your love shall last, will you remain sexually active with her unless ordered otherwise by a qualified physician, and if your time together shall come to an end will you depart from one another in peace and charity, and be content to abide by the judgment of the court?'

'I will,' said Franco, barely audible. 'I will,' said Jonty, rather louder.

When it came to the turn of the brides, Jane could scarcely utter, but Polly sounded quite composed.

I was not sure whether to laugh or to cry, but then I am often in that kind of perplexity these days, which surprises me because I thought you became clearer about things as you got older.

After he had pronounced them man and wife, the mayor kissed the brides and the minister pronounced the blessing. We were turning to go.

'Hold it, folks,' the mayor said, 'this ain't quite the end of the show.'

He clicked his fingers and the unseen organ began to play with an unseen backing group humming along.

'Oh, I love to hear her whisper in the chapel in the moonlight,' the mayor sang in a peculiar rusty voice, melodious in a way but also with an undertone of menace as though prophesying trouble. He insisted we join in the reprise and as we bawled out the dying notes 'the love-light in her eyes', I thought we sounded like a shipwrecked crew whose voices had grown hoarse with dehydration and yelling for help.

After we had said goodbye to the mayor, Jane and Jonty went off to play roulette. They did not lose all the money Jane had won, but they certainly did not come away with enough for the deposit. That did not matter much, because Jonty made a packet when his ISP support business was sold.

Franco did not stay in London when his sabbatical came to an end, but he and Polly are still on good terms, and he often goes to visit Jane and Jonty in the house they have bought in Florida (his old bones crave the warmth).

Wizz died only a few weeks later. A surprise heart attack spared him any long decline. His ashes were mingled with Glen's in Glen's family plot out in Rochester, New York. I was surprised that he had not insisted on being buried with the Shorts or the Stilwells. I did not get to the funeral because by then I had gone home.

Afterthoughts

Sally and Thomas and William

On 1 September 1802 there appeared in the *Richmond Recorder* a piece signed by James Callender, a former political employee of Thomas Jefferson's who had become his vicious enemy. 'It is well known,' the article began,

> *that the man* whom it delighted the people to honor *keeps and for many years has kept, as his concubine, one of his own slaves. Her name is SALLY. The name of her eldest son is Tom. His features are said to bear a striking though sable resemblance to those of the President himself. The boy is ten or twelve years of age. His mother went to France in the same vessel with Mr Jefferson and his two daughters. The delicacy of this arrangement must strike every portion of common sensibility. What a sublime pattern for an American ambassador to place before the eyes of two young ladies . . . By this wench Sally, our President has had several children . . . The African Venus is said to officiate as housekeeper at Monticello.*

So began the media history of the Sally Hemings saga. Two hundred years later it is still running hot and strong, having already inspired a shelf-ful of biographies, essays, reviews, historical novels, not to mention a feature film. For years there was little or no actual evidence for any liaison between Sally and Jefferson beyond the rumour and scandal fomented by Jefferson's enemies in the robust style of the times.

Then in 1873 Sally's son Madison Hemings (1805–77) told his local paper in Ohio, the *Pike County Republican* (13 March), that

> *Maria* [Polly Jefferson] *was left at home, but was afterwards ordered to accompany him to France. She was three years or so younger than Martha* [Patsy]. *My mother accompanied her as her body servant . . . Their stay (my mother's and Maria's) was about eighteen months. But during that time my mother became Mr Jefferson's concubine and when he was called home she was 'enciente'* [*sic*] *by him . . . Soon after their arrival she gave birth to a child of whom Thomas Jefferson was the father. It lived but a short time. She gave birth to four others, and Jefferson was the father of all of them.*

This essentially is the testimony that has persuaded not a few of Jefferson's modern biographers that he fathered some or all of Sally's children over a period of twenty years. Those who were already savagely critical of Jefferson's ambivalent attitude towards the abolition of slavery have found in this supposed clandestine spawning the most damning condemnation of his racism, humbug and exploitation. Garry Wills, for example, while pouring scorn on the 'hint-and-run' method of Fawn Brodie's *Intimate History* of Jefferson, goes along with the thesis of more respectable historians such as Winthrop Jordan and Richard B. Morris that Jefferson did sire most or all of Sally's children but that he was in no way in love with her, regarding her as little more than 'a healthy and obliging prostitute' ('Uncle Thomas' Cabin', *New York Review of Books*, 18 April 1974). Conor Cruise O'Brien in *The Long Affair* (1996), his extended philippic against Jefferson's fanatical support of the French Revolution, argues (p. 22) that Jefferson felt no horror at the idea of miscegenation between white masters and black female slaves. If his brother-in-law John Wayles had sired Sally with his slave Betty Hemings, as was widely rumoured at the time, why should he himself not do the same and sleep with Sally? In an appendix (pp. 326–9), O'Brien accepts Madison's story and expresses the hope that genetics may soon be able to prove through comparison of DNA specimens whether or not Thomas was the father of Madison.

Only two years later, just such an experiment was made and its results reported in *Nature* (5 November 1998, p. 27). Since Jefferson had no legitimate male descendants, the results were obtained by comparing the DNA of the male descendants of his father's brother, Field Jefferson, with the DNA of the male descendants of Sally's three sons. This immediately ruled out the dark-skinned Madison himself because his male-line descendants did not survive the Civil War. But the other two, Thomas Woodson (1790–1879) and Eston Hemings Jefferson (1808–52), did have male-line descendants.

The results in both cases were emphatic. Four out of five male-line descendants of Thomas Woodson showed a haplotype (one with MSY1 variant) that was not similar to the Y chromosome of the Field Jefferson male line but one which was characteristic of Europeans. So Thomas Woodson was definitely *not* the son of Thomas Jefferson, though he probably did have a white father.

By contrast, the single male descendant of Eston who was tested did have the Field Jefferson haplotype, so any one of Field Jefferson's twelve descendants living at the time or Thomas Jefferson or one of his brothers could have been Eston's father.

This interesting verdict was seized on with view halloos by those who were out to smash the idol of American rectitude. Gore Vidal in *Inventing a Nation* (2003) exulted: 'The fact that Jefferson would have six children by Sally (half-sister to his beloved wife, another Martha) has been a source of despair to many old-guard historians, but unhappily for them, recent DNA testings establish consanguinity between the Hemingses and their master, whose ambivalences about slavery (not venery) are still of central concern to us' (p. 77). And the Thomas Jefferson Memorial Foundation blithely claimed (26 January 2000) a 'high probability that Thomas Jefferson fathered Eston and most likely was the father of all six of Sally Hemings's children'. Some time later, in 2003, troubled by the furore its hasty verdict had aroused, the Foundation revised its conclusions in a more agnostic direction, but the damage had been done.

Before we examine the DNA evidence a little more closely, let us go back to the deposition that Madison Hemings gave in old age. He says that Sally came back from Paris pregnant by Jefferson but that the child lived only a little while. Yet in reality Thomas lived to a ripe old age and he is the one child of Sally's whom DNA evidence confirms was not Jefferson's. And it was Thomas's parentage, too, that provoked Callender's original allegation, which sparked off the whole scandal. Madison and Eston were not yet born at the time of the article in the

Recorder. Faced with this difficulty, Jefferson's more entrenched enemies assert that Sally did not become pregnant until some time after her return to Monticello and that therefore Thomas Woodson was not her son and indeed was never at Monticello because his name does not appear in Jefferson's carefully kept records. But Callender in 1802 specifically names Tom as Jefferson's son, clearly insinuates that the affair began in Paris and states that Tom is still alive.

So apart from casting doubt both on Callender's veracity and Madison's, this latest version of the increasingly tortuous accusation makes Jefferson's next moves rather peculiar, if we are to believe his slanderers. There he is, well into his sixties and by now President of the United States, already *wrongly* accused in the public prints of having fathered a bastard by his slave some twelve years earlier in Paris. What does he do? He goes and repeatedly has sex with this same slave, by now a mature woman and the target of what we would today call intense media speculation. And she bears him several more children. This is surely a strange course of behaviour for one who, as O'Brien is the first to point out, was always painfully solicitous for his public reputation and did not disdain the arts of spin to maintain the purity of his image. Yet such is the logical position of those commentators such as William Safire (and indeed Professor Eugene Foster and the other geneticists who carried out the DNA tests). For what they are saying is that Callender was wrong about Thomas Woodson but was right about the parentage of Eston who was born eighteen years after Thomas and six years after Callender's accusation was published. I find that assertion frankly incredible.

So if Jefferson was not the father of either Thomas Woodson or Eston, who was? Well, the historians who were hastily assembled to form the Jefferson-Hemings Scholars Commission to rebut the even hastier judgements of the Thomas Jefferson Memorial Foundation concluded (12 April 2001) that there was insufficient evidence to link Thomas Jefferson with any of Sally's children but that the most likely candidate for Eston's father was Thomas Jefferson's much younger brother Randolph (1755–1815), who was notorious for hanging around with the slaves at Monticello, singing and playing the fiddle – and so why not other malarkey too? This would, among other things, explain why Jefferson himself never issued any formal public denial of the

Sally stories. What would be the use if his denial only exposed Randolph as the culprit? Then as now the revelation of scandalous behaviour by a President's brother would be an embarrassment, especially if it revealed him as belonging to a family who routinely abused their slaves.

But what about Thomas Woodson Hemings? If he was Sally's son, then he was conceived in Paris. And his mother, barely sixteen years old at the time, is known to have been in two places and two places only during the period in which his conception must have occurred: either waiting on Patsy and Polly at the Abbaye de Panthémont, where the girls were under the strictest possible supervision, or at the Hôtel de Langeac, which was a surprisingly small town house and, so far as we know, contained at the time only two young men: Sally's brother James, the minister's cook, and William Short – the only European around. So William becomes the obvious candidate for father of Thomas Woodson. For two centuries he has escaped being so fingered, I believe, only because he is not one-hundredth as famous as Thomas Jefferson.

If William was indeed Thomas's father, then again Jefferson would have wished to keep the matter dark and avoid any scandal that might injure the chances of his protégé. So would William, assuming that he ever knew Sally had borne him a child. Neither man would have dreamed of mentioning the matter in their letters when Jefferson was back in America, since the mails were so avidly read by spies and censors.

If you want any further pointers, consider the strong and surprising tradition that Sally had been reluctant to return to the United States with her master. She was pregnant, unmarried, very young and, as far as we can tell, knew little or no French. Why on earth would she wish to stay behind in Paris unless it was to be with the father of her child? And who else was remaining at the legation but William Short?

Finally and rather sadly, why should William be so reluctant for the rest of his life to visit his ageing patron and adopted father at Monticello? Yes, the older he became, the more this lifelong *ami des noirs* kept to the northern states, hating to see the despicable institution of slavery in action. But how much more sickened might he have been to be reminded of the consequence of his own actions?

Debts and Farewells

The Condor's head still stares down in chilly disdain on the proceedings of the American Philosophical Society in its fine old red-brick house in Philadelphia's Independence Park. Along with Greuze's poignant portrait of Benjamin Franklin in old age, it made an excursion in October 1997 to a little exhibition at the Frick Collection in New York. The exhibition catalogue (*Franklin and Condorcet*, Philadelphia, 1997) contains Johanna Hecht's first-rate account of how the bust came to Philadelphia via William Short and his little Duchess. Since 1952 the American Philosophical Society has also sheltered the extraordinary letters between William and Rosalie, the vast majority from her to him in her firm neat hand in ink that has faded to the colour of old blood (most of his to her were burnt during the Revolution – to her great chagrin, as we have seen). Thus the head is no longer separated from the documents of the heart which brought it to Philadelphia. The correspondence has never been published in English (the translations are mine), though a selection was published in French, edited by Doina Pasca Harsanyi (Paris, 2001).

William Short never threw away a scrap of paper or an account book. The huge bulk of his papers is shared between the Library of Congress and his old university, William and Mary in Williamsburg. The Historical Society of Pennsylvania down the road from the head also has valuable Short material in the Gilpin and Dreer collections. I am very grateful to the Librarians of these institutions for allowing me to consult their collections. There is no trace left of the addresses on Walnut Street where William first lodged and in his last years built his own house.

For the story of William's life, the pioneer was Marie G. Kimball, 'Jefferson's Only Son', *North American Review* 133 (September 1926, pp. 471–86). This is largely superseded by the only full-length biography, the invaluable *Jefferson's Adoptive Son, the Life of William Short, 1759–1848*, by George Green Shackelford (Kentucky, 1993). For William's earlier affair with Lilite, see Yvon Bizardel and Howard C. Rice's 'Poor in love Mr Short', *William and Mary Quarterly*, Third Series, 21 (1964) pp. 516–33. The same volume also contains Arthur Schlesinger's fascinating little note, 'The lost meaning of "the Pursuit of Happiness"' (pp. 325–7). Notable portraits of William are by Rembrandt Peale (College of William and Mary, 1803), and in old age by John Neagle (Historical Society of Pennsylvania, 1839). Bizardel and Rice, like Doina Pasca Harsanyi, assume that no serious relationship with Rosalie developed until after William's return from Italy in May 1789. This cannot be right. As early as 1787 Madame de Tessé was criticising William's over-frequent visits to the Hôtel de la Rochefoucauld. And the repeated references in the letters between Jefferson and Short during William's Grand Tour show beyond a doubt how tense the matter had become and how hugely relieved Jefferson was to pack Short off to the south and then to hear that the affair had ostensibly come to an end (see in particular the *Papers of Thomas Jefferson*, vol. 13, p. 636 and vol. 14, p. 43 and pp. 276–7). Even Shackelford, who does not make this mistake, seems oblivious of the enormous strains caused by the great length of the courtship, from their first meeting in July 1785 to the consummation a full five years later.

What we know of William's life in Paris outside the great love affair of his life comes largely from his correspondence with his employer Thomas Jefferson, when one or other of them was away on his travels. All those letters and a great deal more are preserved in the magnificent *Papers of Thomas Jefferson*, edited by Julian P. Boyd et al., 31 vols, Boston, 1940–. These volumes, more than the six volumes of Dumas Malone's monumental biography, *Jefferson and His Times* (Boston, 1948–81), give a marvellous picture both of Jefferson himself in all his vigour, curiosity, benevolence, nobility and blindness, and of his young secretary, cool, diligent, ambitious, both hard-headed and sentimental. For Jefferson in Paris, *The Paris Years of Thomas Jefferson* by William Howard Adams (Yale, 1997) is superbly complemented by Howard C. Rice's lavishly illustrated *Thomas Jefferson's Paris* (Princeton, 1976).

There is no need to list here all the general histories of the French Revolution from Thomas Carlyle and Albert Sorel, through Richard Cobb and Georges Lefebvre to Simon Schama and François Furet, but certain biographies of leading figures should be acknowledged: *Condorcet Un Intellectuel en politique* by Elisabeth and Robert Badinter (Paris, 1988), *Lafayette* by Michael de la Bedoyere (1933) and *Saint-Just* by Norman Hampson (Oxford, 1991). The liberal aristocrats who did so much to engineer the French Revolution and shape the later

French Republics have been largely erased from history. Conor Cruise O'Brien, for example, in *The Long Affair* conflates the two La Rochefoucauld Dukes, both pivotal figures. They are among those commemorated in Boniface de Castellane's somewhat old-fashioned *Gentilhommes Démocrates* (Paris, 1891). Otherwise one must rely on the equally creaky *Biographie Universelle,* which is not a patch on the *DNB.* I must also mention the memorable account of August 1792 in François de La Rochefoucauld's *Souvenirs du 10 août 1792 et de l'armée de Bourbon* (1929). Further information on Marie Antoinette's last days is to be found in Antonia Fraser's life. The details of Condorcet's last days come from the meticulously recorded official depositions. For Josephine and her court the best sources are Madame de Rémusat's *Mémoires 1802–08* and the many biographical studies by Frédéric Masson and Joseph Turquan, especially Masson's *Madame Bonaparte 1796–1804* and *Impératrice et Reine 1804–09.*

For other Americans in Paris, there is Gouverneur Morris's remarkable *Diary of the French Revolution* (2 vols, Boston, 1939) and *John Paradise and Lucy Ludwell of London and Williamsburg* by Archibald B. Shepperson (Richmond, 1942). For Gouverneur's life, there is Richard Brookhiser's *Gentleman Revolutionary* (New York, 2003).The best biography of Anton Mesmer is by D. M. Walmsley (1967), but a fuller picture of the whole story is given in *The Evolution of Hypnotism* by Derek Forrest (Forfar, 1999). The clearest introduction to the Physiocrats is *The Economics of Physiocracy* by Ronald L. Meek (1962).

For the architecture of the time, Anthony Vidler's *Architecture de C. N. Ledoux* (Paris, 1983) provides a good conspectus of that extraordinary fantasist of the rational. Four of his customs pavilions survive: the rather lumpy pairs at the place de la Nation and the place Denfert-Rochereau, both sets swamped by traffic, the Rotonde de la Villette off the place Stalingrad, Ledoux at his purest neoclassical and now a haunt of dossers, and, the prettiest of the four, the Pavillon de Chartres, a charming little kiosk at the entrance to the Parc Monceau, which doubles as a public toilet. The Désert de Retz caught my fancy in John Harris's account in his memoirs of trespassing there (*Echoing Voices*, 2002), but it had been first introduced to English readers by Osvald Siren in his trailblazing article in the *Architectural Review* (November 1949). Diana Ketcham provides an up-to-date account of the Désert's history and present fortunes in *Le Désert de Retz* (Cambridge, Mass., 1994). At the time of writing, the whole demesne is closed behind high walls and fences awaiting further restoration and the resolution of a legal dispute. For a closer acquaintance with its mysterious magic and for a great deal else on this and other excursions I have to thank my wife Julia who showed me the way over the fence.

The chateau of La Roche-Guyon is still in the family. It belongs to the descendants of the Liancourt Duke, since his cousin had no children by either of his wives. There is not much to see inside except the usual crappy videos. The young American who spent the best years of his long life there is not mentioned. But you can still look out from the terrace to the meandering Seine, over Rosalie's Jardin Anglais, now nicely replanted. And you can still climb the twisting chalky stairway to the old fortress.

Wm is far away in Laurel Hill cemetery overlooking the wooded cliffs of the Schuykill river, a few miles upstream of the city of Philadelphia. It was on this stretch of the river that Thomas Eakins painted the scullers with their scarlet kerchiefs round their heads, here that Wizz did his coxing, here too that Grace Kelly's brother Jack trained for Henley regatta where they barred him because he was only a bricklayer's son from Philadelphia. William's white tombstone is right by the cemetery fence, threatening to topple over into the traffic roaring along the freeway below, his situation as precarious in death as it so often was in life. The lettering on the tombstone is, like its occupant, almost effaced by the abrasions of time. But the curator of the cemetery kindly gave me a transcript of the inscription. What it says is:

Sacred to the memory of
William Short
Born at Spring Garden, Sussex County in Virginia
on the 30th day of September 1759
Died at Philadelphia on the 5th day of December 1849.

His life, public and private, was distinguished by ability, probity and industry never questioned. HE RECEIVED FROM PRESIDENT WASHINGTON WITH THE UNANIMOUS APPROVAL OF THE SENATE

> THE FIRST APPOINTMENT TO PUBLIC OFFICE CONFERRED UNDER THE CONSTITUTION OF THE UNITED STATES AND FROM PRESIDENT JEFFERSON, WHOSE AFFECTIONATE FRIENDSHIP HE ALWAYS LARGELY POSSESSED, PROOFS OF SIMILAR CONFIDENCE. These public trusts he always fulfilled with a sincere patriotism, a sagacious judgment and a moderation and integrity which deserved and assured success.
>
> In private life which for many years he fondly coveted he was social, intelligent, generous and urbane.

Well, nothing untrue there, nothing too overblown, at least not by the standards of tomb talk. But don't all those capital letters protest a little too much, as though there was after all something to hide? I wonder who wrote it. That phrase about fondly coveting private life surely has a touch of William himself. He would have taken a sardonic pleasure in composing his own epitaph. And he would not have wanted his disappointments to lie as heavy on him in death as they had in life: President Washington choosing cynical old Gouverneur Morris to supplant him in Paris, for example, or the Senate voting not to send him to Russia, or Mr Jefferson's never really lifting a finger on his behalf, or Rosalie's refusal to marry him and come to America, that above all. Certainly Philadelphia society would have been scandalised if there had been any mention here of Rosalie except as Mrs Wm Short. 'For many years the devoted companion of the Duchess de La Rochefoucauld'? No, good heavens no. Even putting aside the flagrant and habitual adultery, not something to be lightly put aside on Society Hill, Philadelphia did not have much truck with duchesses in any shape or form. So there William reposes in solitary eternal eminence. Far below him the scullers with their headbands still skim along the ravelled waters dreaming, if they dream at all, of Thomas Eakins or Grace Kelly and not of William Short.

Ferdinand Mount
London, 2006